THE BLOOD OF SEVEN

ISBN: 978-1-970121-02-5 (Paperback)
ISBN: 978-1-970121-03-2 (Paperback)

Library of Congress Control Number: 2019902624

Cover Art by Claire L. Fishback

Book Cover Design and Interior Formatting by Melissa Williams Design

Printed in the United States of America.
First edition. June 2019.

Dark Doorways Press, LLC

info@darkdoorwayspress.com

PO Box 620514
Littleon, CO 80162
DarkDoorwaysPress.com

THE BLOOD OF SEVEN

CLAIRE L. FISHBACK

ALSO BY CLAIRE L. FISHBACK

Lump: A Collection of Short Stories

For

Angela Alsaleem who witnessed the spark

Pat Carroll who demanded more pages

and

Lisa Baker who made all the threats

CHAPTER 1

Friday

Fake it till it feels right again.

Or run as far and as fast as possible to try to escape it. Detective Ann Logan, if she could even call herself a detective anymore, ran along the trail, gravel crunching beneath her feet. Lodgepole pines towered overhead, blocking out most of the stars still visible in the early morning sky. According to her GPS watch, she was on mile three, but the nightmare images from the Salida Stabber case threatened to break her mind further than they already had.

She pushed faster. Sometimes it took only one mile, sometimes five, sometimes a sixer of her favorite brew. Her therapist urged against the latter. So, Ann ran deep into the San Isabel National Forest in Colorado's Rocky Mountains.

The usual nightmare had awoken her at three in the morning and left her shaking under the sweat-filled sheets. It was the version in which Bruce, her old partner, came back from the dead to tell her his death was all her fault. Then, the Stabber's last victim—Elizabeth Bradshaw, seven years old—did the same. Even though Ann didn't believe in zombies or ghosts or anything like that, the dream wormed its way under her skin where it ate away at her sanity little by little.

They said two words over and over again. The same two words she chastised herself with.

Too late, too late, too late.

Their voices chanted in her ears in rhythm with her footsteps and the bouncing light from her headlamp. She hit mile four, and still they chanted. Images from the case flipped through her mind like a grotesque slideshow. She shook her head and squeezed her eyes closed. When she reopened them, she broke into an all-out sprint.

A tree root arched over the trail in the light's beam. Ann jumped too late. It snagged her foot and sent her sprawling onto her stomach. The air rushed out of her body. The voices stopped. She rolled onto her back and looked up at the stars peeking through the trees.

After a few gasping breaths, she got her wind back and climbed to her feet. She walked a little way to catch her breath before breaking into a run again.

The clearing where she usually turned around to get six miles out and back came into view. The crescent moon hung in the sky like the Stabber's sadistically perfect smile. Ann stripped her running jacket off and tied it around her waist, despite the fact that her breath puffed in front of her face with each exhale.

She walked in circles to keep her legs warm while her lungs returned to a normal breathing pattern and turned to head back down the trail when a tingling sensation spread over her skin. Ann rubbed her arms, but her flesh was free of goosebumps. The moonlight illuminated her skin. But no, that wasn't it. The veins just beneath the surface glowed blue-white. She rubbed at it again, but the illumination didn't go away. She lifted her shirt, then her pant leg. Her whole body glowed.

The tingling intensified. It burned. Like lava flowing through her nervous system.

She dropped to her knees, closed her eyes against the agony, and let out a low wail of pain. Static filled her ears.

Through the crackle, a voice compounded of many voices said, *"Protect her."*

Ann opened her eyes. Bright light flooded her vision, blinding her. A thin black figure appeared in the distance. It came closer until it resolved into the silhouette of a young girl around six or seven—long, curly hair stood out around her head. Her eyes glowed the same blue-white. Her hands moved, and she lifted something, a book, the interior gilded with the light. The book flew toward Ann. Scribbled words filled the pages. One of them flared, blinding Ann even further.

Sophia.

Ann's heart boiled inside her chest. She cried out again.

Then the book and the girl faded away, replaced with a flash of light that burned three familiar mountain peaks—the Royal Mountains outside her hometown—onto her retinas. When she regained her vision, the clearing came back into focus. No girl. No book. No Royal Mountain peaks. Just the clearing surrounded by towering pines.

Ann's breath came in short, painful gasps, as if she had just arrived in the clearing from the previous sprint. Her head swam. She must have pushed herself too hard out on the trail. That was all. Her brain was signaling a blood sugar crash or something. Her stomach growled as if to confirm.

She jogged back down the trail.

Or maybe it was stress. Stress did all kinds of things to people. Couldn't it cause hallucinations? A second failed psych evaluation *had* taken its toll on her psyche.

Inside her truck, Ann pulled on her jacket. The fabric rubbed over a sore spot on her chest. She touched it and winced. The skin was raised and felt raw. She flipped open the collar and peered down at it. Then she grabbed the rearview mirror and jerked it in her direction.

At first, she thought the two-inch-long, raw and red brand was an Egyptian Ankh, but on closer inspection, it sort of resembled an upright Jesus fish. Three bands encircled where the lines met to become the tail.

"What the fuck?" Her voice rode on gasping air. "No, no, no. What is this?" She poked it again and winced. Nothing had touched her out there. She hadn't even crashed into any overgrown bushes. She looked at it again in the mirror and then angled the reflective surface away from her. She gripped the steering wheel. Tears sprang to her eyes. She willed herself to keep it together until she got home and could assess the situation. Figure out the facts—what happened and what didn't.

The keys jangled in her hand, but she managed to get the right one in the ignition.

She wasn't ready. She knew that. No matter how ready she may have felt before this, no matter how ready she was to take another eval—she couldn't go back to work. Her mind went into preservation mode. Her Lieutenant would understand. He already thought she was back too soon. She called him from her truck once she pulled up to her apartment building. He told her to take two weeks. Longer if she needed.

Ann shuffled to her front door, eyes on the ground in front of her. Footsteps took off down the corridor. She looked up, but they were gone around the corner already.

A box about two feet square sat on her doorstep. UPS was on top of it today. She'd never received a package during the night. On closer inspection, however, there was no postage of any kind. Just her name scrawled on the top in black marker.

She jogged to the end of the corridor, but the person who must have dropped it off was long gone.

Ann squatted next to the package and examined the outside. She took it to the coffee table in the living room.

Using her keys, she sliced open the tape and folded back the flaps.

The first thing she noticed was the smell.

CHAPTER 2

Teresa Hart sprayed furniture polish onto a rag and wiped dust from the crib. "Dusting day." She sang and hummed a lullaby.

After wiping down the nursery furniture, she rearranged and fluffed the stuffed animals at the foot of the crib. She folded down the edges of the pink and white blankets. She stood back and admired how inviting the tiny bed looked waiting for the baby to be tucked inside.

"'Blessed are they who mourn, for they shall be comforted.'" She kissed the cross hanging from a chain around her neck and left the basement.

At the top of the stairs, she closed and locked the door with the key she wore on her wrist. In the bathroom, she made herself beautiful for her husband, Derrick. She met her clear blue eyes in the mirror and wondered when the lines had formed around them. When did her frown become so permanent? Someone once told her the lines on one's face were a road map to the life the person lived. She stopped a scowl from emerging at the thought and smiled instead.

Hair perfectly coiffed, makeup expertly applied, she went into the kitchen to pack lunch for Maggie, their adopted six-year-old. By the time she finished the peanut butter and jelly sandwich it was already a quarter past seven, and Maggie hadn't come downstairs.

Teresa went to the landing. "Maggie, you're going to be late."

Back in the kitchen, she flipped on the coffee pot. When she turned around, Maggie stood behind her. Her long dark hair stuck out from her head in frizzy ringlets, a stark contrast to Teresa's smooth blonde lob. That mess would take twenty minutes to comb out.

"What took you so long?" Teresa asked.

"I didn't sleep very good," Maggie said. She yawned.

"You didn't sleep very *well*." Teresa corrected her. "Here's your lunch. Your backpack is in the living room."

Maggie went around the breakfast bar and pulled her backpack onto her shoulders. She started toward the hallway.

"Maggie," Teresa said. "Where's my hug?"

Maggie shuffled back to Teresa, gave her a half-second embrace around the waist, and turned back toward the front door.

Derrick's footfalls came from the stairs. Teresa watched from the kitchen. He met Maggie in the foyer. Her face lit up.

"Hi, Daddy," she said. She hugged him tight. She looked up at him and whispered, "She forgot breakfast again."

Teresa sighed. Rearranging her routine to make the child lunch every morning was hard enough, but breakfast, too?

Derrick said something about the muffin store in a low voice, and Maggie smiled and nodded. He pulled her hair back into a ponytail and fastened it with a pink scrunchie. When he glanced toward the kitchen, his mouth turned down at the corners.

"Wait on the porch. I'll be right out." He came into the kitchen while Maggie went outside.

"Good morning," Derrick said. He pulled a travel mug out of the cupboard and filled it with coffee. He turned to Teresa. "What's wrong?" His tone suggested, *What's wrong this time?*

Teresa busied her hands with the dishes in the drying rack. Derrick touched her wrist and stopped her. She didn't look at him.

"What's wrong, honey?" The softer tone, the nicer one. He was pretending to care.

"Maggie doesn't like me."

Derrick shook his head. "Not this again." He put his mug on the counter and crossed his arms. "Why do you think that?"

"She doesn't hug me like she hugs you." Teresa fiddled with her necklace. "She rarely makes eye contact." What else? Oh yes. The most important. "She never calls me

Mommy."

"Don't be silly," Derrick said. "She's just getting used to us."

"She's been here for three months." Teresa dropped her arms. "How long until she settles in?"

Derrick shrugged. "I need to get to the clinic. I have an eight o'clock."

The usual excuse to not deal with things. To leave the situation. To leave her. Harmony was a fifteen-minute town. It took him five to walk Maggie to school, another ten from there to the clinic.

He brushed a kiss across her cheek and grabbed his briefcase from the living room.

"Derrick," she said, her voice cracking. "You know what today is, right?"

He shook his head. So easy for him to forget now that he had a replacement daughter.

"The baby . . . our baby's . . . anniversary . . . of her . . . of her death." She held the tears in, but her voice hitched.

"Oh, Teresa." Derrick came back to her, hugged her. "I'm sorry. I forgot. I know how important it is to you."

But not to him.

He kissed her forehead and released her, turned to leave but stopped. "You know," he said, then paused.

Teresa knew what he was going to say. He was going to tell her to get over it. That's what it always came to. He didn't understand. He didn't know what it was like to grow a human inside his body only to have it ripped away. But he reached for her again and awkwardly held her by the shoulders. His voice softened.

"It's been seven years. Maybe you should . . . I don't know . . . call your therapist. Start seeing him again."

He wants me medicated.

"Or you could come help out at the office. Perhaps some . . . normalcy . . . or a new routine would help."

"It was so easy for you to move on, wasn't it?" Teresa said in the voice she used when she wasn't sure if she really wanted Derrick to hear her. "So easy to be *normal* again. To forget our baby."

"It was *never* easy, Teresa." His nostrils flared. "I just . . ." He lifted his hands, then dropped them. "Never mind. I have to go. I don't have time for this."

She stood in the kitchen and listened to the front door open and close. At least he didn't slam it this time.

Teresa scurried to the front room and looked out the window. Derrick and Maggie strolled down the sidewalk and out of sight. His smile was for her now. Teresa sat on the love seat. Across from her, an upright piano stood against the wall. Pictures in silver frames sat in a cluster on top of lace doilies from Bruges, from another time, another life. Pictures of them, together. Happy. Smiling. Carefree. She and Derrick.

Tucked in the middle, partially obscured by the music stand, captured for the rest of time in black and white, was Teresa holding the baby. They had the same fair skin and pale hair. She was only seven weeks old.

A tear welled in Teresa's right eye but didn't fall. She went to the bathroom, snatched a tissue from the box on the counter, and dabbed, careful not to mess her makeup.

Mommy . . .

A distorted voice, like a child talking into a fan.

Teresa whirled and peered out into the hallway. Across from the bathroom, the basement door stood wide open. She checked her wrist for the key. Still there. No one else had a key. She knew she locked it. She always locked it. The only other way to unlock it was from the inside.

She slid to the door and peered down the darkened staircase.

A shadow drifted by at the bottom. Prickly chills washed over her scalp.

"Who's down there?" Her voice cracked. "Maggie?" she called, even though she knew she was home alone. Her mouth went dry.

Teresa took one step down the stairs and stopped. She didn't want to be the idiot bimbo in a horror movie. She backed out into the hallway, closed the door, and locked it, jiggling the handle to ensure it was secure.

The water heater, the furnace kicking on, wind in the ducts, rats . . . She'd call an exterminator.

Glass shattered in the front room. She spun toward the noise.

No, the kitchen. She found a tipped glass in the sink. Nothing broken. She rinsed it under the tap.

Mommy . . .

She shut off the faucet and listened, holding her breath. Her hand went to the cross at her neck.

The clock on the wall ticked off the seconds. Ten. Twenty.

Mommy . . .

From the front of the house. Teresa nearly shrieked. She took small, slow steps back down the hall. She stopped at the doorway and peeked into the front room.

The frame with her and the baby lay on the hardwood floor surrounded by pieces of glass. The other pictures remained untouched in a circle around a now empty space where the portrait had been.

There had to be an explanation. She just couldn't think. Not with a mess on the floor. She knelt and picked up the larger pieces but needed a broom. She took one step toward the hallway and tripped over something soft and yielding.

Teresa caught herself on the doorframe, turned, and gasped. The antique stuffed bear she'd had as a child stared up at her.

Big Bear.

She lifted him to eye level. What was he doing here? Derrick had put Big Bear in the garage. He'd wanted to throw the stuffed toy out, but she begged him not to. It had been hers when she was little. It hadn't been in the house since . . .

Since the baby died.

"Mah-mee," Big Bear said in the voice she'd heard.

Teresa dropped him. He landed face down. The pull string on his back slid inside his body. She let out a relieved laugh and tucked Big Bear on the love seat and arranged the pillows around him.

"Mommy."

The voice came from behind her. Not distorted. A child's voice. Crisp and clear. Not from the bear's old voice box.

Teresa turned around and froze.

A girl in a frilly white dress stood in the doorway. A black ribbon held her long pale hair away from her face. Dark eyes peered up from beneath a fringe of blunt-cut bangs.

"Mommy," the girl said in a sickly sweet voice. She cocked her head. "Why did you kill me?"

CHAPTER 3

The scent of a reptilian terrarium mixed with death filled Ann's nostrils. Packaging peanuts hid the contents of the box. She had to find the source of the smell, but at the same time, she didn't want to just plunge her hands into unknown depths. She pushed away the top layer of peanuts and uncovered a leather bomber jacket with a paper bag tucked inside the collar. The jacket was her dad's. Part of the Bram Logan signature style. Ann pulled the paper bag from the jacket and unfolded the top flap. She opened it and peeked inside. Nothing dead and rotting. She dumped the contents onto the table. A passport and wallet.

She pulled the jacket out of the box, and the smell of decay intensified. Ann reeled and covered her nose.

Jeezus fuck. There'd better not be a head in here.

Two parcels remained at the bottom. One, a plain brown package about six by six inches, tied shut with a piece of thick twine; the other five inches long, roughly cylindrical, wrapped in newsprint. She tugged the corner of the newspaper, and one of her mother's angel figurines rolled out. They were usually lined up on the mantel at the house where she grew up.

The angel held a little girl in a protective embrace. Ann set the figure on the couch next to her and lifted the other package, fumbled with the twine and unwrapped it. A blue velvet jewelry box and an incredible stench. Good Lord. Her stomach twisted.

Ann opened the lid. Her mouth filled with saliva. She dropped the box, ran to the bathroom, and heaved into the bowl. She rested her head against the roll of toilet paper.

Hallucinations, glowing veins, burn marks—now this. Cold sweat broke out under her eyes and across her upper lip. Ann wiped her forehead on the back of her arm. She got the first aid kit from under the sink, rifled through it, and found a jar of menthol rub. She dabbed some under each nostril and returned to the little box of horrors.

One, two, three. She opened the lid.

Even though Ann's mother died thirty years ago, Bram Logan never took off his wedding ring. Not even now. Her dad's ring finger, still wearing his custom-made band, had been crammed into the neck of a decapitated rattle snake. The snake's body coiled around the inside of the box like a macabre necklace.

Ann's brain worked to make sense of what she was looking at while desperately searching her memories.

Is it really a finger?

What was the last thing she said to her dad? She

struggled to remember.

It can't be his finger.

When was the last time they spoke cordially? It had to be the night before she graduated.

Christ, it's his finger.

When was the last time she hugged him, saw his smile, heard his laugh, gave him the time of fucking day?

Her rational mind forced its way to the forefront. She needed a print to be sure it was his finger. She snapped the box shut, and as her lungs took in short bursts of air and she worked to not break down completely, she dumped the rest of the Styrofoam out. There had to be an explanation. A ransom letter. A business card from the mob boss in Harmony.

Harmony didn't have a mob.

She grabbed her cell phone, still tucked in the armband from her run.

Call it in. Take everything to the station. Start a case. Find him now.

Instead, she called her dad. His voicemail was full. She hovered her thumb over her Lieutenant's number in her recent calls.

Maintain control. No body, no murder.

Not entirely true, but she had to tell herself something.

The right thing to do was call the police, she knew this, but at the same time, she didn't want someone like Anderson assigned to the case. That greasy-haired fucktard would screw everything up. Ann didn't understand how someone so incompetent could be a cop.

Who else could she call? Six months ago, she would have called Bruce.

She took a deep breath. Maybe someone in Harmony had seen her dad. She sat up straighter. Sheriff McMichael, her dad's best friend. She didn't have his personal number, but she could easily call the Sheriff's Department. She did. He wasn't there. Too early. She left a message with the bored dispatcher and scrolled through the rest of her contacts.

Joey Rigsby, professional hacker. Worked for the CIA for a while even and never let anyone forget it. Not a good secret-keeper, so it hadn't worked out.

She shook her head. No. She hadn't left things great with him either.

That's your way, isn't it? Burn your bridges until you have no one left.

She examined the outside of the big box again. Someone packed it, someone delivered it. There had to be prints. She ran out to her truck and grabbed her kit. But the box and its contents were clean. She examined every packing peanut, every nook and cranny inside the box, every inch of each item for any clues. Nothing. It was like the box had been packed in a vacuum.

She lifted the angel figurine. It was definitely one from the house in Harmony. When she was six, she thought the angels needed faces. This was the one she had started on. Her dad caught her before she could draw the second eye, but he'd let her finish it anyway.

Summon your angel, Dad. I guess that really worked, didn't it?

It was his phrase. *Summon your angel.* All her life he had used it to remind her she had a guardian angel who would protect her.

Ann scoffed. Angels, right. Protection, sure. She stared at the figurine, then focused on the passport.

Her dad was a world traveler. He was in law enforcement. He was careful and smart and observant. She rubbed her thumb across the angel's face. She had to go home.

After nearly fifteen years of being away, she had to return to Harmony, Colorado.

CHAPTER 4

Teresa backed up until her legs hit the love seat. She sat down on Big Bear, and he groaned something in his mechanical voice.

The girl came closer.

"Mommy," she said. "Why. Did. You. Kill. Me?" She enunciated each word as if English wasn't Teresa's first language.

"I–I don't know what you're talking about. How did you get in here? Who are you?"

The girl put her small hands on her hips and raised an eyebrow at Teresa, an expression Teresa had used many times with Maggie. Teresa's mother made the same look throughout Teresa's childhood and beyond. Disbelief, disappointment, and a healthy dose of are-you-completely-incompetent-or-just-stupid.

"Once upon a time, Mommy," the girl said, shaking a finger. She took a step toward Teresa, and Teresa pulled Big Bear onto her lap.

"Don't call me that," she said. "I don't know you."

The girl only laughed. "Once upon a time, you had a baby, and you were so sad." She exaggerated the words, drew them out. "Then you killed me, and here I am as I would be if I hadn't died. Aren't I so cute?" The girl twirled around, skirt and hair flying outward.

"It was an accident," Teresa whispered. "I only left for a second. I needed air. I needed . . ."

"Why did you replace me? And on my birthday, too." She crossed her arms and pouted.

Maggie had arrived three months ago on what would've been the baby's seventh birthday.

"I didn't . . . I never . . ." Teresa cringed behind the stuffed bear. "Daddy decided. Not me."

Partially true. When they couldn't get pregnant again, Derrick brought up adopting a child. Perhaps he didn't trust her to be around babies. He never believed her about what happened. He never said those words, but she could tell. She only said yes to please him. To make him happy. All she ever wanted was for him to be happy.

To love me again.

"Never mind that now," the girl said. She pranced toward Teresa and shoved Big Bear off her lap. She placed her hands on Teresa's. "Here I am, and maybe I forgive you." The girl grinned.

Teresa searched her face. The dark eyes—Derrick's eyes. The pointed chin—her chin. The pale hair. The dress—white and lacy and frilly. It was a replica of the dress she'd buried the baby in.

"T–Tiffany?" Teresa tested the name she hadn't said in so long. The name she refused to even think. Saying the baby's name in her thoughts made it hurt that much more.

The girl nodded.

"How is this possible?"

"I have a friend who lives in the old house outside of town."

"The abandoned funeral home?" Teresa asked.

Tiffany nodded. "He is glorious in all his power." She grinned.

Teresa pulled her left hand free and held the golden cross at her neck. Tiffany placed her hands on Teresa's knees.

"He will give us another chance to be together. We just need to help him."

A second chance? Teresa's heart fluttered at the idea. "What do I have to do?"

Tiffany stomped over to Big Bear.

"If you love me, you'll do anything to have me back." She kicked the bear onto his side. "Say yes and we can be together again. Don't you want to be with me?"

Bring back the baby. Then what? Would it be like nothing ever happened? Would it repair the damage? Would Derrick love her again?

Tiffany's dark eyes gouged into Teresa's soul. Teresa wanted to say yes. So often she said no. Back when she was naive and stupid and believed her life would be perfect if she just followed the rules. Graduate from high school, get married, buy a house, have a baby . . . No one ever told her the next step. Not even her mother, who ingrained the first four rules into her brain to such a degree she felt if she didn't follow them she would be a failure. A complete failure.

The baby died. Doesn't that make you a failure?

She looked at the girl standing before her. Seven-year-old Tiffany. Teresa cocked her head. "Why does your friend live in the abandoned funeral home?"

Tiffany stomped her foot. "Mommy, say yes." She clenched her little fists.

Babies don't come back from the dead as half grown children.

"No." It burst from her lips. "No. This is some joke, isn't it? Some sick . . . joke." She went to the doorway. "I don't know how you got in here, or who put you up to this, but this is . . . disgusting." She pointed into the hall toward the front door. "Get out of my house."

The girl shrugged. She stopped right next to Teresa, crowding her in the doorway with her chilly presence. Teresa pushed herself against the frame.

"You'll change your mind. He always gets what he wants, and . . . So. Do. I." She stepped into the hall, into a beam of sunlight coming in through the slender window by the door, and faded to nothing.

A trick of the light. That's all.

But Teresa knew better. The door never opened.

And no one but she knew the truth behind the baby's death.

CHAPTER 5

The Royal Peaks, a small mountain range in the Colorado Rockies, loomed in the distance as Ann pulled down the road to Harmony. King Mountain, the tallest peak in the trio of fourteeners, already had snow from its tree-line to craggy top.

Ann parked in the driveway of the two-story "cabin" where she'd grown up and turned off the truck. She sprinted to the front door, turned the knob and pushed. Her shoulder rammed against it.

No one locked their doors in Harmony—no one had a reason to.

Okay, so Dad locked up before he went wherever he went to get his finger cut off.

A strange sensation spread through her belly, and she almost laughed. At the same time her eyes filled.

Keep it together, Logan.

She went around to the back of the house and checked the rear entry. Locked, too.

Back at the front of the house, she checked under the welcome mat, felt along the top of the door frame, and finally found the key in a fake stone by a pot of dead mums. She unlocked the door and went inside.

Her training taught her to observe, orient, decide, and act. She scanned the living room, adjoining dining area, and kitchen.

The furniture from her youth begged to be updated. Log framed couch and chairs. Log framed beds. Log framed logs. Even the bathroom carried on with the same motif. Thank goodness the toilet wasn't made of wood. She took care of business and went back into the living room. Her dad would never change a thing her mom had had a hand in, even though she'd been gone for so many years.

In the kitchen, a key with a yellow tag key chain sat on the counter under the family bulletin board. The tag advertised the local storage facility. It must have fallen off one of the push pins. She hung it back up, and it fell again, so she stuck it in the junk drawer at the end of the counter.

She opened the fridge. Empty aside from the obligatory crusted condiment bottles lining the door and an unopened case of Fat Tire. Nice.

The master bedroom was on the first floor with a direct line of sight to any intruders. Her grandpa had designed the house this way so he could protect his family. He and Dad always had that protector gene, which suited them well in their roles as Castle County Sheriff and the years they served in Harmony. She was supposed to follow in their footsteps, but she wanted bigger, better things. She wanted the hell out of this claustrophobic town.

Ann crossed the living room to the master and flicked on the light. The bed was unmade, but everything else seemed in order. She opened the top dresser drawer. Empty save for a couple pairs of underwear. The other drawers didn't appear to be missing anything, not that she had a full inventory of her dad's clothing. She slid the closet open. A collection of empty hangers were interspersed throughout. She rifled through them and noted his favorite cargo pants were missing, as were the shirts he usually wore during his travels.

"Where did you go, Dad?" A shirt clinging to a hanger for dear life dropped to the floor and startled her. Ann chastised herself for being so jumpy.

She went upstairs to search the rest of the house. Nothing was out of place. In fact, it all seemed like a time capsule from fifteen years ago. She wondered if her dad ever went to the upper floor. The place started to feel too small, so she ran outside and took in gulps of fresh mountain air. Her phone buzzed in her pocket. She had a couple voicemails. Damn cell service was shit. She listened to the messages.

The first one was from her therapist hoping she was okay. She said she was there if Ann needed to talk. The second was from Sheriff McMichael.

"Hey, Annie!" He always sounded so cheerful. "Got your message. Damn, kid. Good to hear from ya. Give me a holler, yeah?" He didn't leave a number. Back inside the house, she dialed him from the land line. The dispatcher said he was out responding to a call.

Ann got her suitcase and the box of her dad's stuff out of her truck. The box with the finger-snake was double bagged in a gallon-sized plastic bag. She put it in the freezer next to a bottle of spiced rum. Then she sat on the couch to fully investigate the remaining contents.

She flipped open the passport to the identification page—her dad's toothy grin smiled out at her. Most of the pages had stamps from Egypt, of course. His wallet contained his Colorado State driver's license, a credit card, a handful of small bills, and a Miles & More frequent flyer membership card from Lufthansa Airlines. A crinkled snapshot of her mom was tucked into an interior pocket with a folded twenty. Her mom had been an Egyptian goddess. Ann inherited a lighter tone of her mom's skin as well as her dark hair, but had her dad's blue eyes. The interesting combination usually made people ask her about her origin.

Colorado born and raised.

Ann searched the remaining pockets. She wasn't surprised to find zero pictures of herself even though she'd sent him one of her graduation from the Denver Police Academy. Her relationship with her dad was almost nonexistent the past few years, and completely nonexistent the past six months when she needed him the most. Numerous voicemails—at least one a day—pleading for him to call her all went unanswered. No calls, no texts, no emails. Nothing. No support in her first use of deadly force. He was MIA.

Ann stuffed his wallet and passport into the left pocket of the jacket and hung it on the coat hook by the front door. She took the angel to the mantle to return it to its proper place and paused.

All the other angels were missing. A layer of dust covered the shelf with ten roughly circular shapes where the wood grain showed through. Angel footprints. She swiped her finger through the grime. Her dad hadn't dusted in months. She wiped down the shelf and put the figurine in the middle, so lonely without its companions.

Ann sat on the couch, but the quiet of the house was unsettling. To combat the feeling, she headed to the diner for a late lunch. Maybe being around the people of her home town would make things feel better.

CHAPTER 6

Ann wandered down Forest Parkway, the main thoroughfare through town, and marveled at the complete lack of change. How were some of these shops still open? Mrs. Baker's Scrapbook Store, Mike's Shoe Repair, Mullen's Bait & Tackle. In high school she joked about the shops being fronts for drug operations or money laundering. After being in law enforcement for the past fifteen years, it actually made sense.

She briefly wondered who from high school had stayed, who else had left, which old lifers had died. What events happened in her absence that would live on in infamy, like the Billy Rogers incident of '99, Carl Conrad's dog from '58, and the fire of 1912?

Harmony was a town that never forgot.

The streets were empty. The town folk were all probably still at work this time of day, but the general absence of people gave her goosebumps. A thought that everyone had abandoned the place crawled through her mind.

She left that thought at the door when she entered Mac's Diner, the town's only real restaurant. It was full of the early supper crowd. White hair at every booth. Ruthie Gill, a girl Ann went to high school with, almost dropped her coffee pot when she spotted Ann in the doorway.

"Ann Logan? Is it really you?" she said with a huge smile. Though they hadn't been close in high school, she hugged Ann, then turned to the dining room. "Ann's home!"

All the guests looked up from their greasy meals and clapped. Some even stood. A sharp whistle came from the back of the restaurant. She wasn't a war hero. She wasn't a hero at all. Surely, they read the paper.

Heat flushed across her clavicle and instantly cooled. She peeled off her coat, hung it on the coat rack by the front door, and pushed her sleeves up.

She glanced at the exit. But she couldn't allow the creeping anxiety to turn her into a hermit.

"You can sit wherever you want." Ruthie touched Ann's arm. "We're not that fancy."

"Can I just get a sandwich to go?" Ann asked. "Chicken salad if you have it?"

Ruthie nodded.

Ann willed her internal thermostat to function properly. Cold and heat chased each other through her core. She ignored the faces beaming around her by alternately looking at the old stained carpet and up at the ceiling tiles.

Ruthie came back. "Bobby's on it. He makes damn

good chicken salad."

"Hey . . . have you seen my dad?" Ann asked.

Ruthie turned to her, mouth open to answer the question, but someone across the restaurant cried out. Ruthie shoved the half-empty coffee pot into Ann's hand and rushed to the scene. Ann peeked around a divider.

Ruthie patted an old lady's back. "Don't worry, it's just water." She dropped a stack of napkins on the spill. Then brought the lady a fresh glass and went into the kitchen.

Ann briefly wondered why they hadn't been friends in high school and remembered Ruthie had been the type who drifted from clique to clique, except for the more exclusive ones. Like the jocks and cheerleaders. Ann hung out with the jocks, but not the cheerleaders. She always felt more like one of the guys than one of the girls.

Ruthie came back and retrieved the coffee pot. "I know I'm grinning like an idiot, but we're all so proud of you," she said. "Our own being the one to catch the killer."

"My partner caught tons of bad guys last year," Ann said and took in a quick breath. No training could ever prepare a cop for notifying next of kin, or how grief or pride could be overshadowed by blame. By guilt. Bruce's wife never forgave her.

"I'm sorry about what happened to him." Ruthie touched Ann's arm again. "I'm sure folks back in his home are damn proud of him, too." She nodded solemnly. "I'll go check on your sandwich." She hurried off.

Ann went outside and chuffed her boots against the

sidewalk. The cool air chased the anxious heat from her body. She rubbed her arms.

"Hey, Magnum PI!" an all-too-familiar voice shouted. Ann looked up. Derrick Hart peered at her from across the street. "Ha! I knew that was you!"

Fifteen years had passed, but it was like she'd left him yesterday. A giddy feeling trembled in her gut. She wanted to ignore him or run back into the restaurant or hide in the bushes, but it was too late. She suddenly didn't know how to stand normally. She tucked her hands into her pockets. Derrick trotted over and opened his arms. Ann grabbed his hand and shook it.

"What . . . a handshake?" He pulled her into an awkward hug. Then he pushed back and held her by the shoulders at arm's length. His dark eyes darted all over her face as if taking inventory to make sure she still had two eyes, a nose, and a mouth.

Eye contact didn't feel natural. "If it isn't Doogie Howser," she said, a slight waver in her voice. "I didn't think you'd still be here." She didn't know what else to say.

Derrick released her and ran his left hand through his hair, messing it up. He'd done that all through high school too. She used to love it for some odd reason. Until she didn't. Until everything she loved about him became annoying.

The sun glinted off his wedding band.

"I came back." He shrugged.

"Your wife let you drag her here?" Ann laughed because

it seemed like the right thing to do, but it sounded as fake as it felt. He looked at his left hand and crossed his arms as if to hide it. "Who'd you end up with, anyway?"

"No one from here," he said. "After you left . . . me . . . I . . . uh . . . had to split town too." He looked at anything but her. "So I went to med school, got married, had . . . a kid . . ." The words rushed out and then tapered off. He glanced at her, then back at the ground, and rubbed the back of his neck—his tell for discomfort. He was just as nervous at seeing her as she was at seeing him.

"What about you?" he asked. "Take the plunge?" His face flushed.

Ann shook her head. When she moved away right after high school graduation it shocked everyone in town. They all thought she and Derrick would be together forever. Everyone had some predetermined life picked out for her, trapping her here in a place where potential got stunted. So she'd left and hadn't been in a serious relationship since.

"Married to my career," she said.

"Me, too." Derrick's lips momentarily frowned, then smiled again. "Hey, I opened my own clinic here in town." He waved vaguely over his shoulder. Ann glanced that way. The Post Office and Sheriff's Department were on the same block.

"That's great. Hey, have you by chance seen my dad lately?"

To treat a bloody stump perhaps?

The diner door pushed open, the bells clattering against

the glass. Ruthie came out juggling a paper bag in one hand, a to-go cup of coffee in the other, and Ann's jacket tucked under one arm. She halted briefly and smiled at the two of them while the door banged shut.

"Oh, you two," she said in a gosh-oh-gee voice. Ann took a step away from Derrick. Ruthie looked back and forth at them. She opened her mouth to say something, but Ann intervened.

"See you around," Ann said to them both. She took the items from Ruthie and hurried across the street to the Sheriff's Department.

CHAPTER 7

The dispatcher, a bored-looking woman, probably in her early twenties, glanced up but didn't smile.

"Hi, Rachel," Ann said, reading the name plate on the girl's desk. "Is Sheriff McMichael here?"

"He's still out on patrol." Her eyes shifted upward over Ann's shoulder. Ann turned to see a clock on the wall. "He should be about done. You might find him out the road." Rachel's gaze focused on her computer screen while her mouse hand clickity-clicked.

Ann thanked Rachel, left the station, and walked west to the dirt road that ended at the old funeral home. She ate her sandwich on the way, juggling the bag and the cup of coffee.

The air grew chillier near the narrow creek that dipped over and ran alongside the road. When she was a kid, she thought it was the ghosts from the old cemetery. Harmony stopped using that cemetery in 1912 after a fire swept through town and they ran out of room. Now, it was overrun by ponderosa and lodgepole pines. Grave markers, some blackened like rotten teeth, jutted up among the trees.

The abandoned funeral home, which had been spared in the fire—contributing to local folklore about the house and the man who'd lived there—still slouched among the foliage, shrouded in darkness. The warped front steps gave it a sinister grin. The two windows on the upper level lent the old house a pair of eyes. They glared at her. She glared right back.

After what she'd been through, the stupid old house no longer scared her.

A stick snapped in the darkness. Ann inhaled a shriek, dropped her coffee and chips, and reached for her gun—which, of course, was back home locked up tight in her closet. She had thought about bringing it, but the more she'd stared at the black metal, the harder her heart pounded. She wondered if she would ever be able to fire her weapon again.

"Sorry to scare you like that." A man in Castle County Sheriff's Department khaki came out of the woods. Ann would recognize that voice anywhere. Frank McMichael had a deep baritone that rumbled from his barrel chest.

"Just the man I was looking for," Ann said.

He tipped back his wide brim hat. "Well, I'll be. Little Annie Logan, back in Harmony." He came out of the gloom and stepped over the creek onto the dirt road.

"In the flesh," she said. He surprised her and pulled

her into a quick hug. He didn't often show affection. A pat on the head or a handshake. His wife, Lisa, rest her soul, was the one who gave out hugs—and candy. Ann's hand brushed his gun. She ignored the quickening of her pulse.

Twenty years had been rough on the old sheriff's waistline, but the twinkle in his eyes hadn't dimmed in all that time. Clever eyes for a clever man.

"Little jumpy," McMichael said with a grin.

"Just a tad." Ann couldn't help but smile back. Being near him was like being next to her dad. They were best friends their entire lives. McMichael was more uncle than anything else.

"With reason—the Salida Stabber. Boy howdy, what a case. Followed that one day and night. We were all rooting for you, Annie. Whodathunk a gal from a small town like ours would make the Denver Post?" He grinned, rocking forward onto his toes and back onto his heels. The only thing missing was a hearty *a-yup*. "How're you holding up?"

Ann bent to pick up the dropped coffee cup and ignored his question. "What are you doing out here?"

"Oh, just makin' sure no pesky kids are using the old funeral home." He squinted his eyes toward the woods. "Got your phone call." He turned back to her. "What's going on?"

Ann glanced down the road toward town. "It's about my dad." They started walking and Ann filled him in on the details of the box.

"You send in a print?" He scoffed. "Of course you did, you're Bram Logan's daughter." He winked at her. "Did you call it in?"

Ann winced and shook her head.

"Why the hell not?" He stopped walking.

"I don't trust the other cops in Salida." She looked anywhere but at his eyes. "I wanted to see what I could find out first. If I called it in, they would have taken it away from me. He's *my* dad." She shrugged. "Besides, I sort of did call it in, didn't I? I called you. Bram Logan is from Harmony, not Salida."

"Fair enough, young lady." He continued down the road. They meandered in silence for a few seconds.

"I would be lying if I said I'm not worried," Ann said. "I know a finger isn't a body, but . . . It's not good. Is it?"

"No return address, no stamps, no fingerprints—he'd never be without his bomber," he said, as if the jacket was more of a tell than the severed body part.

"I haven't heard from him in months," Ann continued. "After the Stabber, I called him every day. I thought if anyone could coach me through my first use of deadly force it'd be him." She stopped, and McMichael turned to her. "He never called me back." She looked into his eyes.

I'm struggling McMike. Please help me.

"Maybe he'll still show up." McMichael looked doubtful. He took a few steps ahead of her. His next words came out a whisper. "I should have been there."

"What was that?" Ann asked, though she heard him.

"Oh, nothin'." He smiled at her.

"When did you last see him?" Ann stopped herself from grabbing his arm. The begging tone in her voice irritated her. They'd reached the edge of town.

McMichael slid his hat from his head and scratched his scalp. "Few months. Six? Eight? Not sure. Sometimes he breezed through without stopping in." The corners of his mouth dropped. McMichael motioned toward the diner.

"Can I buy you another coffee—seein' that I scared this one right out of your hand?"

"Does the station have coffee?" She lifted one shoulder. "Save you a couple bucks?"

The sheriff grinned. "You betcha. It'll melt the skin off your tongue, but we've got it." He patted her on the shoulder. "I'm sure your dad is fine," he said in a low voice.

"How can you be so certain?"

"He's a smart man. Strong, intelligent, observant. I don't think anyone could get a jump on him."

Ann thought about the contents of his wallet. The Lufthansa mileage card. "What if he was in Egypt when it happened?"

"You think someone in Egypt sent you his finger in a box with no postage?" He lifted an eyebrow at her.

Ann pursed her lips to the side. Good point. They reached the Sheriff's Department, and McMichael opened the door for her.

"Afternoon, Sheriff," Rachel said. "Did you get the bad guys?"

McMichael introduced Ann to Rachel. This time, the young woman acknowledged she knew who Ann was—the lady who got the Stabber—and offered Ann a sincere congratulations before returning to the game of Solitaire open on her computer. McMichael motioned to a seat at one of the desks in the main area and disappeared behind the saloon style doors Ann knew led to a kitchenette.

"Your dad asked me to keep his locker for him," he called over the doors. "Sweaty socks and dirty underwear, I reckon, but you're welcome to try to open 'er up. It's number seven."

Ann wandered back to the locker room where four full-size lockers stood across from filing cabinets. They were numbered one, five, seven, and ten.

Ann tried various number combinations to no avail. She went back to the main office and sat down opposite McMichael.

"No luck?" He pushed a cup of black lava toward her.

She shook her head, took a sip, and cringed. The sheriff was right. Her tongue would never be the same again.

"So, what's new?" Ann asked.

"Just the usual. Louise Marga calling in suspicious activity every couple weeks, though honestly, I haven't heard from her in a few months." He looked at his watch. "I'd say we're due for something. Usually it's just kids yelling in the woods, raccoons in the attic, a butterfly fart—who knows with her." He chuckled. "I seem to recall your daddy calling me one night 'cause you went missing."

Ann laughed. "I'm sure we were out there tapping on Looney Lou's windows with sticks." She and Derrick and Derrick's goon friends, who'd given her the sort-of-cruel nickname. Louise lived on the other side of the old cemetery. It was all too easy to stir her up. "I can't believe she's still alive."

"And sharp as a pair of fresh-honed shears. Still stirs up the town from time to time. End-of-the-world bullshit." He sipped his coffee, and they sat in an amicable silence for a few seconds.

Ann nodded to a stack of files on his desk. "Any good cases?"

"Nothing big since an infant death a few years back. Accident my ass. Never believed a bit of that woman's story, but, you know how it goes. Lack of evidence, good lawyers." His mouth twisted in disgust.

"Anyone I know?" Ann asked.

He took a breath to answer when the front door burst open and a burly guy ducked inside. He hung his Castle County Sherriff's ball cap on a hook by the door. When he turned around, he met Ann's eyes and froze. She glanced over her shoulder in case someone was about to attack. Her heart sped up. There was no one there. He was staring at her.

Damn.

"Is that . . . is that . . ." the man said. He pointed a thick finger at Ann. "Is that Detective Ann Logan of the Salida PD?" He rushed over and grabbed her hand. "Deputy

Riley. George Riley. It is an honor and a pleasure."

He couldn't be older than twenty with his baby face and smooth skin. Ann pulled her hand out of his grasp. Deputy Riley pulled a chair over and sat facing her. He placed his huge hands on his knees, brushing her knee caps with his knuckles. Ann pushed her chair back, but it hit the desk. Trapped.

"How'd you do it, Detective?" Ann darted a glance to the door. "I read the paper, but I want to hear it from you. Straight from the horse's mouth as they say. I think that's what they say." He cocked his head.

What did he want? A play by play?

"I have a case—do you think you could take a look at it?" Deputy Riley leaned over Ann. His badge brushed her nose. Ann did everything she could to stop from pushing him out of her personal space while he rifled through a stack of files. Finally, he sat back to flip one open across her lap. "See if you confirm my suspicions?"

"Aw, George," McMichael said. "Leave her alone, will ya?"

George looked at Ann and pulled the file away. "I'm sorry, Detective. Am I outta line?"

"Maybe another time." Ann stood and maneuvered around him. "I gotta go."

"Don't let this buffoon scare you away." Rachel flipped a hand in George's direction. "He's harmless."

The office had suddenly grown too small with George Riley and his big goofy grin hovering around. Ann backed away to the door.

McMichael stood. "It was great to see you, Annie." He pulled her into another hug and whispered, "I'll subpoena your dad's phone records, okay?" Ann pulled away nodding. She mouthed a thank you and left the stifling office.

On the sidewalk, she took in a deep breath and turned to head home when the girl she saw in silhouette that morning ran across the street toward her.

CHAPTER 8

Teresa convinced herself the entire exchange with the strange little girl had been a dream. She often fell asleep during the day. She was asleep on the couch in the family room when Derrick called to tell her he'd made it to Aspen.

"Aspen?" Teresa said. "What are you doing there?"

He made a frustrated sound. "I told you, Teresa. I'm at a seminar on small practice management today."

Oh, right. The seminar. He signed up for it to make her feel guilty for having quit the practice a few years ago. Teresa had managed the business side of things—at least once her patients stopped coming to see her and before she stopped going in.

"I put it on the family calendar," he said. Teresa wandered into the kitchen to the bulletin board. It was there, not only circled in red marker but highlighted, too. He knew she'd miss it.

"I'll be home tonight," he said. "Late."

"What am I supposed to do with Maggie?"

Silence on the other end. She could only imagine what was going through his head. Probably the same thing she was thinking. Take care of *Maggie*? She could hardly take care of herself. But that wasn't true. She always made sure to beautify herself for him. Just like her mother taught her.

Always look your best for your husband.

"Don't forget to get Maggie from school," he said. "Oh, and Teresa?" His voice wasn't soft. "Make an effort." He hung up.

Make an effort.

She made plenty of efforts. She packed Maggie's lunch every day. She made sure dinner was on the table every night. She made sure the house was clean and presentable. What else was there? What else did she have to do to show him?

Later that day, Teresa walked to the school. The late afternoon air held the chill of an oncoming first snow. Teresa scowled. The only thing she hated worse than the cold was snow. She stood outside the school and waited for Maggie to come out. The girl bounded down the front steps and looked around. When she spotted Teresa, she froze. Her face fell, and she all but dragged herself over to Teresa.

"Hi," she said in a quiet voice. "Where's Daddy?"

"Derrick isn't going to be home until late tonight." She paused. "Looks like it's just us girls." She tried to put excitement in her voice.

Maggie only stared at her.

"Um, what would you like for dinner?"

Maggie cocked her head up at Teresa and narrowed her eyes—as though trying to peer through the *effort* Teresa was making.

"Pancakes?" Maggie asked in a hopeful question.

Pancakes? Seriously? For dinner?

"I have a nice roast in the fridge," Teresa said, even though it would take hours to cook. "Or, I can order pizza."

Maggie perked up. "Pizza? Oh goodie."

Teresa smiled because it seemed like the right thing to do. "What toppings do you like?"

"Last time Daddy took me I had the red circle things." She held up her fingers in a circular shape.

Teresa didn't even know when *Daddy* had taken Maggie for pizza. He certainly hadn't invited her along. She swore he didn't invite her to things on purpose, forcing this distance between her and Maggie. Why was it so easy for him to bond with children?

"Teresa?" Maggie said, her voice small.

"Huh? Oh, pepperoni," Teresa said. "Please, call me Mommy."

"Okay," Maggie said.

Across the street, the door to the Sheriff's office opened, and a woman Teresa had never seen before stepped out onto the sidewalk. She had an exotic look to her—tan skin, shiny dark hair. The woman shoved her hands into the pockets of her jacket.

"Who's that lady?" Maggie asked. "I need to meet her." She pulled away, and Teresa tightened her grip on the girl's hand. But Maggie jerked out of her grasp and took off across the street.

"Maggie!" Teresa called, looking up and down the street for cars. An image of Maggie getting hit flashed in her mind. Derrick would never forgive her. Maggie talked to the woman like they had met before.

"I'm Maggie, by the way." Her high-pitched voice bounced off the brick wall of the Sheriff's Department. "I live down the street that way. Do you live here? I've never seen you before. I like your coat. I got mine from Daddy when I moved here. I like pink. Do you like pink? What's your name?"

"Ann Logan," the woman said. She shook Maggie's hand. Maggie tugged the woman down into a crouch and whispered something in her ear. Ann got her hand free and backed up a step.

"I'm so sorry," Teresa said. She took Maggie by the shoulders and pulled her back.

"It's fine." Ann rubbed her hands together and shot glances at Maggie. "Ann Logan." She held out her hand.

"Doctor Teresa Hart." Teresa gave Ann's hand a quick squeeze. She crossed her arms and met the woman's bright blue eyes. "Aren't you the detective who caught the, what was it, Saliva Slaughterer?"

"Salida Stabber," Ann said. "That's me." She paused. "Hart? Are you Derrick's wife?"

Teresa narrowed her eyes. How did this woman know her husband?

"Yes," Teresa said, eying Ann up and down. She stood shorter than Teresa. The jacket hid her body, but her jeans were tight enough to show off shapely hips and thighs.

"So, you caught the killer, you saved the day, but you didn't really, did you?" Teresa had read the local paper. The town made Ann out to be some kind of hero, but Teresa saw the truth. Ann let her partner *and* the killer's last victim die. Heroes didn't do things like that.

Ann took a step forward. "Excuse me?"

Teresa smiled. "Oh, never mind." She waved a hand. "Serial killers are not a topic to discuss in front of a six-year-old."

"I'm seven now." Maggie grinned at Ann. "Today is my birthday."

"Happy birthday," Ann said, though she didn't smile.

"Why do people want to kill cereals? They're delicious. Especially Lucky Charms."

Teresa patted Maggie's head. "Tell me, Ann, how do you know my husband?"

"Your husband? Oh. Uh . . . we went to school together." Ann smoothed her fingers over her eyebrow. "I grew up here."

Teresa heard what Ann didn't say.

You didn't grow up here. You don't belong here. You're an outsider.

"Well, Detective," Teresa said. "I need to get this one

home and fed. Enjoy your stay." Teresa took Maggie's hand and led her down the sidewalk. Maggie stumbled along behind Teresa, looking over her shoulder at Ann.

Another person Maggie liked better.

CHAPTER 9

Back at the house, Ann burst inside and slammed the door. She leaned against it. Maggie's breath still tickled her ear.

I've been waiting for you.

Ann changed into her cold-weather running clothes and followed the road out of town. She focused on her panting breaths and footfalls to no avail.

Maggie was definitely the girl from the vision. Ann picked up speed. Maggie's breath in her ear had made the mark on her chest tingle. She shook her head to rid it of the memory and kicked into a full sprint.

A mile down the road, she passed Harmony Storage. She glanced at the main office. A person inside waved at her. She waved back, then halted. The yellow key tag with Harmony Storage had been sitting on the kitchen counter at her dad's house when she arrived. She thought it had fallen off the bulletin board, but maybe he left it there on purpose. She sprinted back to the house, gasping for air in the high altitude.

The key with A257 scrawled on the Harmony Storage tag sat right on top in the junk drawer she'd thrown it in.

On the short drive back to the storage place, the memory of the fight she and her father had the morning she'd left for the police academy swirled around in her head. He wanted her to stay in Harmony, follow in his footsteps, become his deputy, and eventually run for sheriff. Ann wanted so much more than that. She'd set her sights higher. They parted angry. She hadn't seen him since.

Ann pulled into the lot. She drove past the office and up and down the lanes until she found A257 in the back corner.

It was a smaller unit with a regular door instead of the typical, garage-style roll-up. She took a deep breath and stuck the key in the knob. With a little bit of jiggling, she got it unlocked and went inside.

Ann clicked on the light and surveyed the stacks of boxes. Years' worth of dust covered everything except a trail of footprints leading toward the back. Some kind of work boot, by the pattern of the tread. The tracks couldn't be more than a month or two old, based on the amount of dust.

She followed them to an unmarked box and flipped open the lid. Mom's angels, half-wrapped in newspaper, filled the box. She unwrapped a few and considered taking them home. Dad kept them on the mantle Ann's entire childhood to keep Mom's presence in the house. She was six when her mom died in a hit-and-run.

The key *was* a clue. Along with the missing angels. He'd expected her to put the two together. So much for being a great detective.

Ann closed the box and turned it around. Her dad's tidy but looping handwriting on the backside read, "Tchotchkes." Ann let out a snort. Her mom called all of her knickknacks by that name. There were a lot of boxes to go through, and Ann had no idea what she was even looking for. Something, anything, to give her an inkling of what happened to him.

After three and a half hours of searching through mostly unlabeled and mildewed boxes—at some point there must have been a leak—she found what she was hoping for in the one directly under the tchotchkes. Another mental smack.

Come on, Detective *Logan.*

She pulled a leather-bound journal filled with pages of her dad's handwriting out of the box. The stiff, warped pages crinkled under her fingers. Water damage had smeared or dissolved most of the writing.

The vanishing lines of writing turned to illustrations of what appeared to be reliquaries, but a lot of the words were indiscernible. The last drawing talked about how the necklaces—oh, necklaces, not reliquaries—were used as identifiers among the P-something. She flipped the page. They used ultra-violet lights. Something about how the necklace glowed under UV light. Silvery-blue.

Like my veins.

How could veins be inside a necklace? The necklace looked like it could hold something, and whatever that something was, glowed. She rubbed her arm for a second, thinking hard when it came to her. It wasn't her veins that glowed. It was what was inside them. It was her blood.

Normal blood appeared dark, almost black, under UV light unless sprayed with a solution like Luminal. So, a P-something's blood must glow, like hers did. But naturally.

She flipped ahead a few more pages toward the back where the writing became even more illegible. One page had SUMMON THE ANGEL written over and over again. A small key was taped to the opposing page along with a collection of signatures. Ann peeled the tape and put the key in her pocket. Then, she perused the names, but—of the ones she could decipher—she didn't recognize any of them. With the journal in hand, she left the storage unit, got in her truck, and drove to the little office just inside the gate.

An old man, the one who'd waved at her, glanced up. He had a pair of glasses perched on the end of his nose. "Hiya," he said with a smile. "What can I do you for?"

"I was wondering if you have any kind of record of who comes and goes around here. Or security tapes. Something like that."

"Oh, dear. Has someone broken into your unit?"

Ann shook her head, then reconsidered. "Kind of. They didn't steal anything, but they put a box in there. It had to be someone my father knew."

"Number?" he asked.

"A257."

"Let me see here." He opened a filing cabinet and flipped through some folders. "Bram Logan, A257—here we are." He stood and peered over his glasses. "You don't look like Bram Logan." He clicked his tongue and slapped the counter. "You must be Ann! Last time I saw you, you must have been in pigtails. Now you're catchin' killers and saving the world." He grinned. "One town at a time, eh?"

"Yep," Ann said.

"What did you need? Oh, yes. Some kind of record or security footage." He shrugged. "We don't have either."

She should have known. They didn't even have a computer. No electronic records of any kind.

"You wouldn't happen to know when my dad was here last, would you?"

He looked at the upper corner of the room. "I think I remember him driving by a few months ago. Didn't stop in to say hello like he usually does, I don't think. Memory's going, you know. Old age and all." He laughed like it wasn't a joke the elderly used all the time. "Coulda been him."

Though it wouldn't explain why a box of her mom's stuff was inside, she asked, "Who had the unit before my dad? Maybe they still have access."

The old man opened the file and flipped through it.

"Oh... the people who had it before your dad don't have it anymore because they died." He shook his head. "Death.

And taxes."

"Do you keep record of maybe other people who have keys?"

He shook his head. "All we keep track of is who's rentin' which unit. What they do with their keys is their business."

Ann's shoulders slumped. She gave the guy a brief smile. "Well, thank you. He must have stashed it there before he left town last time—or something."

"You drive safe out there. Looks like we're finally gettin' that snow storm the weather lady's been yappin' about."

Ann drove through flurrying snow. Back at the house, she grabbed a beer from the fridge, popped off the cap, and chugged over half of it before coming up for air. She sipped the rest of it while flipping through the journal again but didn't find anything new. The little key was her only hope, and she had no idea what it opened.

Ann finished off beer number one and grabbed another. She sat on the couch and leaned back. She wanted this to be her safe place. Sure, she came here to investigate her dad, but she also came to get away from her life's bull shit. Recoup. Recover. Get back in the game. She tried to see herself from the viewpoint of everyone who heard only the media's version of the story, but all she came up with was that her supposed courage led to a dangerous decision and the loss of two innocent lives.

An inventory of events from *the* night followed. The knife, the blood, the gunshots. How her legs shook so hard from the surge of adrenaline she could hardly stand.

Condition black—not able to do anything about the Salida Stabber's knife sticking out of the victim's chest. It pulsed as the girl's heart beat its dying rhythm. The life leaving her eyes.

The victim's eyes were brown with flecks of gold, fringed with thick black lashes. They locked Ann in their fear-filled gaze while the seven-year-old gasped for air that wouldn't fill her punctured lung. Ann would never forget those eyes.

She would never forget the way the blood spread across Bruce's white shirt or the way he looked at her with a combination of surprise and sadness.

Or was it regret?

The hot, prickly sensation in her eyes should have meant tears, but no tears came. Fine with her. Tears meant feeling. She took a long pull off her beer and let the numbness coat her emotions. But the sensation wouldn't subside.

The phone rang, and her beer bottle slipped from her hand. It hit the coffee table and toppled to the floor. A puddle of amber liquid foamed across the hardwood.

"Shit." Ann dashed to the kitchen and grabbed a towel and the cordless phone. "Hello?" She knelt to wipe up the mess.

Static and emptiness on the other end. A heavy breath. She sat back on her heels.

"Real funny, perv."

"Hello?" a man's voice came through the static.

"Dad?" She dropped the towel and gripped the phone with both hands.

"It's Asim Raghib." The voice was slightly accented. Ann slouched. She didn't know any Asim Raghib.

"What can I do for you?" Ann continued wiping up the mess. "If you're selling something, I don't want it."

"I knew your father," the man said. Ann froze. *Knew* your father. "It is a danger for me to call you. I have information for you." He paused. "Ann Logan."

He knew her name. He knew to call her at her dad's house. Just like the Stabber knew to call her at home that night to taunt her. Ann hung up the phone and tossed the cordless handset onto the couch. She wiped her hands on her pants.

For all she knew this was the guy who cut off her dad's finger. Or—because of his use of the past tense—much worse.

CHAPTER 10

Teresa served pizza onto Maggie's plate, and, like a barbarian, the girl picked up the greasy slice and shoved the end into her mouth. Teresa sat down at the opposite end of the table with knife and fork.

"I think we should invite that lady for dinner sometime," Maggie said with her mouth full. She took another bite before swallowing the previous one. "She's nice."

"Don't talk with your mouth full," Teresa said. She cut her pizza into small pieces. "And I don't think that would be appropriate. We hardly know her."

"*I* know her," Maggie said in a low voice. Teresa ignored her, and they finished their dinner in uncomfortable silence.

The rest of the evening passed without event. Maggie played in her room, which left Teresa with the opportunity to do some digging. She went to the garage and pulled down an old box with Derrick's handwriting on it. She opened it and found his high school yearbooks.

"Ann Logan . . ." she whispered, sliding her finger down the index. She flipped to the first page mentioned and found Ann's face among the line of smiling heads. Then she found Derrick's. There was a heart around his picture, and when she saw the message Ann had written, she dropped the book.

I will love you forever. —Ann

She tore through the other three yearbooks and found similar notes in all of them. Except the last one. His senior picture only had a heart next to it. No love note. Even still . . .

They weren't just a couple. They were high school sweethearts. Homecoming king and queen, no doubt. They were probably supposed to get married and have a family and grow old in the same godforsaken town they'd grown up in.

Together forever.

She put the books away and went back into the house. Upstairs she *made an effort* and checked on Maggie. The girl slept in the rocking chair in her room with a large book open on her lap.

The dirty old book had arrived hand delivered from the agency in charge of Maggie's welfare shortly after she'd moved into the house. A cryptic letter from Maggie's grandfather accompanied it. Both were written in another language, by hand, with heavy ink characters.

Teresa only knew who the letter was from because Maggie told Derrick, and Derrick told Teresa. It was

Maggie's only possession from her life before the Harts rescued her from an unknown fate.

When Teresa shifted the book to get a better look at it, Maggie stirred. The book slid to the floor where it landed and closed with a heavy *thump*.

"Maggie," Teresa said in a soft voice. She touched Maggie's shoulder. "Time for bed."

Maggie woke up just enough to slide off the rocker and climb into bed. She hit the pillow face first and was out. Teresa covered her prone form and smoothed her hair away, surprising herself with the small gesture of affection. It seemed a natural action. Perhaps *making an effort* was easier than she thought.

Easy enough when the child was asleep—and Derrick wasn't watching and analyzing and judging her every move.

She sat on the edge of the bed. He didn't trust her around Maggie. She saw it in the way he watched her. Almost as if he were looking for a reason to question her mental state again. To send her back to that hell. Back to Mountain View.

She shuddered and, with Maggie in bed, went to draw a bath. Nothing like near-scalding water to remove the chills from the day. The day-mares and the thoughts of the baby. Seven years gone. She slid lower into the water and closed her eyes, listening to her respirations and heartbeat in the muffled silence. When she finally sat up in the lukewarm bath, pale moonlight shone through the window.

Maggie's voice came through the wall. Teresa got out and pulled on her robe. Maggie giggled and talked, as if responding to someone. Teresa looked at the clock as she passed through the master bedroom. After midnight. Derrick must have come home and awoken her.

Mother would not have allowed it. *Let sleeping babes sleep*, she always said.

Teresa crept down the hall, curious to hear what they were talking about. What was so important he had to wake her? She peeked through the cracked door. Maggie sat on the floor by a large plastic dollhouse Derrick had gifted her for no reason at all.

"The mommy goes in the kitchen. She likes to make purple Jell-O with tangerines." Maggie dragged out the last word to a high note. Teresa heard a faint whisper, but it wasn't a man's voice. Maggie laughed. "No, silly. The daddy goes in the family room with the horses. I want a horse. If I had a horse, I'd name her Butterscotch and I would ride her to school. My grandpa had goats, but you can't ride them. They might eat your shoes."

Teresa pushed the door open an inch more, and the hinges creaked. Maggie jumped and looked up at her. No one was in the room. Kids had imaginary friends, still, didn't they?

"What are you doing out of bed?"

"I had a bad dream and couldn't go back to sleep." She placed the doll from her hand in the doll house bathroom. "I dreamed about the lion man stealing my light again."

She cocked her head at Teresa. "Teresa? Why does the baby go in the basement?" She held up one of the littlest of the dolls.

Teresa knelt on the floor and took the baby from Maggie's fingers. "She doesn't. She goes in the nursery." Teresa placed the doll in the little pink crib. It rocked back and forth.

"But . . . *she* said to move the baby stuff to the basement. Like you did."

"She said? She who?"

"Tiffany. She's right there." Maggie pointed to the corner where the rocking chair sat.

No. It couldn't be. It had been a dream. A nightmare.

Tiffany waved at Teresa with only her fingers, her eyes black spots on her face in the moonlit room. Her lips, pulled down into a disgusted frown, eased up at the corners into a sneer full of malice.

Teresa took a deep breath. "Maggie," she said. "Would you please come with me?" She didn't want to alarm the girl, and even though her pulse pounded in her ears, she fought the desire to snatch her up and rush her into the master bedroom. Tiffany's grin only deepened.

"What's the matter?" Maggie asked. Teresa flicked her eyes to the rocking chair.

"Just, please, come with me." Teresa held out her hand. Maggie took it, her brows knit together with a blend of worry and curiosity. Teresa took Maggie to her and Derrick's room and closed the door behind them.

"I thought it would be . . . fun . . . for you to sleep in here tonight." Teresa indicated the king-size bed.

"But . . . I'm not tired. Tiffany—did you see her?" Maggie climbed onto the bed but didn't crawl beneath the blankets. "Who is she?"

Teresa didn't know what to tell her. The truth was more frightening than a lie. That was certain. Teresa touched her golden cross and cleared her throat. "I didn't see her. Is she your invisible friend?"

Maggie's eyebrows screwed up in confusion.

"Try to get some sleep, okay?" Teresa said before Maggie could say anything else. She pulled the covers back, and Maggie crawled beneath them.

"I'm not even tired," the girl muttered.

Teresa turned off the light. A few minutes later, soft snores drifted from the mound of blankets.

Teresa went back to Maggie's room, but Tiffany was gone.

"Please stay away from Maggie," she whispered.

If anything happened to the girl on her watch, Derrick would send her back to Mountain View. Or leave her. She gasped and held back a sob. What would people think of her then? Unable to hold onto a child. Unable to hold onto a husband. Unable to hold onto her . . . sanity.

CHAPTER 11

Saturday

Ann followed Looney Lou Marga into her house, juggling a grocery bag and the woman's shawl full of oranges. Inside, a handful of cats looked up from their slumber. A tabby trilled and prowled over to them. It circled Louise's ankles then jumped on the table.

Music played from somewhere. A small, tinny sound. A closed door with a heavy bolt took up a section of the wall to the right of the entry. Ann cocked an ear toward it. That's where the music seemed to come from.

They went into a small kitchen off the main foyer, and Louise shooed the cat from the table. Ann set the oranges down. She handed the now empty shawl to Louise, who pulled it around her shoulders. A leather-bound book sat in the center of the table. *Gnostic Bible* had been embossed in gold leaf on the cover. Interesting choice of reading material.

"I can't thank you enough," Louise said, giving Ann a bony hug. The scent of cinnamon wafted from her. She released Ann but held her arm in a frail grip. "I would have been out my daily vitamin C if it weren't for you." She smiled a gruesome yellow smile and then busied herself filling a kettle. She put it on a lit burner.

Ann had gone for a run that morning and helped Louise when the old woman's grocery bag split and spilled her oranges into the street. Louise had all but begged Ann to join her for tea as a thank you for her kindness in "wrangling the wayward citrus."

"Please sit." Louise motioned to the table. "Just push her off."

Ann pulled the chair out and nudged a ginger cat to the floor. Louise smiled at her from the other end. The kitchen opened onto a sunken living room crammed full of bookshelves and toppling stacks of files, newspapers, and magazines. The room screamed *hoarder.*

How many cats are dead among the piles?

"So lovely to see you, dear," she said again. "I read the article about you in the paper. Our small-town hero." She smiled at Ann. "I wondered if you would ever come back. I know your father was awfully sad when you left."

"Yeah, he was. He didn't want me to go."

"Well, with your mother gone so many years, you're all he has." Louise looked up at her. "When people get older, loneliness can take quite a toll." A tear dribbled from her eye. Ann didn't know if it was from sadness, or because they were just watery old-lady eyes.

The kettle whistled. Louise poured hot water into two delicate tea cups. They rattled on their saucers as the old woman turned and set them down. Ann pulled one toward her. Her eyes lingered on the book on the table.

"The *Gnostic Bible*," Louise said. She pulled the book closer. "I studied the secret texts in college. Comparative Mythology major."

"Are these the codices from the Nag Hammadi library?" Ann asked. Louise nodded and smiled, her eyes crinkling. Ann's father had been big into the secret texts, which shed new light on the Bible. The texts were found in Egypt back in the 1940s. Bram had tried to teach her about them, but she was a rebellious teen when he broached the subject, so she didn't pay attention.

What I'd do to hear his voice now.

She ventured a sip of tea. Spicy cinnamon. It tasted like she was drinking Louise. She gently pushed the saucer a few inches away.

"Every culture has a creation myth." A black and white cat jumped into Louise's lap. She stroked its head. "Usually an entity of some kind creates the world, and in one way or another, life is born unto it." Louise sipped her tea with a noisy slurp. Her eyes grew serious. In a low voice, she murmured, "There are things we cannot see. Great forces that tug at the world and its fibers in directions we cannot fathom. Beings that have been fighting a war since the creation of the material world." Her eyes shifted and met

Ann's. Ann flinched. "I have a story you must hear."

Ann leaned back in her chair to distance herself from the serious lunacy that had entered Louise's voice and expression.

"Okay," Ann said. Louise flipped through the pages of the book but didn't read from them.

"The creator of the physical universe was a demiurge," Louise said.

"Demiurge?"

Louise paused in her page-turning and met Ann's eyes. "A heavenly being, subordinate to the Light, or Supreme Being, if that makes more sense."

"Uh, sure."

Uh, no.

"The demiurge's mother, Pistis Sophia, Faith Wisdom, created him without the help of her partner, nor the consent of the spirit, the Supreme Being." She paused and sipped her tea, her other hand still on the cat. "He was born disfigured, with the head of a lion and the body of a snake. When Pistis Sophia saw what she had created in her ignorance, she cast him from her and hid him in a cloud with a throne at the center. It's rather sad, really. She cast her child from her. She did not love him."

Ann furrowed her brow. Was this an allegory for what Ann did to her father? To Derrick? Or was she reading too much into it? No, she loved both of them when she left. Even though it hurt her to go, she had to. She needed to live her own life.

"The demiurge was known by three names."

"Why three?" Ann asked. She tried the tea again but couldn't get past the taste. Cinnamon tea would never be the same again.

"Mythology, dear. No reason for anything, really." Louise shrugged her shoulders. "He was called, Samael, meaning *blind god*, Sakla, meaning *fool*, and, as I like to call him, Yaldabaoth, meaning *child of chaos*." Her eyes twinkled.

"When Sophia cast him away, he stole some of her power, and with that power, he created the seven heavens and seven sons to rule them. When one of them left to be with Pistis Sophia's daughter, Zoe, Yaldabaoth created Death as his replacement. Death created his own children, all named after undesirable things, like jealousy, wrath, and suffering. Zoe countered Death's progeny with her own virtuous children, whom she named after good things, such as truth, love, and faith. Do you need more tea?"

Ann glanced at her still-full cup and shook her head.

"It can be said, then, since Pistis Sophia created both Zoe and Yaldabaoth, she is in fact responsible for creating all the bad and all the good in this world. In humanity."

Louise paused and took a sip before continuing. "Yaldabaoth and the rulers of the seven heavens feared mortal man. They feared he would eat from the tree of life and learn the rulers weren't as powerful as they claimed to be. Yaldabaoth claimed to be god. He believed he was the greatest power of the aeons. He didn't know there was anything before him."

"What was before him?" Ann asked.

"The Light."

"Like, god?"

"If that's what you believe." Louise's smile disappeared behind her tea cup.

"I believe in science," Ann said. "Evolution and facts."

"Of course, dear." Louise reached across the table and patted her hand. "Your father believes in angels." The patting became bony fingers clenched around Ann's hand.

Ann sucked in a breath. The cat fled.

"You were drawn here," Louise said. Her eyes widened and her face went slack. "Drawn by a force greater than you or me. Listen to me, Ann."

Ann pulled at her hand, but Louise had a tight grip. Maggie's words drifted through her mind.

I've been waiting for you.

"There are things in this world. Terrible things. The worst is yet to come." Louise took in a wheezing breath, released Ann's hand, and sat back, breathless.

"Are you okay?"

Louise adjusted her shawls and nodded. She brushed her hair out of her face.

"Upon hearing Yaldabaoth claim to be god," Louise continued as though she hadn't just had some strange out of body demon possession thing happen, "Pistis Sophia called forth a fiery angel to bind Yaldabaoth and send him to Tartaros."

"Tartaros is . . . Hell?" Ann asked.

"Why, yes dear. Aren't you clever." Louise smiled.

"It's an interesting story," Ann said. "Thank you for sharing it. I should probably get going now."

"You were unaware of this story?" Louise asked.

"I think some of it seemed a little familiar," Ann said. "But for the most part it's the first I've heard it."

Louise cocked her head. "Interesting."

"How so?" Ann asked.

"I thought your father would have told you about it."

"I think he tried." Ann's skin prickled. "Why do you think he would have—"

"Because of who he works for, Ann," Louise said.

"My dad? He's retired. You know that. Frank McMichael took his place years ago."

Louise's brow furrowed. Then she smiled. "Of course, of course. What was I thinking?"

CHAPTER 12

Teresa woke in the not-so-plush armchair in the corner of the bedroom, her neck and back stiff. She looked at the bed.

Maggie was gone.

Teresa jumped to her feet, shoved the door open, and ran to Maggie's room. Not there, either. Then she heard giggles from the first floor—and Derrick's voice. The scent of bacon wafted up the stairs.

Teresa sat on the top step and listened to them. Even though she couldn't hear what they said, their tones were joyous. She wanted to cry. With relief? With fear? With jealousy? She didn't know.

She went to the bathroom and prepared herself to greet her husband. When she finished the final touches on her hair and makeup, she went downstairs. Typically, she would be up well before Derrick and Maggie, and she would go into the basement. Maybe read one of the baby's books to the silence. Maybe hold the nursing pillow on her lap. Maybe just sit in the rocker and wish.

In the kitchen, Derrick was at the stove making pancakes. He flipped them over singing, "Pancakes, pancakes."

Maggie giggled. Teresa wanted to smile, wanted to be in there with them, happy, laughing, taking part in the family.

Making an effort.

She would walk in, kiss Maggie on the top of the head, sing along with Derrick. Hug him from behind. Kiss him. She would smile. They would smile with her. They would all be happy. Yes.

After the events of last night, her effort with Maggie, she could see those things happening more easily than ever.

She positioned a smile on her face and stepped into the kitchen.

"Hey." Her voice cracked.

Maggie looked at her. Derrick paused mid-flapjack-flip. Neither one of them smiled. Neither one of them greeted her. It was stupid of her to think she could walk in and become part of them.

The pancake on Derrick's spatula dropped onto the floor. He turned his eyes to Maggie.

"Man down!" he said. Maggie beamed.

They were happier without her. She should just leave. Go to the basement and lock herself inside and not come out until they left to go do daddy-daughter stuff together. Things she wasn't allowed to do with them.

But no. She was *making an effort.* It wasn't her fault they made it so damn hard. She straightened her blouse and sat next to Maggie at the breakfast bar.

"What's the plan for today?" she asked.

Derrick busied himself at the oven. Pulled the tray of bacon out, poured off the grease, clattered the tray back inside.

"It's supposed to be warmer today, so we thought we'd go fishing," Derrick said with a tight smile.

He knew she didn't care for fishing. "Oh?" she said. "Can I go?"

Derrick's smile faltered. His eyes darted to Maggie then back to Teresa.

"Uh, sure." He cleared his throat. "But we only have two poles."

Maggie was in their bed when he came home, wasn't she? Didn't that tell him anything about the effort she was making? Didn't that tell Maggie she could view Teresa as her mother? Her guardian? She'd rescued Maggie from a ghost, for Pete's sake!

"I can get one," she said. "What time does Mullen's open?" She got up from the stool to retrieve her purse.

Derrick's eyebrows came together. "Mullen died three years ago. His shop's been closed ever since."

Teresa dropped her eyes to the counter top and bit her lip. When she looked back up at her husband, she heard the words behind his frown

Don't you ever leave the house? Don't you read the

community paper? Don't you care about the town you live in?

"Maybe next time," she said in a quiet voice. "Excuse me."

She went to the front room and sat on the love seat with Big Bear. Outside the window the sun warmed the night's dew. Clouds of steam rose from the ground like awakened spirits.

Derrick's singing and Maggie's laughter drifted down the hallway.

We can be together again. Tiffany's words whispered in her mind. *Just say yes.*

Laughter. Singing. Smiles. Happiness. Where did she fit in with that? What did she have to do to wedge herself into their lives? To be part of this family?

Say yes, Mommy.

Teresa lifted her hand to the cross at her throat. A tear dripped down her cheek.

God, forgive me.

"Yes," she whispered. "Yes."

CHAPTER 13

Derrick and Maggie left with backpacks and fishing poles and smiles. Teresa waited until the family car pulled out of the driveway and disappeared down the road. Then she tiptoed into the hallway.

"Tiffany? Are you here?" She peered into the front room. "I'm saying yes. I want another chance. Please come out."

Nothing.

She sighed and looked at Big Bear. Seeing him sitting there amongst the pillows jarred her memory. Tiffany had said her friend was staying in the abandoned funeral home. Maybe Tiffany was staying there too. She took a light jacket from the coat closet and went outside.

Derrick and Maggie went south. She went north into town. Derrick was right. She rarely left the house. Why would she? There was nothing out here for her. The people didn't even care for her.

"Good morning, Mrs. Hart," someone shouted from

across the street, as if to prove her wrong.

"It's *Doctor* Hart," she said. The person's smile faded. Teresa pulled her jacket tighter and kept her eyes on the sidewalk until she reached the dirt road that led out to the old graveyard.

When Derrick first brought her to Harmony, he'd given her the grand tour of the place. Back then she was just happy to have a new husband and a new future ahead of her. Happy to be living her life according to her mother's plans. His tour included the abandoned funeral home, mainly because that's where he and his high school buddies did all of their underage drinking.

He probably took Ann there, too. Is that where they shared their first time? Teresa shook the thought from her head and lifted her chin.

The damp ground squelched under her feet. She wiggled her toes inside her ballerina flats, and, undeterred by her lousy choice of footwear, picked her way between the muddy potholes.

Despite her careful attempt to keep her shoes clean, they were a mess, and her toes were numb by the time she reached mile marker one. She turned and peered into the forest. Then she stepped over the little creek and stood among the trees.

The old house sat tucked back away from the road. The front porch steps bowed in the middle, the rusty nails no longer able to hold them to the frame. It made the house look as though it smiled. The front door hung open to the left on a single hinge, inviting her in.

Teresa wondered if Tiffany was inside, if Tiffany's friend was home. The friend who would reunite them and make everything better. Fix it all. Bring back her happiness.

Teresa approached the porch and ascended the steps.

"Tiffany?" she called, though her voice only came as a whisper. "Are you here?"

A sudden chill in the air tingled over her skin, and she tugged her jacket tighter. She peered through the darkness into the entry but couldn't see anything. The remnants of caution tape hung from a staple in the upper right corner of the door frame. She put one foot over the threshold. No turning back.

This is what you want.

Inside the house, the air warmed. Much warmer than it should have been. The stench of mildew and urine permeated her nostrils. Teresa crinkled her nose. This was no place for her daughter to live.

The farther she ventured inside, the warmer it got. Teresa loosened her jacket. It had to be nearly as warm as Derrick kept the house.

"Tiffany?" Teresa's voice seemed too loud in this damp, muted place. She closed her eyes. It wasn't real. It *had* been a dream. Of *course* it had been. Since when did dead daughters appear seven years after their death asking for help to come back? Teresa let out a long breath and opened her eyes.

Fire light licked from torches set in stone. Stone walls?

She turned around. The doorway was still visible, centered on a crumbling plaster wall, flanked by windows. But when she turned back around, the walls dissolved into sandy stone. Toward the back of the cave, a pool of water reflected the light, and a tunnel led off into complete darkness.

"Hello?" she said. Her voice traveled far away. She reached for one of the torches.

"Mommy!" Tiffany's voice said from behind her. "You came!"

Teresa turned, and Tiffany ran to her and danced around her, beaming with delight. What a difference from the malice that adorned her face the previous night.

"I knew you would come." She grinned up at Teresa. Teresa dropped to one knee. The firelight danced across Tiffany's beautiful, pale face.

"Yes, I'm here," Teresa said. "And my answer is yes. I do want to be with you again. I will do anything to have you back."

Tiffany's eyes sparkled in the flickering flames. "I know."

"Where is your . . . friend?" Teresa looked around. "I'd like to meet him."

"He's not here." Tiffany danced away in a circle. "You don't need to worry about him, anyway." She twirled back to Teresa and stared into her face. "I will come to you tonight, and we can get started."

"Get started on what?"

Tiffany threw her head back and laughed a girlish cackle. "It's a surprise, Mommy! I can't tell you everything!"

Teresa didn't like not knowing what was expected of her. She wanted all of the details, the requirements, to get her daughter back. But Tiffany's face, her beautiful expression, told her, just this once, she could let go of that control.

"Okay," Teresa said. She watched her daughter dance in the firelight. Her grace and beauty in direct contrast to the rough and dirty cave. "Would you be more comfortable at the house?"

Tiffany shook her head. "I can't be away from my friend for very long. I get so weak." She drooped her body forward. Then she snapped upright again. She patted Teresa's head. "Go home, Mommy. I will see you tonight."

"Oh . . . okay." Teresa stood and backed away, not wanting to leave her baby. She turned and stepped onto the front porch. At the steps, she looked back. Inside, the room was dark, but she could just make out old living room furniture, a door, and a staircase.

"I'm losing my mind," she whispered. "I've completely lost it." She trudged back to town, ignoring the puddles and the muddy sections of the road. When she reached the roundabout, her pant legs were wet halfway up her shins, her feet covered in mud. She'd have to throw those shoes away. There was no saving them.

CHAPTER 14

After going home to change clothes—she couldn't have possibly gone to Tiffany's grave covered in mud—Teresa wandered to the new cemetery west of town and turned left at the winterized fountain near the entrance. The absence of the trickling water cast an eerie silence over the grounds. She shivered against the chilly morning and slipped her hands into her pockets.

Tiffany's grave wasn't too far. With everything going on yesterday, she'd forgotten to stop by. She always visited twice a year. Tiffany's birthday, and the anniversary of her passing. It was part of her grieving process, like cleaning the basement nursery every week and sitting in the rocker most mornings.

She followed the path to Tiffany's grave. The casket beneath her feet was smaller than the massive white marble tombstone Derrick had picked out.

A sob bubbled up at the thought of the tiny pink box holding her daughter's remains. She stifled it. Soon enough they would be together again. No need for tears.

She knelt on the ground, cleared away the debris around the grave, and straightened the white river rocks decorating the outer border. For Tiffany's birthday, she always brought flowers. For the anniversary, she brought guilt and sorrow.

She cleared her throat and prepared to recite her usual prayer.

"My little blessing," she whispered. "God has you in his arms now—"

Footsteps crunched on the gravel path, and three teenagers, two boys and a girl, laughed their way past her. Teresa scowled. Such disrespect to laugh in a cemetery. They stopped at a large grave marker ten yards away and leaned against it. The first boy flicked a lighter and lit a cigarette. He took a long drag and held his breath before letting it out. A skunky scent wafted over to her, carried on a slight breeze.

The boy said something, and the other two laughed again.

"Show some respect," Teresa said, loud enough for her voice to carry to them.

One of the boys peered at Teresa and took a few steps in her direction. The girl tugged at his arm and pleaded with him. Teresa heard it in the whine of the girl's voice. The boy pulled out of her grip. "Excuse me?"

Teresa turned back to Tiffany's tombstone, traced the letters of her name. She closed her eyes.

"Excuse me? What did you say?" Gravel crunched as he took a couple more steps toward her.

She ignored the kids, pretended she couldn't hear them, bowed her head, and clenched her teeth.

One boy said, "Oh jeeze. Do you know who that is?" One of them sucked on the marijuana cigarette they were sharing. On his exhale, he said. "It's Teresa fuckin' Hart."

"Is that her dead baby's grave?" The other boy said in a voice Teresa hoped was supposed to be a whisper.

Teresa touched her collarbone, found the chain of her necklace, and held the cross in her hand.

"Guys, shut up. She might hear you," the girl's voice whined.

Without turning to them, Teresa shouted, "You kids get out of here!" She wished they would leave so she could make her annual peace.

Another round of inhales. Out of the corner of her eye, Teresa saw one slap the other on the shoulder with the back of his hand.

"Hey, hey, Paul." He let out an unharnessed laugh. "How do you put a baby in the blender?"

Paul laughed so hard his voice cracked, and all that came out was airy huffing. "Feet first," he said with a gasp, "so you can see the expression on its face."

Teresa's throat went dry. Her heart beat so hard and so fast, she swore anyone with eyes could see it pound. Her ears tuned in on every word they spoke.

"Hey, Ryan, what's worse than a pile of dead babies?"

Teresa refused to give any sign she was listening to them.

"Oh god, I love this one." Ryan laughed. "A live one at the bottom, eating its way out. *Nom nom nom.*"

The girl tugged at the first boy. "Please, you guys. Ryan, stop. You're being so mean."

I should leave.

But Teresa wouldn't. She couldn't. She would have to walk right past them to get to the front gate. And if she left now, they would win.

"Wait, wait, wait," Paul said. In her peripheral vision, he turned to Teresa and smiled a devil's grin.

"When is the best time to bury that baby you killed?"

Teresa's fingernails bit into her palms. Her heart thundered behind her eyeballs.

Ryan snorted. "When it . . . when it . . . when it . . ." He couldn't get the last part out through his laughter. "When it starts talking to you again."

Teresa's head involuntarily jerked in their direction. The boys stopped laughing and stared at her with evil sneers. The girl stood off to the side, gripping her elbows, as if not to be guilty by association. She looked at Teresa with sadness. Pity.

The boys doubled over, howling and slapping their knees.

"Please, Ryan, stop it," the girl said. "I'm so sorry, Mrs. Hart," she whined at Teresa.

Teresa stood and faced them. "That's *Doctor* Hart."

The girl took off, leaving her male comrades behind. Teresa wanted to mock *them*—words that would hurt—but she leaned against Tiffany's gravestone in resignation.

Her eyes focused on a rock. Her mind carried her away.

What if I just threw it at them?

She imagined doing so. Imagined the rock sailing through the air and hitting the boy named Paul in the foot. His dance backward while Teresa picked up a second rock. She'd throw it as a warning, a threat. But it would fly through the air and hit Ryan clean in the nose. He would cry out and grab his face, blood dripping between his fingers . . .

"Fucking crazy lunatic!" Paul shouted.

She shook herself from the dream to find she'd approached them a few steps. Blood gushed from Ryan's nose.

The boys kept their eye on her and edged out of the graveyard.

"Well, I *am* a doctor," Teresa shouted. "Or did you forget that, you little shits?"

"I'm calling the sheriff!" Paul shouted over his shoulder, ushering Ryan away.

"For what? To tell him you were smoking pot and being disrespectful to the dead? Go ahead!" She strode after them a few paces, hurrying them on their way.

On her way back to the grave, she found one of the stones shot with rose quartz from the site and picked it up. Someone had defaced it with red paint. She put it in her pocket along with some other refuse to throw away later. Then she knelt again and bowed her head to deliver the annual prayer.

"My little blessing. God has you in his arms now, to love and protect you as one of his own angels. As the angel you are and always will be." Then, she recited Ecclesiastes, *for everything there is a season,* and bowed her head to sit in silence.

CHAPTER 15

Teresa woke curled in a ball on the ground, disoriented until her eyes landed on the gravestone. She placed her hand on it, a loving caress across Tiffany's name. A silent vow to free her. Then jerked up and looked around. No one was there. Hopefully no one had seen her sleeping in a public place. Imagine the rumors *that* would cause. She straightened the stones around the grave.

When is the best time to bury that baby you killed?

She sucked in a breath. A tremor shook her hand as she laid the last stone.

It didn't happen. It was a dream, or vision. A sick carrying away of thoughts. She got to her feet and crossed her arms, clamping her hands in her armpits to stop the shaking. The air grew chilly.

Bury that baby you killed.

She shook her head. A nightmare. She had fallen asleep, after all. It was a dream.

That baby you killed.

That joke didn't even make any sense.

Baby you killed.

"I didn't kill any baby!"

A sob escaped her. Then a second. A third. She sank to her knees and rested her forehead against Tiffany's name. "We'll be together again soon." She kissed the smooth stone and wiped her eyes.

* * *

Ann chose her usual booth in the back corner of the diner. Louise had mentioned she'd seen Ann's dad at the diner a while back, reminding her she'd never gotten a response from Ruthie about when she'd seen him last.

Ruthie came by with a coffee pot, which seemed to be an extension of her arm, and filled Ann's cup.

"How're you settling in?" Ruthie asked, placing a menu on the table.

"Little at a time." Ann tore open a creamer cup and stirred it into her coffee. "It's weird being back in my old house, but I'm getting used to it. Hey, when was the last time my dad came in?"

"I remember exactly," Ruthie said. "Three months ago, Wednesday, the same day Bobby set fire to the cook top trying out a new recipe." She rolled her eyes. "Your dad jumped to action and stopped Bobby just in time. He was going to throw water on a grease fire."

Ann winced.

"Yeah. Bram grabbed the class B and put it out lickety-split."

"Bobby still work here?"

Ruthie dropped her head back and groaned. "Yes. He knows the menu. He's just not allowed to experiment anymore."

Ann snorted. "Plus, it's Harmony. Not like people are flocking here for work, right?"

Ruthie winked and placed her hand on Ann's shoulder. "I'll be right back to take your order."

Ruthie rushed around the dining room, refilling coffee, chatting and laughing with the other guests. Ruthie was a staple in this town. The people could count on her, and she obviously enjoyed having that role in the community. It was all over her smiling face and in the sound of her voice.

* * *

On her way back through town, Teresa found a small two-top by the kitchen in the diner to warm up, the afternoon's dream nearly forgotten.

"Doctor Hart!" Ruthie's voice said to her left. Teresa jumped and turned. "It's so good to see you."

Teresa composed a courtesy smile on her lips. "Thank you, Ruthie."

"Coffee?" Ruthie held out her coffee pot, and Teresa nodded. "I know it's not my place to say or ask," she said. "It's just . . . I know Derrick offers exams now as part of annual physicals and all, but I'm not comfortable with male doctors, and I hate driving all the way to Pine Valley. I just don't have the time." She pulled a couple sugar packets from her apron, set them on the table, and met Teresa's eyes. "When are you coming back to the clinic?"

"Oh." Teresa twisted her coffee cup on the table and watched the contents swirl. She thought people knew her license had been revoked. She thought that was why they shunned her. "I'm not sure." She took a sip.

"Well, you have a patient in me when you do," Ruthie said.

"You would be the only one," Teresa whispered as Ruthie walked away.

Ruthie had always been nice to Teresa. Teresa thought it was just part of her job, but back when Ruthie had been her patient, she always took the time to catch up and inquire about Derrick and how Teresa's pregnancy was going. She always asked to touch Teresa's belly *before* touching it. Teresa placed her hand on her flat stomach. Back then, she didn't mind things like that. Now she could hardly stand being in this place with its fried grease smells and collection of wrinkled regulars. The thought of veined, knobby hands touching her, groping at her belly, turned the corners of her mouth down.

Ruthie bustled around the diner, stopping to chat at each table. Laughing, filling coffee, gasping in surprise at a young woman's ring finger. She worked the diner day and night, Sunday to Sunday. If she wasn't careful, she would work herself to death.

Did Ruthie look thinner than Teresa remembered?

The menu Ruthie left on the table listed an array of greasy, fried foods, a section of food smothered in gravy, and a small selection of salads with fried chicken strips. For just two dollars more you could smother it in gravy. Teresa scowled and pushed the menu away.

Just as she finished her coffee, Derrick and Maggie came in. Derrick's face lit up, but he wasn't looking at her. Teresa followed his gaze and found Ann sitting in a corner booth. After a second, Teresa's family sat down with Derrick's ex-girlfriend.

Well, isn't this just perfect?

Teresa considered confronting them, but the diner was full of people. How might that look? Baby killer, jealous wife. She left a few dollars on the table and slid out of the booth.

She slipped into the kitchen before sneaking out the side door undetected.

* * *

Ann looked up and saw Derrick come in. Maggie bounced along behind him, holding a massive book, her long dark curls springing with her steps. Ann's gut twisted. The girl. And now the book. Maggie spotted Ann in her faraway corner and came toward her. Derrick followed.

Oh no.

"Hey, Ann," he said, slipping out of his jacket.

"We went fishing," Maggie said, her cheeks rosy. "I got a big one, but Daddy let it go." She slid into the booth and sat on her knees, placing the book on the table. It had a worn leather cover. The yellowed pages inside were wrinkled and warped like a paperback left in the rain.

"Maggie," Derrick said. "Ann didn't invite us to sit down."

"It's okay, Daddy," Maggie said. "She was going to ask us." She opened the book and flipped through the pages.

"Sorry," Derrick said. "Do you mind?"

Yes, she did mind, but motioned to the opposite bench.

"This is my daughter, Maggie," Derrick said.

"We met yesterday," Ann said. "It's good to see you again, kiddo."

"You, too." Maggie perused the book, her body fidgeting on the bench. Derrick asked her if she wanted to take her coat off—a puffy pink jacket—and helped her out of it.

"What are you reading?"

"A book my *baba* gave me." The tip of her tongue poked out the corner of her mouth. Then she said, "He's dead."

Derrick raised his eyebrows and shook his head. "A few weeks after we adopted Maggie, a member of the adoption agency hand delivered this book, which was kind of weird, actually. It had a letter with it explaining her grandfather had passed." He shrugged. "I can't read a word of it, but she seems to be able. She's read a few passages to me. Sounds like it's some kind of religious book." He huffed air through his nose. "I haven't told my wife. If she knew Maggie was reading some religious text other than the Bible there would be a holy shitstorm from hell."

"Daddy—language," Maggie said without looking up. Derrick covered his mouth in mock shame. Ann laughed. Ruthie came back over and glanced from Derrick to Ann and back.

"Hey, Doc. Teresa's sitting across the way." Ruthie glanced over her shoulder, and Derrick followed her gaze, the smile gone from his face. "Or not. I guess she was in a hurry."

Visible relief washed over him. He shifted his weight on the bench and cleared his throat, the tips of his ears bright red.

Ruthie flipped to a new page in her notepad. "I already know what Miss Maggie wants." Ruthie bent over. Maggie draped herself across the table, and at the same time they said, "Pancakes!"

Ann closed her eyes and tried to stay calm. This was all too small-town-perfect.

Ruthie righted herself and looked at Ann. "Detective?"

"I'm good with the coffee, thanks."

"You need to eat," Ruthie said. "I'll bring you the special. On the house, hero." She winked.

"I'll pay," Ann said.

"And for the hungry doctor?" Ruthie looked up from her notepad at Derrick.

"I'll do the BLT, extra B," Derrick said. He winked at

Ann. "Cholesterol shmolesterol, right?" He laughed, so did Ruthie. Ann did her best to not look as uncomfortable as she felt.

"You got it." Ruthie rushed off.

"Is there some joke I'm missing?" Ann asked Derrick.

"What do you mean?" He raised an eyebrow.

"So much winking going on around here, just thought I missed something."

Derrick laughed. "Nah." He waved his hand. "You haven't missed anything. I'm sure you've seen nothing's changed around here."

Ann nodded and wished he'd stop smiling at her.

"It really is great to see you." To her shock he slid his hand across the table and clasped hers. She pulled away, and his face sobered. He cleared his throat and sat back as if to get as far away from her as possible. Thank god.

"So, did you meet my wife yesterday, too, or did Maggie's teacher walk her home?"

"Your wife. She seems—interesting," she said for lack of anything better to say. "She's . . . well . . ."

"Unfriendly. Unpleasant. Self-centered." Derrick said under his breath.

Ann cleared her throat. "Should we be talking about this in front of Maggie?"

Derrick leaned over and petted Maggie's hair. He pulled her against his side and hugged her. She gazed up at him with adoration in her eyes.

"I need to hit the bathroom," Derrick said. "You don't

mind watching Maggie, do you?"

"Sure." She did mind. She minded a lot.

Maggie hummed random notes while she flipped through the book, her eyes darting across the text. The handwritten words on the page weren't English by any stretch. But, to Ann's relief, they weren't scribbled nonsense, either. Not like the book from her dream.

"What language is that?" Ann asked.

"Coptic Egyptian," Maggie said, pronouncing each syllable carefully. She turned the book sideways for Ann to get a better look. "My baba helped the Protectors. They are people like you."

"People like me?" Ann asked. Then she got it. "Oh, you mean cops?"

Maggie shook her head and leaned closer. She lowered her voice. "Protectors of the Knowledge." She tapped her temple.

Ann sat back. Her heart beat painfully hard a couple times. She rubbed the center of her chest.

"At first I thought it was Daddy," she said, her eyes on the book. "Then I met you, and now I get it." She met Ann's eyes. "The book told me—just like Baba said it would."

You were drawn here . . . I've been waiting for you.

A dull roar started in Ann's ears. The lights seemed to brighten. She closed her eyes and rubbed her temples. The roar escalated until all of the voices in the room combined into mumbled rumbling.

I'm having a stroke.

"You're broken on the inside," Maggie whispered, crisp and clear, in her ear. "But you'll heal."

The roar stopped. Ann opened her eyes. Maggie was gone but the book remained. She sat up straight and surveyed the room. Where did the little shit go?

"Maggie?" she called. "Maggie?"

Shit. She'd lost her ex's daughter. She tore out of the booth. Laughter came from the center of the restaurant along with Maggie's clear, high voice reciting something that sounded like a poem.

"'Light and darkness, life and death. But the good are not good, the wicked not wicked, life not life, death not death. Those who live above the world cannot fade. They are eternal.'" She turned, and her eyes bored into Ann's. "'Wisdom is mother of the angels.'"

The guests clapped, and she took a bow, grinning. Derrick stood behind her, clapping as well. He guided her back to their booth. Ann swallowed the wad of burlap in her throat and took deep breaths to stop her heart from racing.

"Excellent, Maggie," Derrick said, leading her back to the table. "Where did you learn that?"

"From Baba's book." She placed her palms on the pages and looked at Ann. Ann forced herself to smile.

Ruthie brought their lunches, and even though her appetite had once again vanished, Ann forced herself to eat. The special was a slab of chicken-fried steak smothered in gravy, served with a salad. As if the salad would cancel out the entrée.

When they'd finished eating, Derrick grabbed the bill and took it to the front to pay before Ann could protest.

Maggie stared at her. "I want you to have this," she said. She pushed the book across the table.

"I can't take that," Ann said. "Your . . . Baba gave that to you. I can't even read it."

"You can't?" Maggie sat back. Her eyebrows knitted together in confusion. "But the book said . . ." she started, but then Derrick came back and sat down.

"Did I miss anything this time?" he asked, nudging Maggie. "Did you recite more poetry?"

Maggie shook her head. She flipped the book shut.

"I'd like to go home now," she said in a small voice.

Derrick looked at Ann and shrugged. "Her Majesty gets what Her Majesty wants." He smiled.

"Thanks for lunch," Ann said.

Derrick helped Maggie with her coat and led her by the hand. Maggie looked over her shoulder at Ann, much like the way she had when Teresa hauled her away. But this time her expression wasn't so excited as it had been then. Her face held a different expression now. Disappointment.

CHAPTER 16

Teresa got home and paced up and down her hallway like an angry lioness. How dare he? How. Dare. He. She took deep breaths and tried for rational thoughts, but her mind was overblown with worst-case scenarios.

He's cheating.

No. Not cheating. Not yet anyway. A public place with a child was not exactly an affair.

Teresa went down to the basement and clicked on the nursery lamp. She sat in the rocker with the nursing pillow on her lap and worked to shift her mind to Tiffany.

"We'll be together again soon," she whispered. "We'll have our life back the way it was before. We'll be happy again. All of us." She hummed a lullaby and stroked the pillow.

She rocked in the chair until she heard Derrick and Maggie's arrival home above her. Then her throat went dry. How could she bring up what she saw? How could she confront him? Wretched despair weighed her down.

Maggie's rapid footsteps ran up the stairs, and Derrick's heavier footsteps stomped down the hall. A hard knock came from the other side of the basement door. Then Derrick's muffled voice yelled through it.

"Teresa, come out of there," he said. "Now."

She didn't like his tone. He had no right to yell like this. She hadn't done anything wrong. He had. She went upstairs and opened the door. Derrick stood in the hallway, his arms crossed tight.

"I ran into Sheriff McMichael today after lunch," he said through his teeth. His nostrils flared.

"Sherriff McMichael?" She didn't know what the significance of this might be.

"He said you assaulted some kids at the cemetery."

Her scalp tingled. "I did nothing of the sort." That man would do anything to continue to tarnish her reputation, like he'd first done when the baby died. She pushed past Derrick into the hallway and went to the kitchen.

"He said one kid's mother called him. Said you threw rocks at them." He followed her and grabbed her arm. She jerked away from him.

"I didn't do anything. I went to Tiffany's grave since it was seven years ago yesterday she *died*." Teresa instilled her voice with scorn and balled her fists. "I cleared away the leaves and straightened the stones." Her voice hitched on the last word. Derrick's face didn't change. "You don't believe me, do you? You never believe me. You always take the other person's side."

She stormed down the hall to avoid his glaring eyes and racked her brain, trying to figure out if any of the dream had been real. She got her coat out of the closet by the front door.

"Where are you going?" Derrick followed her. "You can't leave. We need to talk about this."

Teresa reached into the pocket of her coat and drew out the paint-spattered rock. It dropped from her trembling hand and hit the hardwood. Not paint. Blood. She covered her mouth and sank to her knees.

"What's that?" Derrick picked up the rock. "What is this?"

"Oh God," Teresa whispered.

"Is this . . . blood?"

"They were taunting me." She hated the way her voice trembled. "They told horrible jokes about dead babies. I felt threatened. I had to protect myself."

"Goddammit, Teresa, they are kids. *Kids.*" He walked away, turned, and came back. "What is going on with you?" His voice drained of anger. His eyes softened. Placing his hands on her arms, he helped her stand. Was he finally going to listen?

Don't be fooled.

"I saw you at the diner," she said. "With another woman."

He halted and stared at her. "Ann? She's an old friend I haven't seen in decades. We were just catching up."

"She was your high school sweetheart, Derrick." Her

voice was an octave too high, bordering on hysteria.

"Teresa, please," Derrick said. "I married *you*. I chose *you*. Don't you trust me?"

Did she? She never had reason not to. Not until now.

"I try, Derrick." She gripped his sleeves. "I try so hard." The opportunity had arrived, and she found herself unable to tell him what she wanted to say. How she did everything for him. How he pushed her away. How even when she did try it wasn't good enough. "It's never enough," she whispered.

"What's never enough?" he asked. The usual tone returned, full of disdain.

"The effort I make," she said. "Making lunch, taking care of the house, looking nice for you." Her voice grew smaller, became a whisper. "It's never enough for you. Is that why you're . . . having an affair?" She stared at the front of his shirt.

He threw his hands up. "Lunch with a friend is not an affair." He shook his head and paced. Here it was. The disbelief. She was wrong to think he would understand her pain.

"What happened to us?" she asked. Hot tears spilled down her cheeks. She wiped them away. "Why do you hate me so much?"

He barked a short laugh.

"You sit in your damn dark basement and brood." He didn't deny hating her. "You sit down there, and you feed yourself lies and stories and stupid . . . shit! Then you come up here and fill this house with your pain. *Your* pain." He held out his hand. "Give me the key."

Teresa backed away. She held the key to her chest, attached to her like an umbilical cord by a coiled lanyard around her wrist.

"No," she said. "No, you can't."

"Give it to me, or I swear to God, Teresa." His fists clenched.

Derrick had never struck her or ever threatened to. Her mother's words screamed through her mind.

Keep your husband happy, and he will never have a reason to discipline you.

"No, you can't have it. You can't take this from me." She dodged by him and ran for the kitchen. Her socks slipped on the hardwood. Derrick grabbed her arm and pulled her against him.

Fire in his eyes, he grabbed her wrist. She squeezed her hand so tight the key dug into her palm. He pried her fingers open and jerked it. The lanyard dug into her skin then broke. His breath came in bursts through his flared nostrils. He went to the basement and locked the door, then came back to her, a crazed look in his eyes. Teresa backed away from him until she bumped against the counter.

"You will not be going down there anymore. Do you understand me?" He stuffed the key into his pocket. "Monday, you are coming to work." Teresa opened her mouth to remind him she couldn't come back. He held up his hand. "You will come back to work to help out in the office. I had to let Whitney go, remember?" He didn't let her reply. "You will be a part of this family from now on, and you will stop *obsessing* down in the basement. Do you understand?"

She wanted to yell that he needed to include her if he wanted her to be a part of the family.

They were both panting from the grapple over the key. He was treating her like a child. She felt scolded, like she should cower before him and beg forgiveness. She felt something she hadn't felt in a long time. Sensations that heated her through. She wanted to kiss him. To touch him. To *feel* him.

"Kiss me," she said, meeting his eyes for the first time since his accusations.

"What?" Confusion replaced the anger on his face.

"Kiss me."

His confusion dissolved into a combination of disgust and disbelief, like she was some kind of monster. She knew her makeup was smeared and runny from her tears, but it couldn't be *that* bad.

"Please." She stepped toward him until she stood right in front of him. She tilted her face up and closed her eyes.

Please.

She waited for what seemed like long minutes, wishing and praying he would just kiss her. His arms wrapped around her. His heart beat in her ear.

"Listen to me, Teresa." His voice rumbled under her cheek. He stroked her hair. "Things need to change."

They stood in silence for a time.

"The parents of the kids you assaulted aren't going to press charges. For that, you're lucky." He took a deep breath. "You need to wake up."

Make an effort. Wake up.

She couldn't do anything right.

He loosened the embrace and looked into her eyes, then lowered his mouth toward hers. Anticipation tumbled in her stomach. They hadn't shared a moment like this since Maggie arrived. Derrick had been too preoccupied with getting the girl settled in. The whisper of his breath caressed her lips.

"Can I come down?" Maggie called from the top of the stairs, her voice timid.

Derrick released Teresa. "Yeah," Derrick called. "Come on down."

No kiss. The moment gone. Defeat sank into Teresa's body and pulled her into unfathomable depths. She stared at the basement door, and ragged anger fought to break through the wall despair had built inside her.

Maggie tiptoed into the kitchen with wide eyes. Derrick asked her something. Maggie responded. Teresa couldn't understand their muffled voices as she walked past them. They didn't notice her. She was a ghost.

She climbed the stairs and, in the master bedroom, picked up the phone on the nightstand. She hesitated over the numbered keypad. It had been years since she dialed this number. She put the phone to her ear.

Her mother answered on the third ring. Her voice filled Teresa with relief.

"Hi, Mom." She sat on the edge of the bed and bit her thumbnail.

"If it isn't my long-lost daughter." Mother didn't sound angry or sad. Just matter of fact, as usual. "What happened?"

"What do you mean?"

"I don't hear from you for years and now you decide to call. Something dreadful must have happened. Are you ill? Are you dying?" Her mother's voice broke from its happy-go-lucky-borderline-told-you-so tone that was stereotypical of the 1950s housewife.

"No. I'm fine. My husband is mad at me. He did something horrible." She filled her mother in about Ann and taking away the key.

Mother's regular tone returned. "It sounds like you're the reason he's upset. I told you, Teresa, time and again. Keep your husband happy. I gave you all the lessons you needed to become a good housewife and make a decent life for yourself."

"Mom, I—"

"Cook, clean, keep the children clean and quiet, please him. You're allowed to enjoy sex, too, don't forget."

Teresa could see her mother counting these things off on her fingers.

Sex. Indeed. When was the last time?

"Are you doing these things?" her mother asked.

"Yes."

"All of them?"

Teresa sighed. "No. Not all of them."

"Teresa, dear. A happy husband means a happy home. You know that. Have you forgotten everything I taught you? Have you forgotten what the Bible says?" She cleared her throat. "Ephesians 5:22 to 5:23. Say it with me."

"'Wives, submit yourselves unto your own husbands, as unto the Lord. For the husband is the head of the wife, even as Christ is the head of the church.'"

"Very good." Pride in Mother's voice. "Now, darling, go make amends. Make that husband of yours happy, and keep him that way. Do everything right and you're guaranteed marital bliss."

Her mother hung up before Teresa could say another word. Teresa looked at the phone. Sadness welled inside her chest.

"I'm sorry," she whispered. She put the phone down and thought of Tiffany and her powerful friend. Tiffany said he could help her.

You need to change.

Oh, things would definitely change.

CHAPTER 17

Ann pulled her dad's jacket off the coat hook and tugged it around her body like a hug. She sniffed the collar where remnants of his aftershave still clung to the wooly fibers. She closed her eyes, breathed it in, and wrapped her arms around herself, pretending they were his.

Something in the lining poked her back. She took it off and prodded around it. Near the bottom cuff, she found some large haphazard stitches.

Ann grabbed a pair of scissors and cut through them. Inside, still stuck to a safety pin, was a square envelope with her name on it. The envelope contained a writable DVD and a folded piece of paper.

The paper was a copy of Maggie's adoption certificate naming Derrick and Teresa Hart as the parents, signed by someone named Gail Park.

Heart pounding, Ann turned on her dad's old tube TV and the DVD player. She put the disc inside and sat back on her heels.

The video was dark at first, the recording grainy, then the strike of a match and the glow of fire. A figure entered the frame and sat down. Ann grabbed the sides of the television.

Her dad sat before the camera. He wore a scraggly beard and his favorite Indiana Jones-style hat, a little worse for wear. His eyes sparkled in the flickering light.

"I hope this thing's working," he muttered. He focused on the lens and rubbed the corner of his right eye.

"Hey, Angel." His pet name for her. "If you're watching this, I'm probably dead. How cheesy is that?" He smiled and let out a laugh that held no mirth. "But it's true." His eyes shifted down. "Where to start . . . There's too much to tell you. I don't have a lot of time." He cleared his throat and blinked his eyes hard.

"I'm sorry this is going to be so cryptic, but I know you'll figure everything out. You're smart. If this gets into the wrong hands . . ." He shook his head.

Bram Logan sighed on the screen. The sigh was full of weary exhaustion. Ann sighed with him.

"I'm so tired," he whispered. "I've been running . . ." He cleared his throat again. His eyes twinkled with tears and jumped to the lens. "I am so proud of you and what you have accomplished. I'm so sorry I couldn't be around for you when you needed me. I listened to every one of your voicemails. Saved them. Every time I heard your voice, your plea for help, my heart broke."

Ann's eyes welled with tears.

"It was for the plan. It was all for the plan. You needed to come home. I hope you are home." He looked to the right of the camera then back. "I *know* you're home. You have to be . . . the book, the girl . . . the angel in the box." His brow furrowed. "There are forces at play beyond most people's understanding. Beyond *your* belief system."

Ann slouched a little. Was he going to go into some strange rant like Louise now?

His eyes drifted from the camera, and he looked into the middle distance. "God, I hope she's safe." He leaned forward in a conspiratorial way, and when he spoke again, his voice was lowered.

"I took care of both records, and I put something for you in the angel's hideout." He nodded one slow dip of his chin. "It might be helpful. If she's safe, all is well."

The video went silent. Her dad stared off again. She touched his face on the screen, wishing she could feel the stubble of his beard.

"I know you have a lot of questions, and I wish I was there to answer them for you. To fight by your side. I don't even know if you'll get this in time, or at all. I have to believe, though."

He sighed, and Ann let out a long breath at the same time.

"If you're watching this, Raghib followed my instructions and contacted you. You can trust him."

She paused the video and stared at her dad's mid-word face. She'd hung up on Raghib without even thinking to get his contact information. With no idea where he was or how to get in touch . . . She'd killed her only lead.

Way to go, Detective.

She pressed play.

"I have to go now, Annie. I . . . Remember . . ." His eyes met the screen, and for a few seconds, Ann felt like they were in the same room. The silence continued as if he were waiting for her to respond that she was listening—the way he always did.

"I'm listening," she said, despite herself.

"You must believe, Ann. Summon your strength. Summon the angel." His eyes bored into hers. "Summon the angel. It is the key. I hope you get this."

He reached forward, and his hand obscured the screen. The television displayed the DVD player's menu.

Ann stayed on the floor staring at the menu options but not seeing them. He really was gone. Grief spilled into her body. She got up and grabbed a beer from the fridge, drank it as fast as she could, then another, and another, until her belly filled with gas and she let out a horrendous belch, followed by a giggle. Then she drank the last one.

Numb. Just the way she liked to feel, but her woozy brain kept cycling through key points of the video.

The book, the girl. Angel's hideout. What the hell was the angel's hideout?

Then the patch of healing skin over her heart started to burn again. The blue-white glow spread from her heart down her arms to her hands. Ann doubled over, prepared for the onslaught of pain, but it didn't come. The feeling subsided and the glow dimmed until it disappeared altogether.

CHAPTER 18

Teresa woke when the temperature dropped. The clock read 3:12. She climbed out of bed, careful not to disturb Derrick, and slid her feet into a pair of plush slippers. She pulled on a micro-fleece robe and shuffled into the hallway to check the thermostat.

Before she could touch the screen, Tiffany's giggle came from downstairs. Teresa followed the disembodied voice to the front room.

"Hello, Mommy," Tiffany said in the caramelly sweet voice she always used. "Are you ready to begin our journey?"

"Journey?" Teresa pulled her robe tighter around her. Tiffany gave her an exasperated expression.

"The one that will bring us together again."

"Oh, yes, of course." Teresa shivered and wondered if the thermostat was malfunctioning. She'd have Derrick check it in the morning. "What do we need to do?"

Tiffany grinned and presented an oversized

hypodermic needle from behind her back. The barrel lay across both of her hands like an offering. Teresa took the syringe. The needle was as big around as a pencil and longer than one used to administer an epidural by about five centimeters. She'd never seen a needle this big in her entire medical career. The barrel, cold and heavy in her hands, was made of crystal-clear glass, the plunger stainless steel.

"What am I supposed to do with this?" She winced at the thought of finding a vein with the thick point. She looked at Tiffany.

Tiffany grinned. "We're going to play a game."

"What kind of game?"

"A doctor game."

Teresa gulped. "What are we going to use this for?"

"We are going to collect souls."

The hypo dropped from Teresa's hand and landed with a heavy thud on the rug. "Souls? You didn't say anything about collecting . . ." She couldn't even fathom what Tiffany meant. What the task entailed, how this massive hypo would factor in.

"You said you'd do anything to have me back." Tiffany stomped her foot. "You made a deal."

Teresa thought back to the abandoned funeral home. It felt like so long ago. Was it only yesterday? Did she make a deal?

"What are they for?" she asked. "The souls, I mean."

"Payment to bring me back."

Teresa picked up the syringe. "What do I do with this?"

"You'll see," Tiffany said. "Let's go. I can't be gone for too long, remember?"

Teresa followed Tiffany to the front door, flipped the deadbolt, and opened it. On the front porch lay the end of a glowing milky-red rope the size of the lines they used to tether cruise ships to docks.

"What is that?" Teresa crouched and poked it with the syringe's plunger before picking it up. It pulsed like a carotid artery. The glow brightened and dimmed with each throb. She dropped it and wiped her hand on her robe, though the rope wasn't slimy like she thought it might be. It was so smooth, like healing skin after a bad burn.

"Follow it," Tiffany said.

Teresa followed the line out of the neighborhood to the diner and then behind to a small house. Her chest tightened when the line disappeared through the front door. The stainless-steel plunger rattled in her shaking hand.

"Doctor Mommy," Tiffany said in a PA system voice. "Paging Doctor Mommy." She laughed.

"What do I do?" Teresa asked.

Tiffany pointed to the oversized vein and used a sing-song voice. "Follow the glowing red zoe."

Nausea swirled in Teresa's stomach. She lurched to the bushes and dry-heaved. Tiffany's cold essence touched her shoulder.

"I know you can do this. I know how badly you want to be with me."

Teresa nodded and wiped her mouth on the sleeve

of her robe. She stood and went to the front door, took a deep breath, and tried the knob. Unlocked. Of course. No one locked their doors in Harmony. Everyone was family. Except her. That's why she *did* lock her doors. Even when she was home by herself.

The line, the zoe as Tiffany called it, trailed inside. Teresa stepped into the house. Warmth washed over her, and her skin prickled with the blood rushing to its surface. A small table near the door held a stack of mail. Most of it was addressed to the diner, but one had a name on it.

"Ruth Gill," Teresa whispered. "Ruthie. Oh God, not her." Ruthie was always kind to Teresa. She was the only one in town who still welcomed her after the baby died.

Ruthie is nice to everyone, not just you.

It was true. She had to be, otherwise her diner wouldn't do such great business. Or maybe since it was the only restaurant in town, it would still do well, but still. There was some measure of niceness Ruthie showed all her customers, even Mr. Proast, the most despicable man in town.

"I can't do this," Teresa said. "I can't take Ruthie's . . ." She couldn't say soul.

"Follow the zoe. It's easy." Tiffany pranced into the house. She leaped back and forth over the line, almost like she couldn't touch it herself. She came back to Teresa and took her hand. "She won't die," Tiffany said. Her eyes sparkled in the dim light. "I promise." Her voice dripped with saccharine sincerity.

Teresa nodded and followed the line down the hallway

into the single bedroom. Moonlight spilled in, casting everything in an eerie blue light. Ruthie lay on the bed on her back, the covers thrown off of her. The milky-red line led straight into her chest. Teresa gasped and gripped the door frame. She closed her eyes.

"Stick the needle in her heart," Tiffany said. "That's where the soul lives."

"She won't die?" Teresa asked incredulous.

Ruthie stirred. Teresa sucked in a breath and froze. Ruthie rolled onto her side, then onto her back again. Teresa let out her breath.

"She won't die," Tiffany said.

Teresa didn't understand how someone could live without their soul, but she trusted her baby wouldn't lead her astray. She crossed the room to the bed and stood over Ruthie, so quiet and calm in her slumber. Teresa glanced at Tiffany, her expectant face, her glittering eyes and porcelain skin.

My little dolly.

Teresa raised the needle over her head. Her arms shook. She dropped them back down.

"Do it," Tiffany urged.

Teresa closed her eyes, raised her arms again, and plunged the needle into Ruthie's chest up to the luer.

Ruthie's body convulsed. Her arms and legs jackknifed together, and a gurgling gasp escaped her throat. Teresa jumped back. The arms and legs relaxed, but Ruthie's back arched, her chest rising high off the mattress.

"Pull the thingy," Tiffany yelled, motioning with her hands. "Quick!"

Teresa rushed forward, gripped the plunger, and pulled. A milky-red glowing substance oozed into the barrel, thick and sloggy like cold maple syrup. The farther she pulled the plunger, the more shriveled and shrunken Ruthie's face became.

Plunger fully retracted, Teresa withdrew the needle. Ruthie's body lay rigid on the mattress. Her papery skin hugged the bones of her face.

Teresa backed away. Something crunched under her slipper. The milky rope that had led her to Ruthie was crispy, shriveled, and black in the moonlight.

Ruthie lay still as stone. Teresa leaned over her to listen for breath. She turned her head to Tiffany.

"You said she wouldn't die."

"She's not dead—look." Tiffany pointed. Teresa turned her head back.

Ruthie's eyes popped open. They were black and bottomless. Teresa jumped back. A tortured keening issued from Ruthie's dry, cracked lips. Teresa stumbled backward toward the door. She stopped to look at the shell of a person that remained. Ruthie sat up.

"Mommy," Tiffany said in a calm voice. "Time to run."

CHAPTER 19

"Run, Mommy! Now!"

Teresa barely heard her baby's voice over Ruthie's hollow scream. Ruthie's mouth stretched impossibly wide, tearing the papery skin and creating a cavernous hole in the woman's face.

Tiffany tugged Teresa's hand. Teresa's body stiffened. Her heart palpitated. She regarded the hypo, its contents glowing and pulsing inside. Tiffany ran away.

Ruthie stood and lurched toward Teresa on unstable legs. Teresa unfroze and sprinted to the door and out into the night, where the cold air smacked into her, icing her lungs.

"This way!" Tiffany darted across the town square toward the dirt road leading to the abandoned funeral home.

Teresa's lungs burned. Her legs ached with each forward push. Her foot splashed into a mud puddle, soaking her slippered foot. She tripped. Her body pitched forward, and she landed on her stomach. The syringe flew from her hand and clinked and clattered on the rocks a few feet away.

"No, no, no!" Teresa gasped for air and crawled over to the glass syringe. Gravel poked and pierced her knees. The glass remained intact.

Ruthie screamed. Teresa chanced a look. A stick-like figure lurched along about ten yards behind her. How could Ruthie move so fast? Teresa launched to her feet and took off.

"Mommy! This way!" Tiffany leaped over the ditch at the side of the road and dashed into the forest. Teresa dug deep and pushed herself through the woods. She dodged tree trunks and finally came to the old cemetery near the abandoned funeral home. She dropped to her knees.

"We made it," Tiffany said in a gleeful whisper. She enveloped Teresa in a cold hug. Tiffany pulled away and twirled in a slow circle. Then Teresa saw them. Fuzzy green lights bobbed and danced in the night. Their green glows illuminated the headstones, tree trunks, and even Teresa herself.

"Do you like them?" Tiffany asked. She reached out a hand and poked one. It puffed away, leaving behind incandescent smoke.

"What are they?" Teresa asked. She held out her free hand to touch one. It landed in her palm and tingled against her skin. Others floated over and landed on her or hovered close by. They covered her torso like a sweater vest.

"They're lost souls," Tiffany said. "They are drawn to you."

Lost souls also collected around the barrel of the syringe. When she moved, they darted away, but drifted close again, like moths drawn to light.

"They want to free her," Tiffany said. She stroked the syringe. "Let's get inside."

Teresa glanced back just as Ruthie jumped across the creek and took two steps before she seemed to meet resistance. A crackle of electricity coupled with Ruthie's pained screams disturbed a handful of nesting birds. She pushed forward and stumbled four more steps. Her body smoked. She clawed at her arms and torso like she was covered in bugs and ran back across the creek. She paced along the bank like a hungry hyena.

"She can't stay in here," Tiffany said. "You have to have a soul, or be one, to cross over."

"She has no soul . . ." Teresa dropped to her knees again and moaned. "What have I done to her?" She watched Ruthie lurch and stumble along on legs so thin it seemed they should snap off at the knees.

"You did what needed to be done so we can be together again. You do want to be together again, don't you?" Tiffany's dear sweet face held a sad, expectant expression.

"Yes, of course, baby." Teresa looked over at Ruthie. "But I've destroyed her." She looked at the hypo in her hand. Could she stick the needle into Ruthie and give it back? A tear coursed down her face, and she sobbed.

Tiffany touched her cheek.

"Don't worry, Mommy," Tiffany said. "She will be just fine, and you and I will be together again." Her hand left a cold trail on Teresa's skin. "Time to come inside."

Teresa nodded and followed Tiffany. At the door, she cast a glance at Ruthie one last time and at the lights of the lost souls dancing and bobbing. So many of them. She looked at the soul in her hand and stepped through the doorway.

The meager light in the living room dimmed until Teresa could see nothing. Then torches on the walls sprouted flames, lighting the cave with a warm, flickering glow. Tiffany was gone.

"Tiffany?" Teresa called.

A deep and resonant voice answered. "She's gone to bed." The words filled her chest and caressed her heart. "She is a child and tires easily."

A man wearing nothing but a loincloth stood by the pool at the back of the cave. Dark hair caressed muscular shoulders, which flexed when he turned around and met her stare with yellow, predatory lion's eyes. With his physique and only a loin cloth covering his necessary elements, he belonged on the cover of a romance novel about cavemen.

A half-naked man in a darkish place? A flicker of fear shuddered through her. She backed away from him.

He laughed, deep and rumbling. A soothing sound. "Don't be afraid—I know my appearance can be . . . off-putting."

Off-putting? He was gorgeous, ageless in his beauty. Teresa relaxed but only a little.

"Who are you?" she asked.

The man only smiled. His bright white teeth tapered to sharp points.

"You have what I need." His voice slithered like ribbons of silk falling to the ground.

Teresa gripped the barrel with both hands and held it against her chest. She backed away from him. "Tell me who you are."

"I'm the one you're helping," he said. "If you wish to see Tiffany, to be with her, you must give me the zoe."

Teresa retreated until she hit the opposing wall where the door should have been but wasn't anymore. While she was distracted by the sudden realization she was trapped, the stranger pounced and penned her with a hand on either side of her shoulders. She looked into his eyes.

"You don't . . . you don't scare me," she said. It was meant to come out strong, but it came out breathless. She couldn't avert her eyes.

"I'm the one who has given you the ability to see your daughter, to spend time with her." His voice filled her, warmed her. Heat flushed her skin. Teresa closed her eyes and swallowed hard.

"I'm the one who will return her to you."

His breath on her neck. His lips on her mouth. A small moan escaped her. She wanted to resist, but she couldn't.

She tried to lift her arms, to push him away, but found herself pulling him toward her instead, returning his kiss. Everything inside her screamed no, but she couldn't stop.

His hand enveloped hers, and she released the hypo. He pulled away from her, leaving her breathless and ashamed.

"Go home now."

"But Ruthie . . ." she said. "And Tiffany. I want to see my baby."

"Ruthie no longer wants you." He smiled. "You will see Tiffany again very soon."

The uneven cave wall at her back changed shape, and the door to the outside took form. She took the knob in her hand. Everything in her wanted to say, no more, she couldn't do this, but when she met his eyes, she asked, "How many do you need?"

The stranger smiled. Something in the expression made her cringe.

"Seven bloods, seven souls. Six more."

Ruthie's soulless shell no longer prowled outside the cemetery. Teresa staggered home in a daze. Her mind couldn't understand what she'd just done. What she'd just seen. None of this was real. It couldn't be. She would wake up in the morning and none of it would have ever happened.

CHAPTER 20

Sunday

A small group of people stood outside Mac's Diner. Ann didn't expect the masses until after eleven when church let out. She scanned their faces and body language. These people weren't waiting for breakfast.

"What's going on?" Ann asked the first person she encountered.

"Ruthie didn't open the diner," the young woman said. She turned and met Ann's eyes. Recognition flashed across her face. "Hey! I heard you were back in town."

Ann didn't fully recognize the young face, but something in the girl's smile was familiar.

"My parents watched every news story that aired." She held out her hand. "Marcie Berg," she said. "Roger and Betty's daughter."

Ann shook Marcie's hand. Roger Berg graduated Ann's sophomore year, but she knew him well enough. He'd been the class Valedictorian that year and had done well for himself all through high school in both sports and academia.

"George and Sheriff McMichael are at Ruthie's," Marcie said.

Ann slipped through the group and peered down the hill toward Ruthie's house. George stood around, shifting his weight and repositioning his hands like he didn't know what to do with them.

McMichael wandered out of Ruthie's house carrying a small evidence bag. Ann's curiosity piqued, and she ducked under the sagging police tape.

"We told you to stay back." The sheriff was still looking at the contents of the bag. He turned. "Oh, Ann." He indicated the bystanders. "Thought you were one of them."

"What's going on?" Ann asked.

"Got a call from Ruthie's mom this morning. Ruthie didn't show for Sunday breakfast. Came down to the diner to check on things, and the place was still closed up."

Ann could deduce the rest, but McMichael went on.

"When I got down here, the door was wide open, and Ruthie wasn't home."

"Any sign of forced entry?" Ann asked.

"Nope, not at all. It's like she forgot to shut the door behind her."

"Or," George said from right behind Ann. She nearly jumped out of her shoes. "The perp forgot to shut it."

"*You* need to shut it," the sheriff snapped. He led Ann

into the house.

McMichael handed Ann the evidence bag.

"Found this in her room and traces of it ground into the carpet leading from the front door to the back bedroom."

Ann held the bag up to the light. The substance inside looked like strips of old scabs. Pieces had flaked off just from handling it. "What do you think it is?"

"Not sure. I'm gonna have George drive it to Pine Valley to have the lab rush it."

"How long will it take to get results?" she asked.

"Historically? At least a week," McMichael said. "Ruthie'll probably show up with a perfectly good explanation by the time we hear back."

"Does she disappear often?" Ann asked.

McMichael took off his hat and scratched his head. "Not often, but every once in a while she sort of runs off."

Ann raised an eyebrow.

"Now, now, hear me out," McMichael said. "Ruthie always calls her sister, Debbie, to run the restaurant whenever she plans to run off, and that's what concerns me. And she certainly wouldn't leave her mama worrying either." He replaced his hat. "Ruthie is one of our best."

"Did anyone call Debbie? Maybe Ruthie *did* call her."

McMichael nodded. "She hadn't heard anything from Ruthie. She's on her way to open up."

"What did you tell her?" Ann asked. She would have mentioned Ruthie missing but would have reassured her and told her not to worry.

"I told her the truth," McMichael said. "That Ruthie didn't show up to open this morning."

Ann stepped toward the door. "Let me know if there's anything you need a second opinion on."

Outside, the fresh air filled her lungs. She hoped McMichael knew what he was doing. Per protocol, all law enforcement officers were trained in crime scene investigation. At least enough to not screw things up. But this was small town nowhere, and McMichael was, well, old.

George stood by the evidence kit sitting open on the Jeep's hood. He blew a kiss toward the top of the hill. Ann followed the direction. Marcie pretended to catch the kiss and held it to her chest.

"How old are you?" Ann asked. She narrowed her eyes at him. George turned to her.

"Twenty-one next Tuesday," he said with a nod. Ann looked up the hill where Marcie still stood. George followed her gaze and stopped smiling. "She's seventeen," his eyes widened. "She'll be eighteen before the end of the year. And I haven't done nothing with her, honest. Just kissing and stuff."

Ann smirked and walked up to Forest Parkway, stuffing her hands in her pockets. There was a small grocery store down the street. A package of bacon, a carton of eggs, and a few other essentials would at least get her fed and give her something to do.

"Are you helping them find Ruthie, Detective?" someone asked her.

Ann looked up. A young male, late teens to early twenties, held a notepad with a pencil poised over a blank page.

"For the community paper?" Ann asked. The community paper was a home-printed-and-stapled affair with news about upcoming events, a classified ads section, and pictures from around town.

He shrugged. "Sort of. More like a pet project, really." He held out his hand. "Brent Winter. Can you tell me anything about the case?"

Ann shook his hand. The remaining crowd turned their way.

"Yeah, there is no case." Ann took a step.

Brent blocked her way.

She sighed. "I offered my professional opinion. End of story."

"Can I take your picture?" He pulled a camera out of his jacket pocket.

"No, I don't think that's—" Ann held up her hand to stop him, but Brent took her picture anyway.

"Thanks, Detective." He looked at the digital display. "That's exactly what I need."

A shiny white SUV pulled up in front of the diner, and Ruthie's sister climbed out. She unlocked the restaurant and let the people inside.

"Hey, Debbie," Ann said, holding out her hand. Debbie looked at the hand, took it in her own, then looked at Ann's face.

"Ann . . . oh my god, what are you doing here?" Her

eyes widened. She gasped. "Is Ruthie dead?" Debbie clutched the sleeve of Ann's jacket.

"She's probably fine," Ann said, gently removing Debbie's hands. "Sheriff McMichael is looking into it. Besides, Ruthie isn't technically missing yet. The local law's just antsy to do something besides break up bar brawls and warn bothersome neighbors to keep quiet. Right?"

Debbie wiped her eyes and nodded. "I better get inside," she said between sniffles. "Knowing you're helping out—I'm sure you'll find her."

Ann walked to the grocery store feeling like she couldn't escape herself. If it hadn't been to investigate her dad, she wouldn't have come here. And, sure, she could leave anytime, follow protocol, and give the case to the police. But she knew she had to be here. Harmony was where she was meant to come.

Louise's voice rang in her mind.

You were drawn here.

"Dammit."

Drawn here my ass.

* * *

Ann returned home with a bunch of frozen meals. The front door hung wide open. She dropped the groceries and grabbed the tire iron out of her truck, then stood to the side of the door and peeked around the jamb.

The couch cushions lay askew, and the drawers on the

TV stand had been removed and dumped out. The roll-top desk in the corner spilled its contents out onto the floor. Her copy of the Salida Stabber case file lay open on the coffee table. Crime scene photos spread out like a macabre table cloth. She'd almost forgotten she brought it.

Ann sneaked inside holding the tire iron out in front of her. She cleared the master bedroom, then turned quickly into the bathroom and tore aside the shower curtain all in one swift movement. Half the rings came off in the process. Lower level cleared, she crept up the stairs.

At her old bedroom, a dark shape filled the crack between the hinges. She sidled inside and jerked the door away from the wall, ready to clobber whoever might be hiding there. Just a jacket on a hook.

After destroying the shower curtain in the second bathroom, she sat at the bottom of the stairs. Anger replaced adrenaline as she surveyed the mess. Anger and a sense of violation that someone had come into her private space and destroyed it. They had broken in—or found the key by the mums.

Ann gritted her teeth and dug her fingernails into the lip on the edge of the step. She got a jolt of pain on her fingertip. A sliver of wood protruded from beneath her nail. She felt along the underside. It was rough.

On her knees, she leaned down to see why it wasn't smooth like the rest of the wood. The word *Angel* was crudely carved into the lip.

She bent sideways to get a better look. The tip of a wire

stuck out. She pushed it, but nothing happened. It wasn't sticking out far enough to pull. She shifted it sideways and heard a soft click. The top board popped up.

There was a message carved on the bottom. The same message she'd seen a lot of lately, it seemed.

Summon the Angel.

Angel's hideout. How did her dad expect her to put that together on her own? A wooden box sat in the bottom of the space. She pulled it out.

Carvings adorned the lid, intricate and detailed, depicting an angel standing at the edge of a pool of water. She held her hands out, not in offering, but palms down. Below the surface of the water, a snake with a lion's head writhed in pain. Yalda-whatever. The demiurge that created the physical world in Louise's whacked-out mythology.

Ann opened the box. Cobalt velvet lined the inside, protecting a crusty piece of paper rolled up like a scroll, and a necklace. She lifted the necklace by the chain and examined it. Antique silver vines enclosed a glass cylinder about one-inch long. It looked like the drawings in the journal she'd found in the storage unit.

Her father didn't wear much jewelry. Usually just his wedding band and a watch. The only other item was this necklace. Ann remembered seeing it twice in her life. Once when it fell out of her dad's shirt when he was kissing her goodnight, and the other time when he was drunk.

He had pulled it over his head and held it in his hand. Ann remembered the expression on his face. He wanted to tell her something. Instead, he sighed heavily, tucked the necklace away, and hugged her. That was fifteen years ago, right before she left Harmony to go to the police academy. Right before their huge fight.

Ann slid the chain over her head. The vial rested between her breasts.

She unrolled the piece of paper. It was a list of names followed by two dates. Ann figured they were birth dates and death dates.

At the very bottom, a diagonal tear took off the left corner, but her father's first name had been saved. None of the other names on the list were familiar.

The door creaked open. Ann spun around.

An old man in a canvas jacket peered inside. His gray hair stood out from his head. His eyes met Ann's and he held up his hands.

"I am Raghib," he said. "I'm very sorry to bother you, but I need to talk to you about your father."

CHAPTER 21

Teresa dug under the bed trying to find her golden cross necklace. It must have fallen off somewhere. She lifted the bed skirt, and all thought of her necklace vanished from her mind.

Her slippers. Caked with dried mud.

The reality of the previous night's activities rushed to the surface of her mind and left her breathless. Her entire body trembled, and a chill slithered through her.

She dashed to the bathroom and threw up.

"'Submit yourselves therefore to God. Resist the devil, and he will flee from you,'" she said in a shaking whisper. The rest of James 4:7 escaped her. She brushed her teeth.

Tiffany and her friend had told her Ruthie would be fine. Teresa spit into the sink and rinsed. Ruthie wasn't dead. She was okay. Teresa would go to the diner and prove it. Her hands continued to shake so hard she nearly poked her eye out with the mascara wand.

Downstairs, she turned toward the kitchen to see if

Derrick and Maggie were there and froze. The door to the basement stood wide open.

Teresa tore downstairs. A panicky feeling tightened her lungs. The baby's furniture. Gone. All of it. The crib, the dresser, the rocking chair, the nursing pillow. All the stuffed animals. Every. Last. Memory.

No. Not all of it. She ran back upstairs to the front room. Big Bear still sat on the love seat. She grabbed him, hugged him to her, and laughed. The bear responsible for the baby's death was the last piece of the baby she had left. The irony was cruel. She wondered if Derrick knew Big Bear was even in the front room. She tucked him among the pillows on a chair in the corner.

Tiffany would be hers again soon enough. But her stomach turned at the thought of taking six more souls. She covered her mouth with her hand and sobbed only once. That's all she allowed. Part of being a wife was to present oneself with elegance and poise. Her husband was not to see her distraught, only happy. She'd slipped up lately, but not anymore. She had more strength than that.

Teresa went back to the basement door and closed it. She strode down the hall and pulled on her coat. The air outside nipped her cheeks.

The sign in the diner's window flashed its red letters. Open. She smiled. Ruthie *was* okay. Alive and well. Teresa went inside. The tables and booths were packed. She frowned. The church crowd? She checked her watch. She could count on one hand the number of times she'd missed church.

The person who greeted her with a harried hello and a hand flung toward the dining room was not Ruthie.

"Sit wherever you want," the woman said. She resembled Ruthie in every way—except she had fashionable clothing and styled hair. Ruthie wore jeans and flannel and always had her hair in a pony tail. This woman wore a button-down blouse and black slacks. Her hair curled slightly around her shoulders.

Teresa sank into the bench of a small booth and willed herself not to jump to conclusions.

Perhaps Ruthie was just out sick.

She gazed around the restaurant at the patrons. The greasy food here probably kept Derrick's clinic in business with gut ailments. Sheriff McMichael sat in a corner booth shoveling something smothered in gravy into his mouth. A side of fries, also smothered in gravy, sat in a basket nearby.

He's so . . . fat. Look at the size of his belly flopped over his belt like that.

Her frown deepened.

The waitress came to Teresa's table and filled her coffee cup.

"Who are you?" Teresa asked.

"Debbie. Ruthie's sister," the woman said. "You know that, Doctor Hart. You delivered my first baby."

Teresa cocked her head to the side. "Oh, yes, Debbie." She touched the spot on her breastbone where the cross usually hung. "I'm sorry I didn't recognize you."

"Three kids later," Debbie said with a half-hearted laugh and a light touch to her stomach, though it was flat.

"Three?" Teresa said. "Who delivered the other two?"

Debbie's mouth dropped open, closed, opened again.

Teresa smiled and waved a hand. "That's not important." She forced a laugh. "The important question is, where's Ruthie?"

Debbie looked at the coffeepot in her hand. Her lip trembled. She looked at Teresa with tear-filled eyes. "Excuse me." She dashed off toward the kitchen.

Teresa reached for her necklace again. Her eyes welled with tears. Her cross was gone.

Ruthie *is gone.*

Teresa gasped. Her necklace had to be at Ruthie's house. She slid off her chair, hurried to the front of the restaurant, and dashed outside. Police tape lay on the ground at the top of the hill. A cold breeze set it writhing across the ground like a dying snake.

Her chest tightened. This was happening. It was real. She stole Ruthie's soul and gave it to some handsome stranger in the abandoned funeral home so she could get her dead daughter back.

Teresa jogged down the hill. Police tape sealed Ruthie's front door. They'd already searched it. They'd already found her cross. They would find her out. They would know.

A rattling whisper spoke behind her. "What have you done?"

Louise, the town loony, stood behind her—close

enough that Teresa saw the wrinkles etched deep into the old woman's skin. Her sharp gray eyes widened.

It wasn't quite a question, though. It was a reprimand. The way a parent would address a child's mess. Louise took a few steps back and stopped. Her eyes narrowed for a moment, then widened again.

"What did you say?" Teresa's mouth went dry. She took a step toward Louise, and the old woman backed away. The wind lifted her scraggly gray hair, adding a little more lunacy to her already crazed expression.

"You don't know what you're doing."

Teresa frowned, even though she knew it caused lines to form on her forehead. Louise kept backing away. Teresa followed. The old woman scrambled to the front of the diner and gave one last alarmed look at Teresa before dashing inside.

Teresa swallowed away the dryness in her throat. How? But no, Louise wouldn't know. How could she know? She couldn't. No one was out that late. Ruthie's screams, though. How did they not wake the whole town?

Teresa's heartbeat pulsed along the edges of her vision. She couldn't let this woman spread rumors about her. She followed Louise inside and stood by the door.

The crazy woman yelled, "Darkness—it has come! The End of Days shall be upon us! Have you repented for your sins?"

The patrons shied away. If Ruthie had been there, she would have nicely guided Louise to a booth and given her a free breakfast. But Ruthie wasn't there. Debbie was.

Debbie, harried by the rush of breakfast-goers, pointed the coffee pot at Louise, then the door, sloshing coffee onto the floor. "I will *not* have you disturbing these people. Please leave, or I'll call the sheriff and have you removed," she yelled.

Teresa looked around. Sheriff McMichael had already left. He made short work of that breakfast.

Louise, not missing a beat, turned her gaze to Debbie and took two staggering steps toward her. She lifted a knobby finger.

"Your sister was the first of many—"

"Get. Out. Now." Debbie said. "Bobby! Call the sheriff," she yelled toward the kitchen.

"I'll leave," Louise said. "But you mark my words." She swung around, addressing the entire diner now, pointing her hand as she went. "A great darkness shall descend! The End of Days! They are upon us!"

Teresa backed out the front door and into the cold. Louise did the same and wandered away. Teresa followed, but at the town square she stopped. Louise hadn't said a thing about Teresa or what she thought Teresa had done. Her comment about Ruthie was close but innocent. Sort of. Teresa, lost in her worries, didn't realize she had gone directly to the abandoned funeral home.

CHAPTER 22

Unable to speak, Ann stared at the grizzled old man standing in her doorway.

"May I come in?" he asked, his voice accented enough to prove he wasn't American.

Ann nodded and motioned him inside. "Sorry about the mess. Someone broke in." She wiped her hands on the front of her jeans to hide their shaking.

"Is anything missing?" Concern etched the lines around Raghib's eyes.

Ann shook her head. "Not that I'm aware of," she said. "Uh, can I get you something to drink?"

"A glass of water?"

Ann went to the kitchen and filled a glass from the tap. "Ice?" she called toward the living room.

"Please."

She opened the freezer. The bottle of spiced rum lay at an angle instead of tucked against the wall like it had been. She shoved it aside and shifted the ice cube trays and frozen dinners around. The finger was gone. She dropped the glass. By the grace of whatever power, it didn't break, but water spilled all over the linoleum. Raghib appeared in the doorway.

"What's happened?" he asked.

Ann threw a handful of paper towels onto the puddle and mopped it up with her foot. "I, um . . ." Ann ran her fingers over her eyebrow. "Butterfingers." She shrugged and got a fresh glass, managed to get ice and water into it without dropping it, and handed it to Raghib. He drank greedily.

"How did you know to find me here?" Ann asked. "How did you know to call me at this number the other day?"

Raghib held up a hand. "Is this place secure? I mean . . ." he ducked his head and glanced around at the mess, "from listening? Did the intruder plant any bugs?"

Ann hadn't considered that. She didn't have a reason to. Did she?

"We can go outside." She pulled on her jacket.

"In the back," Raghib said. "I can't risk being seen."

Ann took him down the short hallway toward the rear of the house, through the laundry room and a small mudroom. Raghib followed her outside. A couple of Adirondack chairs sat on a covered patio facing an expanse of forest. A large gray cloud loomed in the west. Tiny flurries twirled in the air. Ann zipped her coat.

Raghib took full advantage of his chair, propping his

legs up and everything. Ann stayed on her feet and towered over him.

"Who are you? How do you know my father? And what do you have to tell me about him?" She paused. "And how the hell did you know I was here?"

"I told you who I am." Raghib took a deep breath. "Asim Raghib. I was very close to your father. He saved my life." Raghib stared ahead, the daylight making his light whiskey-colored eyes glow.

Ann narrowed her eyes. "Did you leave a box on my doorstep in Salida a few days ago?"

Raghib's face distorted and he began to cry. "It was my duty to send a box to you upon your father's demise," he said. "It was to be my last act for him. A promise I made to him during our last encounter. Someone attacked me and stole the box."

"Who?" If he had a description, she had a lead.

Raghib shook his head. "It all happened so fast. I was struck from behind and knocked out. I never saw a single part of them."

Lead gone.

Ann sat on the other chair and leaned forward, elbows on her knees. "When did you last see or talk to my dad?"

Tears followed the deep wrinkles in Raghib's cheeks. "Many months ago." He wiped at his face.

"Do you know what the box had in it?"

He shook his head. "It was not my place to know."

"My father told me I could trust you." Ann got up

and paced. "The box had a message in it." And his finger, but she didn't tell Raghib this just yet. Who came to her house? Who stole the finger? Was it his ring they were after? Raghib showed up at a coincidental time.

"How do I know you're really who you say you are?"

Raghib sat up. "Your father knew you would be—what is the word—skeptical." He smiled a toothy grin. "I understand your reluctance to trust me." He pulled out his passport from the side pocket of his cargo pants and handed it over.

She flipped to the photo page. Asim Raghib. In the flesh. "This could be forged." She handed it back.

Raghib sighed and nodded. "He knew you'd say that, as well." He reached toward his back, and Ann reached for her gun. Raghib held his hands up, as if she had a weapon on her hip.

"I'm reaching into my back pocket for my wallet," he said with a nervous smile.

Ann nodded. He pulled his wallet out and produced a small photo.

"This is secondary proof." He handed the picture to Ann. It was a photo of her dad with his arm slung around Raghib. She let out a breath and handed it back to him, then sank down onto the chair.

She turned her eyes to his. "Is my father . . . dead?"

Raghib nodded. "Sadly, it is true, but his death was no accident. He was assassinated while performing his duty as a Protector."

"Assassinated? Do you mean murdered?" Ann asked. "Did he die here in Harmony?"

Raghib shook his head. He looked down at his hands clasped over his belly. "He died in Egypt."

Yeah, he went to Egypt a lot. But Egypt was well outside of his *protector* jurisdiction by thousands of miles. What could he be protecting there?

"My father was in Egypt helping people," Ann said, but her voice had lost its conviction when she recalled her conversation with Maggie. Maggie had used the same term, Protector, to describe Ann. And Maggie hadn't meant because Ann was a cop.

Raghib sat up and shifted his feet to the concrete pad their chairs sat on.

"Where did he do this helping?"

"Upper Egypt," Ann said.

"Are you familiar with the secret texts? The Nag Hammadi library?"

Ann nodded.

"The library was named after the town where it was discovered. In Upper Egypt."

Ann sat up straighter. She hadn't known that particular detail.

"Do you know the story of Sophia?" Raghib asked. "From the secret texts?"

"I recently learned that particular story, but what does that have to do with my dad? What was he protecting in Nag Hammadi?"

"Nag Hammadi was headquarters for an organization called the Protectorate. They were the enemies of the Messengers of the Light. It was they who tried to kill me. The ones your father saved me from. But wait." He held up his hands in a halting gesture. "In order for any of this to make sense, I must return to the beginning." He leaned back onto the chair and propped his feet up again.

In the beginning, Ann expected him to say.

"I am ashamed of my past," he began. "I worked for the Messengers of the Light for many years. Not until my son's wife gave birth to my granddaughter did I realize the way of the Messengers was all wrong." He gazed out into the distance. "They assassinated my son and daughter-in-law for their abandonment. They would have killed my granddaughter, too, but I spirited her away to the only place I knew she would be safe—Protectorate Headquarters."

Ann nodded and motioned for him to keep going.

"You see, the Messengers and the Protectorate used to be one organization, but differences among the leaders divided them into two factions. The Protectorate was not a malicious group. Not like the Messengers. The Protectorate was forgiving."

Raghib had begged them to give Maggie sanctuary despite his affiliation with the Messengers. He begged their forgiveness and vowed he would never work for the Messengers again.

"Even in their distrust of me, they allowed me to swear allegiance to them."

"How did the Messengers take your treason?" Ann asked.

"They never found out until I was gone."

"You were a double agent."

"Indeed. It was your father's idea. Mr. Bram devised the most intricate, most well-thought-out plans. They never failed."

Ann scoffed.

Sure they didn't. And that's why he's dead.

She let Raghib continue.

"As part of my allegiance, I was forced to live at Protectorate Headquarters for several months. They called it rehabilitation. You see, the Messengers were cult-like in their ways. They used brainwashing techniques to ensure we were serious—devout, I think is the word?" He shook his head. "Their devotion consisted of using full sensory deprivation—pulsing white noise, blindness with black-out goggles—to torture their members into submission."

"Shit," Ann whispered. "I can't imagine." The loud ocean waves her therapist played in the waiting room was torture enough. "And you went through this . . . brainwashing?"

"Yes, when I was much younger. I do not think I would survive it now." He took a sip of water. "It was to strip us of what we thought we knew about the world. To take us to an ignorant state, so we could be rebuilt. The Messengers believe ignorance binds us to the material world, and once we shed this ignorance we will transcend to the heavens to be with who they believe to be the one true god."

"Yalda-whatever," Ann said. "Right?"

"Yaldabaoth. Samael. Sakla." He spit the last name like a curse. "The Messengers believe that in their devotion he will spare them in the End of Days when he seeks vengeance upon Pistis Sophia for banishing him to Tartaros."

"So, was the Protectorate successful? You don't have any loyalty to the Messengers anymore?"

"The Protectorate was thorough. They kept me under surveillance until they knew they could trust me. Once they were sure, I was allowed to become a Protector Allegiant and serve your father whenever he was in Egypt, and as his, as Mr. Bram said, feet on the street, when he was away."

Her dad's right-hand man, so to speak.

"He was a very passionate man, your father," Raghib said.

Ann thought back to her dad's desperate pleas to keep her in Harmony resulting in the fight that ultimately sealed her decision to leave. She was well aware of how passionate he could be. Passionate, stubborn, bullheaded, whatever.

"He saved my granddaughter, and in doing so, discovered who she is." He finished off his glass of water. "Any time she cried, any time she was in distress of any kind, his blood inside his Protector necklace lit a glorious blue-white."

She pulled the necklace from beneath her shirt.

"That is it. When filled with blood it will glow."

Glowing blood. Ann looked at the back of her hand. "Did his veins glow?" she asked.

"Veins? No. Just the blood in the vial." Raghib paused. "Why do you ask?"

"Mine did. A few days ago. They tingle every once in a while, too." She stuffed the necklace back into her shirt. "I also got a mark over my heart. Like a brand." She pulled her shirt collar aside.

Raghib sucked in a breath. "The *Sa*," he whispered.

"What is this? What does it mean?"

"The Sa is the mark of the Protector. Does it hurt?"

"Not anymore. But it burned like hell when I first got it."

"Did you see anything—any visions?"

"Nothing too concrete," Ann said. "A silhouette of a girl and a book. The mountains here." She gestured vaguely around them.

Raghib nodded. "And when did this happen?"

"Friday."

"She turned seven on Friday," Raghib said, his eyes intense. "Seven is an influential number in the Gnostic world. What time of day was it?"

Ann shrugged. "Early morning. Like three or four." She walked to the edge of the patio.

Raghib made an affirmative sound. "Just as I thought. Your blood activated at the exact date and time she was born. The exact moment she turned seven."

"She who?" Ann asked over her shoulder.

"My granddaughter," Raghib said. "My Magdalene."

Ann spun around. "Magdalene . . . ?"

"Mr. Bram called her Maggie."

Ann's heart triple beat, and she almost choked on her next words. "As in Maggie Hart?"

Raghib nodded. "She is who you are bound by blood and soul to protect."

Ann fell onto the chair and gripped the arm.

"This is why you are here now," Raghib said. "Mr. Bram told me much about you. That you are as stubborn as him—but also a realist. He said you might not return to Harmony. But you were called, were you not?"

Ann opened and closed her mouth. Was she? She certainly needed to get away from Salida, from her trauma. Harmony was the only place she thought of to go. Because of the box.

"My dad—the stuff in the box. That's what brought me here."

Raghib shrugged. "Your father's plan, I assure you. He knew you might not heed the call of Sophia. The vision, Ann."

She sat in silence, trying to let this sink in, but Raghib spoke again.

"Did she give you the book?"

Ann sighed. "She tried, but I didn't take it. I didn't understand why she wanted to give it to me."

"You must keep both of them safe," Raghib said. "The Messengers will be looking for the book. If it is in Maggie's possession, they will hurt her to obtain it."

"Why the hell does she have it then?"

"We could not trust anyone else." Raghib scratched his beard. "I stole the book from them, and they learned I was working for both sides. Fortunately, this was my last duty before going into hiding. Before all of us went into hiding." The way he said the words indicated it was a euphemism for something else.

"Why are you saying it like that?"

"The Messengers had grown in numbers and power. Our members, the Protectorate's, were in danger. Bram devised a plan to remove us in an impermanent fashion before the Messengers could do so permanently. They'd already started killing us off, one by one."

The Protectors had all faked their own deaths. Left their families behind without a word. Disappeared. Started over somewhere else with alternate identities.

"Even Protector Allegiants, those sworn to serve the Protectors, were told to do it."

"That explains why Maggie believes her baba dead."

"The Messengers started coming after the Allegiants to find the Protectors. They started targeting our spouses and our children to gain information about the Protectors, and when we didn't give them what they wanted, they killed us, too."

The way he spoke gave her chills, as if he had returned from the grave to tell her this.

"We did what we had to do to keep our families safe. To keep our secrets, safe. To keep the book and the passages safe. To keep Maggie . . ." he hitched in a breath, "safe."

"Are you sure my dad didn't fake his own death?" Her mouth went dry. She searched Raghib's eyes. He searched hers.

"I am certain he is gone, but even if he was still alive, you would never find him."

"I would spend the rest of my goddamn life looking for him." She jumped to her feet again. "I have connections. I could find him."

"Your energies are best spent in protecting what your bloodline is meant to protect."

"If there are other Protectors, can they help me? Can I maybe call one and learn what there is to learn about this?" A sudden anger toward her father filled her. "I need information, Raghib. My dad didn't tell me shit." Ann paced at the edge of the concrete pad.

"They can't help you, Ann," he said with sad determination. "As I mentioned before, no one knows where they went, or where they are today, or if they are even still alive."

She growled. "What the hell am I supposed to do then? Stumble through this on my own?"

Raghib stood and stopped her with raised hands.

"You must retrieve the book from Maggie. It will show you the way."

"Enough of this cryptic bullshit."

"I am a Protector Allegiant, nothing more. I do not understand all of the operations of the Protectorate. My duty is to act as ally. To assist the Protect—"

"I'm supposedly the only Protector not in hiding. You say it's your duty to assist me, so assist me. What am I supposed to do?" Ann hated the frustrated desperation clinging to her voice. She turned and faced him.

"You are not just the only Protector," he said. "You are *the* Protector."

Ann's scalp prickled. "*The* Protector. Not *a* Protector."

"Yes." He took in a deep breath. "Your mother and father were both Protectors. Your unique combination of genes has marked you as—for lack of a better term—The One."

"You're goddamn crazy," Ann said. "The One? Like Neo in *The Matrix*?"

Raghib gave her a confused look.

"Never mind." Ann unzipped her jacket and let in some of the cold air. "My mother was part of this, too?" She sat down hard on the chair. "How did I not know any of this?"

"After your birth, your mother left the Protectorate to focus her attention on you," Raghib said. "It is Bram and Mary's combination of genes that is the reason your veins glow, the reason for the mark over your heart." Raghib sighed as if delivering this piece of information lifted a great weight from his shoulders.

He moved to sit but glanced at his watch. "I've been here too long. I must go."

"How do I find you in case . . . in case of whatever?"

"I'm staying in room six at the Harmony B&B," he said. "Get the book. Protect my granddaughter."

CHAPTER 23

Teresa bounded up the steps of the abandoned funeral home.

"Tiff—" Her voice caught in her throat.

Inside, she didn't find the cave lit by torches. She found an old, lumpy couch and a floor littered with plaster from the crumbling ceiling. An old sleeping bag lay balled up in the corner with some burned newspapers scattered around it. The place smelled of urine and dead animals. She held her hand over her mouth and nose and backed out of the house.

Maybe the cave only appeared when Tiffany was with her. Or Tiffany's friend. She didn't know his name. A breeze blew across the front porch, though the near-by trees remained still. She glanced back into the house expecting the view to have changed, but it remained the same. She let out a defeated sigh and walked back to town.

With the baby's furniture gone from the basement, Teresa didn't know what to do with herself. Most mornings she sat down there for hours. It seemed like a lifetime ago. So much had happened.

At the town square she turned to the new cemetery and sat at Tiffany's grave. Now that Tiffany visited her, the grave didn't hold the same meaning. There were only remains inside. Tiffany's soul was with her. Guiding her so they could be together again.

Teresa didn't know where else to go, so she went home. Derrick's car was in the driveway. Finally. Where had they gone? She was surprised to find she actually wanted to hear all about it. Things *were* changing. Mother would be proud.

For a brief moment, she wondered where they took the baby's furniture. Probably the donation center in the church so another family could benefit from her pain. She frowned, then thought twice. It was just furniture. Her baby would return to her soon.

"I'm home," she called when she walked in the front door.

No one answered. She hung up her jacket.

"Hello?"

"In here," Derrick's voice called back. It wasn't a happy, here-we-are-thank-goodness-you're-home kind of voice. It held that same disappointed tone he seemed to use more and more with her lately. What had she done this time? What *hadn't* she done?

Teresa sighed and shuffled down the hall toward the family room, but she stopped in the kitchen. Her mud-caked slippers sat on the back mat. She looked at Derrick in the living room with Maggie. His shoulders tensed as if he sensed her gaze.

Maggie leaned over a piece of paper and some crayons on the coffee table. Derrick patted her on the back.

"Keep at it. I need to talk to Teresa for a minute."

"Okay, Daddy."

Angry lines formed between his forehead and around his mouth. He came toward Teresa, and when she backed away, he stopped. His shoulders slumped. The lines disappeared.

"Can we talk?" Weariness filled his voice.

Teresa nodded and slinked to the back door. She stepped out onto the porch and crossed her arms. Derrick followed.

"What happened to your slippers?" he asked.

"I . . . don't know." She lowered her eyes. Derrick stepped closer. A tentative, sliding step like he was trying to catch a frightened rabbit.

"Is everything all right? Are you sleeping okay?" He reached toward her and touched her arm. "I can prescribe something . . ."

Teresa broke then. She knew her face became hideous when she cried, so she covered it with both hands. Derrick pulled her against him, his body strong and warm.

"I don't know what's going on." She wanted to tell him everything, confess her sins, but she couldn't. He would think she was crazy. Instead, she melted against him and relished the fact that he was there with her. Right now. He wasn't off with Maggie having fun without her. Teresa closed her eyes and smiled and wrapped her arms around him.

"Where did you go today?" she asked. His heart beat in her ear.

"Gold Bowl, that little ghost town near Pine Valley." No further details.

She looked up at him. "Did you have fun?"

"Yeah. It's a cool little town." Derrick let go of her, leaned against the porch rail, and crossed his arms. Why was he being so distant now? It was like he didn't want to share any details, because then she would be a part of it. A part of *them.*

"What else did you do?" she asked.

He shrugged one shoulder. "Grabbed some lunch. The library had a kids' day thing, so I took her there, stopped for some ice cream, and came home."

"Sounds like fun." Teresa rubbed her arm. "I wish I could have gone with you."

"Yeah," Derrick said. "Why are you avoiding the real subject?"

Teresa took a step back. "Real?"

"The slippers?" He motioned to the door where they lurked on the other side. "What's going on? First the bloody rock and the kids, and now your slippers. Just tell me. I want to help you."

"I–I just . . ." At a loss for words, she shook her head

and shrugged her shoulders. "I took a walk and didn't realize it had snowed."

"You took a walk in your slippers?"

Teresa scratched the side of her neck and avoided his eyes. She gazed out over their back yard and through the neighbors' glass door. They were sitting down to dinner as a family. They probably ate all of their meals together.

"Why don't we do things together anymore?" she asked in a small voice. "Remember back before Tiffany—we used to go on dates, and kiss, and hold each other, and . . ." She shrugged. "Make love." She glanced at him. His brows were creased with confusion.

"That was all before Mountain View." His voice was hoarse. He cleared his throat. "Before the drugs changed you into someone else." His voice didn't match his lips, like a badly dubbed movie. Teresa couldn't figure out how that could be. She closed her eyes and massaged her eyelids. When she opened them, Derrick was looking at her with an expectant expression.

"I'm sorry, what? Did you ask me something?"

"You're not even listening to me." He let out an exasperated sound, reached for her, then dropped his hands. "I'm trying to talk to you, Teresa. I'm trying to connect with you here, and you're off in La La Land." Now he looked at the back yard.

"I was listening. You said something about Mountain View and the drugs," she said.

He faced her, and the movement made her shy from

him. "I didn't say that. I didn't say anything like that."

"Yes, you did."

"No, I didn't. I'm not arguing with you like this. It's childish." He rubbed his hand on his forehead, then through his hair. "I'm taking you back to Mountain View."

Again, the words didn't match the movement of his lips.

"I've had enough of your crazy behavior. Your mother would be ashamed of you, making me unhappy like this." Even his gestures didn't match. He held out his arms to her. Now *he* was crazy. There was no way she was going to hug him now, not after what he just said.

The back door opened a crack.

"Daddy?"

"Not now, Maggie," Teresa said, her voice sterner than she'd meant. Maggie looked at her. "We're having an adult conversation. Go back inside."

Maggie looked at Derrick.

"Don't look at him. I am your mother." Her voice rose in pitch. "You do as I say."

Maggie startled away from the door. It clicked shut.

"Don't talk to her like that," Derrick said. "She's a human being." He thrust a finger at her. "We aren't through here."

Teresa followed him inside. "Yes, we are. You are not taking me back to Mountain View."

"Maggie?" Derrick called. He turned to Teresa. "I didn't say a goddamn thing about Mountain View." He ran down the hall to the bottom of the stairs. "Maggie?" He ran upstairs and back down a few seconds later. "She's gone," he shouted. "Mag—" his voice cut off when he ran outside and slammed the door behind him.

Teresa flung her hands in the air. She grabbed her muddy slippers and threw them in the trash.

CHAPTER 24

After Raghib left, the temperature dropped. Flurries accumulated in the grass.

The One.

What a cliché. She couldn't believe it. Wouldn't believe it. She didn't buy the concept of—what was this even called? Magic?

She didn't feel like The One. *The* Protector. She couldn't protect jack shit.

Just ask Bruce's wife, or Elizabeth's parents.

Ann had a sudden need to make sure Maggie was okay. Elizabeth had only been Maggie's age when the Stabber cut her life short. She jumped in her truck, turned it on, and ran the wipers. The snow was still fairly light, but that could change in an instant. She cranked up the heat, flipped on the headlights, and set off toward the other side of town to the newer residential district where the houses were only forty years old instead of eighty-plus.

The snowflakes thickened. Visibility worsened as the

sun slipped behind King Mountain. The defroster in the old beast wasn't up to snuff. Ann wiped at the glass, and her headlights caught the figure of a child walking with her shoulders hunched against the storm.

Ann swerved. The truck spun and thudded to a stop when the ass-end slammed into a telephone pole. She jumped out and ran to the sidewalk.

"Holy sh–crap, kid," Ann said. Maggie stood shivering and wet without a coat. Ann tore off her own jacket and wrapped it around the girl. She stuffed her into the truck.

"What are you doing out here without a coat?" Ann demanded.

Maggie's teeth chattered so fiercely she couldn't talk.

"I'll get you home," Ann said.

"No!" Maggie yelled. Her face contorted, and she started to cry. The mark tingled. "They were fighting. Teresa hates me."

"Okay, okay. Calm down, please calm down. I'll take you to the station, warm you up, and we'll call your dad."

Maggie leaned forward to adjust the vent, and Ann's jacket fell away. She had the book clutched against her chest.

"You carry that thing with you everywhere?"

Maggie didn't answer. Ann maneuvered the truck back onto the road. A minute later, she drove past the station.

"That's the sta—hey, where are you going?" Maggie asked.

"I'm sorry, kid. Protocol. I gotta check if your parents

are home first." Guilt settled in Ann's gut. Maggie kept shivering despite the blasting heat.

At Derrick's house, lights flooded from the front room. She peeked in the window next to the door and thought she saw movement down the hall, but she couldn't be sure. She knocked, rang the bell, and waited. No one answered.

Ann climbed back into her truck.

"Wh–Wh–where are we g–going now?" Maggie asked.

"The station to call your parents."

Maggie slumped back against the seat. Her teeth chattered so violently Ann thought she might break a tooth. Her lips were a little blue. Ann needed to get the kid warmed up, and from what she'd seen, they didn't have a lot of options at the station.

"Change of plan," Ann said. "We'll call your dad from my house."

Two blocks later she pulled into her driveway and lifted Maggie out. She carried her to the front door. The book radiated against the mark on her chest.

"It knows . . ." Maggie whispered through her vibrating jaw.

Ann gently shushed her and went inside. She deposited Maggie on the couch and pulled a bunch of blankets out of the linen closet.

"Can you put the book down?" Ann asked. Maggie released it, and Ann put it on the coffee table on top of the Stabber file. She threw all six blankets over Maggie's shoulders and tucked them around her. "You are now a Maggie burrito," she said.

Maggie smiled through the chattering. "W-what h-h-happened in h-here?" she asked.

Ann glanced around. Oh, yeah. The house was still wrecked.

"Oh, just looking for something." Ann went to the kitchen and opened the freezer, not sure what she was looking for now.

"Did you find it?" Maggie asked. "The necklace, right?"

Ann closed the freezer door. "What." The question came out without the inflection.

"Did you find your dad's necklace?" Maggie asked again.

"What are you talking about?" Ann's voice was an octave too high. Her ears were on fire.

Maggie nodded toward the book since her arms were swaddled against her body.

"Flip to the last page," she said.

Ann sidled into the room and sat on the couch next to the little burrito girl, who struggled and finally got her arms free. Maggie opened the book and flipped through the pages.

"See?" Maggie pointed. All but the lower left corner of the page was missing. Ann leaned in closer to read the word "Logan" followed by a comma. The shape of the tear was familiar. She retrieved the rolled-up paper from the wooden box. If it fit, lined up exactly, she would likely pass out. Or maybe just, who knows, die, or something.

Ann unrolled the piece of paper and held it to the book. Perfect fit. Ragged edges and all. Logan comma Bram. Beneath that, *Bram Logan's Offspring.* Whoever wrote the list wrote it before Ann was even born.

"The missing part," Maggie whispered. "Mr. Bram is your dad, right?"

Ann nodded, uncertain of what might fly out of her mouth if she dared open it.

Maggie flipped to the middle of the book.

"You can read this now, can't you?"

Ann looked at Maggie. The girl's eyes sparkled with urgency. Ann glanced at the book. Though it was still in—what did Maggie call it?—Coptic Egyptian, words flashed in her mind as her eyes darted across them.

She took a deep breath and exhaled.

"Yes."

Maggie jumped out of the blankets and hugged her. "It's you! I knew it. The book told me—like Baba said it would. It's you!" Her little fingers toyed with the chain at the back of Ann's neck. She leaned away and pulled the necklace from beneath Ann's shirt. Her eyes widened.

"This is it," Maggie said. "This was Mr. Bram's Protector necklace. You don't need it, of course, because you're you." The little girl shifted her hand to Ann's shirt collar and pushed it aside. Ann swallowed hard. "The mark."

Maggie pulled her own shirt collar down and showed Ann she had a similar brand on her chest in the shape of an Ankh. The most popular Egyptian symbol—meaning "the breath of life."

"Bonded by blood and soul," Maggie whispered. "Did it hurt?"

Ann nodded, afraid to speak.

"Mine, too. It happened on my birthday." She let go of her shirt. "I didn't tell my dad."

"Why not?"

Maggie shrugged and met Ann's eyes. "I think I knew he wasn't the one." She scrunched her nose. "He probably would have freaked out."

"Where did you learn all of this?"

"My Baba told me. When he sent me away, he said you would find me," she said. "Daddy didn't *find* me. I was given to him." Maggie touched the necklace. "Baba told me you would know what to do." Maggie's honey-colored, bright and expectant eyes met Ann's again.

Ann didn't want to tell the girl she didn't have a damn clue what to do, that she had just learned all this herself from someone Maggie thought was dead.

"Let's call your dad." Ann got to her feet and stumbled to the kitchen. She held onto the counter and reached for the phone. "What's your number?"

Maggie shook her head and clamped her lips shut.

"I have a phone book. I can just look it up."

"Please, Ann. Please don't call him yet."

"He's probably worried sick. Don't you want to at least tell him you're safe?"

Ann opened the phone book and flipped to the H

section. She dialed D. Hart. The phone rang and rang and finally went to voicemail.

"Hey Derrick, it's Ann. I found Maggie wandering the streets in this storm without a coat. We're at my place if you want to come get her." She hung up. "He's not there." She moved back into the living room. "He's probably out looking for you."

Ann knelt in front of the TV and started picking up the DVDs to avoid talking to—or even looking at—Maggie.

"You have to take the book," Maggie said. "You have to keep it safe. It's your job as the Protector."

"I am a whole lot of things. But I really don't think I'm a Protector." Denial was still her defense.

"But the book says—right there." Maggie pointed to the torn page, which, without someone holding it down, had curled up. "You're Bram Logan's daughter. You're next on the list."

"Just because my dad's name and his offspring are on some old list doesn't mean anything."

"I can prove it." Maggie's voice had taken on a smart-ass tone Ann didn't like. The girl was determined. She'd give her that.

"How are you going to prove it?" Ann paused in alphabetizing the DVDs.

"You'll see." She crossed her arms and looked smug. "Come closer."

Ann sat on the coffee table again, across from Maggie.

"Let me see your hand," Maggie said.

Ann held out her right one. Maggie brought it close to her face. Ann jerked away.

"I'm not gonna to bite you." Maggie laughed. Ann raised an eyebrow. Then she held her hand out again.

Maggie leaned in and blew a steady stream of air onto Ann's skin. A silvery-blue glow blossomed in her palm.

CHAPTER 25

The mark on Ann's chest pulsed. Maggie sat back and looked up. Her eyes burned brighter than the light coursing through Ann's veins.

"How the fu–heck did you do that?" Ann asked.

"I don't know how it works," Maggie said with awe in her voice. "I only know what it means." Her eyes locked on Ann's. "You are the Protector. *My* Protector. It's you—just like I said. Just like the book says." Her eyes faded back to their usual light-gold color.

"How? Why?" This couldn't possibly be happening. Shit like this *didn't* happen. Ann squeezed her eyes shut and opened them. The light in her veins faded. "How did you know this would happen?" Ann asked. "How do you know it means I'm . . ." she gulped, "the Protector?"

In a voice full of wisdom for such a young girl, Maggie said, "Life breathes light. Light is life."

A voice not Ann's own whispered in her head. The same voice from the clearing—what felt like ages ago.

Protect her.

"I can't believe I'm going to ask this—I can't believe I'm even considering any of this is real."

"It *is* real, Ann."

"Assuming it is . . . What does it mean to you? Me, being your Protector or whatever."

"I told you. You have to protect the knowledge," Maggie said. Her eyes twinkled. "The book." She pointed at it. "You have to keep it safe and hidden." She leaned forward and retrieved the tome. "Baba said, if you have the book, if you keep it safe," she took a shuddery breath, "then *I'll* be safe, too."

Ann lifted the book. It was still warm, though it had been sitting on the coffee table for some time now.

"Safe from whom?" Ann asked. Or *what*, based on the story Louise had told her. This Yalda-character. Ann rubbed her forehead, smoothing her fingers across her eyebrow.

Maggie opened her mouth, but someone knocked on the front door. They both jumped. Ann got up and peeked through the peep hole.

"Your dad's here." She raised an eyebrow at Maggie and then opened the door. Derrick stood on the porch, his eyes wild and hair sprinkled with snow.

"I need your help." His voice came out rough. "Maggie—she ran off."

"She's right here." Ann stepped aside. Derrick ran to Maggie and pulled her close.

"Daddy, you're so cold and wet!" she squealed.

"Thank god you're safe," he said in a ragged voice. He looked up at Ann. "Where did you find her?"

"Down the street." Ann omitted the fact his daughter nearly became road kill. He stood, and the relief on his face changed to a scowl.

"Why didn't you call me?" The accusatory tone took her back to the bickering they did in high school and how he always wanted a phone call to let him know where she was after they parted.

"I left a message." Ann moved back to the dining room and sat at the table. Derrick deposited Maggie on the couch. Then he sat at the table opposite Ann.

"What happened in here?" Derrick flung a thumb over his shoulder at the mess of DVDs on the floor.

"They were out of order," she said. "Want a drink?" Without waiting for a response, she retrieved the bottle from the freezer. Sailor Jerry. The Captain Morgan wannabe—albeit stronger. She snagged two glasses from the cabinet and brought everything to the table.

Derrick examined the label. "I took you for a Bacardi girl."

She glanced into the living room. Maggie had fallen asleep in the nest of blankets on the couch.

Ann set the glasses on the table, and Derrick poured a splash in each.

"Sorry, I don't have any mixers." She took a sip and grimaced.

He downed his, coughed, and stuck his tongue out. "I think the last time I drank this stuff was when we sampled my dad's liquor cabinet back in high school." He shook his head and groaned. "Capful by capful."

He poured another and sipped it.

"Didn't we sneak off to torment Louise afterward?" Ann asked. "All buzzed and full of great ideas."

"Oh yeah. We were *not* nice kids." Derrick smiled behind his glass. "Totally going to hell."

They reminisced on old high school memories for a while, sticking mainly to stories about Derrick's dumb friends and the shit they got into, while skirting around any talk of who they were back then. They finished half the bottle in the process.

Maggie shifted position on the couch.

"She's an interesting kid." Ann nodded toward the girl and took a long pull of rum. The slight buzz was slowly working its way to full-force drunk.

"She's a sweetheart. I couldn't have asked for an easier kid." His voice left something unsaid.

"But . . ."

"Teresa's having a hard time adjusting." He lifted his glass but set it down without drinking. "We had a baby." He met Ann's eyes. "She died seven years ago." He drank.

"I'm so sorry." Ann usually sucked at sympathy, but the rum helped. "How?"

"One of her stuffed animals—this obnoxiously giant bear Teresa had as a kid—fell on top of her, and when she tried to struggle out from under it, she ended up pressed against the crib . . ." his voice broke, and he took a deep breath, ". . . bumper. She suffocated." He tossed back the rest of his rum. "We tried again, and nothing came of it. Turns out our baby was a miracle. Teresa is infertile. This may be TMI, but, her cervical mucus has a low pH. The acidity makes for a hostile environment." He sighed. "Then she had cysts on her ovaries and had to have one of them removed before it ruptured. The other one was so malformed—they said she would never get pregnant."

"So you decided to adopt?"

"Yeah." He looked thoughtful for a second. "Actually, oddly enough, your dad put the idea in my head."

"My dad?" Ann sat up straighter.

"Yeah. Huh, I just remembered that." He looked thoughtful for a second. "We had dinner together a couple times after you left. Misery loves company and all." He looked down at his glass. "I saw him around town a few times. Then nothing. I thought he moved away, too." He shook his head. "Anyway, a few years after our baby died, he called me. I think to check up on me. I'm sure Sheriff McMichael kept him in the loop about what was happening around here."

Ann patiently waited for Derrick to get to the point, but she couldn't stop herself from asking, "When was the last time you saw him?"

He looked at her. "A year, year and a half ago? We met for drinks. I told him everything. How Teresa was in bad shape. He mentioned adopting. How it might help her heal." Derrick's lips moved into a tight mirthless smile. "I wasn't sure how to broach the subject with her, so I just decided that's what we'd do. I didn't give her a choice. She was a wreck." He huffed out a mirthless laugh. "She's still a wreck. It's been seven years. Maggie joined us three months ago. Nothing's changed. Teresa still hasn't come back to work. She just broods." His voice had taken on a disgusted tone. "Things aren't good. She's . . . not right." He frowned and shook his head.

"Wait . . . How did you adopt a kid if Teresa isn't right? Don't they do, like, home studies or something to make sure the environment is friendly? Don't they conduct interviews and do background checks?"

Derrick shrugged. "Somehow we passed. The advocate, who we never even spoke to, signed off on all the home study and family assessment paperwork." He shrugged. The signed form from the Angel's hideout came to mind. "Also, I think Teresa knew I really wanted this, so she was always on her best behavior."

"Sounds like she isn't as bad as you make her out to be," Ann said. She took a swig.

Derrick made a face.

"She had all of our baby's furniture in the basement, arranged like a nursery. She sat down there doing god knows what." He looked at Ann. "I got rid of it this morning." There was some sick pleasure in his smile, like taking something like that away from Teresa made him happy.

"Derrick, Derrick, Derrick." She let out a groan. "You can't do that to her. You're fucking with her grieving process."

His voice took on a defensive tone. "Maybe, but she didn't say anything about it." He shrugged and changed the subject. "She accused me of having an affair. She saw you and me at lunch together."

"You've got to be kidding me," Ann said. Derrick frowned, and she wondered if he wished it were true.

"I told her I was catching up with a friend, but she also knew about us—that we were together back in high school."

"Fuuuuhhh," Ann said under her breath.

"Don't worry," Derrick said. "I smoothed things over."

Because you're so *good at that.*

Derrick glanced over his shoulder toward Maggie's sleeping form. When he turned back to Ann, his eyes were sad.

Uh-oh.

When he spoke again, his voice was soft as if he were only thinking out loud. "This reminds me of when we were together," he said. "Us, talking like this, hanging out."

"Except, usually we'd be on the couch with your hand up my shirt." She laughed and took a drink.

"Why did you leave?"

Ann almost spit her rum out. "You know why." She wiped her mouth.

He shook his head. "I really don't." He lifted his eyes

from his empty glass to her face but failed to make eye contact.

"I felt trapped." Ann slouched back and let out a long breath. "Everyone had this life planned out for me and never really considered what I actually wanted."

"I thought I was what you wanted." His voice had softened, lowered.

She leaned forward. "You were." Might as well put it all out on the table. "But, junior and senior year, you were a little controlling." She winced.

"Controlling?" he said with disbelief. "I was not."

Ann reminded him of the phone calls.

"I didn't want to worry about you." Then she reminded him of the other things. The time or two he told her not to hang out with certain friends of hers, his constant decision-making on her behalf. How he pouted when she didn't want to hang out with him every second of every day. How he made it a point to always touch her in some way in public, as if to show everyone she belonged to him. How he tried desperately to persuade her to stay in Harmony to follow her dad's plan for her and become the sheriff.

"I didn't want to be a sheriff. What I wanted, I couldn't have if I stayed here. I wanted to solve cases and lock away really bad people. Not just the town drunks."

"Okay, okay. Point made." Derrick twisted his glass on the table. He lifted it and attempted to drain a few nonexistent drops into his mouth. "I know you didn't want to be the sheriff. Remember? *Magnum PI*?" He smiled. "Though, come to think of it, he was a private investigator."

She let out a soft laugh and shrugged. "We both had our plans, Derrick. You wanted to be a doctor, I wanted to be a detective."

"I know." He sat back. A few seconds of silence settled over them. Derrick sighed, and in a voice almost a whisper said, "I would have waited for you." He met her eyes, leaned forward, and jabbed his finger into the tabletop. He spoke through his teeth. "I would have come to you in Denver or wherever it was you went. I would have done whatever it took to be with you." His voice softened again. "I would have waited for you—if I knew you were coming back."

"I wasn't planning on coming back," she said. "There's nothing here for me." Especially now that her dad was gone. She shrugged. "There's nothing for me in Salida, either. I had nowhere else to go." She rambled on.

Damn you, Sailor Jerry!

"You're a hero, though," he said, as if that made any sense after what she'd just told him. "You saved the children of Salida from a terrible man. You made the town safer."

She glared, shook her head, and pointed at him. "Don't you start that. I'm no hero, Derrick. I'm a failure. I'm here to—I don't know—figure shit out, I guess. Get my shit together." She leaned her head against the chair back and closed her eyes. The room spun.

Derrick was quiet for a minute, looking at her, probably trying to figure her out. No. That's what *she* would be doing if the situation were switched. Can't take the detective out of the detective.

"I think we better head home," he said.

Ann rolled her head back and forth along the back of the chair. Without looking at him she said, "It's snowing. You're drunk. I'm drunk. Maggie's sleeping. I have two spare rooms upstairs."

"Are you asking me to spend the night?"

Ann snapped her head up. "I'm asking you not to risk your life out there." She got up and snatched the bottle from the table. After two tries to twist the cap back on, she jammed it on and set the bottle on the counter. She went to the master and shut the door a little harder than she meant.

Derrick had been in her dad's house before. He knew where her old bedroom was at least. A tear sneaked from her eye and she brushed it away.

Why are you crying?

Ann flopped backward onto the mattress. She examined her palm, breathed on it like Maggie had, but nothing happened. How did Maggie do that? What did it mean, Protector of the Knowledge? What knowledge?

The book, dumbass.

She already had the answers—sort of.

The front door shut. Hopefully Derrick had the mind to at least wrap Maggie in a blanket or two. Ann went into the living room, but the mess in there turned her back around. She sat on the edge of the bed.

Something in her pocket poked her in the hip. She dug out the small key she had found taped in her father's journal. She'd forgotten about it after yesterday's talk with Loony Lou, lunch with two-thirds of the Hart family, and today's chat with Raghib.

Tomorrow, she would hopefully get some answers.

CHAPTER 26

"Wakey, wakey," A little voice said. A cold finger trailed across Teresa's cheek.

She opened her eyes and smiled at Tiffany in the low light.

"Hello, baby," Teresa said.

"Time to go."

The happiness at seeing her baby dissipated. Already? Couldn't she rest a day or two before taking another person's . . . Teresa gulped.

"Yaldabaoth is so pleased with you," Tiffany said, her voice brimming with excitement. So *that* was his name. She pranced to the doorway and turned to Teresa. "He has given you a choice!"

"A choice?" Perhaps she could choose to just spend the night hanging out with Tiffany instead of running through the woods stealing souls.

"Yes, a choice." Tiffany beckoned her to follow. Teresa went into the foyer. She pulled on a pair of winter boots, her coat, and a pair of leather gloves lined with sheep skin.

"Open the door," Tiffany said.

Teresa took a deep breath, let it out, and opened the door. The breath sucked back in.

Draped over the picket fence and winding through the yard, at least fifty zoe lines led off into the distance in different directions.

"Look at them all!" Tiffany squealed with delight. "You get to pick one!" She jumped up and down and clapped her hands. So pleased. So excited. How could Teresa break her little spirit?

"How do I know who they lead to?" she asked, dreading the response.

So much happiness in such a small little face. "You don't!" Tiffany said. "It's a surprise!" She grabbed Teresa's hand. "Isn't this fun?"

Teresa ignored the queasiness in her stomach and gave Tiffany a weak smile.

"Yes," she said, her voice catching in her throat. "So . . . fun." She stared at the veiny ropes pulsing on the ground. Snowflakes drifted down, landed on them, and immediately melted. Who would be sacrificed tonight?

"Pick one, Mommy." Tiffany danced and hopped over them, so careful not to touch them. Teresa wondered what would happen if she did.

Teresa swept her gaze across the lines. Which one? Did it even matter? One life was just as valuable as the next. Wasn't it? She crouched and examined them for a sign that one might be weaker than another, or different somehow. If she could figure out which one might lead to an elderly person, someone who had lived their life, that might make it easier.

But they all held the same vibrant, pulsing red color.

"Try this one," Tiffany whispered in her ear, pointing. "Or that one." She pointed at another. "Come on, we don't have all night!"

Teresa closed her eyes and reached her hand forward, flinching back when she grazed the smooth rope. She wrapped her hand around it. Her stomach lurched at the warm pulsing. She opened her eyes. Long furrows in the snow where the rest had lain were the only sign they had been there at all.

"Very good," Tiffany said. "Let's see where it leads."

Teresa held onto the zoe and used it to guide herself, gathering the rope in her arms. Its warmth pulsed against her body.

The moment she stepped outside of the yard, someone screamed an unearthly sound, half mountain lion, half human.

"Uh-oh," Tiffany paused in her back and forth leap over the zoe. "Ruthie knows."

Teresa halted. "What do you mean?" she asked, unable to hide the terror in her voice.

"She can sense you are going to take another," Tiffany said. "We have to hurry!" She took off running along the glowing strand. Teresa followed, jogging and coiling until she slipped, fumbled, and dropped the whole yarn. She gave up and ran, following it, down Forrest Parkway right on Ponderosa Boulevard, deeper into the older residential area full of rustic homes hidden within the trees.

Each shriek from Ruthie came closer and closer. Teresa glanced over her shoulder. Ruthie—her shriveled, stick-like form—lurched after them. Teresa gasped and stumbled over a coil of the zoe, caught herself, and kept running. Tiffany darted ahead and turned onto the front porch of the house where the zoe led.

"Quick. Once we're inside, she can't get us!" Tiffany reached her hands toward Teresa. Teresa dashed up the steps and, despite her desire to burst through the front door, opened it slowly and stepped inside. She held her breath and clicked the door shut just as Ruthie clambered up the porch steps, claw-like fingers reaching. Teresa threw the deadbolt and leaned against the door.

Once she caught her breath, she peered through the darkness. Blue light flickered from a room down the hall. Teresa tiptoed to the doorway and peeked inside.

Sheriff McMichael lay in a recliner in the corner wearing only boxers and an undershirt. A snore escaped his parted lips. The zoe led straight into his chest.

Teresa ducked back into the hallway and pressed herself against the wall.

He was old. In his seventies at least. Aside from the fact that he never believed her story about what happened to the baby, she really didn't know him very well. Did he have a wife sleeping in the next room?

It wouldn't do to have someone wake up and catch her stabbing a giant needle into the man's chest.

"Should I search the house for others?" she asked Tiffany.

"You can only take one, Mommy."

"That's not what I meant." Teresa crept down the hall and checked the other rooms. She went back to where the sheriff was still fast asleep.

Ruthie scratched at the front door.

Tiffany handed Teresa tonight's oversized hypo. Her hand shook when she took it.

"Just like last night." Tiffany made a stab and pull motion.

Teresa nodded and tried not to throw up. She positioned herself next to him, raised her arms, and was about to plunge the needle into his chest when an orange cat jumped into his lap with a trilling meow.

Teresa jumped back with a loud gasp. The cat held her gaze.

"What in the hell are you doing in my house?" the Sheriff's voice hollered. He struggled to sit up, bucking the recliner in his flailing. The cat launched to the floor.

The sheriff's left hand reached toward the side table. His gun, still holstered, sat on top of a *Hunting & Fishing* magazine.

Teresa leaped on top of him and pushed against his chest. Their combined weight tilted the recliner back as far as it would go. It knocked over a floor lamp, fell to the side, and spilled them onto the floor.

McMichael landed on top of Teresa, crushing the wind from her lungs. They locked eyes.

"You," he said. His cheeks were flushed. He struggled to his knees and lunged sideways for his gun. Teresa, still wheezing, sat up and shoved the needle into his chest.

His torso swung back toward her. His limp hand caught her in the chin, rocking her head back and to the side. The sheriff grabbed at the syringe while his mouth opened and closed, his lungs pleading for air.

Teresa yanked the plunger. The barrel filled with glowing red zoe.

He didn't shrivel like Ruthie had. Instead, his skin turned a putrid green. The vessels in his eyes burst, changing the white to a blotchy red. His tongue swelled up and flopped out of his parted lips. Bloat tightened his skin. He stopped moving.

The smell of death and decay seeped from his overstretched pores. Teresa gagged and withdrew the needle. The zoe swirled like a mini hurricane inside the barrel.

They couldn't leave the way they came in. Ruthie would get them. She clawed the door as if sensing Teresa's conundrum.

Teresa ran down the hall, Tiffany close behind. In a bedroom at the back of the house, she opened the window, pushed the screen out, and went through feet first. Something gouged the back of her left leg.

Teresa cried out and landed on her side, jarring her shoulder and rattling her teeth.

Ruthie shrieked from the other end of the house. Panic pushed Teresa to move. She ran toward town, slipping on the accumulated snow.

At the town square, Teresa doubled over and gasped for breath. The cold air pierced her throat and lungs. Her whole left side ached.

"Come on, we're almost there!" Tiffany said. She took off into the darkness.

Ruthie shrieked again before letting out a low, rumbling moan. Teresa looked over her shoulder. The sheriff hobbled after them on bloody bloated feet.

"Go," Teresa whispered, gritting her teeth. "Go, dammit!" Her legs listened, but sharp cramps riddled her quads and calves.

She ran down the dirt road, now sloppy with snow, and dodged to leap over the creek. Her push-off foot slipped, and in her attempt to stop herself from falling, she twisted her ankle and tumbled to the ground.

"Oh God," she cried. She reached for her ankle, but something cold and hard gripped it first.

Ruthie had hold of her foot. Teresa screamed.

CHAPTER 27

An intrusive sound in the wakeful world alerted her, and Ann fought the stranglehold of sleep, slipping in and out of consciousness. A vibrating boom brought her upright.

Ann groped the night stand for her gun. It was missing. She wracked her brain for where she left it. Hanging on the door with her belt and holster? At the station in her locker?

A deep grogginess shrouded her vision and mind. She tried to get her bearings, but the room was unfamiliar. Then she remembered.

Harmony, not Salida. Dad's house, not your shitty apartment.

Of course her gun wasn't on *this* nightstand.

The clock showed wee-hours-of-the-morning early. Three thirty. The TV flickered from the other room. She hadn't even turned it on earlier. She cocked an ear and listened. The page of a book turned.

She sidled to the door and peeked into the living room.

Her vantage point revealed the dark TV screen. The light came from somewhere else.

Ann dropped to her knees and peered under the bed.

Bingo.

She gripped the handle on her dad's Louisville Slugger. Baseball bat in hand, she grabbed the knob, jerked the door open, and lunged into the living room with a still-drunk war cry.

No one was there.

Maggie's book lay open on the coffee table, a blue-white light radiating from the pages. The same color her veins had glowed when Maggie breathed on her palm. The light wasn't like a halo or a beam or anything. The pages themselves seemed to be made of it. A low hum, more felt than heard, emanated from the book. Or maybe from the light. Or maybe in her head.

A page turned of its own volition.

Ann backed into the bedroom and shut the door. When she released the knob, her hand shook.

"You didn't see that. It could be light from the window and a breeze from . . . the furnace vent." She swallowed and nearly choked on the dryness of her throat. "You're tired. You're stressed. Still a little drunk. You. Did. Not. See. That."

Everything in her wanted to go back to bed, to curl beneath the covers and sleep off the residual effects of Sailor Jerry, but one little piece of her wanted to prove to herself it wasn't real. The part of her that needed to see something to believe it. Her rational, detective mind. She tore the door open.

The book still spilled forth angelic light. The feeling of the hum increased, vibrating inside her body.

"Dammit."

She leaned toward the coffee table and used the bat to flip the book shut. The light turned off. She went back into her room. Behind her, the pages fluttered. The light pulsed twice then stayed steady.

Ann froze. She turned around an inch at a time, eyes wide. That didn't happen, and yet, her rational mind couldn't come up with an explanation. She didn't believe in this stuff.

Keep telling yourself that.

Seared mark, glowing veins, Maggie in the vision. All things she couldn't explain, but believed anyway.

Ann let out a sigh, propped the bat against the couch, and sat. The light sucked into the center of the book, leaving the room in darkness. She picked it up and turned on the nearest lamp.

The leather cover was warm, and for a sickening second, it almost felt like human skin. The open page was about a third of the way in.

Just as before, when Maggie showed her the book, she could read it. The pages spoke of Sophia and the Protectorate.

Ann skimmed the text. *Sophia* meant knowledge and wisdom, and this *Sophia* and Louise's *Pistis Sophia* were the same person—a person who might actually exist.

The day Sophia is born into being, manifesting in physical form, returning to the material world to protect us from darkness, our duty as Protectors increases tenfold, for Yaldabaoth shall rise again and destroy the material world, for it was not only his creation, but also his demise. Should Yaldabaoth come to full power, he shall seek vengeance upon Sophia. Should Sophia expire before her time, the End of Days shall be upon us and all of humanity shall be smote from the earth.

Ann snorted. The End of Days. And Yaldabaoth again. What did Raghib say? He would be vengeful toward Sophia for defeating him. Assuming she believed any of this, if Sophia manifested while Ann was Protector, Ann's job was to save the world. She let loose a bark of a laugh.

"I'm still drunk." She had to be if she considered believing any of this.

She flipped to the back of the book to the list of names and dates. The page her dad left her was the last one.

Bram Logan's offspring.

She flipped back several pages to where the list began.

The title heading read: *A Genealogical Study of the Protectors of Sophia.*

The first date was so long ago, Ann thought Jesus probably walked the earth at that time. Assuming Jesus had actually walked the earth or even existed to begin with. The name with that date was—oh, surprise—Yeshua.

Bull. Shit.

The second name was John. Ann thought back to her brief time dating a churchy guy and thought she remembered John was an apostle.

"This can't be real." She needed to say the words out loud to the silent room. Maggie said her grandpa did the study. Ann wondered if the Protectorate had given him that task during his rehab. Seemed like a good method to get someone's mind involved in a new way of thinking.

Lines drawn in the margin connected names to other names. For some Protectors the line connected to the word *offspring* instead of a name. Some of the *offspring* entries had dates listed next to them.

Protectors' children whose names had not been recorded?

For other *offspring* no date was listed.

Maybe Protectors who never had kids.

Or maybe they were killed before they could pass the torch to their offspring.

Like Dad.

All of the names had "deceased" written next to them, except Bram Logan. For a second, Ann thought maybe he really was still alive somewhere, living under an alias. After all, she only had a dismembered finger and a video message.

While the video message sort of confirmed his death, it wasn't an official document stating as such. She'd accepted he was dead, though, because if he was alive somewhere and had been ignoring her calls for help this whole time—well, that would hurt even more than him being dead and gone.

Then a thought occurred to her. What if he *couldn't* call? Raghib said they'd all gone into hiding to protect their families, but how could he do that to her?

The safety deposit box, if there was one, *had* to have answers. Something to discount the message in the DVD, an explanation of where he was and why he couldn't be there for her. An explanation of the finger. Anything. Something.

She flipped back to the page about Sophia and reread the passage. Ann didn't want to believe it, but the truth was as clear as the light that had shone from the book.

Maggie said if Ann had the book and kept it safe, she would be safe too. Raghib's words confirmed it. Bound by blood and soul.

Ann had to protect Maggie.

She sat back against the couch. The book in her lap warmed her thighs. On a whim, she lifted her hands from the edges and spoke to the pages.

"Show me how to protect her."

The book didn't budge. Ann flipped through, but the only passage she could read was the one the book had just shown her. The rest remained in Coptic Egyptian. Ann turned to the back pages and studied the list of names again. Ran her finger down the columns as if she could divine something by osmosis through her fingertips.

The book cooled in her lap. It must've been done telling her its secrets for the night. She closed it and set it on the coffee table.

Protect Maggie, keep the book safe, save the world.

"All I want is my normal life back." A tear slid down her cheek. "I can't even look at a gun." Her words filled the silence, but they didn't help her answer the questions swirling through her mind, addled as it may be with the lingering effects of too much cheap spiced rum.

She lay down on her back and stared at the popcorn ceiling. Sometimes she imagined she could see faces in the texture. Sometimes she tried to find them. Tonight, the ceiling faded to dark as mental exhaustion overtook her.

CHAPTER 28

Teresa kicked with her free foot, but Ruthie had a strong hold. The sheriff lumbered over, his skin tight and bloated. He didn't even look like the old man anymore. He bent down to grab Teresa's other foot, his sausage fingers groping. Teresa kicked his hand away. He stumbled sideways and stepped on Ruthie's head, crushing the side of her face. Ruthie's shriek gurgled from her unhinged jaw. She let go of Teresa and grabbed what was left of her face. Teresa crab-walked backward until she hit one of the many tombstones.

She let out a scream, lunged onto her knees, and crawled as fast as possible through the brush and forest debris until she reached the stairs of the funeral home.

Fear and panic and exertion caught up with her. Somehow she'd managed to keep hold of the hypo. The zoe inside undulated like a lava lamp filled with coagulating blood. The green lights of the lost souls hovered around her, drawn to the zoe.

I can't do this. I can't do this. I can't do this.

Ruthie stalked along the barrier, holding the side of her crushed head. The sheriff stared in Teresa's direction.

Would they always be there, waiting for her every time?

Five more . . .

The thought filled her with desperation. With dread.

"Mommy." Tiffany's touch trailed along Teresa's cheek. "You are so brave. Yaldabaoth is very pleased."

Teresa clenched her jaw and looked into her precious baby's eyes. Then she looked at the dead people waiting for her beyond the barrier. She looked at the hypo in her hand. This was for Tiffany.

She limped up the steps and followed her daughter into the abandoned house. Inside, the sandy brown cave walls with torches appeared.

"I'll go get him." Tiffany skipped down the dark corridor, leaving Teresa in the flickering torchlight.

Teresa tested her ankle. She could put most of her weight on it. Some ice and elevation and she'd be good as new.

She wandered to the edge of the pool and peered into the black water. She couldn't see the bottom and wondered how deep it was. The water rippled. She stepped back and into something solid but warm.

"You have pleased me this night," Yaldabaoth said.

She turned around to face him. He stood too close, trapping her between him and this fathomless pool. With great reluctance, she looked up into his eyes and clenched her jaw.

"Take this. I'm done." She slapped the hypo against his bare chest and tried to push past him. He took it but didn't move out of her way. His amused chuckle vibrated through her.

"Done, are you?" He let her pass, but the doorway back outside was gone. "What about Tiffany?"

He snapped his fingers. A scream came from deep within the cave and ripped straight through Teresa's resolve.

"Tiffany!" She ran toward the corridor, but it was too dark. Impenetrable. And she was too afraid of what might lurk there. "Stop, please!" She rushed to Yaldabaoth and tugged on his arm. Tiffany's screams died, but her daughter wept in residual pain.

"Mommy . . ." she moaned.

"Tiffany," Teresa called. She paced at the mouth of the corridor like Ruthie had at the invisible barrier. "I'm here, baby, I'm here." She held out her hands. "Come here."

"She can't," Yaldabaoth said. "Your inability to carry out what you have started will keep her from you."

"I can't do this," she whimpered.

"You already have, twice." He cocked his head and lifted an eyebrow. "You can do this, and you will, or else . . ." He grinned and snapped his fingers again.

Tiffany wailed. Teresa's mouth went dry at the desperate, agonized sound. She covered her ears and dropped to her knees, crying out for her baby.

"Okay!" Teresa shouted. She gasped and sobbed. "Stop

hurting her. I'll do what you want."

Suddenly, he knelt behind her. His arms wrapped around her body and pinned her arms to her sides. He licked her neck and, though she knew she should be disgusted, a thrill coursed through her body. The cave heated. Or was it just her inner temperature?

"Good girl," Yaldabaoth breathed in her ear. Teresa closed her eyes. "Five more and you can have her." The air chilled again. He was gone.

Teresa got to her feet. "Tiffany?" she called down the corridor.

Tiffany didn't answer. Teresa took a torch from the wall and started down the tunnel. After a few yards, she looked over her shoulder. The cave behind her had disappeared into darkness. She continued slinking along the wall until she came to a door. A standard white home interior door. She turned the knob and opened it.

Old lumpy couch, sleeping bag, urine smells. She was in the abandoned funeral home. She turned around to go back, but it was only a closet. She looked at the torch in her hand and found it was just an old wet decayed piece of wood. She threw it into the corner with an angry shriek and stomped outside.

Ruthie and the sheriff had gone back to whatever hell they stayed in when they weren't chasing her. She stumbled toward town and wondered if she ought to return to the sheriff's house and make sure she didn't leave any evidence behind.

Evidence. Worry flashed through her. What if the sheriff had found her necklace at Ruthie's place?

The squeaky crunch of footsteps in snow broke the night's silence.

"Good evening, Doctor Hart. Or should I say good morning?" an old woman's voice asked.

Teresa whipped around. Louise wore a puffy, full-length coat that looked like it came from the second-hand shop down on Forest Parkway.

"Louise!" Teresa gasped. "You frightened me."

"What are you doing out at this hour?" the woman asked.

Teresa reached for her cross. God bless it! Where had she lost it?

Louise smiled and held out her closed hand.

"Looking for this?" She opened her palm. Teresa's cross dropped and dangled by its chain from Louise's fingers.

"Where did you find that?" Teresa moved to grab it, but Louise jerked back.

"Not so fast, Doctor."

"That necklace is mine. Give it to me."

"What were you doing in the old cemetery last night?" Louise held the cross out. A carrot to Teresa's horse.

"How did you know?" Of course. Louise lived over on the other side of the old cemetery from the funeral home. "I've been having trouble sleeping. Walking at night helps me relax."

"Yes, but you were in your robe and slippers."

She knows too much.

If only Tiffany would appear with another syringe—she'd get a two for one deal.

Like a shoe sale.

The thought made Teresa giddy and sick at the same time.

"I don't need to explain myself to you," Teresa said. What did Louise know? What did she think? She took a step back. What rumors would she spread?

"Don't worry, Doctor Hart. I won't tell anyone your secret." Louise held the necklace out to Teresa.

"I don't have any secrets."

"We all have secrets," Louise said. "You should see what's in my basement." She raised an eyebrow, and Teresa's eyes widened. The basement nursery was gone; surely she didn't mean that was one of Teresa's secrets.

Teresa snatched the cross and clasped it around her neck.

"How is our dear Maggie, by the way?" Louise asked. Something in her inflection made her inquiry sound ominous—like the witch asking about Hansel and Gretel *after* she ate them.

"She's . . . fine . . ." Teresa said. "She's settling in. Just fine."

"And you?"

"Me?" Teresa peered through the darkness. "I'm fine, too."

"Okay, then," Louise said. She stepped over the creek and disappeared into the woods.

* * *

Teresa eased the front door shut. She took off her gloves and boots, hung up her coat, and stepped onto the first step to head up to bed. Someone cleared their throat from the front room. Teresa grabbed the banister with a start.

"Who's there?" she whispered.

"Teresa. Come here, please." Derrick's voice, thick and slow.

Teresa stepped into the doorway of the front room. He sat on the love seat. She flicked her eyes to Big Bear, still hidden among the pillows on the chair in the corner.

"Yes?" she said in an innocent voice.

Play it up. You didn't do anything strange.

Derrick held out his hand. Teresa went to him and slid her fingers into his palm. He pulled her down next to him.

"I'm sorry," she said. She flung herself at him and hugged him tight. His arms wrapped around her and moved up and down her back in that comforting way she loved. It filled her with warmth.

"It's okay." Derrick said. "I found her."

Did he think she was out looking for Maggie?

Oh, what luck!

"Thank God," Teresa said. "I'm sorry I yelled at her. At you. I'm so sorry."

He brushed her hair aside and kissed her neck in the same place where Yaldabaoth had licked her. She pulled away in case he could smell the stench of dried saliva.

The moonlight coming in the window twinkled in his eyes. She leaned into him and kissed his lips. He tasted of—what was that—stale alcohol?

"Have you been drinking?" she asked.

He nodded. "Just a little. It's mostly worn off."

"Where did you find Maggie? At Flynn's?"

Flynn's was the town watering hole. She'd never been, of course. Ladies didn't frequent such establishments. Besides, it was a place for the locals, not her.

Derrick shook his head. "She was at Ann's."

Teresa stood and backed away. "Ann? What was Maggie doing there?" Besides making friends with Derrick's ex-high-school-sweetheart.

"Ann found her and picked her up."

"And she didn't think to call us? To let us know Maggie was safe?" Teresa vaguely remembered the phone ringing, but it seemed like days ago.

"Teresa, please," Derrick said in his oh-so-casual-drunk voice. "Maggie didn't want Ann to bring her home."

"And I suppose everyone does what Maggie wants."

"*Because*, if you'd let me finish, Maggie didn't *want* to come home. And besides, we weren't here to answer the phone anyway."

"She didn't want to come home?" Great. Maggie didn't want to be with them anymore, and it was Teresa's fault. Her hand went to her throat, to the cross. But it didn't bring her the strength it once did. "Is she home now?"

"Yes. Upstairs. Sleeping." Derrick tried to get up twice

and finally got to his feet. "And that's what I'm going to do, too." He kissed her cheek and left the room.

"Where *did* you go to drink?" Teresa asked.

Derrick paused in the doorway, and his shoulders raised up like he was bracing for a blow. She could almost hear his mouthed curse. He turned around.

"You know alcohol is not allowed in this house." She crossed her arms.

"Yeah, I know," Derrick said. "Not since Tiffany died."

She dared him to blame her. She even gritted her teeth, expecting it. She'd formed a retort in her mind already, and when he didn't say it, she let it loose.

"Not since you drank yourself into a stupor for months on end, you mean." She was goading him. Did she want him to say the real reason?

"I had no choice," Derrick said through his teeth. "You were in and out of the hospital. What was I supposed to do? I didn't have you, Teresa. I didn't have my *wife*—who I thought I could get through anything with. And when you were back, you weren't you anymore." He stepped toward her and pointed his finger at her chest. "I made promises when I married you. I stuck by your side in sickness and in health." Tears welled in his eyes. Alcohol made him emotional. It always had.

"I needed *you*, Teresa. We needed each other." His voice had softened.

"Seven years—and now you're telling me this?" She failed to keep the snap out of her voice. This was no small thing to keep from her.

He sighed, and his whole body drooped with the exhalation. "What happened to us?" A tear dripped onto the floor.

Teresa stared at where it landed. She didn't know what to say. Tears welled in her eyes now, and when she lifted her gaze to his, they streamed down both cheeks.

"I'm trying, Derrick," she said, her voice low and measured. "All we do is fight." She took a step closer to him, then another. She stood inches in front of him, so close she felt the heat of him.

He pulled her against him and rested his cheek against the top of her head. She cried into his chest. For the briefest moment, she wished they could stay like this forever. It was like before. The way they were in the pictures on the piano.

She stopped crying and relished in his embrace, drank it up. She lifted her chin. He lowered his lips to hers.

The kiss was everything she wanted it to be. She expected it to be rough and lusty—the way he used to kiss her. Though it was gentle, she could feel his need. His hands moved up her back and into her hair. He moved his lips to her neck, his hands to her buttocks. He lifted her, and she wrapped her legs around his waist. He stumbled backward, regained his balance, and lowered both of them to the floor. He lost his balance again and they landed with a *thump* on the rug.

"Oh, sorry," Derrick whispered. "You okay?"

Teresa giggled but stifled it. "Shh. We don't want to

wake Maggie."

She hadn't felt this way in . . . she didn't even remember how long. He gazed into her eyes, then fastened his lips back onto hers while he fumbled at her pants. Taking his cue, she unfastened his belt and brazenly reached into his boxers.

He pulled her hand out of his pants and pinned both of hers above her head. She didn't usually like these kinds of rough games, but this time it brought her thrills. She lifted her hips to him. With one hand, he worked her pants and panties down to her ankles.

Even after he let go of her wrists, she left her hands above her head, surrendering to him, allowing herself this moment.

He teased her with his fingertips while grinning at her with the sweet-yet-devilish-smile he stole her heart with. Then he replaced his fingers with his tongue.

Teresa opened her legs to him. She wound her fingers in his hair. A guttural and primal moan escaped her, uncontained pleasure rippling through her vocal chords. Her ecstasy built, higher and higher, faster than any other time she'd been with him.

At the peak, Derrick lifted his face. She met his eyes.

"Please." She hitched in a ragged breath. "Keep going."

He no longer had a lusty look to his eyes. Had her moan killed the mood? How could it?

"I . . . can't." He lurched to the side and vomited on the rug.

CHAPTER 29

Monday

Ann took the small key straight to the bank, but a crowd was dispersing from the church, even though it wasn't Sunday. Some people looked mad, others afraid. George Riley was the last to leave, red faced and with drooping shoulders. Ann waited for Sheriff McMichael to come out, but he didn't. She followed George into the station.

George paced the length of the office back and forth from the desks to the hallways where the lockers were.

"I can't do this," he muttered. "I can't. They ate me alive in there."

Rachel had her hands up like she was trying to tame a lion without a chair and whip. George's eyes landed on Ann.

"Detective Logan, thank god you're here." He rushed toward her and pulled her into the room. "You gotta help me."

Ann pulled out of George's grip. "Uh . . . what's going on?"

"He's gone. The sheriff is gone. He's missing, just like Ruthie." The whites showed all around his eyes.

"Is that what the meeting at the church was about?" Ann threw a thumb over her shoulder in the general direction of the church.

"The Town Hall was for Ruthie." Rachel sighed. "And George the Giant Doof here may have mentioned the Sheriff is also missing." She rolled her eyes.

"He told me yesterday he called a Town Hall to talk about Ruthie and safety precautions until she's found," he explained, his big hands palms up. "He didn't show up. I called his cell, I called his house. But he didn't answer." He paced over to his desk. "I had to tell folks to lock their doors, but they didn't believe me, so I had to tell them something else." He slumped into his chair. His forehead hit the desk. "They had so many questions." He groaned. "I had no answers."

Ann chewed her lip. "Well, but you know what to do now."

George lifted his head and looked past her toward Rachel. Rachel made an annoyed sound.

George's ears turned red. "Uh."

"Check his house? Check the places he frequents? Come on, George."

He dropped his face into his hands and mumbled, "I panicked. I had no clue what else to do."

"How about start with following protocol," Rachel said.

George lifted his head. "I did! I ran the meeting even though he wasn't there!"

Ann held up her hands. "Children, please," she said in her authoritative voice. They both snapped their attention to her.

"So, the town thinks their sheriff is missing. Big deal," she said to diffuse the tension between Rachel and George. "When he shows up, they'll be relieved. Honest mistake." She shrugged.

George nodded. Rachel sat down and returned to her game of solitaire.

Ann sidled toward George. "We need to go to his house."

George looked at her with big sad dog eyes. He nodded.

"You drive." Ann pushed open the door.

They climbed into the department vehicle, an old Jeep Cherokee, and George drove the minute and a half to the sheriff's house. McMichael's truck was outside. George jumped out and dashed to the front door. He pounded his fist against it.

"Sheriff?" George yelled. "Frank? Are you in there?"

Ann surveyed the area outside the house and went through her mental checklist for footprints, tire tracks, anything unusual. Unfortunately, the snow had covered any signs overnight in a smooth blanket of white. She circled around to the side of the house and peeked in the first window. A recliner lay on its side, and a floor lamp had been knocked over.

She unzipped her jacket and inhaled through her nose and out her mouth a few times.

"George," she called. He appeared around the corner. "I think something's happened."

"What?" Panic in his voice. "What happened?"

"I need you to stay calm." Even though everything inside her wanted to scream and run away, she'd mastered presenting a calm front. "There are signs of a possible struggle. Are you familiar with how to perform a block search?"

He nodded. "Sheriff McMichael did the same thing at Ruthie's."

"Good. Is there a kit in the vehicle?"

He nodded.

"Go get it." Ann moved around the side of the house to the back, scanning the ground, the bushes, the house.

The screen from the back window lay on the ground partially covered with snow. The curtains inside the open window fluttered in a short-lived breeze. Ann's throat tightened, and she worked to accumulate enough saliva to swallow.

Based on the position of the screen, the perp had exited the house through the window.

"Ann? Where are you?"

"I'm at the back. Just stay there." She examined the sill. No pry marks around the edge of the window, though a piece of metal flashing jutted out from the frame. A small amount of some kind of fiber stuck to it. She moved slowly, scanning the area, around to the other side of the house. The first room and the back window were the only signs of anything amiss that she noted right away.

At the front of the house, she told George what to do, but his eyes were wide and glassy, and she didn't think he understood her. Damn kid was going into shock. Whoever gave him the idea to get into law enforcement?

"I need an envelope and some tweezers," Ann said.

He nodded but didn't move. Ann took the kit from him, set it on the front porch, flipped it open, and got what she needed. She went back to the window, pulled on a pair of nitrile gloves, and collected the fiber. At the front, the doorknob turned, but the door didn't budge.

"The deadbolt's been thrown," Ann said.

"Oh, here." George held out the Jeep's keys. "It's the brass one."

Ann took the keys. "Why do you have—never mind." She unlocked the door.

Inside, she found the same dark brown, almost black, crispy substance McMichael had found at Ruthie's house. She collected as much as she could.

In the first room, the recliner and lamp were tipped over as she had observed from outside. The television was on. A side table held the sheriff's sidearm, a Colt .357 Magnum. Ann's palms sweated, and a prickling chill raced over her body. Whoever abducted him probably caught him off guard and overtook him before he could grab his gun. It was likely someone he knew.

They needed to check phone records to see if anyone called ahead of time. They needed to get the samples tested against those from Ruthie's house. The fiber from the window, too. This was all more than a small-town Sheriff's Department could handle.

She took a deep breath. The air in the room held a faint scent of rancid meat.

Something touched Ann's ankle, and she cried out. An orange feline stared up at her, its tail swishing. His purr vibrated against her leg while he snaked around her ankles.

"Hey, kitty." She crouched and held out her hand. The cat bumped his head against her palm, arched his back, circled around, and did it again. She picked him up. "George," she called.

He appeared in the doorway with the look of a frightened child.

"Take the sheriff's cat and put it in the car."

"Remington?" He held out his arms, and Ann handed him the cat. "Hey, Remy." He scratched under the cat's chin. Then he gazed into the room. "He's gone, isn't he? I can't be the sheriff, Ann."

"Just go put the cat in the Jeep."

Ann stared at McMichael's gun. How did the attacker get McMichael out the back window? Why did they leave that way? What about the crunchy substance? Was it like a calling card?

On top of collecting trophies, serial killers often left

hallmarks. Modus Operandi.

The Stabber's MO—Ann took a deep breath—was to leave a page from a book with some letters missing. No title, no author, just a seemingly random page. When Ann came onto the case, her knowledge of ciphers, due to her dad's love of the word puzzles in Harmony's community paper, clued her in. The missing letters revealed the cipher and the number of letters in the key phrase. The solutions, coupled with intel from a literary scholar Ann spoke with at the University of Denver, helped Ann figure out where to find Elizabeth.

But this couldn't be a serial killer. Not in safe, unpretentious Harmony.

They're just abductions, missing persons.

The rational side of her brain tried to pipe in, but Ann knew better. McMichael had been in law enforcement since she knew him. Deputy for her dad, then sheriff for the last ten or so years. They both served their time in the Navy well before Ann was even born.

Ann went back through the house but paused at the entry to the dining room. An envelope and a few pieces of paper lay on the table. She stepped closer. It was a subpoena filled out in McMichael's neat handwriting. She used the tip of her finger to shuffle the pages apart.

He had checked the box for "produce." In the description it said, "Phone records from Colorado Telecomm; 6 months from the date of this request for the party listed below." Ann's eyes jumped to the next section where her dad's name, Bram Logan, was listed along with his phone number, address, and email. McMichael wanted to obtain her father's phone records, just like he said he would, but something happened to him before he had a chance to mail this. Was it somehow related?

Her mind, usually teeming with activity, went blank. She tucked the document and envelope into the interior pocket of her coat and went back outside. George leaned against the Jeep, stroking Remy.

"When will we get the results from the lab on the substance from Ruthie's house?" Ann asked through her constricted throat.

He shrugged.

Ann rubbed the back of her neck. "We need to dust for prints and note anything that seems out of place," she said. "Pay special care to the window in the back. You can do that, right?"

George nodded and put Remy in the Jeep.

When they finished processing the house and surrounding area, Ann said, "Let's seal it up and get back to the station. We'll talk about what to do next there." She paused. "You can break the news to Rachel."

George gulped. "Please, Ann," he said. His face contorted. "You gotta tell her. I can't do this."

"Yes, you can, and yes, you will."

On their way back to the station, Ann had George drop her off at the post office three buildings down. She stuffed the subpoena into the envelope and sent it on its way before walking down the block to the station.

George still sat in the truck. He got out when Ann approached.

"I didn't want to face Rachel alone," he said in his sheepish way.

Ann followed George inside. Rachel read a magazine at her desk but dropped it and stood when they came in. Her face held expectance instead of her usual disinterest.

"What's the word?"

George came in with Remy.

"Is that Remy?"

"George," Ann said.

He hid his face in the cat's fur. Rachel took Remy from him. George slunk away, disappearing down the hallway.

"Rachel," Ann said. "I'm sorry. He wasn't home."

Rachel sank into the chair. The cat purred and bumped his head under her chin. "What does this mean?"

"There were signs of a struggle," Ann said. "We think he may have been abducted."

"Who would do such a thing? This town loves him. He has no enemies—well, I mean, not ones that would kidnap him. That's what you're going to ask, right? If he has enemies?"

Ann nodded. "Is there anyone else we should inform?"

"How can you be so methodological about this?" Rachel asked, emotion creeping into her voice. "He's not just a misplaced sock. He's a person."

"I know this must be hard for you," Ann said. It was

hard for her. McMichael was like family. But she shoved the feelings down deep to maintain a professional front. "Maybe you should go home."

"Are you reciting something you learned in your big bad police academy?" Rachel grabbed her things with one hand and held Remy in the other. She pushed past Ann. "Show a little heart, Detective."

Everyone handles things differently.

She had to stay emotionally distant or risk breaking in two. Rachel slammed the door on her way out.

"That had to be hard," George muttered from behind her. Ann closed her eyes. It was cake compared to Bruce's wife and Elizabeth's parents.

Something inside her cracked open a little. She took in a quick gasp of air and held it until the despair went away. She released the breath and turned around.

George watched her with wide open eyes. She looked past him toward the lockers. Not now. She had a fire to prevent and George was waiting for guidance. Heat flamed through her, dampening her armpits. She paced back and forth, aware of George watching her every move, waiting for her to supply all the answers to their dilemma.

Two missing persons with completely different profiles. Both disappeared within a day of each other. Strange crispy substance. No weapons. No blood. No bodies.

She stopped in front of George. "This is what we're going to do. We're going to call the state police and Colorado Bureau of Investigations and request assistance."

George let out a long breath. "We?"

"Yes, we. You don't think I would turn my back on this town, do you?"

George shrugged. "You're here on vacation—I didn't think you'd want to get involved."

She couldn't very well leave her town in the hands of incompetent George Riley.

Damn you, McMichael. Why couldn't you defend yourself?

"As the sheriff's only deputy, you are now Acting Sheriff," Ann told him, though she suspected he had to know that.

"Oh . . . kay?" George's voice held an uncertain edge to it. Maybe he didn't know.

"My role is consultant."

"How about I swear you in as my deputy?"

Ann shook her head. No way. If the town knew she was involved, they would expect miracles from her. It would be another chance to fail. A chill replaced the heat flashing through her body. Queasiness settled in her gut. She sat and rubbed her temples. Then she leaned back and gripped the arms of the chair.

"I will help in a limited capacity. I do not want to be actively involved, and I don't want anyone outside of you and me to know I'm involved," she said. "You have questions, you ask. You find anything you have the faintest idea might be important, you tell me."

She stood and faced George and clapped her hands

on his shoulders, an awkward gesture given he was over a foot taller than her.

"George, this is your time to shine. To prove to the town you are capable and can do your duty to serve and protect!"

His eyebrows slid to the center of his forehead, giving him a sad puppy look. "But I'm not—I'm a failure. Failed right out of the police academy. McMichael only gave me this job to help me prove to my dad I'm not a complete loser. He never liked my dad."

Jeezus.

"You aren't a failure."

I am.

"You are a man on the edge of becoming a hero. Are you ready to be a hero, George?"

He shook his head and dropped into a chair. This pep talk was not going as planned.

"Think of Marcie," she said. "Don't you want to keep her safe?"

George perked up at the mention of his underage girlfriend. "Of course I do," he said. "She means the world to me. I'm going to marry her someday—as soon as her parents see I'm not just trying to get into her pants."

What a sap.

"This is your golden opportunity then. Town heroes are greatly rewarded." She swore she was channeling Tony Robbins or some other motivational speaker. "Think about it. I'll be right down the hall." She strode to the lockers and glared at the dial on her dad's. If only they were secured with keyed padlocks. She could pick a padlock. Hell, she could cut a padlock. It could take her hours to guess the right combination. What could it be?

She twisted the dial and tried her birthday, his birthday, her mom's birthday, mom and dad's anniversary again . . . What other dates were important?

On a whim, she tried the day she graduated from the police academy.

It worked.

Ann's heart gave a couple of hard beats. The threat of tears stung her nose. Her dad's combination—the day she graduated. She closed her eyes. Now that she was finally here, apprehension filled her. What would she find inside? The fear of disappointment made her pause.

"Ann," George called from the office area. The sound of his heavy footsteps preceded him down the hallway. "I've come to a decision," he said. Ann turned around.

"I'll do it. I'll do it and prove myself to Marcie's parents so I can marry her." He dipped his chin in a single nod, finalizing his decision.

"Fantastic. You know you didn't really have a choice, right?"

"Yeah, serve and protect. It's my duty. I have to embrace it." He took a deep breath. "If not for Marcie, then for Sheriff McMichael and Ruthie."

He made it seem so easy to decide to stand up to his reservations and fears. Ann wondered if his ignorance was a blessing.

"Great. Your first task as acting sheriff is to call state police and CBI," Ann said.

"As acting sheriff, I think we should keep this investigation private until we have more details," George said.

"Nope. We follow protocol. We need help. Go call them." She pushed him out the door toward the desks. "Tell them we are requesting assistance in the disappearance of two individuals, one of whom is a law enforcement officer." She turned back to the lockers.

Before anything could happen to distract or disrupt her, she opened the door.

Her dad's Smith & Wesson M&P 9 semiautomatic pistol—the same gun she preferred—hung from a hook by its belted holster. She reached a hand out to touch it but thought better. An old t-shirt lay in the bottom. That was it. His gun and a shirt. She sank to the floor, picked up the tee, and sniffed it, but it didn't smell like him anymore. She dropped it into her lap and peered into the locker again.

The shirt had been covering a metal lock box. Excitement surged through her. She pulled the little key out of her pocket and stuck it into the lock.

CHAPTER 30

Teresa stepped into the clinic. Metal bells clattered and clanged against the glass. A sign on the desk said, "Please take a seat. We will be with you in a moment." It was punctuated with a grotesque smiley face.

Derrick had to let their receptionist, Whitney, go after the baby died. He couldn't afford to keep her on. It was a zone of contention for them. Teresa always thought he charged too little, but he didn't believe in inaccessible healthcare.

She didn't let those thoughts ruin her mission. The front desk would be perfect for her now. On cue, the phone rang. Teresa hurried around and answered it.

"Thank you for calling Hart Medical. This is Dr. Hart. How may I help you?" she said cheerily into the receiver.

"Uh . . . hi. I was just checking to see what time my appointment is? I didn't get a reminder call."

Teresa nodded, confirming that this could be her job. Derrick was far too busy to manage the office and business side of things without her. Why hadn't she thought of this before?

You were too upset about losing—everything.

Her smile dropped from her face.

The voice on the other end said, "Hello? Can you hear me?"

"Yes. I can help you with that," Teresa said. "What is your name?"

After helping the patient, she took the appointment book to the records room and pulled the charts for the next day. She sat in her old office and started making calls.

Derrick walked past her office to the waiting room.

"Huh." It was a confused sound. He walked right by her office again, stopped in his tracks, and came back. She watched this take place while the dial tone droned in her ear. She hung up.

"Oh, hey," he said. "That was you who came in?" His cheeks flushed. "Uh—"

"You don't need to be embarrassed," Teresa said. "About last night, I mean."

"Oh . . . that." He rubbed the back of his neck and stared at her mouth instead of her eyes. "I cleaned it up."

"Derrick." She rose to her feet. He met her gaze. "Everything's okay."

His brows lifted. One of them arched. An uttered *huh?* would have completed the picture. Teresa took tentative steps toward him and wrapped her arms around him. She gazed up at his chin.

"Maybe we can try again tonight?"

"Oh, yeah, sure." He gave her a small squeeze. "I need to get back to my patient. Sorry." He let go of her and left the room.

Teresa frowned. He was just hungover. As far as she knew, he hadn't drunk like that in at least a few years. She continued making calls until she had confirmed all ten appointments for the next day.

Derrick escorted his patient past Teresa's door. The bells clattered. He came back and stood in her doorway.

"How's it going?" he asked.

"All of your appointments are confirmed for tomorrow, Dr. Hart." She smiled and gathered the appointment book and files into her arms. He followed her to the record room and helped her file the charts. She turned to head back to the front desk, but Derrick grabbed her arm. He pulled her into a hug. She melted against him.

This. This was what she wanted. All this time. This version of them in which they supported each other and showed their love through actions.

He lifted her chin with his fingertips. She winced and pulled back.

"What's wrong?" he asked.

"Oh, nothing. Sorry." She lowered her face. There was a bruise on her chin from McMichael's meaty hand.

Derrick cradled her face in his palms and tilted her head back. "What happened to your chin?" He examined it with clinical eyes. She thought she'd covered it up well enough with concealer.

"I slipped on some ice," she said with a nervous laugh. "Biffed it good, as the kids say."

Do kids still say that?

"I'm fine." She touched his hands. He let go and looked into her eyes, concern etched around his mouth and eyebrows.

"What is it?" Her voice came out small, uncertain.

Derrick backed away. His hand went to the back of his neck and he turned to the door.

"I don't know, Teresa," he said. His soft doctor voice disappeared. "After the kids at the cemetery, I thought maybe you got in a fight with an old man or something."

She sucked in a breath. He turned back toward her, a smile on his face. He let out a laugh. She relaxed. A joke. Funny.

Derrick pulled her into a hug again and kissed her forehead. She could spend the rest of her life there. She lifted her face to his. His lips just touched hers when the bells on the front door jangled.

"Gotta go," he whispered. "But I'm not through with you." He pecked her so light she wasn't sure his lips even touched hers.

Teresa composed herself and stepped out into the hallway. Derrick led Mrs. Grube toward an exam room. The old biddy was complaining about a pinching pain in her backside.

At the reception desk, a stack of mail sat neglected.

Teresa rifled through it. Junk mail and insurance checks. Using a knife-like letter opener, she sliced open the checks and set them to the side. She would deposit them for Derrick later.

The community paper lay on the desk at the bottom of the pile. A four-page newsletter was clipped to the front.

The Local Inquirer written by Brent Winter.

Teresa scoffed. *National Enquirer* articles at a local level. Fun at the town's expense.

The front page featured a photo of Ann Logan talking to Sheriff McMichael outside Ruthie's house. There was a second photo of her close up with her hand raised to block the camera. The story claimed Detective Logan, the catcher of the Salida Stabber, was assisting with a local "misper" investigation.

Teresa scoffed, but couldn't stop the pang of anxiety in her stomach. Ann Logan, the town's beloved detective, was helping out. Of course, this *was* Brent Winter's work. How credible was that? She swallowed the dryness from her throat and turned the page.

The headline on the next page read: *Local Woman Rants About the End of Days. Harmony at the Center of the Apocalypse!*

The article was accompanied by an image of Louise at the diner.

She flipped through the rest and scanned the headlines and found an article about the correlation between the weather—days flip-flopping between snow and warm temps—and extraterrestrial activities. Another claimed the bad cell service in Harmony was part of a social experiment. She paid little attention to the content until she saw a picture of herself. Heat flushed to her cheeks. She gripped the envelope opener so hard it dug into her palm.

Mrs. Hart lives in the abandoned funeral home . . .

The image, though from a distance and through the trees, portrayed her coming out of the house looking over her shoulder. An article didn't accompany the photo. She flipped through the pages and found nothing else. Just a photo with a silly caption. But still . . . If Derrick saw it—after the mud caked slippers—he'd send her back to Mountain View like he said he would.

She remembered their strange conversation on the back porch and scowled. He was so night-and-day lately. One minute threatening her, the next pleasing her.

Exam room one opened, and Derrick escorted Mrs. Grube out to her car. Teresa tore up the newspaper and threw it away.

Derrick came back in, leaned on the front desk counter, and smiled at her. "Thanks for coming in," he said. Warmth spread through her, and she actually felt herself blush. It was clinicals at Harvard Medical School all over again. "I'm really glad you made an effort."

Cold replaced the warmth. She struggled to maintain her smile.

Made an effort.

She dropped her smile.

"What? What did I say?" Derrick asked. "I'm grateful you came in. Truly. Honestly." He straightened and held up his hands as if in surrender. "What did I say?"

She shook her head and tried to smile at him again, but her lips wouldn't cooperate.

"Tell me, Teresa. What is it?"

"I *have* made an effort. The other night when you were out of town . . . Didn't you see Maggie in our bed? I rescued her from a nightmare. I slept in the chair, so she could have our bed. I took care of her. I fed her pizza. You act like I did nothing."

He dropped his head back and sighed. "Teresa, please."

"No, Derrick. Don't you see? You do this to me on purpose. You make me feel like an outsider."

"This again?" Exasperation filled his voice.

"Yes, this again. I just want to be included. I want to be part of *our* family, and you deny me that."

"Deny you?" He let out a sharp laugh. "You denied yourself. Every time you escaped to your messed up little basement you denied yourself. Every time you chose not to come with us to do something you denied yourself. Every time you declined our invitations, you denied yourself. Maggie just wants—"

"Don't you bring her into this."

"She's part of this family now. You agreed to adopting her. You have to accept her," he said.

"I don't *have* to do anything." Teresa came around the counter.

"Stop it," Derrick snapped.

"No, I won't stop it." She took in a breath. "I won't stop until you understand how I'm feeling. I thought we had a connection last night. I was willing to let it go that you threw up on the rug. I was willing to let that go because I thought we were getting better. I thought things were changing."

A cruel laugh seeped from his lips, accompanied by a hateful sneer.

"You think an attempted roll in the hay is going to magically change the last seven years?"

His words cut her. She stepped back.

"I . . ." Teresa resisted the urge to go back to her usual poor-me phrases, the ones she used to turn their arguments around. She wanted to face this head on.

"What can I do, then?" she asked, lifting her trembling chin.

Derrick's sneer dropped from his face. He probably expected the same words she forced herself to swallow.

"I want to make you happy," she said. "I want us to be happy again." She took a step toward him and reached for him. He crossed his arms.

"Dammit, Derrick. I'm trying here." She stomped her foot. "Say something, please."

He met her eyes. "You've been acting weird, Teresa. You must be having some sort of imbalance in your brain. You're acting—"

"Acting what?" She stepped toward him so fast he

stumbled back and fell into one of the waiting room chairs. "Crazy? Is that what you were going to say?"

"I—"

"Go ahead. Call them. Call the doctors. Call Mountain View." She stormed away, flung her hands in the air, and turned her back on him. Derrick shifted. Teresa whirled around and charged in one movement. She tried to push him back into the chair, but this time he didn't budge.

"Put me back in," she said, hitting his chest with flat palms. He raised his arms to block her, but she kept pummeling him.

With each hit, he flinched. "Stop!"

"Get rid of me. I know that's what you want." Her voice became shrill and screechy. "You . . . and Maggie—you don't need me." She raised her hands, fisted now, to strike his face.

He grabbed her wrists and squeezed so hard her fisted hands went limp. His nostrils flared. The muscle of his jaw clenched. She twisted and wrenched, and in the process, rubbed the skin until it burned. But she couldn't break free from his grip.

So different than how he had held her wrists the night before.

"Derrick," she cried. "You're hurting me."

At the sound of her pained voice, his eyes widened, and his mouth opened slightly. He pulled her against him.

"I'm sorry," he said in a demanding tone. "You were going to punch me."

Teresa didn't respond. Her arms were pinned against his chest. The skin throbbed.

When Derrick caught his breath, he swallowed hard. His voice became low and soothing.

"You need to get back on something. Your mood swings are out of control. I'm writing you a prescription."

She shoved away from him and backed out of his reach.

"I can't fill that here." The words burst from her mouth. "I can't. They'll spread rumors. The town will know." Her lower lip trembled. "They'll think I'm crazy."

His features shifted, but not in understanding—in pity. He left her in the waiting room and walked down the hall.

"You *are* crazy," she thought she heard him mutter. He disappeared into his office.

She touched the red marks on her wrist gingerly. Her heart shattered. They wouldn't recover from this. She was better off at Mountain View, drugged up and oblivious.

But who would save Tiffany? Who would bring her back to them?

The entire walk home she struggled to keep herself together. Tears stung her nose and her eyes, but she kept it in until she closed the front door behind her. She sank to the ground, taking ragged breaths and blinking rapidly to keep the tears at bay.

The phone rang. Teresa ignored it. When it stopped ringing, she rose to her feet and shuffled to the kitchen. She stared at the phone for a minute before picking it up and dialing her mother for the second time in as many days.

"Teresa, darling," her mother's voice said. Teresa broke down. Thick, guttural sobs erupted from her throat. She slid down to the floor and dropped her face into her hands. "What's wrong?"

"H–he hurt me. He left marks on my wrists."

"Oh, dear."

Teresa got up and paced the kitchen. Sink to hallway and back.

"You realize this is twice in one week you've upset your husband. Do I need to go over the rules with you again?"

Teresa shook her head and then nodded. "Yes. Please."

"From the beginning. Follow along."

Teresa wiped a fat teardrop from her cheek and took a deep breath. Together they went through the lessons she'd learned many times over.

"Graduate high school, get married, have children." Her mother paused. "What did you do that wasn't in this list?"

"I went . . . to college," Teresa whispered.

"Yes. You did. As a result, your first-born child was punished." Her mother's voice darkened. "You didn't follow the rules."

Renewed tears welled in Teresa's eyes.

"But," her mother's voice took on a happy tone again. "God has forgiven you because in your time of desperate need you turned back to Him."

Teresa let out a breath she didn't realize she'd been holding. The anger and hurt welling in her chest released along with the exhalation.

"Now, tell me. What is your husband's duty?"

"His duty is to provide for our family."

"And your duty?"

"To make sure that is all he needs to worry about."

"Very good, dear." Her mother made kissing sounds into the phone and hung up. Teresa replaced the receiver and went into the bathroom.

The sight in the mirror was frightful. Mascara streaked down her cheeks, muddled with the foundation and rouge, and made a sloppy mess of everything. She looked like a drowned clown.

"Be a good wife," she told her horrifying reflection. "'Now as the church submits to Christ, so also wives shall submit to their husbands in everything,'" she whispered. Fresh tears coursed down her cheeks.

CHAPTER 31

Ann snatched the lid of her dad's lockbox open and pawed through it before realizing she needed a more methodological approach. She didn't know what she was looking for, after all, and needed to slow down.

Her high school graduation picture sat right on top. She wore the maroon robe and mortarboard with a gold tassel. Harmony High's colors. The next day she had left her life in the tiny town behind her—Derrick, her dad, a future of small-town mundanity—and enrolled in the Denver Police Academy. She moved the picture aside.

Next was a small envelope with the RSVP card for her academy graduation. Her dad had checked yes, but he'd never mailed the card. He also didn't attend.

Under the card were three Lufthansa ticket stubs for flights to Egypt. One of them was dated the day before her academy graduation. A tingle prickled across her scalp.

Three trips to Egypt.

Four.

The stub for his final trip wouldn't be in this box. She put them aside.

There were three items left. All were folded sheets of paper. The first one was a grid full of letters. A standard *tabula recta* he probably used to solve the puzzles in the paper. The second was folded in fourths and proved to be the introductory page of an application for an adoption home study. The organization listed at the top was The Protectorate. Their tagline—"Protecting the needs of children everywhere"—appeared beneath their logo.

Ann narrowed her eyes. An adoption agency? Raghib said they were some kind of organization of assassins or something. Not an adoption agency. Even so, why would her dad have an application for an adoption home study? She turned to the last item. The smaller paper was folded in half. Ann unfolded it to reveal a list of names in her dad's handwriting. Some were crossed out. Ann only recognized the first name.

Louise Marga. Louise's name had a question mark next to it. Ann stuffed everything back into the box and shut the lid.

Behind her on top of a filing cabinet, four handheld radios sat in their chargers. She grabbed two of them and turned them on.

"I need to take care of something," she said to George. She handed him one of the radios. "I'm guessing these have a long range?"

He nodded. "We can chat from opposite ends of town

on these puppies."

"Good. If anything comes up, call me." She grabbed her coat and headed out into the chilly late-afternoon.

* * *

Ann drove the station vehicle to Louise's. She took the porch steps two at a time and knocked on the door. Inside, cats wailed.

Louise opened up after Ann's third set of pounding knocks, a little out of breath. Her long hair was up in a bun, but a few strands hung in her face, and a sheen of sweat dampened her forehead.

"Ann," Louise said with surprise. "What are you doing here?"

"Last time I was here you said to come back," Ann said with a smile. "Here I am."

"You really ought to call first. Common courtesy and all." Louise opened the door a little further.

Ann stepped inside. A couple of cats scattered. The little house was meat-falling-off-the-bone hot. That would explain the sweat. She unzipped her jacket.

"Tea?" Louise closed the door softly behind her.

"No, thanks." Ann didn't want a cup of *eau de Louise.* Louise put the kettle on anyway. Old ladies and their tea. Ann took off her jacket and glanced around. Muffled music still played behind the bolted door at the entrance to the hallway, and a seemingly different handful of cats lounged around the immediate area.

"Take a seat." Louise motioned to the little table in the kitchen.

Ann moved toward the chair, tugging at the buttons on her shirt. "You torturing Eskimos in here?"

Louise's eyebrows shot up. "Torture? Torturing? Oh." She laughed. "A joke. Funny." She moved to a wood stove in the corner of the choked living room and opened the hatch. "I haven't used this thing in years. I forgot it put out so much heat. The furnace is broken. Damn rats." She jabbed at the glowing logs with a poker.

Ann scanned the adjoining room before taking a seat at the table, taking note of how many cats were in there.

"You have a rat problem with all these cats?"

Louise laughed. "They're worthless. Completely and totally domesticated. They couldn't even catch flies if they had honey." Louise closed the stove and returned to the sink. "So very nice to see you again, dear, but I really wish you would have called. I was in the middle of something."

"I won't keep you then," Ann said. She put the list of names on the table. "I found this in my dad's locker. Why is your name on this list? Are any of these other names familiar?"

Louise picked it up and examined it. "I've never seen these names before, well, except my own." She smiled. "Your father stopped by a couple months ago—"

"Last time I was here you said it had been a few months, and you thought you saw him at the station or the diner."

Louise stared at Ann. "Oh, I must have forgotten." She pointed at her temple. "I'm old and senile." The kettle whistled. Louise started to stand.

"I'll get it," Ann said.

"Thank you, dear. Tea bags are in the cupboard over the sink."

"What did my dad want to talk to you about?" Ann quietly peeked in each cupboard, unsure of what she might be looking for.

"The Nag Hammadi Library and other secret texts. He knew I studied them," Louise said. "I was interviewed in the paper for being the oldest resident of Harmony. I mentioned I'd studied comparative mythology." Her voice held a smile. Her chair creaked. Ann closed the cupboard she was looking in. Louise had turned around. "Over the sink dear. Like I said."

Ann retrieved the tea bags and glanced in the sink. Two metal bowls sat inside along with an empty can of dog food.

"Where's your dog?" Ann knew full well Louise didn't own a dog. She had a million cats though.

Louise looked at her with a raised eyebrow. "Dog?"

Ann pointed to the bowls.

"Oh, those . . . To poison the rats. They can't stay away from that stuff."

"Your cats don't mess with it?"

She shook her head, staring straight ahead. "They aren't allowed in the basement."

"You seem nervous," Ann said. She put a teabag in a cup and poured hot water over it.

"You caught me at a bad time is all." Louise brushed a strand of hair off her forehead again and looked over her shoulder, smiling. "I'm sorry I couldn't be of more help." It sounded like a dismissal. Ann placed Louise's cup on the table in front of her and moved around to the opposite side.

"Is there something else?" Louise's eyes darted over Ann's right shoulder. Ann turned and followed her gaze to the bolted door.

"What's behind that door?" Ann asked.

"The basement."

"What's in the basement, besides rats?"

Louise shrugged. "The usual things one places in one's basement." Her eyes darted to the door again. "Christmas decorations, old clothes to donate . . ." Her hand shook when she lifted her cup. She set it back down, splashing some tea onto the saucer.

"Mind if I take a look?" Ann asked. She stepped toward the door. Louise glided out of her chair and moved around the table, and somehow reached the door before Ann. She stopped and cocked her head, hand on the knob.

"Do you have a warrant, Detective?" Her face turned smug.

"Should I have a reason to get one?"

Louise retrieved the list from the table and held it out to Ann. "Of course not." She smiled.

Ann reached for the paper. Louise let it go before Ann grasped it. It drifted to the floor. Ann bent to pick it up, and Louise sucked in a breath.

"The Sa," she whispered.

Ann tugged her shirt and stood up. Their eyes met.

"How did you come to have the mark on your chest?" Louise asked.

"It's just a tattoo," Ann said, buttoning her shirt up to her neck despite the heat in the house. "I should be going—unless there's anything else you forgot to mention?"

"Yes, sit. Please." She returned to her seat, and Ann followed suit. "You must keep that mark hidden."

"Why, exactly?" Ann asked.

"Say what you will, but that mark was not created with needle and ink." Louise nodded toward Ann's chest. "If the wrong people find out you have it, you could be killed."

"Explain, please," Ann said.

This'll be rich. End of the world again? Or some other bullshit?

"There are two secret organizations at war," Louise began in her mystical voice.

Ann interrupted her. "The Messengers of the Light and the Protectorate." Ann waved a dismissive hand, then leaned forward. "Did you know the Protectorate is actually an adoption agency?"

Are you fucking with the Loon, or what?

"Believe what you must, dear," Louise said. "But don't be deceived by outward appearances. There are many secrets hidden within."

"I really should get going." Ann got up. "If you remember anything else about my dad. Please give me a call."

Something clanged in the wall behind Ann. She jumped and peered at the door where the music came from. Did the clang come from there?

"Damn rats," Louise said with a flip of her hand. "They get inside the walls and make such a racket."

Ann stayed still and silent, holding Louise's gaze. The radio on Ann's belt crackled and squelched. Both she and Louise startled.

"Sheriff Riley to Deputy Logan. Do you read me?"

"Deputy Logan?" Louise raised her eyebrow.

Ann ignored her and depressed the talk button. "I read. This better be important. Over."

"It is. The results on the crispy stuff came back from the lab. You're not gonna believe what . . ."

That was quick.

"Hold on." Ann went outside onto the front porch. She looked over her shoulder. Louise was there. Ann turned the volume down. "And?"

"They said the results are inconclusive. The report has all these calculations and percentages and stuff, but the lab tech wrote some notes. She said it closely resembles—" Silence. "Do you copy?"

"No, say it again. Keep the button pressed down."

"Sorry. My hands are big and this button is tiny. The lab tech said it closely resembles human umbilical cord."

CHAPTER 32

"Tiffany?" Even though Teresa's voice came out small, it still echoed in the cave. "Come out, my sweet baby."

"Hi, Mommy."

"Oh, my baby." Teresa knelt, and Tiffany ran into her arms.

"Why are you here?" Tiffany asked.

"I needed to see you. I just needed you."

"You are hurt," Tiffany said. "I can feel your pain. What happened?"

"Daddy and I had an argument is all. Nothing to worry about." Mother never would have dragged a child into her messes, and Teresa wouldn't either. She stroked Tiffany's hair. It felt like water running through her fingers.

"You shouldn't come here during the day. Yaldabaoth rests and mustn't be disturbed." She looked over her shoulder at the pool of water. So calm and still.

"Does he sleep in the pool?" Teresa stepped to the edge. Tiffany's hand touched hers.

"No, but be careful. The water is deep and cold, and if you fall in you'll never come back out."

Chills passed through her. Teresa peered into the depths but only saw flickering flames and her own reflection.

"When he regains his strength, he will use this pool to bring us together."

Teresa peered at her daughter.

"How? You said if I fall in I'll never come back out."

Tiffany shrugged. "It's like magic, I guess."

"Okay—and what do you mean when he regains his strength? You told me he is more powerful than God." She touched her cross.

"He was badly injured. But the zoe helps him heal." Tiffany tugged Teresa away from the pool. "Right now, though, you should go. He needs peace."

Teresa looked toward the dark passageway. "Where does that go?" She knew, of course, because she'd traveled as far as she could go.

"Don't question things, Mommy. Just believe in them, like you always do."

Teresa gazed at her daughter one last time. She swept her hand down her baby's cheek.

"Five more, Mommy."

"Yes. Five more." Teresa stepped out of the cave and onto the front porch of the abandoned house. She looked back, but the house's interior already replaced the cave.

So, Yaldabaoth wasn't as powerful as she thought. What if he wasn't powerful at all? Teresa fiddled with the chain around her neck. Did she have the strength, the will, to take five more souls without knowing for certain? What if her next victim was someone she knew well?

I don't know anyone very well anymore.

She walked back to the road toward town.

Seven years had taken its toll on her fragile personal relationships. But she didn't need those friendships. They weren't real anyway. How could she ever be real friends with people whose families had known each other for generations? She didn't belong among them.

When Teresa reached the town center, Ann Logan climbed out of an old SUV of some sort parked in front of the sheriff's department, her long hair loose about her shoulders. Teresa smoothed her hand over her hair, pulled into a low chignon, and sniffed. Only wild things wore their hair untethered. Her mother called them whores.

She was about to head home when movement in the trees caught her attention. Louise stood in the shadows, her eyes focused on the distance. Her gaze shifted, and she met Teresa's eyes. Louise took a step back, startled, but then came forward.

"What are you doing skulking around?" Teresa asked.

"Come with me, quickly." Louise motioned to her. "I know your secrets."

What little warmth Teresa held drained from her body. She rubbed her arms through her jacket sleeves. Louise disappeared into the trees. Teresa followed and soon arrived at the old woman's dilapidated house.

Louise stood on the porch with the door open. For being old, she moved fast. Teresa went up the stairs and inside where the heat chased the chill from her skin. Potpourri did a poor job of covering up the smell of cats. A fat black and white one waddled toward her.

"Sit at the table. I'll pour some tea."

Teresa shed her jacket and hung it on the back of the chair before sitting. The cat rubbed against her leg.

"What do you think you know this time?" Teresa asked.

Louise scurried into the kitchen and shooed a cat off the counter. "You are on an important mission," she said. "But you are taking great risks in carrying out your objectives."

"I don't know what you're talking about." Teresa tried to hide her surprise by looking at the chipped Formica tabletop. Louise set a cup in front of her. Steam rose from the amber liquid in smoky tendrils. She took a sip. Cinnamon and spice. Her belly warmed.

Louise only continued to smile. She sat at the other side of the table. Her knobby fingers wrapped around her tea cup like a claw.

"Your mission began seven years ago when your child passed."

Teresa shook her head. "My name was cleared. I didn't do anything wrong."

"No, please, Doctor, please." Louise's voice took on a softer tone. "Listen. This is important."

Teresa tugged at her cross.

"Seven years ago, your miracle child passed." Louise spoke as if she were a carnival fortune teller. Teresa crossed her arms. "In her passing, a gate to Hell opened, for the miracle child had died at the hands of jealousy and ignorance."

"It was an accident!"

Louise held up her hand. "Now is not the time for blame or digging up the past. I am only listing the facts from the beginning. Your daughter passed. A gate to Hell opened. Facts."

"A gate to Hell opening is a fact?" Teresa's hand found the cross again, though the movement seemed out of habit now, rather than comfort.

Louise shrugged. "Pretend for the sake of this story it is."

I should leave. She's obviously crazy. She knows nothing about my secrets.

But, Teresa leaned forward instead, compelled to hear how Tiffany's death coincided with whatever Louise was about to say. And, she had to admit, the human interaction felt . . . nice.

"This Hell is a special Hell called Tartaros. It contains only one being. A once powerful creator."

Teresa leaned back and crossed her arms again. Ludicrous. "God is the only creator," Teresa mumbled.

"Please, let me finish," Louise said, an edge to her voice. "His mother stole his power and banished him to Tartaros. He resides there now, weakened."

Teresa's mouth fell open. The story rang of what Tiffany had told her about—

"Yaldabaoth," Teresa whispered.

Louise's serene smile spread into a wicked grin.

"Yes, indeed."

"How do you know about him?"

"His is an ancient story, Doctor Hart. The Gnostic faith is followed by many." Louise leaned forward. "Man is imperfect because he was created by an imperfect being."

Teresa gulped a mouthful of tea and coughed. "This is blasphemy." And yet, she believed it. Tiffany was proof. Yaldabaoth was proof.

Louise shrugged. "One person's belief is another person's sacrilege."

"Assuming this is so-called fact, what are these secrets you think you know about me?" Teresa asked.

"You have been helping Yaldabaoth."

"I'm helping Tiffany." The words flew from Teresa's mouth.

"Your daughter is dead, Teresa." Louise hit the table with the side of her fist. "Nothing can bring her back. You don't know what you're doing, what you're getting involved in."

"Tiffany said, if I help him, we can be together again. You don't know what you're talking about." Teresa pushed away from the table and stood. "You don't know him." She ripped her jacket from the chair. The black and white cat took off.

A laugh bubbled up from Louise's belly and burst from her mouth.

"I know far more than you know, you wretched thing. You murderer." She stood, her hunched back straightening with a morbid crackling. Fully upright, Louise was as tall as Teresa.

"If you continue to help him you will risk destroying what I have worked toward these past thirty-seven years."

"You can't stop me from being with my baby." Teresa backed toward the door.

"I can tell the sheriff you're responsible for Ruthie's disappearance."

Teresa stopped and turned. "The sheriff?" She scoffed and went back to the table but didn't sit. "Please. That is hardly a threat."

Your beloved Sheriff is gone.

The thought tickled her.

"Ann Logan is in charge now." Louise crossed her arms. "How does that make you feel, the ex-lover of your husband running this town? They were high school sweethearts, you know. She broke his heart. I wouldn't doubt she is his one-that-got-away." She fluttered her hand through the air.

"You shut your mouth," Teresa said. "She's a failure. She let that child die. Why don't any of you Godforsaken people realize that?"

Louise narrowed her eyes and tapped her cheek in thought.

"My, my. You *are* more observant than I thought." She lifted the saucer and cup and took a sip. "Is that truly how you feel?"

Teresa nodded. "Yes, of course."

"How does it make you feel knowing she and your husband were in love all through high school? That they've known each other their whole lives?"

Teresa clenched her jaw and her fists.

"How do you feel knowing your husband was going to marry her? That she would have carried his children? How does it make you feel, dear Doctor, knowing they've had intercourse?"

"Enough!" Teresa's fingers dug into the back of the chair.

A muted cackle rattled in Louise's throat. "Interesting." She seemed to ponder a moment longer. "You have a darkness inside you." She leaned forward and patted the Formica. "I like it." She stood and sidled past the kitchen table. "I have something to show you. Something to . . . I don't know. I suppose we'll figure that out after you see."

She opened a door with a heavy bolt, and music poured out. The door had a three-inch thick foam rubber pad attached to the inside. Louise stepped inside and turned the music off. A loud hissing issued from beyond the dark entry. Louise turned on a light and motioned for Teresa to follow.

They clopped down a set of rickety wooden stairs. The static hissing became unbearably loud as they descended.

Teresa fought the urge to cover her ears. It was maddening.

"Why the white noise?" she shouted.

"You'll see."

The air chilled, and the scent of urine and excrement increased when they reached the bottom. The source of the noise was a television tuned to a non-channel. Black and white spots danced over the screen. Louise crept into the darkness and flipped a switch. Fluorescent lights clicked and buzzed to life.

Teresa gasped. A filthy bearded man sat tied to a chair in the center of the room, a pair of goggles strapped to his face. His chest expanded and contracted at an alarming rate.

"Who's there?" he called above the static. "Someone's there. I can smell you. Please! Please make it stop." His voice came out strong at first and then sank into an agonized groan. "Stop—please." He swung his head from side to side.

Louise came back and stood next to Teresa. The sterile lights gave her face a ghastly pallor and deepened every crease in her skin.

"Sensory deprivation. Heard of it?" Louise asked. "I just added the black-out goggles today. Punishment for having broken my furnace." She indicated the silent equipment. "They further instill his sense of isolation."

Teresa didn't like the way Louise's eyes changed. Sure, she'd always known the old woman was crazy, but this was a new level of insanity. A prisoner? Torture?

"Who is he?" The words choked out of Teresa's constricted throat. She tugged on her cross. Why would Louise trust her with this information?

"Bram Logan," Louise said with a wicked smile. "Ann Logan's dead father."

CHAPTER 33

Ann went inside the station. Marcie sat on George's lap, but she wasn't paying attention to him or the book open on the desk.

"This is a block search," he said. "We did that with Ruthie's house."

What was it, Dummies Guide to Crime Scene Investigation*?*

Ann cleared her throat. Marcie jumped to her feet as if caught with her pants down. Was that relief on her face?

"Hi, Detective." She grabbed her coat from the back of George's chair and kissed him on the cheek. "Bye, George." She hurried out.

"This is not a make-out site," Ann said.

George held up his hands. "We weren't making out. I was showing her how to investigate a crime scene."

"And she seemed *so* interested. Was she here when you radioed me?"

George somehow managed to make his line-backer-sized-self shrink. "No?"

Ann raised her eyebrow at him.

"Yes, but I went to the back. She was out here looking at the book. She was only here for a few minutes. I swear. She don't know nothing about the case." He closed one eye. "Except that we did a block search on Ruthie's house."

Ann grumbled and sat at the other desk, facing George. "Tell me about the lab report."

George shoved the faxed pages toward her. "I don't know nothing about science stuff. I'm really glad the lab tech wrote her findings in –what do you call it . . . when something is simple?"

George Riley.

"Layman's terms." Ann flipped through the report and came to some pictures of the substance under the microscope.

"Do we have any lab equipment here?" she asked.

George shrugged. "There might be some in storage."

Ann looked at him. "Storage?"

"The holding cell is also storage." He shrugged like it was a normal thing.

Ann held in a groan. This place needed a lot of work.

Not your problem.

She found the holding cell packed with boxes. They were, thankfully, labeled. One had "lab" written on the side. Ann pulled the box out and opened the flaps. Inside lay a dusty old microscope. She remembered enough from science classes to know how to prepare a slide and how to operate the equipment. She brought the box to the office area and took out the microscope.

"What are you gonna do?" George asked.

"I'm going to compare the crispy stuff from McMichael's house to the stuff from Ruthie's to make sure they match."

"What if they do?" George asked.

"The abductor is likely the same person."

"Serial killer?"

"Serial *kidnapper*," Ann said. "No bodies, no murders. Got that?" She didn't believe it, but she also didn't want George spreading rumors or getting his manties in a twist.

George nodded.

"Did you call the State Police and CBI like I asked?" She continued setting up the microscope.

"Yeah." George said. "They said they would send assistance."

"Did they say when?"

"I didn't think to ask," George ducked his head. "Sorry."

Ann went into Sheriff McMichael's old office. The phone on the desk was far more sophisticated than anything else there. She lifted the receiver. The line crackled, but there was no dial tone.

"George, is the phone out there working?" Ann called.

"Nope," he answered, matter of fact.

Then, the phone rang. Ann jumped. She pressed the button next to the flashing light.

"Castle County Sheriff's Department, Ann speaking."

Static filled the line. A deep chuckle rumbled through.

"No one can help you."

A jolt of fear prickled her scalp.

"Who is this?" she asked.

The line went dead. After a few moments of stunned silence, the repetitive tone of a phone off the hook beeped in her ear.

Prank callers. That's all.

Ann set the phone down in an overly calm manner and picked it back up. Dial tone. She called CBI first.

Neither agency had received a call from Castle County. After requesting assistance in their case, she hung up and walked back to the desks in a measured stride.

"George," she said through her teeth. "They said you never called."

George peered up at her and tilted his head to the side. "Yes, I did. I swear." He pressed buttons on his phone. "See? Right there."

Ann jerked his desk phone toward her and read the list of recent calls. Sure enough, both numbers were listed.

"Sorry." Ann frowned. "They said they hadn't received a call from us."

George merely stared at her, his eyebrows crinkled together. "Maybe the same person who abducted the sheriff and Ruthie did something to our phones."

Or perhaps the dispatchers George had spoken to were incompetent or lazy. Ann sighed and returned to the microscope. She paused in setting up the equipment and dialed her cell, let it ring once, and hung up.

The number appeared in recent calls, of course. She wanted to believe George was telling the truth, but he *had* fought her about calling in for help.

Well, now help *would* be on the way. It wasn't her place to manage him. She wasn't his boss.

Thank god.

She flipped the switch on the microscope and the light bulb came on. She let out a triumphant *ha-ha*. Small victories.

She prepped her slide and pushed it under the clamps. George watched her the entire time like she was performing a sleight of hand magic trick and he wanted to catch how it was done. With the photo from the fax beside her, she compared the black and white image to the mottled pink and brown one under the lens.

"Match," Ann said in a low voice, as if speaking too loudly would disturb the cells and change the image. "Same substance for both Ruthie and Sheriff McMichael." She made note of this in the case file.

George sucked in a breath. "That's amazing."

"It's just science and basic deduction, George."

"You're still amazing."

Ann snorted, but inside she warmed a little. Her expertise was needed here if they were going to stop people from disappearing. She could do this. She could redeem herself.

"The problem I'm coming up with is the victims are so different. If they were both women, or both older men, we could build a profile based on gender and age and compile a list of suspects who matched." Ann scratched her eyebrow. She flipped through the scene of the crime photos looking for any other clues.

The sheriff had taken good pictures of Ruthie's house. He paid close attention to detail. She wished he was around so she could talk to him about anything he might have noticed. What he excelled with in photography he lacked in his reporting.

"We need to open Ruthie's house," Ann said. "McMichael might have missed something. Some indicator." She looked at George. "There has to be something."

She knew there would be nothing. Once a crime scene was sealed, the possibility of finding anything was little to none. For the first time in her career as a cop, she wasn't sure what to do. It made her feel helpless. Panic crept up her chest and tightened her throat. It replaced the momentary warmth at having done something helpful.

Once a failure, always a failure.

The thought was stupid, of course, but her mind went to stupid places when presented with helplessness. Elbows on the desk, she clasped her hands in front of her and bit her knuckles.

George stared at her again.

Ann spread the pictures out and lifted a magnifying glass from the pencil cup on the desk.

"What are you doing now?"

"I'm looking for clues."

"Sherlock Holmes," George said with a snort.

Ann glanced up at him.

"He had a magnifying glass, right?"

Ann rolled her eyes, though a smile tried to tug at her lips. She scoured every photo but came up with nothing. George stared at her expectantly the whole time. When she finished the last photo, she sat back. His face fell.

"You didn't find anything?" He stood. "You didn't find anything? What did you do to find the Stabber? Maybe you should do that." He started to pace. "I mean, they didn't find anything until you were assigned to the case. What did you find? How did you find it?"

"George," Ann said.

"Was it a small thing? A big thing? What was the clue? How did you know where to look? How did you know where it led?" His questions dug into her, each one a kick to the ribs.

"George!" Ann slapped the desk. "Stop it. I'm not the fucking hero you think I am, okay?"

He looked at her with wounded eyes. "What do you mean?" His mouth hardly moved when he spoke. He sank back into his chair.

"I'm not here on vacation," she said. "I'm on administrative leave. I didn't pass my psych evaluation. I can hardly look at a gun anymore." Her eyes flicked to the one on his hip and back to his face.

George's mouth dropped open in a way that would have been comical if she didn't feel like total and utter shit.

"Your hero's a pussy." Ann sat back in the chair and avoided eye contact.

"Nah," George said. "You're still a hero."

"I got my partner killed," Ann said.

"An accident."

"I knew McCoy had a gun." Ann had never told anyone why she harbored so much guilt for what happened. Not even her therapist. "I saw him reach for it before I shot him." She squeezed her eyes shut, waiting for a gasp, or some other surprised, devastated, horrified sound. George didn't say a peep.

Ann leaned forward again, and this time, she did meet his eyes.

"Firing my weapon brought my partner into the room, so the Stabber could kill him." She blinked rapidly to keep the tears at bay. "It should have been me." Tears fell. "I tossed protocol out the window and based everything on a fucking hunch."

George scooted his chair around their desks and put his meaty hand on her shoulder. Ann leaned into him.

"I didn't put any of this in the report." She wiped her nose on the back of her hand. "I left out that Bruce let me take the lead even though he was primary. I felt so strongly about that old blue house—I wouldn't let it go. I even threatened to check it out on my own." She took in a gasping breath. "I should have gone alone. He'd still be alive if I'd gone by myself."

"There, there," George said, patting her shoulder. She

let out a tear-filled laugh. Her guts were on the table, and he patted her like the crying baby she was. She stopped leaning against him and wiped at her eyes.

George shrugged. "You still caught him," he said in a soft voice. He took a deep breath. "It's not always about what happened. Maybe it's about what might have happened. Sure, your partner might still be alive, but the way I see it, no more kids died." He shrugged again. "Besides, everything happens for a reason. That's what I believe anyway." He stood and grabbed his hat and coat. "If the whole Stabber thing hadn't happened, you wouldn't be here, now, helping me." He pulled on his coat. "And we both know I need all the help I can get." He smiled a big goofy grin. "I'm going on patrol."

George closed the door behind him, and Ann leaned back in her chair. A heavy weight lifted from her shoulders. Not because of what George said, but because she had finally gotten the whole story out. Every single detail. She finally let go of her guilt.

CHAPTER 34

Teresa dropped her cross and pressed her hand against her throat, as if touching it would help her swallow what felt like a sand-covered cotton ball that had lodged there.

"What is he doing down here?"

"He's paying for his sins," Louise said. She took Teresa's elbow and guided her to the stairs.

Teresa ascended on numb legs. She should tell someone about this. Ann deserved to know her father was here.

Or did she?

Teresa stepped through the warmth of Louise's hallway and to the front door.

"Wait." Louise turned the music back on, closed the door, and bolted it shut. "Where does this leave us, Doctor?"

Teresa didn't understand what Louise meant. Her eyebrows furrowed.

"You have secrets, I have secrets." Louise held up her hands and shifted them up and down like the scales of

Lady Justice.

Teresa sucked in a gasp. "Are you suggesting blackmail?"

Louise smiled with half of her mouth. "Not blackmail, per se. We have dirt on each other. You tell anyone what I have in my basement, the entire town will learn all your secrets, and I don't just mean your part in the disappearance of Ruthie Gill." Louise smiled and moved toward the door. "I know about your sordid past, Doctor Hart, and I'm not talking about your dead child this time."

"What do you mean, my past?"

Louise only gave her a smug, close-lipped smile and shrugged. She ushered Teresa out the door and onto the porch.

"You spill my secrets, I spill yours." Louise closed the door.

Teresa tugged her coat tighter. She stepped down the porch stairs and glanced over her shoulder at Louise's old house, at the crumbly stone foundation. She didn't know what to do. She didn't know what information, what secrets, what rumors Louise had on her.

Teresa wandered toward town. What if Louise knew nothing? What if she knew everything? The whole town would learn . . . something. Rumors ruined her family, her mother's and her father's lives. *Her* life.

When Teresa reached the town square, she walked directly to the sheriff's department and paused outside the door. She considered going in, but passed on by, head down, eyes on the sidewalk. At the end of the block, she looked up.

Across the street Tiffany hopped from side to side. Teresa hurried toward her. What if someone saw her?

A milky-red, pulsing cluster of zoe strands shifted on the sidewalk. Teresa stopped and raised a hand to her mouth. Tiffany jumped over them. Back and forth, back and forth, giggling as if it were an extra fun game. The strands shifted again, and Tiffany squealed and hopped out of their reach. Teresa gagged, composed herself, and finished her trek across the road.

"What are you doing here? Someone will see you!" Teresa threw glances all around. What would people think, Teresa running through town with a little girl who *obviously* wasn't Maggie? Word would get to Derrick. "And what are those doing here?"

Tiffany motioned for Teresa to follow her and ducked down the alley between the pawn shop and a real estate office.

"First of all, Mommy"—Tiffany held up a finger—"no one can see me but you, because you love me so much." She grinned.

Teresa crouched down and pulled her daughter into a hug. "Thank goodness."

"Second of all, those are here because it's time."

"Time?" Teresa pulled back and peered up at the overcast sky. "In the daylight?"

Tiffany pressed her hands against Teresa's cheeks.

"Isn't this exciting?"

Teresa didn't think it was exciting at all. Without the cover of night, it seemed dangerous. She wondered if Tiffany would come again later that night to take another. The thought of taking two lives in less than twelve hours sent chills through her body. Chills both sickening and pleasurable. They frightened her.

The zoe lines had followed them into the alley, writhing and slapping like fat sausages on pavement.

"Pick one," Tiffany said.

Teresa scowled at the mess of coiled ropes. They inched closer to her, and her stomach lurched. She'd never seen them move like that before. She touched one with her toe, and the rest slithered away as if they'd been burned. She didn't like this. It didn't seem right.

"Where's Ruthie?"

"She doesn't come out during the day."

"Is that why you're here?" Teresa asked.

Tiffany nodded. "She scares me." Her daughter hugged her around the waist and buried her beautiful face into Teresa's hip.

"I thought Yaldabaoth rested during the day."

"He does. But you woke him, so he thought he'd put you to work since you seemed so eager to be with me."

Teresa looked down at Tiffany. She would do this. She had to.

She followed the zoe down Forest Parkway toward the square. The line veered again into the residential district. She strolled with her hands in her pockets. Tiffany held her arm and followed. The zoe line veered again, and they followed it to a ranch-style house at the end of Evergreen Avenue. No cars were in the driveway. Teresa swallowed hard. She didn't think the zoe would lead her to an empty house.

The front door was locked. Ruthie missing would definitely be enough in a small town like this to cause alarm. Teresa scanned the neighborhood. It was quiet. Not a soul stirred. Except the zoe line leading into the house. It twitched, like a hose when the water is first turned on.

She crept around to a side window and peered in. A living room. No people. Next window. No one in the exercise room. A fence blocked her from entering the back yard. She went around to the other side where a string ran down through an eye-screw in the wood. She tugged the string, and a gate opened.

Teresa slipped through and closed it behind her. She stood, silent and still, and listened. There had been no *Beware of Dog* signs, so she hoped there were no dogs.

A window toward the end of the house was cracked open. Skunky smoke, the same scent from the kids at the cemetery, wafted out.

She crept to the window and peered inside. A young man sat in a recliner. The zoe line disappeared into his chest. He wore a headset and had a video game controller in his hands. He took a drag off a joint and held the smoke. On the exhale, he emitted a series of shallow coughs before setting the joint in an ashtray.

Teresa ducked when he leaned over to grab a bottle off the same table. Beer. This kid, who couldn't be a day over nineteen, was home alone drinking beer and smoking pot.

"My parents moved to fucking Florida and left me here," he said into the headset, as if responding to Teresa's thought. Perhaps he was older than nineteen then. "Living in their house rent free, bitches." He pushed buttons on his controller.

Teresa went around to the back and tried the sliding glass door. It opened smooth and quiet. The screen, however, rattled and screeched along the track.

A big dog's booming bark came from somewhere inside.

CHAPTER 35

Teresa struggled with the screen. When the dog appeared, she gasped and hurried backward into the yard.

A massive fawn-colored pit bull stuck its head through the partially opened screen and forced its way out. It raced toward Teresa, all pink jowls, snorts and snarls, and sharp teeth. Teresa hustled backwards, stumbled, and fell on her rear.

She held her arms over her head, but instead of a horrific attack, the dog proceeded to slather her hands and the uncovered parts of her face with its tongue. She pushed at the dog, but it only caused the canine to double its efforts. Once she finally managed to sit upright, the enormous beast sat in her lap and gazed over its shoulder at her with a goofy jowly grin. Its tongue lolled from the side of its mouth.

"Aren't you vicious." She patted the dog's solid head. A name tag on the collar read Pinky, and why not? The beast was all pink mouth and tongue and nose. Teresa surprised herself with a laugh and struggled out from under Pinky. A tennis ball sat nearby. She picked it up and threw it. The dog took off after it, and Teresa slipped inside the house and closed the glass.

While she was distracted, the zoe line had recalculated like a GPS route and now sat in front of her. Tiffany had crept inside, too. Teresa followed the zoe down the hallway. Outside the boy's room, she pressed herself against the wall and took a quick glance inside.

Brent Winter, the young man who had captioned the photo about her living in the abandoned funeral home, sat in an overstuffed chair. She could just make him out through the fog.

"Smoking an Israeli joint man," he said into the headset. "I'm so cheesed."

She scowled. Tiffany pressed the hypo into her hand. Teresa looked down at her. Tiffany nodded. Teresa took a deep breath and launched into the room. She stabbed the hypo into Brent's chest. He flailed his arms and pushed her into the side table where his beer tottered and fell to the ground in a fizzy mess. Teresa landed, once again, on her backside.

"Shit. What is this?" Brent held his hand up to the hypo that bobbed up and down with his sluggish heartbeat. He was too stoned to realize he'd been stabbed. Teresa quirked her mouth to the side and got to her feet.

"Just a bad trip." She didn't care if *trip* was the wrong word. Brent looked over his shoulder at the table that held his smoking joint, and Teresa grabbed the plunger.

As she pulled, Brent's skin decomposed at an accelerated rate. His muscles and tissues disintegrated next, body crumbling to the ground and rotting with the sound of someone squeezing the insides from a pumpkin. His heart remained stuck to the end of the needle until the plunger fully retracted. It plopped onto the floor and burst like a water balloon full of blood.

All that remained of Brent Winter was a small pile of rotting meat and some bone fragments on the carpet. The odor turned Teresa's stomach.

"Why did that happen?" she asked Tiffany.

The girl pulled a twisty straw from an empty soda bottle. "It has to do with your mind." Tiffany tapped her temple. "Ruthie shriveled because you thought that's what would happen when you pulled the plunger. The sheriff blew up because you thought he was fat. You thought Brent was wasting his life, so I guess he wasted away."

"I didn't think any of those things," Teresa said. "I didn't know what to expect."

"Your subconscious, Mommy." Tiffany squatted next to the remains and poked at them with the straw. She peered up at Teresa and shrugged. "At least he won't chase us."

"But what do I do with this mess?" She covered her mouth and nose with her sleeve. "The smell." She gagged.

"Leave it."

"Leave behind evidence?" Teresa couldn't. Not with big shot Detective Logan on the case.

"UpNSmoke23? Hello?" A tinny voice came through the headset that had fallen when Brent disintegrated. Teresa looked at the TV where some kind of futuristic battle took place. "Where'd you go, man? We need your help breaching the base."

Witnesses. Or were they? She didn't know anything about video games kids played these days, but she knew they played online. Were the other players strangers? Teresa pulled her sleeves over her hands and picked up the headset. She listened in.

"UpNSmoke23, come on, man."

"Dude, he probably passed out."

"Yeah, Israeli joints? Jesus fucking Christ—he's probably blitzed."

"Should we call an ambulance? Anyone know where he's from?"

The last was followed by a series of negative responses.

She dropped the headset, stepped over the pile of rot, and took her daughter's hand. They left through the front door.

The stink of Brent's putrefaction stayed in her nostrils until she reached the dirt road at the edge of town. She avoided the slushy mud—left after the snow had melted—as best she could. Tiffany hopped from mostly dry spot to mostly dry spot. Everything was a game to her. Teresa wished she could be so carefree.

At the abandoned house, Teresa went inside, and the walls melted as they usually did. But instead of the brown stone, Tiffany's nursery, the real one—not the basement—appeared. The crib, the rocker, the changing table. All of it. Every piece Derrick had given away.

"Mommy! My things!" Tiffany reached over the crib's rail and pulled out Big Bear. She held him up and twirled around.

"I don't understand. How is this here?"

Tiffany twirled. "Yaldabaoth, Mommy. He is glorious."

Teresa closed her eyes and swallowed. The door opened, and Derrick walked in. Teresa gasped and backed away from him. His eyes weren't right, though. They were yellow, not dark brown.

"What do you think?" Yaldabaoth's silky, sensual voice came from Derrick's lips. He held his arms wide and turned a circle.

Teresa grabbed onto the edge of the changing table and pulled in a deep breath.

"Too much?" The grin was not her husband's.

Teresa nodded. "I'm not exactly on good terms with my husband right now."

He moved closer to her and touched her stomach. A pleasant chill ran through her, as if his touch had electrified all of her nerves.

She looked past Yaldabaoth for Tiffany, but her daughter wasn't anywhere to be seen.

"This is what you want, isn't it?" He moved closer still, pressing her against the changing table. "Happiness with your husband? The return of your child?" Yaldabaoth's lips lingered millimeters from hers. His hands roamed to her backside, cupped her buttocks. Her eyes flew open and met his. The spell broke.

"You don't want *me*," she said. "All you want is *this*." She slapped the hypo full of Brent's zoe into his hand and moved away from him. "Stop trying to fool me with your mind games."

The nursery melted into the cave with the pool. Yaldabaoth tilted the syringe back and forth like a seesaw.

"Four more." He laughed.

CHAPTER 36

Ann stayed at the station in case anyone called in. While the coffee machine gurgled and hissed, she considered what George didn't know. If she had stayed in Harmony and followed the path her dad wanted for her, *none* of this would have happened. She wouldn't have even been a detective on the Stabber case. She would have had a relationship with her dad. She would have known about the Protectorate and the Messengers and Sophia.

Maggie.

She wandered back to the lockers for the umpteenth time and opened her dad's, smelled his shirt again even though his scent was long gone.

"I'm sorry, Dad," she whispered. She *was* sorry for everything. For not calling him more. For never coming back. For not following in the family's footsteps and running for Sheriff of this godforsaken town. She slammed the locker and leaned her forehead against the cold metal.

It's not your fault. You wanted a life.

You should have been here.

She lifted her head. McMichael had said something her first day back. Something Ann thought strange at the time.

"I should have been there," he'd said. McMichael probably felt it was his duty to be by Bram's side, having been Bram's right-hand man almost their entire lives. But her dad wasn't on duty when he went to Egypt.

Not sheriff's duty anyway.

McMichael's locker stood next to her dad's. What would his combination be? Ann went to the storage cell, searched for, and found, a crow bar. A set of lock pick tools sat on a nearby shelf. She grabbed those, too.

Less than five minutes later, Ann bent the metal door well out of shape. A bead of sweat tracked down her face. She wiped it away and opened the locker.

A standard gray lock box, like her dad's, sat inside. Ann pulled it out and took a ragged breath to calm her heart, which beat behind her eyeballs. The picks made easy work of the simple lock.

Ann opened the lid, and her breath caught in her throat. She lifted a crystal vial necklace almost exactly like her dad's by its chain. Spots of dried blood stained the glass, but it was otherwise empty. She knew the necklace didn't belong to McMichael for two reasons: the necklace would be full of blood, and he would be wearing it, abducted or not.

Ann returned her attention to the sheriff's box and found a small black address book and a newspaper clipping.

The article dated back eight years: *American woman dies in tragic bus accident.*

The location of the article: Nag Hammadi, Egypt. The woman: Lisa McMichael, the sheriff's wife.

Ann sank to the floor. His wife was a Protector. She was killed. In Nag Hammadi. Which was in Upper Egypt. Where her father died. Her lungs struggled to fill.

Keep it together, Logan.

The little address book sat on the floor where it had slipped from her hand when she read the article. She picked it up and flipped through the pages.

Red pen struck through most of the names. The addresses were from all over the world but mostly Egypt or its surrounding countries. Libya, Sudan, even Jordan and Syria.

One name remained unmarred by red ink: Asim Raghib. Next to his entry a circle enclosed the initials PA. She flipped back through the book and found several other names with PA next to them. PA. Protector Allegiant.

Ann put the newspaper article and the necklace back in McMichael's lock box. She needed to go home to cross reference the names with the list in Maggie's book and the list from her dad's locker. She rushed back to the kitchenette and grabbed a cup to go before unplugging the pot.

She arrived home a few minutes later and immediately flipped to the back of the book. Starting on the first page, she scanned the list and paged through the address book. All of the names that weren't identified as Protector Allegiant were listed in the book, including Lisa McMichael. Another dead end.

The Sa tingled. Ann peeked at it. The edges glowed a little. She should check on Maggie, make sure the girl was okay.

* * *

In the bright glow of Derrick's porch light, Ann rapped on the decorative glass panes set in the door. Derrick answered. Ann didn't like the way he smiled or the way his eyes lit up when they landed on her.

"Hey," Ann said. "So, I have a strange request."

"Yeah? What's up?"

"Can I see Maggie?"

His face fell. "What's this about? Did Teresa say something?" Derrick stepped out onto the porch. Ann stepped back so he wouldn't encroach on her personal space.

"What did she say? Did she tell you . . ." he covered his mouth with his hand.

"Tell me what?" Ann squinted at him. He was hiding something.

Derrick paced down the front walk to the fence and back.

"I lost my temper. No, not my temper. I'm just so . . . so frustrated with her." He stood before Ann, and his eyes told her everything. He was sorry for, and regretted, whatever he had done. "I'm tired, Ann. All we do is fight."

"What did you do?" Ann crossed her arms.

"I think I hurt her—" He held up his hands when she dropped her arms and opened her mouth. "Not too badly. I had her by the wrists and might've squeezed too hard. She was raving and out of control. I needed to get her attention. It wasn't bad. I swear."

"Are you sure that's all?"

His eyes searched the space between them and came back to hers.

"Yes. We fought, I hurt her, she left. I haven't seen her since." He glanced at his watch. "Where is she?" His question came with worry.

"I'm sure she's just with a friend or something."

"Teresa doesn't have any friends here." His voice was so matter of fact. "Not close friends, anyway. She blames me for not fitting in." He shook his head. "Ridiculous."

An uncomfortable silence fell between them. Ann shifted her eyes to the door.

"So, can I talk to Maggie?"

"I told you everything. Why do you need to talk to her?" He crossed his arms and distributed his weight evenly—smack in front of the doorway.

Derrick was Maggie's legal guardian. He had a right to know the reason.

"That old book she carries around. She loaned it to me. I need to ask her some questions about something I read."

Derrick relaxed. "You can read it?"

Ann shrugged.

He let out a breath and motioned for her to go inside. "Down the hall to the right."

Maggie was at the coffee table with a stack of paper and a box of one million crayons, or however many colors Crayola had now.

"Hey, Maggie," Ann said. She sat on the floor next to the girl.

Maggie's face lit up, and she hugged Ann. The embrace made heat swarm Ann's body. When Maggie let go, Ann took off her jacket. Derrick was standing behind the couch, watching. She didn't know how to ask him to leave, that they had something secret to discuss. But she didn't need to.

Maggie turned to Derrick. "Daddy, can I please talk to Ann by myself?"

Shock replaced Derrick's parental curiosity. Ann shifted her eyes to Maggie who smiled bright and sweet at him, then to Derrick who, little by little, melted. He cleared his throat.

"Sure. I'll be in the kitchen." He shuffled around the breakfast bar and leaned nonchalantly against the counter. Ann knew he was still listening.

"Are you okay?" Ann asked in a low voice. "It . . . tingled." She pointed at her chest. Maggie nodded, but her eyes were sad. She pointed to pages of drawings on the table. The drawing on top depicted a cross between a lion, a snake, and a man.

"Is that . . ." Ann swallowed. When she spoke again, her voice came out a whisper. "Is that Yaldabaoth?"

Maggie nodded. "My head is full of pictures of him. I had to get them out." She put her crayon down and looked at Ann with intensity. "He scares me."

Of course he does. He wants to kill you and trigger the End of Days.

Ann swallowed hard. Maggie shuffled through the pages of drawings. All of them were Yaldabaoth.

"I don't think drawing him is helping me get him out of my head," Maggie said in a sad whisper. She kept shuffling through the papers and pulled two out.

"This one came to me two nights ago, and this one last night." Maggie pushed the drawings toward Ann.

The first one showed Yaldabaoth with his arms spread wide. Lightning bolts were drawn all around him. A jagged stick figure, sketched in a reddish-brown color, stood in the background as if watching.

Maggie touched Ann's hand. Then she pointed at the red-brown figure. Ann looked at her face. Maggie's eyes filled with tears.

When she spoke, her voice came out small and choked. "That's Ruthie."

CHAPTER 37

Teresa spent the rest of the waning afternoon at the cemetery on a stone bench near Tiffany's grave. The sun slipped closer to the mountains flanking Harmony. The air cooled. She didn't want to go home and face Derrick. Faint bruising had begun to bloom where his fingers had crushed the skin against the bones of her wrists.

He marked her in anger. What could either one of them possibly say to right this wrong? A simple apology wouldn't cut it this time. She wouldn't accept that. Not for physical harm.

She rose to her feet and left the cemetery. At the town center she paused.

I have nowhere else to go.

For the briefest moment, regret hovered over her. If she'd tried harder, perhaps then she would have a trusted friend to go to in times like this.

Ruthie was the only person she could think of who showed her any kindness lately. At the thought of the now stick-figure-zombie, for lack of a better word, her heart hurt.

Teresa gazed in the direction of Louise's house. Louise shared the secret of Bram Logan with her, sure, for her own ulterior motive, not out of friendship.

It was worth a shot. Teresa walked with purpose to Louise's house, and arrived as the mountains swallowed the sun. At the door, she raised her knuckles and rapped against the wood.

"Who is it?" Louise's voice, sing-song and muffled, came from inside.

"It's Teresa."

Louise opened the door, her face a beaming ray of horribly wrinkled sunshine.

"What can I do for you, Doctor?"

Teresa touched her throat, unsure of what to say, how she would ask.

"I . . ." Teresa shook her head. "Never mind. I'm sorry I bothered you."

Louise stepped aside and waved Teresa into the house.

"Come in—have some tea, dear. Let's talk." Louise motioned to the table. Teresa sat.

Louise filled the kettle and put it on the burner.

Click. Click. Fwump.

She smiled at Teresa. "You have nowhere to go, do you?"

Teresa twisted her wedding ring and shook her head.

"No worry. I'm glad you stopped by. I wanted to discuss

something with you."

Teresa perked. "Oh?"

"We have a common interest." The kettle screamed, Louise lifted it. "Tea?"

"Yes, please."

Louise prepared tea for two and set the cups on the table.

"I believe we can help each other," Louise said. "I work for an organization called Messengers of the Light." Louise shooed a calico cat off the chair across from Teresa and sat. "It is our goal to find Yaldabaoth and bring him back."

"But you said I would destroy thirty-some years of work. Besides, aren't I already sort of helping you?"

Louise shook her head. "You have no idea what the procedure is. A process must be followed."

"What have I done wrong?"

Louise tossed her head back and cackled. "You are more deluded than I thought asking that, dear doctor."

Teresa sat back, confused. "But I haven't—Oh." She looked at her cup.

"There's more to bringing Yaldabaoth back to power than murdering people." Louise leaned back in her chair and leveled her eyes on Teresa, scrutinizing her.

"I wouldn't call it murder," Teresa said in a small voice. She twisted the tea cup in its saucer.

Louise cackled again. Teresa frowned.

"What do you call it then?"

"Tiffany calls it 'taking their zoe.'" She lifted her cup

and sipped.

"Zoe means life, Doctor Hart."

Teresa inhaled a drop of tea and coughed. Louise filled a glass from the tap and passed it across the table.

"I didn't know that," Teresa said through her coughs.

Louise's eyebrow lifted.

"Fine. I knew. He called them souls. Seven bloods, seven souls—I think that's what he said."

Louise nodded in what looked like approval.

"What needs to be done once the seven zoes are collected?" Teresa asked.

"I'm not sure." Louise lifted a fat Siamese-looking cat onto her lap. "You see, for the past thirty years or so I've been looking for an artifact that will tell us what to do. It was inside the vessel containing the Nag Hammadi codices."

"Nag Hamma—"

"Gnostic texts," Louise said. "That's all you need to know." She lifted her cup but put it back down.

"Among these texts was a book called the *Origin Codex*. It was an expansion of the scripture titled, "On the Origin of the World." We had it in our possession for many years, waiting for any sign of Yaldabaoth. The book contains the instructions to harness him once he regains his strength. But, someone stole it. Took it right out of the vault we kept it in. None of us had taken the time to memorize it. We were complacent in our power." She smirked as if this were some inside joke and shook her head.

"Without this harness, Yaldabaoth will destroy the entire world out of hatred and revenge. The End of Days shall truly be upon us."

"What? Like the Rapture?" Teresa asked.

"Sort of, but only if he is harnessed. Then he will spare all those who serve him. Those who do not shall be smote from the earth." Louise's part-dreamy-part-adoring smile gave Teresa a chill.

"Have you ever met him?" she asked.

Louise shook her head. The dreamy look melted away. "I have not had the honor."

Something in Teresa's stomach fluttered. Yaldabaoth came to her, someone who believed in a different God. Not his loyal follower.

"Tell me more about this book," Teresa said.

"It's old. Papyrus pages bound in leather."

Teresa gasped.

Maggie's old, dirty book.

"I know where it is."

Louise straightened in her chair. "You do?" A horrendous grin spread across her face, then slid away. "That's rather unfortunate." The corners of her mouth turned down. "All this time I've been torturing Bram Logan for information I could have easily gotten from you. Huh."

She cleared her throat and shrugged with one bony shoulder.

"Well, there are *other* reasons I've been torturing him." Her wicked smile returned.

CHAPTER 38

Teresa caught herself scowling again. She worked to relax her face while standing at Louise's kitchen counter with two aluminum dog bowls.

One for vegetables, one for meat.

She opened a can with a dog on it. Beef Tips and Gravy. It didn't smell like beef or gravy. She dumped the contents into the bowl.

Louise didn't tell her the other reasons behind keeping Bram Logan prisoner in her basement. The old crone told Teresa she'd find out in due time. Teresa asked if she could stay the night, and Louise had agreed, as long as Teresa took Bram his dinner.

The frown returned. She briefly wondered what Derrick made Maggie for dinner.

Pancakes, no doubt.

She filled the other bowl with scraps from a metal canister labeled *compost*. The vegetables inside were slimy and rotten. She picked out a few larger pieces. Her mouth filled with saliva, and she gagged.

"It's not all that bad," Louise said behind her. "At least I'm feeding him. If you ask me, he doesn't deserve even that dog food."

Teresa picked up the bowls and went to the bolted door. Louise opened it for her, and Teresa descended into the basement.

The old television was still on a channel full of static with the volume turned up full blast. The flickering screen gave a strobe light effect that made Teresa dizzy. She put the bowls down and crossed the space, reaching her hand out to find the light switch.

"Who is that?" Bram's rough voice called through the noise. "You're not Louise. You smell different. Tell me who you are."

Teresa sniffed her shirt where the sharp scent of stress sweat clung. She moved to the television and turned it down just enough to make it more bearable. She couldn't imagine having to endure that noise for so long. And virtual blindness on top of it?

"I brought your dinner," she said.

Bram coughed, deep and lung rattling, and spit out a glob of sputum. "Who are you?"

"I don't think I should tell you who I am."

"Fine." He spit again. This time more out of anger than to clear his throat. "Did she tell you to untie my hands, or are you going to hold the bowl by my face so I can eat like a fucking dog?"

In response, Teresa shoved the protein toward him, and he gobbled the chunks of meat product and sauce. She gagged. When he finished, she grimaced at the rotten vegetables.

"I don't think you want to eat these," she said.

"Give 'em."

Once again, she held the bowl near his face. Every last slimy, partially decomposed vegetable disappeared. He sat back, out of breath.

"Water," he said. Teresa glanced around, spotted a case of bottled water on a work bench, and grabbed one. She unscrewed the cap and tilted it toward his lips. He drank the whole thing. Teresa moved toward the TV to turn it back up but hesitated.

Whatever he had done to Louise must have been horrid for her to torture him like this, but he hadn't done anything to Teresa. Unless fathering Ann counted. She touched the knob but dropped her hand and went to the stairs.

"Why are you helping that monster?" Bram's words came out as a croak.

Teresa stopped and looked at him. Thin and dirty and pathetic. If he was part of this, he would know who Yaldabaoth was, but Teresa figured he was likely referring to Louise.

"I have no other choice."

"There's always a choice."

Teresa flicked the light off and went up the stairs.

Louise had set the table with plates of salad. Teresa joined her.

"What did he do to deserve this inhumane treatment?" A scowl worked its way onto her face, causing wrinkles like Louise's. She relaxed her features.

"He killed my husband." Louise took a bite. "Along with many others in the organization." Her gray eyes met Teresa's. "He was a skilled assassin. He took out more of my operatives than anyone else like him."

"Operatives?"

"The Messengers of the Light. A centuries-old organization. Smaller than the CIA or FBI, sure, but we compare ourselves to them. Our methods, our technology—we even had people on the inside who could use the CIA's computers to hunt people down. Then Bram Logan came along. He worked for the Protectorate. A much smaller group than the Messengers but more skilled in the field. In war. In protection. Far more skilled than my group of intelligence agents and doomsdayers."

"They are your enemy."

Louise nodded. "They were. Bram and Ann are the only ones left. He never told her about them."

Teresa lifted her fork, but after watching Bram wolf down rotten lettuce a few minutes ago, her stomach turned at the thought of eating salad.

Louise swallowed and continued. "Several years ago, Bram started taking trips to Nag Hammadi. On one of his trips abroad, I sent several operatives to find out what he was doing." She took a swallow of tea to wash her food down. "I had him followed." Her eyes grew misty as if the memory pained her. "They discovered he was assassinating the local Messengers, working with a traitor named Raghib. Word got back to me Raghib had the book. That's why I thought Bram would know where it was. He must have told Raghib to give it to someone else and keep the location secret."

"He must have given it to Maggie, if it's the same book," Teresa said. "But, why?"

Louise looked at Teresa. No, not at her, through her.

When she spoke again, her voice was hesitant, almost like she was thinking out loud.

"To protect it. Why her, indeed?" Louise stood and unbolted the basement door. Teresa followed. Louise dragged a table near Bram and set a gooseneck lamp on it. She tore the goggles from his head and shined the light in his eyes.

Bram cried out and tossed his head back and forth with his eyes closed.

"Why did Raghib give the book to Maggie?" Louise asked.

"I don't know!" Bram cried. Louise picked up a riding crop and smacked him in the face. Teresa flinched.

Louise switched him again. "Tell me or you will die down here. Right now. You'll never see your precious Ann ever again." A low chuckle vibrated up her throat. "Did I mention she's in town?"

"Fuck. You." He attempted to spit, but saliva swung

from his lips and hit his chin. It dribbled onto his filthy shirt.

Louise leaned in close, her body blocking the light. Bram opened his eyes. The pupils remained dilated from prolonged exposure to darkness. Louise grabbed the arms of his chair.

"Did I tell you she's learned about the Protectorate? She knows she's the one, Brammy." She said his name in a sing-song voice.

His eyes widened.

"I've earned her trust. She'll lead me straight to the book. Straight to Sophia." Louise pointed over her shoulder in Teresa's direction. "Teresa Hart's daughter has the book. How did she get it?"

Teresa backed up several paces at the mention of her name. She swallowed hard. Now he knew who she was.

I have to kill him.

The thought surprised her.

Bram tucked his lips inside his mouth and shook his head. Louise swung her arm and backhanded him. Blood splattered from between his lips, speckling the concrete floor.

"Please, stop," Teresa said. "I can't watch this."

"Then go upstairs." Louise raised her hand again. Teresa lunged forward and caught Louise's arm.

"Stop. Please. He doesn't know."

The old woman's eyes were wide and crazy. Spittle collected in the corners of her trembling mouth.

"Like hell he doesn't." She jerked out of Teresa's grasp.

Instead of carrying through with another backhand, she reached for a toolbox and pulled out a pair of pruning shears. She went behind Bram, allowing the light to blind him again. "Tell me. Now."

Teresa backed away until she was at the bottom of the stairs. She didn't know what Louise was doing, but she could wager a good guess.

"No." He spat the word.

Louise's face contorted, and her body moved like she was applying pressure on something. The shears *snipped*. Bram screamed. Blood streamed onto the floor.

"That's two. Eight more to go." She tossed Bram's pinky aside.

Teresa winced and covered her eyes. "Louise! This is barbaric!"

"This is the way of the Messengers, Teresa. At least I haven't killed him. Yet." She gritted her teeth.

Teresa peeked through her fingers. "Death would be better than this!"

Bram let out an anguished cry. More blood dripped.

"No! Okay. Stop. Stop!" he shouted.

Louise relaxed.

"Raghib . . ." Bram panted. "Raghib is Maggie's grandfather." Sweat dripped down his face and neck, drawing lines in the grime caked on his skin. "I told him . . . I told him to give her the book."

"Why?" Louise asked. When he didn't answer right

away, her jaw tensed again.

"Wait, please. Stop." He let out a sob, splattering sweat and spit toward the lamp. "No more, please. No more." He groaned. "I need water."

Louise nodded at Teresa. She grabbed a bottle off the counter and helped him drink, and while she blocked the light, he met her eyes.

"Doctor, please," he whispered.

"I can't help you," she said and moved out of the light. He grunted and squeezed his eyes shut against his tears.

"Why did you tell Raghib to give the book to Maggie?" Louise asked.

"We sent Maggie to the States. The Protectorate had everything necessary to hide her—new identity, travel papers, everything. They gave Maggie to the Harts, even though Teresa, here, didn't pass the necessary evaluations."

Teresa dropped the bottle of water and covered her mouth.

"We needed to get Maggie to Harmony. For it to look real, she had to be in the system for at least a few months. Kids don't typically enter the system and get adopted right away. It takes time." His face contorted with pain or something else.

"She stayed in a foster home in Denver. From there, the Protectorate forged the documents, and the Harts were approved." He took gasping breaths.

"Why did Maggie need to be in Harmony?"

"To give the book to Ann." Bram's face contorted. His

body shook with sobs.

"Maggie only arrived three months ago," Teresa said. Louise glanced at her, then back to her hands.

"Your story makes no sense, Bram." Louise jerked, and another finger fell into the puddle of blood pooling around Louise's feet.

He cried out again. A long, low wail that ended with gasping sobs. His body trembled.

Teresa tried to keep her eyes from drifting to the newly severed finger lying on the floor and the pinky that had rolled into the corner.

"Please—It's true."

"Louise," Teresa said, her voice breathless. "Let him explain."

"Ann left fifteen years ago. Maggie didn't arrive until three months ago. Explain yourself or lose another finger."

He took in several gasping, shuddery breaths.

"How did you know Ann would come back?" Louise shouted.

"I just knew, okay? I knew she would." Spittle flew from his lips, snot from his nose. Sweat beaded and dripped down his colorless face.

"For all that work, it seems rather risky to place all your bets on your daughter returning to a place she loathes." Louise tensed. Bram screeched a high wail.

"Stop!" Teresa said with force. He was right. It all made sense. "I believe him. At least about Maggie and her adoption."

Louise peered at her with narrowed, questioning eyes. "How so?"

The best way to say it was to just say it. "I don't think I could have ever passed a psychological evaluation."

She lifted her chin and came to terms with what she was about to say.

"I don't think the state would have awarded a child to a woman who had killed her baby."

CHAPTER 39

Maggie pointed at the other drawing she had pushed toward Ann. This one showed Yaldabaoth in the same powerful pose—arms spread wide, lightning bolts shooting down at him—along with a figure that appeared to be the Michelin Man drawn in the same red-brown as Ruthie.

"Who's this?"

"That's Mr. Sheriff," Maggie whispered.

Ann swore her heart was going to burst out of her eye sockets. She swallowed the pound of sand in her throat.

"Is Yaldabaoth being struck by lightning?" she asked.

Maggie shook her head. "He's . . . I don't know how to explain it."

"Try. Maybe I can help."

She looked into Ann's face, her gaze shifting back and forth from eye to eye, then back at the drawing.

"He's using their zoe," Maggie said with a shrug. "Sometimes my brain tells me things, but I don't know what they mean." A tear trembled on her lower lashes and spilled down her cheek. She rubbed both eyes with her fists.

Ann patted her back.

"They're both gone, aren't they?" Maggie asked.

A cold prickle ran over Ann's scalp, and heat dampened her armpits. "What do you mean?"

"Ruthie and Mr. Sheriff," Maggie said, wiping again at her cheeks. "They're gone, right?"

"They're just out of town right now," Ann said through the dryness in her throat and mouth. "When you saw them in your dreams, were they okay?"

Maggie shook her head.

"They were scary," she said with a whimper. "They were okay at first, but when Yaldabaoth used their zoe, they changed and looked funny." She pulled Ruthie's illustration back out. "Ruthie was really skinny, and Mr. Sheriff was puffy."

They were fine until he used the zoe. Ann knew the *name* Zoe, but not the *thing* zoe. Louise had mentioned the name the first time Ann went to see her.

"There's a story you might know—it's about the origin of the world?" Ann hoped Maggie was familiar with the story.

Maggie nodded slowly. Her eyes glistened with residual tears. "I think so. My baba used to tell me stories all the time." She sniffled. "That's the one with Yaldabaoth and Pistis Sophia, right?"

"Do you remember Pistis Sophia's daughter's name?"

Maggie twisted the crayon in her hand, then cocked her head up at Ann.

"Sophia's daughter's name was Zoe," Ann said.

Maggie's eyes widened. "Oh yeah . . . She made all the good in the world."

Maggie's insight surprised Ann. It was true, though. Zoe had created all that was good in the world when she countered Yaldabaoth's creation of Death, who then created all the bad in the world; therefore, Sophia was indirectly responsible for all the good and all the bad, having been the mother of both Yaldabaoth and Zoe.

Human Pandora's Box.

Sophia let it all out into the world.

"Maybe if we find out what zoe means, it'll help us figure out the rest." Ann got up.

"Where are you going?" Maggie asked.

"I'm going to ask your dad if I can use his computer." She turned to go find Derrick, but he was already there, laptop in hand. Ann wondered how much of their conversation he'd overheard. Derrick handed her the computer but didn't let go.

"I don't even want to know what you two are up to," he said. "Well, yeah, I do. I can't say I'm not slightly jealous of what seems like a deep, philosophical conversation with my daughter." He smiled. "So . . . what *are* you talking about?"

Ann glanced over her shoulder at Maggie who scribbled absently on a piece of paper. "Has she told you about her dreams?"

Derrick nodded. "They wake her up. They seem to be getting worse. Before they were about the lion man stealing her light. Now, she just cries and won't tell me what they're about. I'm beginning to wonder if I should take her to a therapist; maybe her nightmares are manifestations of abuse. Who knows what kind of life she had before she came to us."

"I'm sure that's not the reason," Ann said. Derrick gave her a quizzical look. She ignored it. "Thanks for letting me talk to her and for letting me use your computer."

Derrick released the laptop. Ann sat down and opened the lid and typed "zoe" into the search engine. About a million and one results returned

A Mexican band, an actress, and the meaning of zoe, which led to a baby names website. Ann shrugged. Why not? She clicked on the baby names link.

She read the page. "It says here Zoe means 'life.'"

Maggie leaned closer and rested her head against Ann's arm. A chill shuddered through Ann's body.

He's using their zoe.

He's using their life? She thought back to the story Louise told her. If Zoe created all the good in the world, was Yaldabaoth using goodness? Her deduction got her nowhere. The helplessness started to return.

"What are you thinking?" Maggie asked.

"I'm just trying to figure out what it means for Yaldabaoth to use someone's life."

Maggie set her chin on her forearms. "He's trying to get strong." She shuffled through her papers and showed Ann what resembled a cave with a black circle inside. The crayon had been lain on so thick the paper wasn't visible through it.

"What's that?" Ann pointed to the black circle.

"The abyss." Maggie looked at her again. "Another thing I don't know. What's an abyss?"

"A bottomless hole or something."

"It's scary." She lifted the picture. "In my dream I fell into it." Her eyes shifted to Ann's. "You know how sometimes when you dream you trip and it wakes you up?"

Ann laughed. "Yes. I have those all the time."

Maggie didn't laugh. Her face remained serious. "If you don't land, you don't wake up."

She pushed the picture back under another one of a dog—or some other four-legged animal.

"Who's this?"

"Pinky. Brent's dog. I saw her in my mind," she said. "I've never met Pinky, and I don't know who Brent is."

"Dinner time," Derrick called from the kitchen. "Ann, you're welcome to join us."

Ann thought about what Derrick had said. Teresa thought they were having an affair. She closed the laptop and stood. "No, that's okay."

"Please, Ann? Please stay." Maggie gripped Ann's hand.

The child's expression made her change her mind. Maggie was terrified. Who wouldn't be, with the nightmares she'd been having? With the load she had to bear? Ann didn't think Maggie knew the full extent of what it meant to be the human manifestation of Sophia.

And yet, at times, the girl seemed so wise.

"Okay, fine. Dinner, and then I have to go."

Maggie hugged her and bounced to the table. Ann waited for Derrick to sit. Then she sat as far from him as possible. An uneasy anxiety clawed at her belly. She sat up straight in her chair and cast glances toward the front door, fully expecting Teresa to burst in at any moment and catch her husband eating dinner with another woman. Her appetite was gone, but it had been so long since she'd eaten a nice home-cooked meal. She'd been surviving on frozen entrees since she got to town. Her stomach growled at the scent of spaghetti. She dug in and relished the flavor.

After dinner, Derrick offered dessert, but Ann passed. Maggie didn't. He served her some ice cream. Ann struggled to find a graceful way to leave, but something kept her from going. Her duty to protect perhaps? It was in her blood, after all. She absently rubbed the mark through her shirt.

When Derrick took Maggie upstairs to bed, she had the perfect opportunity to leave, and yet she didn't go.

What is it you think you want here?

Derrick came back and gave her a weary smile. "I'm worried about Teresa." He sighed.

"Does she do this often?" Ann asked.

Derrick shook his head. "Never. She's always home. I

mean, lately she's been venturing out a little more. That or she just doesn't answer the phone when I call." He slumped onto the corner cushion of the L-shaped sectional.

"That's not what I meant, though," he said. "She's been . . . just . . . I don't want to burden you."

Ann didn't say anything, but in the back of her mind she wondered if she would find Teresa's like-human-umbilical-cord crispy substance in the near future.

"I'd offer you a drink, but Teresa doesn't let me keep the stuff," he said.

"That's okay." Ann leaned forward. "I should probably get going, anyway."

"Stay," Derrick said. Ann let out a laugh.

"Stay? What am I, a dog?" She got up.

"Please, Ann. I've been so . . . lonely these past few years. I don't have anyone else to talk to."

Dread flooded Ann's body. She gazed at the front door—so far away at the end of the hall—then back at Derrick, dejected and weary.

He held up his hands. "I don't want anything more than some adult conversation."

Ann's body relaxed. "Okay, fine. I'll stay for a few more minutes, but if Teresa comes home . . ."

"She'd be home by now if she was coming."

"Do you want to go search for her?" Ann thought about Ruthie and the sheriff. "Aren't you worried she may have been kidnapped like Ruthie?"

"Have you found anything?"

A subtle change of subject. Ann shook her head. Maggie's drawings lingered in the corner of her vision. The girl had stacked them back together and pushed them inside a folder, but the corners stuck out the side.

"Does Maggie talk to you about her drawings?" Ann asked. She flipped the folder open. The abyss was on top.

If you don't land, you don't wake up.

Derrick moved closer, sitting right next to Ann. His leg brushed hers. She couldn't deny the rush of heat that raced through her, or her heart rate picking up, but she wouldn't allow herself to get wrapped up in those feelings.

"She shows them to me, but she doesn't explain them." He flipped through the pages. "I didn't think a parent was supposed to ask what a kid's drawing is. I feel like I'm supposed to be able to figure it out, like asking would hurt her feelings, you know?" He turned his head.

Ann could see him looking at her out of the corner of her eye. He was too close. Far too close. She moved over half a cushion.

"I'm not sure how to explain this to you, Derrick—"

"I know, I know." He moved a full cushion away from her. "I'm married—you're not a home wrecker."

Ann snorted. "That's not what I was going to say. I mean, yeah, I refuse to do anything . . . like that. But what I meant was, Maggie is . . . special." She cleared her throat and reached for the drawings. "Her dreams—there's some truth to them."

Yaldabaoth and Ruthie's picture appeared in the stack

Derrick flipped through.

"This one, see? She said that's Ruthie."

"She knows Ruthie from the diner," Derrick said. "That's not unusual."

"Does she know Ruthie is missing?"

Derrick shook his head. "I haven't told her. It would break her heart. She loves Ruthie."

"She knows things she can't possibly know." Ann got up and grabbed her coat. "Keep an eye on her for me, okay?"

"Of course." He walked her to the door.

Outside, the cold air felt good. She pulled on her jacket and walked home, letting her thoughts take over.

Yaldabaoth was using their life. But what did it mean? How did he use life to get stronger?

They're gone, aren't they?

Ann shivered at the thought of Maggie's words and zipped up her jacket.

CHAPTER 40

The door to her house was open a few inches. Ann listened at the crack. Someone was inside, sobbing in the dark.

Ann picked up the fake rock with the house key in it and eased the door open enough to see a large shape sitting on the couch. She kicked the door and threw the fake rock as hard as she could. Direct hit.

"Ow!" said a man's voice, husky from crying.

Ann flipped on the light. George Riley turned his red and blotchy face toward her.

"What the hell, George?"

"I'm sorry, Ann. I didn't know who else to talk to."

"You have violated my privacy." The words came out calm despite the anger. Adrenaline shook her body. She leveled her gaze on him. "What are you doing here?"

"I broke up with Marcie." His features contorted into an ugly cry face.

"Probably not a bad thing," Ann said.

George looked at her, then burst into renewed tears

accompanied by a high-pitched whining.

Oops. Probably not the best thing to say.

"I found a positive pregnancy test in her trash can."

Ann clenched her jaw. "You broke up with her because she's pregnant?" What was wrong with the men in this town?

He held up his hands. "No, no that wasn't the reason." He swallowed. "She kept pressuring me to . . ." The last part he mumbled.

"Stop mumbling. You came here to talk to me, so talk to me." She tried to keep the frustration out of her voice. Ann paced over to him, but she didn't sit.

He gave her a desperate look. "I wouldn't have sex with her." His red face turned three shades redder. He stood and paced. "She kept pressuring me. She did everything she could to entice me—"

"Please, save the details."

"But I stuck to my guns. I know it's old fashioned, but I want to save myself for the girl I marry."

"Why didn't you ask her to marry you?"

George's shoulders slumped. "Because . . . her dad hates me." He looked up at Ann. "I was trying to get him to like me better. But I guess maybe I got tired of tryin' so hard?"

Ann considered this for a moment. "So deep down maybe you knew she wasn't the one."

He opened his mouth to retort, but Ann stopped him.

"Just listen," Ann said. "If you really thought she was the one, and you really loved her, you would have done anything and everything to prove yourself."

He got a distant look in his eyes. Ann could smell the gears grinding in his head. He focused his gaze on her.

"I guess you're right." He wiped his eyes with the back of his hand and nodded. "You're right."

"So, no need to be heartbroken." Ann resisted the urge to wipe her hands together.

That's that—now get out.

George didn't move.

"Besides, if she didn't respect your values, she's not the right girl. It's been a long day for both of us. Go home, get some sleep. I'll see you in the morning." She motioned to the door with a sweep of her arm.

"But the test." His face contorted again. "It's not my baby."

Ann put a hand on George's shoulder.

"She's not worth it, George. She's not worth it." Poor George. She took back any ill thing she'd ever said about him, in her private thoughts or otherwise.

The kid deserved so much more than he got.

"I know . . ." The words came out in a moan. "But, why is my heart so torn open?"

"That's how heartbreak works." She patted his shoulder. "You love the idea of having a girlfriend, of her companionship. Love becomes a habit. Something you grow used to and comfortable with." She spoke from experience. "It blinds you."

George looked up at her with red-rimmed eyes.

"She betrayed your trust and everything you'd built her up to be. Your girl wasn't one hundred percent yours." She went to the door and George followed.

"You'll find the right girl, George. One who devotes her entire life to loving you the way you deserve to be loved, and you won't think twice about two-timing Marcie Berg."

Before she could stop it from happening, he pulled her into a hug. Every muscle in her body tensed. She patted him on the back, and he pulled away.

"Thanks, Ann."

She closed the door behind him and immediately switched gears from George's heartbreak to the case. That's what the job required. Leave the personal bullshit at the door and focus. She got a notebook and pen from the junk drawer and wrote down a list of facts. Ruthie and Sheriff McMichael's disappearances. The crispy substance—like human umbilical cord.

All the facts.

Then she drew a line and wrote out a list of all the . . . well . . . *other* shit.

The book pulsing in the night. The glowing veins. The mark. The story Louise told her about Yaldabaoth. The passages from the book and Sophia's physical manifestation. Messengers of the Light. The Protectorate. Everything she had seen or heard or read but couldn't explain or prove, even Maggie's drawings.

Yaldabaoth using Ruthie and the sheriff's zoe. Their forms changing when he did.

Brent's dog Pinky. Why would Maggie have drawn a picture of Brent's dog? Did Yaldabaoth steal Pinky's zoe? She put a question mark next to that item. Perhaps a visit to Brent's house was in order. She looked at the time.

Tomorrow. Definitely tomorrow. Tonight was spent.

Ann went to the bookshelf, then the now re-alphabetized DVD collection, but nothing grabbed her interest. The truth was, even without a passing psych evaluation and her inability to fire—look at—a gun, when she wasn't thinking about the case, when she wasn't *working*, she didn't know what to do with herself.

Maybe I'm healing.

The thought gave her hope.

Maybe it's a breakthrough.

Then the book, still sitting on the coffee table, flipped open. Ann jumped and grabbed the armchair prepared to, what? Throw it at someone?

The pages turned faster and faster, then stopped at about the halfway point. Ann moved around the chair and sat in front of the book. Her eyes scanned the characters.

Seven souls shall be collected. Seven souls shall resurrect His Greatness. Our One True God. A physical body shall become his vessel. He shall become whole. He shall walk the Material Realm amongst us. He shall destroy that which destroyed him.

Ann's heartrate picked up. Raghib had said the book would show her the way.

Blood of the Ancient. Blood of the Pure. Blood of the

Tainted. Blood of the Loving Servant. Blood of the Bastard. Blood of the Blind Fool. Blood of the Devoted.

In the aftermath of his destruction, we shall rise with him to the True Kingdom. We shall shed that which binds us to the material realm and transcend as Perfect Beings.

We shall live on in Him.

Seven bloods, seven souls. Ann grabbed her notebook from the table and wrote them down in the "other" section.

Ancient, Pure, Tainted, Loving Servant, Bastard, Blind Fool, Devoted.

The sheriff could likely be the ancient, given his old age, or the loving servant due to his serving and protecting Harmony. No, Ruthie was obviously the loving servant. What about Pinky, if she'd been taken? A dog could certainly be considered pure. Or devoted.

She sat back and rubbed her palms over her face. Too many questions without answers. Too many unproven, unexplainable elements. The hopelessness began to seep in, but she refused it entry.

I can figure this out. She told herself. Then she said it out loud to give it power over that voice telling her she would fail. The page turned. Shit. There was more.

Seven blood. Seven soul. Seven Son and Daughter.

An illustration had been inked onto the lower half of the page. Yaldabaoth stood, arms wide, just as Maggie had drawn him, in a pool of water. Seven naked people, drawn in such a way that they looked like ghosts, hovered around him, three on one side, four on the other. A dark line connected each of their chests to the water. The figures had both male and female characteristics.

The page turned.

Upon the rebirth, He shall be vengeful and unharnessed. In His natural state, He shall seek only to destroy. Unless controlled, His rage shall reign until none will stand to contest him.

A sacrifice. A vessel. He shall live again.

The passage ended there, and the next chapter, though in the same Coptic Egyptian she'd just been reading, didn't decipher, as if the book only allowed her to read what it wanted.

CHAPTER 41

Louise smiled A crooked, half-wicked smile. "So, you finally admit it."

Teresa clamped her lips shut and nodded her head. Tears flooded her eyes, distorting the view of the basement horrors.

"I couldn't handle the crying." Teresa gasped and covered her mouth with her fingers. "She wouldn't stop. I left her alone. I don't know when she stopped crying. I swallowed a couple over-the-counter sleep aids. Washed them down with whiskey." She met Louise's eyes. "I just needed some sleep. Some alone time." She looked away again. "When I awoke, I found Derrick doubled over the baby . . . my Tiffany. He was—he was sobbing and rocking over her stiff body." The last words rode on a horrendous bawl. Big Bear had fallen on top of Tiffany.

Louise stroked her shoulder. "Good girl," she said. "Doesn't it feel nice to finally admit the truth—that your child died because you neglected her?"

Teresa couldn't deny it. Whatever she'd bottled up with that truth finally came out along with it. All this time she'd been lying, even to herself.

"How the hell did you get out of that?" Bram asked in a weak voice.

"The best lawyers," Teresa said. "They played up the post-partum depression angle. I wasn't charged with anything." Just years in Mountain View and the loss of herself and her medical license.

Sheriff McMichael never believed her innocence.

Too bad for him.

Louise stood and tossed the pruning shears onto a work bench.

"There's a first aid kit in that cubby." Louise pointed to the corner. "Bandage him up." She paused at the bottom of the stairs.

"A first aid kit?" Teresa moved the light around to examine Bram's hand. She shook her head. "He needs stitches, antibiotics." She moved to the workbench, picked up the shears. "A tetanus shot!"

"You'll find everything you need in the kit." Louise disappeared up the stairs.

The standard unit contained bandages, gauze, antibiotic ointment, and the like. A sterile package contained a curved needle with some cat gut sutures.

Teresa moved around behind Bram and looked at the mess Louise had left.

"I–I can't save the fingers."

"Do what you can." Bram's voice was low and gentle. His labored breathing moved his entire body. "Is there any morphine in there?" He grimaced. Or maybe it was a grin. She dug around and found a bottle of pills.

"All I have is Tylenol," she said. Bram nodded. She shook four into her palm and helped him swallow them down with some water.

"Cauterize the stumps," he said. "Smear some of that antibiotic ointment on the burns. Wrap everything up." He winced. "Fuck. My hand. It's on fire." He held his breath, then let it out. "At least it was the left one."

At that, he laughed, a low chuckle that crescendoed into a full-out belly laugh. Shortly after, the laughter turned to quiet sobbing.

Teresa moved behind him. He only had his index finger and thumb left. Where had the third finger gone? She doused his hand with hydrogen peroxide. Bram wailed as if she'd cut off another finger. The solution hissed and bubbled.

"Sorry," she said.

While the peroxide did its job, she searched for something she could use to cauterize the wounds. She found an old iron, doused it with alcohol, and plugged it in.

When it heated up, she brought it over to him.

"Brace yourself." She stuck the hot surface onto the bloody stumps. The skin hissed and let off an offensive smell that soon turned to rank burned meat. She hardly noticed his cries.

After bandaging his hand, she packed up the first aid kit in silence, turned off the television and the lamp.

"Thank you," Bram whispered.

Teresa cleared her throat. "I'm just doing my duty as a doctor. I may not be actively practicing, but I still took the Hippocratic oath."

Bram laughed. "You swore to do no harm, did you?" He spit on the floor. "You shouldn't be helping her. She's evil. She will turn on you."

Teresa went upstairs and bolted the door behind her. She stank of stress sweat. Fear. Louise was at the table.

"I think . . . I need to go home," Teresa said. She fiddled with the hem of her shirt.

"That's fine, dear doctor," Louise said. "Maggie has the book I'm after." She met Teresa's eyes and cocked her head to the side as if inviting Teresa to read her mind.

"You want me to steal it."

Louise righted her head and smiled. She took a sip of tea. "Naturally."

"Derrick—he'll have questions. When I get home." She swallowed hard. "What do I tell him?"

"The truth, of course."

Teresa let out an exasperated scoff. "I can't tell him the truth. He'll never believe me. It'll just start another fight." She held her forearms. "He hurt me—did I tell you that? Today, at the clinic. He marked me." She pulled up a sleeve to show Louise.

"I don't blame him," Louise said.

Teresa couldn't stop her mouth from dropping open. Louise moved from around the table, pulled Teresa's jacket from the coat rack, and guided her to the front door.

"Go home. Make amends. Even if you don't mean it. We need to keep things as normal as possible in order to succeed."

She opened the door and gave Teresa a gentle push onto the front porch. The door snapped shut.

Teresa looked at her watch. It was late. Perhaps Derrick had already gone to bed. Perhaps she could sneak in, shower, and climb into bed next to him without disturbing him. She zipped her jacket shut against the cold and wandered home.

* * *

Inside the house, she closed the door quietly behind her. All movement seemed amplified in the silent, sleeping house. She crept upstairs and peeked into Maggie's room. Maggie slept with reckless abandon. Her limbs hung over the edge of her mattress. Her blanket tangled around her legs. Teresa took a cursory look around the moonlit space but didn't see the book in its usual spot on the nightstand.

She tiptoed to the master bedroom and into the *en suite* bathroom. Once there, she let out her held breath and switched on the light. Her dirty face, smudged from sweat, looked back at her. Bram's blood speckled her sleeves. She peeled her clothes off and got into the shower, wincing when the water shrieked through the pipes.

After her shower, she pulled on a nightgown and slid into bed next to Derrick. He jerked awake.

"Teresa?" He groped under the covers for her. "Oh, thank God." He pulled her close to him, pressing his body against her. "I was so worried."

Teresa lay still. He wasn't mad at her. He wasn't mad she'd disappeared. He'd been worried. His lips found her neck and kissed softly.

"I'm so sorry," he whispered, his voice thick with residual sleep.

Teresa relaxed and melted against him. A smile slid onto her lips. The warmth of his body against hers sent a thrill through her.

She rolled over and faced her husband, held his face between her hands. His dark eyes searched hers. He didn't ask where she'd been. Instead he kissed her on the lips. He deepened the kiss and rolled her over on top of him.

Their typical, and rare, love-making sessions were usually hasty and habitual. They didn't hold the passion of their youth or the spontaneity. But this . . . *this* was like old times. His hands explored her body. He was slow and passionate, tending to her needs. When they'd finished, the briefest glimmer of her old self came back. The self before the hospital and years of living in a medicated state of numbness.

"I guess what they say is true," she said, surprised by her light tone.

"What's that?" Derrick kissed her shoulder.

"Make-up sex is the best."

He laughed. And she did too. The sound carefree. A sound Mother would have scorned.

Ladies don't cackle.

Forget Mother.

Teresa wouldn't let her mother's lessons destroy this joyous moment. Oh, she felt so free. She felt so . . . loved. Wanted. She kissed Derrick again, craving him now that he'd given up what she had desired for so long.

"I miss this," Derrick said.

"Me, too," Teresa nestled against him. His arm wrapped around her shoulder and pulled her tight.

"We can be like this again," he whispered.

Teresa nodded, smiling. Everything would be okay.

But her smile faded as the carefree Teresa melted away, replaced by who she was now. A murderer.

Everything wouldn't be okay. It would never be the same again.

CHAPTER 42

Teresa awoke with a start. The alarm clock flashed midnight. Did the power go out? Derrick's side of the bed was vacant, the covers thrown back. Faint light seeped through the blinds. She lay back against her pillow.

He must have let her sleep in. She didn't smile, though. She couldn't assume last night would fix everything. He, himself, had told her that.

What had he called it? An attempted roll in the hay?

Well, maybe that was all *he* needed.

Teresa dragged herself out of bed and shuffled into the bathroom, took care of the necessary, and applied some makeup.

"Hello? Anyone home?" she called.

Her voice sounded strange, echo-y and muffled at the same time. A disquieting stillness filled the house. She shivered and tugged her robe tighter around her body. The microwave clock also flashed midnight.

Teresa went into the front room where an old,

hand-wound Victorian clock sat on top of the piano with the silver-framed pictures. The clock had also stopped at midnight.

This couldn't be right. She held it to her ear and listened for the second hand to *tick tick tick* around the face. She set the clock down and backed away from it.

The room flickered. Teresa squeezed her eyes shut, then opened them. For a second, she thought she saw—

She ran to the front door and opened it.

A creek trickled in the early morning quiet. Glowing lost souls danced among the lodge pole pines, illuminating their trunks and the crooked tombstones. The sun hadn't even started to peek above the mountains.

In a daze, Teresa stepped onto the sagging front porch and down the three stairs. Her footsteps crunched on pine needles. She tried to pull her robe around her, but she no longer wore it. Instead, the same blood-stained clothes from the previous night covered her body. Not the previous night. This same night. How much time had really passed?

A few feet from the front porch, she turned around. Though she already knew what she would find, the sight of the abandoned funeral home brought dread and grief.

It hadn't been Derrick.

It was *him.*

She'd *fucked* Yaldabaoth.

"No." The sound moaned from her throat. She doubled over, covering her face with her hands.

This is a dream. A nightmare. You went home.

The night didn't dissolve around her. She didn't wake up.

"Mommy," Tiffany's voice whispered. The sight of her daughter made her stomach twist.

"What have I done?" Her voice gasped the words. A tear let loose from her blurry eyes and journeyed down her cheek. "What happened? I went home—" Her breath hitched in.

Tiffany came closer. So pale in the moonlight. Teresa only hoped she wasn't here to present another syringe.

"You did come home," Tiffany said, indicating the house behind her. "Yaldabaoth fixed the inside. He thought you would like it. Do you like it?"

Something in Tiffany's tone told Teresa she should say yes. She nodded, instead, afraid her voice would betray her.

Tiffany placed her cold fingers on Teresa's cheek and wiped away the tear.

"Good." Tiffany smiled. She pulled away and pirouetted with the lost souls. "It's a glorious night."

"I need to go home," Teresa said. "I have to go home."

Tiffany stopped. "You *are* home."

"This is not my home." Teresa stood and staggered toward the creek.

"I wouldn't do that if I were you." Tiffany sang from the trees.

Teresa didn't listen. She jumped across. Instead of

standing on the dirt road, she faced the abandoned house again. She turned and leaped over it again with the same result. And again. And again. Every time she tried to cross the creek onto the dirt road, she was back on the same side, facing the house.

I'm trapped.

"Let me out of here. Now," she yelled. Tiffany giggled from the darkness of the pines. The front door opened, and Yaldabaoth stepped into the moonlight.

"It is quite a glorious night, is it not?" His silky voice both terrified and delighted Teresa. It made her dizzy, distorted her thoughts. She wanted to run away from him. She wanted to run toward him. Teresa gripped the sides of her head and closed her eyes.

"Please, leave me alone," she whispered, covering her face with her hands.

Yaldabaoth's hands touched her arms, slid up to her shoulders. One cupped the back of her head. The other tilted her face up to his.

"You have work to do, my dear." He dropped the hand at her neck and produced a syringe.

"I can't," Teresa whispered.

"You can," Yaldabaoth said, his lips inches from hers. "And you will."

She closed her lids, squeezing tears out. His touch vanished. Teresa opened her eyes. He was gone.

One throbbing zoe line lay at her feet. She willed herself to follow it, but her legs wouldn't obey. Tiffany danced into her sight. She approached Teresa with wide, innocent eyes. The girl took Teresa's hand.

"Come on, Mommy. You can do it. I'm here to help you." Tiffany pulled Teresa down the length of the line. When they left the forest, Ruthie's mountain-lion-like shriek tore through the silent night.

"Oh, I forgot," Tiffany said. "Run."

Teresa wanted to lie on the ground. She could hardly walk, her legs trembled so hard. She didn't know what would happen if Ruthie caught up, but the sight of the mummified woman lurching after her was enough to pump adrenaline through her system and get her moving.

They ran toward town, then into the residential district. They followed the line and ended up on the front steps of Betty and Roger Berg's house.

She wondered which Berg would get it tonight.

"Open the door," Tiffany said.

Teresa jiggled the knob. It was locked.

Ruthie screamed—closer now.

Panic set in. Not knowing where Ruthie was made things that much worse.

Tiffany led Teresa around the house. Teresa peeked in the windows trying to see the continued zoe line inside, see where it led.

At the back of the house, Tiffany stood on her tiptoes and peered inside. Teresa looked. The red line crept under the blankets on a bed where Marcie Berg slept.

Teresa pressed her palms against the glass, praying the

window was unlocked. It slid. She boosted Tiffany up and inside, then launched herself, kicking her legs for leverage.

She dropped to the floor. Marcie tossed over in her bed and tugged the covers over her ear.

"Be careful," Tiffany said from the foot of the bed. "Her parents might wake up."

Teresa slid the window shut just as Ruthie appeared at the glass. She took a moment to catch her breath. Then she pulled back Marcie's blankets.

The zoe line ended in Marcie's young, flat stomach. Teresa plunged the needle into the young woman's belly.

Unlike Ruthie or Sheriff or Brent, Marcie didn't move a muscle.

Teresa pulled the plunger, sucking the milky red zoe into the barrel. Marcie's eyes flew open and turned black. The irises, the sclera, everything. But she didn't shrink or bloat or disintegrate.

When Teresa withdrew the needle, the young woman's eyes returned to normal. She moved her hand to her stomach where Teresa had stuck her and curled into a ball around it. A pained moan poured from between her lips.

Then the bleeding started.

Not bleeding like Teresa had seen in miscarriage or in birthing. Blood gushed from between Marcie's legs, soaking the girl's nightgown and sheets. Marcie gasped. Her mouth opened, and her face turned red. The cords in her neck went taut as if she was straining, pushing, giving birth. Tears trickled from her eyes. No sound came out, no sound went in.

Still, the blood poured. A broken dam.

Teresa looked at the syringe. What had she done? She hadn't thought twice about where the zoe line ended. Was Marcie pregnant?

Ruthie screamed at the window and clawed the glass, beat it with her bony fists. Teresa jumped.

"Goddammit!" A man's voice shouted from somewhere in the house. "George Riley, if that's you making all that racket, I swear to Jesus I'll have your hide."

The knob rattled.

"Marcia Victoria Berg, you open this door right this minute," Roger Berg hollered. Teresa looked at the window where the not-crushed side of Ruthie's face pressed against the glass, her thin lips pulled back in a vicious sneer.

Roger pounded on the door again. The whole thing shook in its frame.

Teresa cast about for a place to hide. She knelt and peeked under the bed. There was too much stuff under there.

"*Psst,*" Tiffany motioned Teresa over to a closet with slatted, accordion doors. They stepped inside, trampling on piles of shoes.

The door to the bedroom burst open just as Teresa eased the closet shut.

"Where is he?" Roger shouted. Teresa peeked through the slats and saw him approach Marcie's bed. "Jesus Christ!

Marcie!" He held her, then turned to the hallway. "Betty. Call 911," he yelled. "Something's wrong with Marcie. I think George must've done something to her. Oh, my baby. Please—what happened?"

Marcie's face had gone white. Her eyes stared at nothing in particular.

Check her pulse.

Teresa willed the words. She couldn't just stand by and watch someone bleed out, but she couldn't burst out of the closet to save the day either. There was nothing she could do except crawl back to Yaldabaoth and deliver the fourth soul.

With Roger's face buried in Marcie's hair, Teresa slipped out of the closet and scurried into the dark hallway. The hall light came on, blinding her. She dove sideways into the bathroom as Betty ran by with a phone pressed to her ear. Her shouts of Marcie's name joined Roger's wails.

"There's no answer! Doctor Hart isn't answering."

Teresa paused. Where was he, drinking with Ann?

"Dammit, Betty. I said 911, not Doctor Hart!"

Tiffany pulled Teresa into the hallway and toward the front door.

"I can help them," Teresa said, looking over her shoulder toward their cries.

"No, Mommy. You can't."

Outside, they ran back to the old house. Ruthie shrieked behind them, gained on them. Tiffany led the way. Her pale form glowed in the moonlight. Teresa's lungs burned.

Her legs burned. Her head swam with the flashing shock of instant regret. She could have helped them. She could go back now and help. Besides, she didn't want to go back to Yaldabaoth.

Ruthie's footsteps thumped behind her. Teresa glanced over her shoulder just as Sheriff McMichael, still bloated, crashed through the fence surrounding the neighbor's back yard.

Teresa had never run so fast in her life. Ruthie shrieked. It seemed like she was inside Teresa's head.

On the dirt road, Teresa turned and leapt over the creek. The lost souls bounced and bobbed among the tombstones. She fell against a marble epitaph to some long-lost ancestor of the town and caught her breath.

Inside the abandoned funeral home, Yaldabaoth stood by the pool, gazing into its still depths.

"Here, it's done." Teresa pushed the hypo into his hand. She turned to leave, but he grabbed her arm and pulled her against him.

"You're upset with me," he said, his breath—laced with lavender and honey and something unsavory—washed over her.

She pulled away from him. "You *deceived* me." She started for the door but turned back. "You made me . . . unfaithful." She reached for her throat, but he caught her hand.

"You knew the whole time," he said. "It was what you wanted."

Teresa backed away, shaking her head. "No. I didn't—I didn't know and I didn't want it. I just want to be happy. With my husband and our daughter." She cast around for Tiffany. "Where is my baby?"

Yaldabaoth laughed again. "She is in her room." He indicated a white door that had appeared on the cave wall. "Take a look." He was suddenly behind her, whispering the words into her ear, holding her arms in a gentle grip. A grip full of tethered power. She resisted the urge to lean back and press against him. He let go of her.

Inside was the nursery again. She knew it wasn't real. She stormed to the door, opened it, and stepped out into the hallway in her own house.

No, not her house. Still the cave. The cave of illusions. Yaldabaoth was toying with her. She went downstairs to the front door, and when she opened it, she was on her front porch, looking out onto the residential street.

Teresa's breath came in panicked gasps.

Where are you, really? Home? The cave? Mountain View?

She went back inside, and the stone walls reappeared.

"Stop this!" she screamed. Yaldabaoth's chuckle echoed, but he was nowhere to be seen.

"I have so much power over you, my dear," he said, suddenly behind her, stroking her arms again, breathing on her neck. "You are mine."

"Please," she said. "Please let me go home." Derrick would be worried. Or furious. She had to let him know she was okay. "I need to go home."

The room melted into the moldy interior of the abandoned house. She let out a sobbing gasp and ran to the door, into the forest, across the creek, onto the dirt road.

She glanced back at the house. It glared down at her. How had she ever thought the front steps looked like an inviting smile?

CHAPTER 43

The phone rang. Ann jerked awake. It rang again. She jumped up and ran to the kitchen. The clock on the microwave read 4:08. She picked up the receiver.

"Hello?"

"Detective Logan? It's Whitney? I'm the night receptionist at the station?"

"Oh . . . hi . . . What's going on?"

"I got a call from the Bergs? I guess something's happened to their daughter?"

"Marcie," Ann whispered.

* * *

Ann pulled on a clean pair of nitrile gloves and carried her kit to Marcie's room.

Flight for life had arrived shortly after she finished taking statements from Betty and Roger Berg. Ann was able to convince Roger that Marcie's state couldn't have possibly been drug induced, but he still heard a bump in the night that he swore was that damn Riley kid sneaking in. Betty rode in the chopper with Marcie, and Roger took the car to meet them in Aspen.

Ann surveyed Marcie's room. A desk sat against the wall with stacks of celebrity gossip rags and teen fashion magazines towering over a laptop.

She grabbed the camera out of her bag and set about following protocol for taking pictures.

By Marcie's bed, Ann dropped to her knees. The crispy substance lay in a line, shattered to pieces. She took several pictures of the stuff, then collected as much of the substance as she could in a little envelope. She pulled out the fingerprinting kit and got to work.

The inside of the window only came up with prints on the latch and the two areas where one might pull the window open or push it closed. Probably Marcie's. Outside, she dusted the exterior of the glass.

One full flat hand print revealed itself in the powder. Ann held her hand up to it for comparison and found it to be about the same size. Not George's then. His hands were like a bunch of bratwursts. Maybe Marcie? If she'd sneaked out, this was probably how she got back in. Ann collected the print on the tape and hoped the station had the equipment needed to analyze it. Otherwise, she'd be calling in a favor to an old friend.

She collected Marcie's laptop from the desk. If nothing else, she could compare any prints pulled from the machine with the ones from the window.

A piece of paper stuck out from under a stack of textbooks. Ann pulled it out and unfolded it. She gave a short laugh through her nose.

The Local Inquirer.

Photographed, Written, Compiled, and Printed by Brent Winter. How the community paper allowed him to use their equipment, Ann would never know. Someone scrawled a hand-written note across the top.

Meet me behind the library at noon tomorrow. Love, Pinky's Pal.

A secret note. Not so secret name, though. Ann shook her head. Good job, Brent. Now you're a suspect.

Ann flipped through the pages and found four pictures amongst the articles with ridiculous headlines: Ann herself, Louise in the middle of the diner with her arms spread wide, and Teresa Hart coming out of the old funeral home. Ann collected the newspaper as evidence.

A visit to Brent's house was definitely in order. Not just to question him, but to see if Pinky, in fact, was a victim in Yaldabaoth's grand scheme.

She also wanted to see Derrick, find out why he had been *unavailable*. Teresa, too. Maybe they were preoccupied with mending their relationship. She could only hope.

She finished collecting anything she felt was evidence and packed it out.

Next stop, the sheriff's department to drop everything

off. Tomorrow she would search the storage cell. She hoped if they had a microscope they had other equipment, too.

CHAPTER 44

Tuesday

Fingers tucked Teresa's hair behind her ear. She opened her eyes. Derrick pulled his hand back like she'd snapped at him. He sat on the edge of the couch with a cup of coffee in his other hand.

"Hey," he said in a soft voice. Teresa sat up and shifted away from him. Was it really him, or was she still trapped in the old funeral home, Twilight Zone, Hotel California?

"Hi." Her voice rasped. She cleared her throat. He handed her the cup of coffee. "What time is it?"

"Nine," he said.

"Maggie," Teresa glanced over her shoulder at the kitchen, worried about having failed to make breakfast and lunch for the child. Wondering how she'd slept through their morning preparations.

"I took care of her," Derrick said.

He picked up another mug of coffee from the table

and sipped it, staring straight ahead at the fireplace across from the couch.

"Gave her some lunch money and stopped at the bakery on the way to school." He glanced at her. "Where have you been?" His voice held tender curiosity, but the muscle in his jaw jumped.

"I was . . . I . . ."

"Don't lie to me, Teresa." Tenderness gone. He knew. He could smell her indiscretions. Yaldabaoth. He knew everything. No. He couldn't know. She bit her lip.

"After you *hurt* me," she said, sliding into a sitting position and holding out the wrist with the most bruising for him to see, "I went to a friend's house."

"A friend?"

You have no friends here.

"Yes." She smoothed her hand over her hair. Oh, God, what kind of mess was her hair right now? Her make up? She imagined she looked fresh out of a horror movie and glanced at her shirt. She remembered then. Coming home and throwing her bloody shirt in the trash. She'd pulled on one of Derrick's souvenir shirts from Steamboat Springs.

"I made a friend the other day."

"Who?"

"Is it so hard to believe I can make friends, Derrick?" She got up and edged toward the hall bathroom, but Derrick grabbed her wrist. He immediately let go when she shied away from him.

He sank onto the couch. Silence for one beat, two beats.

He stared into his coffee cup.

"I'm sorry," he muttered. "I didn't mean to hurt you."

"If you're going to apologize, at least have the decency to look me in the eye."

He didn't. She left.

The bathroom mirror reflected a not-too-horrible version of her usual self. Her makeup had managed to stay in place, and her hair, though a little mussed, held a sort of careless order to it. She shrugged. Not bad, actually.

When she came out, Derrick was in the hall.

"You look pretty," he told her. "By the way—I don't think I tell you enough."

She straightened her shirt and lifted her chin. "Thanks."

"I like it when you don't try so hard." He looked into her eyes. "I'm sorry—for bruising your wrists." He lifted his hand, and she watched it near her face. He tucked her hair behind her ear again and opened his arms to her.

Teresa scrutinized his face, his eyes, the faint scar on his chin from a frat boy drunk fest in college, before stepping into his embrace. He rested his cheek on the top of her head. He held her like that, wrapped in his arms, safe and comfortable and familiar.

She could forgive him, yes. She could forgive him for what he'd done. They could move on. A smile came to her lips. A real one. Not a prearranged version for appearances.

He shifted again and kissed the top of her head, took a deep breath, and let it out slowly. Something else was coming.

"I think we need to take a trip to Mountain View," he said in a soft voice. His arms tightened, as if predicting she'd pull away. She did and backed into the bathroom doorway. She gripped the frame.

"What? Mountain View? Why?"

"Just for an analysis. That's all."

"An analysis? What does that mean?" Her voice had gone shrill, and she hated the way it sounded. Fear tremors rippled through her.

"You haven't been yourself lately. You refused my offer of pharmaceuticals. I just want to help you." His face saddened.

"By doping me up? Is that what you want? You want the zombie version back?" She stormed past him to the kitchen and stood at the sink. "Four years, Derrick. Four years I spent in a drug-induced fog behind those walls. Two more out here, at home. I can't do that again. That wasn't living. That wasn't even *existing*." She swiped a hand across her forehead. "You can't tell me you want that version of me." Tears sprang to her eyes.

"I don't," he said after a few seconds. "I want the version before Tiffany . . . died." His shoulders dropped. He looked weary.

Teresa didn't know what to say. She didn't remember who she was back then. Her only clues were the pictures on the piano. Their smiling faces and endearing gazes. A distant memory of being happy and carefree. Six years spent in a drugged haze. In the end, after weaning off of all the anti-psychotics, anti-depressants, anti-*living* drugs, all she was left with was what her mother taught her about being a good wife.

Tiffany would restore their happiness. She snapped her eyes to Derrick.

"I can be that version again. I will be, soon," she said.

Three more.

She gulped.

His eyebrows came together. "What do you mean?"

"I'm working on some things," she stepped toward him. "Things that will bring us great happiness again."

He raised one eyebrow and cocked his head at her. "What are you working on?"

What, indeed.

"Just . . . things." She shrugged and toyed with her necklace.

Derrick let out a long, slow breath. "I need to get to the clinic." He turned, hesitated. "Whatever you're up to . . ." He sighed and didn't finish whatever he was going to say. "I'll see you later." He continued down the hall.

At the door, he turned again. "Consider what I said. About an analysis. Please?"

Teresa nodded, though she couldn't even consider it. She would never go back. Not even for an analysis. Derrick closed the door behind him.

Teresa paced. She needed to get this done or risk going back to her personal Hell. She needed to finish her business with Yaldabaoth, bring Tiffany back . . .

Then Derrick would know. He would see. They would be happy again.

She needed to speed things up. But how? Tiffany always came to her with the next task. She stopped pacing.

Yaldabaoth had sent Tiffany.

Though the thought of seeing him again so soon filled her with unbelievable dread, Teresa went down the hallway to the front door, pulled on her coat, and left the house.

CHAPTER 45

When Ann arrived at the station, George was already at his desk with his face smashed against his hand. She closed the door, and he heaved a great sigh.

"Hey, George," Ann said. "Where were you between three and four a.m.?"

"Sleeping." He lifted his head and looked at her. "Why?"

Ann pulled her chair over to his desk and sat near him.

"The station got a call from Betty and Roger Berg," she said. George sat up a little straighter. "Something's happened to Marcie."

"She's gone? Abducted like Sheriff and Ruthie?" George moved to stand, but Ann put a hand on his shoulder and made him stay.

"Hold on. Let me finish," she said. "Marcie is alive but in shock. She lost a lot of blood. Flight for Life took her to Aspen General Hospital." Ann considered her next words. Would George want to know? Would he care? "She lost the baby."

"I have to go to her," George said, rising again.

Ann stood and pushed him back down into his seat. She leaned over him, hands on the arms of his chair, a posture she'd used before when questioning stubborn suspects.

"Listen to me, George. You can't go to her. Her parents think you poisoned her or stabbed her or did something to cause this. To be honest, it makes sense why you'd do that, but I know deep down you never would."

He opened his mouth.

"Shush. Listen to me. I know you wouldn't, but there are implications. So tell me, right now—is there anyone who can vouch for where you were last night? Specifically between the hours of three and four in the morning?"

George blushed and nodded. He let out a lip-flapping breath.

"I was here most of the night," he said. "With Whitney. She's the night receptionist." He glanced at Ann, then away. His face turned full-on crimson.

"Were you here when she got the call from the Bergs?"

He shook his head. "I left close to four."

Ann went back to her own desk where she'd set the evidence.

"We played strip Go Fish." He grinned, Marcie's plight apparently forgotten.

Ann held up her hand. "I don't need the details, thanks."

"It was her idea."

"Please." She glanced at him out of the corner of her

eye. "Good for you," she muttered. "For . . . moving on. Or whatever." Ann pulled out the prints she'd collected. "Do we have any way to analyze fingerprints?"

"We have a scanner and an old computer in the sheriff's office," George said. "But no way to analyze stuff. That's what the lab is for."

Ann let out a long breath and went into the office. The beast of a computer sat on the floor. The monitor took up half the desk, the scanner the other half.

"It's slow," George said from the doorway. "But it works—after a while." He leaned against the frame. "What are you gonna do?"

"Scan the prints I collected and send them to a friend."

"FBI?" George seemed impressed. "CIA?"

Ann shook her head. "Not quite." She turned the computer on, and it whirred to life with a high-pitched whine.

A burp and a fart later and the operating system finally booted. George came around behind her.

"Click that icon there." He touched the screen, smudging the layer of dust. "The program for the scanner will open."

"Thanks." Ann clicked it and, after the computer percolated a pot of coffee, the software opened. She scanned the prints and waited while the processor rendered the images.

When they came up, she picked up the phone and looked at George.

"Give me a minute?"

He shrugged and left the office.

Ann dialed her ex-CBI friend's cell number. She chewed a hangnail on her thumb while the phone rang. Joey Rigsby could have been the top analyst in the state, possibly the country. He'd graduated from high school two years early, attended prestigious colleges, held a job with the CIA before CBI. Then, he got shit-canned for his penchant for marijuana and inability to keep secrets. His voicemail picked up, and while Ann left a message, he called her back. After their usual banter, he convinced her to have dinner with him the next time she was in Denver in exchange for hacking the various systems and running the prints.

Ann hung up and went out to her desk to examine the other evidence. George swiveled in his chair to face her.

"What else did you find?" he asked.

"I have her laptop, but listen, George." She touched her eyebrow. "I don't think you should help me with this case. It's too personal to you, and I don't want your perceptions to cloud your judgment."

He nodded along with her. "Okay, but I might be able to help you."

"If I run into anything you can help with, I'll ask."

"What do you want me to do then?"

"Don't you have other cases?"

He shrugged. "It's Harmony."

"Answer the phone if anyone calls. I have a feeling Rachel won't be coming back anytime soon."

Betty said Marcie didn't have a cellphone, due to the crappy service, so hopefully her laptop had something to go on. Ann pulled it out of the evidence bag.

George shuffled over to Rachel's seat and twisted back and forth in the chair.

Marcie's laptop prompted Ann for a password.

She tried *PinkysPal* and *BrentWinter* and even combinations of George's name, but none of them worked.

"Hey, George, do you know what Marcie might have used for a password?"

"Yeah," he said. He'd opened Solitaire. "PV6LUV."

Ann tried that. It worked.

"Thanks."

"Wait, it worked?" He turned around.

"Yep," she said.

"Our first kiss was in Pine Valley in June last year." He sighed. "I thought she might have changed it. Why did she have to cheat on me? Why'd she have to go and get pregnant and leave the test where I'd find it?"

Ann shrugged. "She's young, George. She doesn't know what she wants right now." Except Brent Winter, who Marcie also probably kissed in Pine Valley when she was there this past June, according to Betty.

Now logged into the computer, Ann opened Outlook.

Besides a whole lot of spam, there wasn't much. She clicked through some of the folders but found nothing interesting. Nothing from Pinky's Pal or Brent Winter. Nothing even from George.

"Marcie has an incredible lack of email," she said. "There's nothing in here even from you."

"Kids these days," he said, as if he weren't a kid himself. "With bad cell service, they write notes on newspapers or something silly like that." He turned to her. "I kept all the ones Marcie gave me."

Ann picked up the bag with *The Local Inquirer* in it. Pinky's Pal. There was a "contact us" address on the back. She jotted it down in her notepad, then went to the supply closet and stuffed a pair of latex gloves and some evidence bags into her pocket. Just in case.

"I'll be back later," she said, pulling on her coat.

George sighed. "I guess I'll be here . . . waiting."

"Is your radio on?"

He checked and nodded.

"I'll call you if I need anything, and you do the same."

CHAPTER 46

Ann walked past the clinic. She paused outside the door, then went inside.

"Derrick?" No answer. Ann took a few steps down the hallway. His muffled voice came from behind a closed door labeled Exam Room 1.

She sat in the waiting room and flipped through a *People* magazine from two months ago. Derrick came out a few minutes later, escorting a mother with her child. He gave her some instructions in a quiet voice, and the woman thanked him and left with her son.

"Ann," Derrick said, his voice full of surprise. "Are you ill?" He lifted an eyebrow and smiled.

Ann stood. "Where were you last night, between the hours of three and four in the morning?"

"Whoa. Okay." He rubbed the back of his neck and paced around the counter, putting the reception desk between them. "I was at home."

"Why didn't you answer the phone?" Ann asked.

His face turned hopeful. "Did you call me?"

Ann shook her head. "No. But Betty Berg did. No one answered."

"What happened?"

Ann dropped her head back and thought about how much she should tell him.

"Their daughter was sick and needed help," Ann said.

"Is she okay?" He turned around and rifled through the records behind him, pulled a chart, and opened it. "I should call them." He picked up the phone.

"No," Ann said. "Flight for Life came. They took her to Aspen General Hospital."

"Flight for—shit. What happened?" The phone fell back into the cradle.

"I'm not at liberty to discuss it."

"She is my patient. I have the right to know."

"Call the hospital. I'm more concerned at this point about where the hell you were. You are the only doctor in town and you didn't answer the phone?" Ann couldn't stop her voice from rising.

Derrick rubbed his neck again. His mark for discomfort, embarrassment. Good. His face flushed.

"I was drunk." He slumped into the chair behind the desk. "After you left, I found a bottle of scotch in the garage and had a few."

"You've got to be kidding me," Ann said.

"Nope. Not kidding. Things have been strained at home."

"Yeah." Ann scoffed. "I never pegged you as a guy who'd harm your wife." Anger boiled in her words. "What if Maggie had gotten hurt while you were sleeping it off?" Ann wondered if the End of Days would be triggered no matter how Sophia was killed, or if it had to be at Yaldabaoth's hand.

"I'm sorry." He didn't meet her eyes. "I guess I just needed a night off."

"You are a father," Ann said through gritted teeth. She wanted to scream it, to shout at him, but it wouldn't help anything. "You don't get nights off from that."

Derrick shrugged one shoulder and turned away from her. Ann bit back the response she wanted to throw at him.

His eyes landed on her. "I need to ask you a favor."

Ann crossed her arms and raised her eyebrows.

"I was wondering if you wouldn't mind watching Maggie tonight."

"Why?" She relaxed her arms.

"It's . . . private."

"If you're going to ask me a favor of this magnitude, I need to know why. It's my right, don't you think? I mean, since I cleaned up your mess last night and all."

Derrick looked from her left eye to her right, then down at the desk. He took a deep breath.

"I need to take Teresa to Mountain View." He looked up at her again. "For analysis. She's been acting strange."

"You did take away her coping mechanism."

A puzzled expression crossed his face.

“The furniture?” Ann prompted. “You took away her special room. What does she have left?”

Derrick’s eyes went to the desk again. “Oh. Right.” He sighed.

An uncomfortable silence settled on them. Ann didn’t know what to say, so she waited. Silence made people talk.

Derrick gazed at the space between them. “I’ve come to accept that Teresa will never be the woman I married ever again, but at the same time, every day that goes by I can’t help but hope maybe today she’ll smile again, maybe today she’ll give Maggie the same motherly affection as she did our Tiffany.” He let out a short, mirthless laugh. “The more I hope and the more I wish she would, the further away she seems to go. I don’t know what to do.” His pleading eyes darted up to Ann’s.

She let him sweat for a few seconds. “I’ll watch Maggie,” she said. “But not so you can deposit your wife at a mental health facility. I’ll do it so you can take the time to sort things out with her.”

And to keep Maggie safe.

Derrick nodded. His lips tightened into a single line bordering on a frown. Ann shook her head. The asshole just wanted to get rid of his wife. He didn’t want to deal with her. Ann hoped it wasn’t because she was back in town.

“There will never be anything between us,” she said, to be certain. “I just want to put that out there in case you think there will be.”

His mouth opened.

Ann held up her hand. “You need to work things out with Teresa.”

He closed his mouth and nodded. “Maggie gets out of school at three. I’ll go home and get some of her things together.” He frowned. “Can I drop her off at your house? In case Teresa’s home?”

Ann nodded and left before he could say anything else.

Outside, she took in a long pull of crisp air before turning toward Brent’s house. An unsettled feeling drifted down on her. On the one hand, Maggie was the person Ann needed to protect. What better way to protect her than to babysit? On the other hand, she didn’t know the first thing about the care and feeding of small children.

She’d have to go to the grocery store. While Ann could live on a sixer of her favorite brew and a frozen entree, a seven-year-old child could not. They needed nutritious stuff. Like fresh vegetables.

Ann rounded the corner and peered at the house numbers. Brent’s was on the left. She went up on the porch and raised her hand to knock.

The door wasn’t latched.

“Hello?” she called. “Castle County Sheriff’s Department. Is anyone home?”

A dog—big by the sound of it—barked and lumbered out of a room down a main hallway to greet her.

Don’t show fear. Ann stood her ground. The dog trotted to her and sat at her feet. It looked up at her, pawing the air near her leg. Dried blood and small cuts marred the top of its head.

"Pinky?" Ann said, crouching down. The dog's ears perked, and she cocked her head to the side. So, Pinky wasn't a victim after all.

Why did Maggie draw—

Ann stood so abruptly Pinky barked and went on high alert. Then she relaxed and looked up at Ann with a big, pink-mouthed grin.

"Where's Brent?" Ann asked the dog. "Why do you have blood on your nose?"

Pinky ran down the hall. Ann grabbed a poker from the fireplace and cleared the living room and the dining room.

In the kitchen, the glass on the sliding door was shattered, which coincided with the cuts on Pinky's head. The poor dog had been left outside.

She crept down the hallway, where she cleared a bathroom, an exercise room, and master bedroom. The last room was the one Pinky had come out of. It reeked of stale pot, despite the cracked window. Pinky was licking the carpet. Ann pushed her away, but the dog was persistent. Ann shoved the beast out of the room and closed the door.

A brownish mark stained the rug. Ann wondered if the dog had defecated there. She'd heard of some dogs eating their own feces and grimaced. The room didn't smell like shit, though. It smelled like rancid meat.

She crouched down for a closer look.

The indescribable and distinct scent of death came from the carpet.

To the side of the stain, nestled among the thick pile, sat a molar.

CHAPTER 47

Teresa sprinted to the abandoned house. Inside, the walls melted into the cave. She let out a relieved breath.

"Yaldabaoth," she said, "I need to speak with you."

The walls swirled and the nursery he'd constructed for her appeared. He sat in the rocker with his fingers tented before his face—his eyes, as always, full of sexual malice.

"My dear, dear Teresa." He stood, and a wicked grin slithered onto his lips. "Back for more so soon?"

She backed away from him. "I need to discuss speeding up the process."

He gasped in mock surprise. "Just last night you were over this whole charade."

"I'm over *your* charade. Your deception." Teresa peered into the empty crib. "Where is my Tiffany? Let me see her."

Yaldabaoth approached her. "You don't need her right now." He slid the back of his fingers down her cheek. Teresa took in a gasp of air at his touch but pushed his hand away.

"How can I get this done faster? Can I take more than

one a night?"

Desperation clawed at her insides at the very thought of returning to Mountain View. She couldn't go back there. She wouldn't. She would rather die.

"You send Tiffany to me. What drives your decision to send her?"

He didn't answer but watched her thoughtfully. He seemed to be enjoying her desperation.

"Some were at night, one during the day. What makes you decide when?"

"That is hardly important," Yaldabaoth said. "I am impressed by your desire to succeed, to finish. Please, come." He guided her to the door, and they stepped out of the nursery into her own formal dining room, complete with the table and chairs she'd picked out back when they first moved in.

He pulled a chair out for her to sit. She accepted, and he sat across from her.

"You need not know the ins and outs of this," Yaldabaoth said. "You only need to know that every time you give me a soul I am that much closer to the powerful being I once was, that much closer to giving you what you seek."

"What happened to you?"

"My mother. She cast me from her. She sent me here, to Tartaros. It was a misunderstanding. I took some of her light. I needed it to live." He leaned forward and clasped his hands on the table. "When my mother sent me away, I was but a shred of my former self. A wisp. A fragment. A fractioned soul." His voice had grown distant.

"But then, I used her small amount of light and multiplied it. With each creation, I gained more power. First, I created seven heavens. Next, seven sons and daughters, then they too multiplied by seven more. I took my power outside of the seven heavens and formed the material world."

Teresa knew better than to yell blasphemy like she had with Louise.

She met his eyes, and for once, she saw more than evil. There was a sad hope. She leaned forward and almost touched his hand, but she pulled back before the motion carried her away.

"My mother has always been so much more powerful than I." He looked away from Teresa. She could relate. His jaw twitched, and when he looked at her again, the hope and sadness were replaced by rage. "She will pay."

"The sooner to bring you to power, then?" Teresa ventured.

"Yes. Yes, of course." He flipped a hand. "But you must understand." He stood and pulled her to her feet. "The zoe is strong. It takes time for me to absorb it. To truly revel in the ecstasy." He pulled her close to him and tilted her chin. "You understand—don't you?" He lowered his lips toward hers but didn't kiss her.

She closed her eyes and yearned for him to close the small gap, but at the same time her mind screamed in terror.

"Yes," she whispered. He released her.

"Tiffany will appear when the time is right."

The cave reappeared, and he pointed toward the doorway.

Outside, she bent over and gripped her knees. Her body, heated by Yaldabaoth's touch, shook with pleasure and fear. He was right. He had *so* much power over her.

With no way to speed up the process, Teresa returned home. Derrick's threat of taking her back to Mountain View loomed in the forefront of her mind.

"I can't live that way." She picked up the pace and made it home in less than ten minutes.

In the kitchen, she picked up the phone and called her mother. It rang three times before her mom answered.

"Hello, Teresa. What have you gotten yourself into now?"

Teresa ignored her mother's snide remark.

"Derrick wants me to go back to Mountain View for analysis. I can't go back there, Mom. I don't know what to do."

"You've angered your husband. You need to make things right with him. He is your topmost priority. A happy husband is a happy home." Recycled advice. She'd heard the same so many times in her life and on the phone these past few days.

"Yes, but . . ."

The front door opened, and Derrick walked in. "Oh, hey. I forgot my lunch—who are you talking to?"

"I have to go." Teresa hung up.

"Who was that?" Derrick asked.

"None of your business." She crossed her arms.

"Tell me who you were talking to."

Teresa lifted her chin and tightened her lips.

"Was it your new friend? Who is she?" Funny he would assume her new friend was *female.*

Teresa relented. "I was talking to my mother, if you must know. I called her earlier in the week, after you took the baby's furniture, and apologized for the years of silence. I had to talk to *someone.* Since you seem to believe I *have no friends.*"

Derrick's face turned white and his mouth dropped open. Was it that much of a shock that she would call her mom? He closed his mouth and swallowed. Teresa actually saw and heard his Adam's apple bob up and down.

"What's wrong? You look like someone danced on your grave."

"Teresa." Derrick's voice was low and soft. It was his doctor's voice. She hated when he used that voice on her. "You can't have called your mother."

Teresa tightened her crossed arms. "And why not? I have every right to call my family if I want to."

"No, it's not that you're not allowed . . . It's just . . . Teresa . . . your mother is . . ." He swallowed. "She's dead."

CHAPTER 48

Ann pulled the gloves on and collected the tooth. In the bathroom, she grabbed a couple of cotton swabs from a glass jar on the counter. She used them to collect a few samples of the stain in the carpet, specifically a chunk Pinky had missed. Ann didn't want to jump to conclusions, but it resembled subcutaneous fat.

The dog whined and pawed at the door. Ann examined the cotton swab samples. It could be blood. Blood mixed with dog saliva.

A guttural lurching sound came from the other side of the door. Ann opened it just as Pinky threw up the contents of her stomach. Swimming among the pieces of bloated kibble and clumps of undigested grass were more teeth and gobs of other unrecognizable substances.

Ann put her hand over her mouth and turned away. The task at hand required some assistance. She pulled the radio from her belt and pressed the talk button.

"George. I need backup at Brent Winter's address.

Bring a kit." She waited. "George, do you copy?"

"Oh, hey, Ann. Yeah, I copy. I'll be right over after I beat this game of Solitaire."

"No. You'll be here immediately. When I request backup, drop what you're doing and get over here."

George arrived minutes later in the station vehicle. Ann was on the front porch. She'd pushed Pinky into the back yard and barricaded the door with some chairs. She knew dogs sometimes liked to recycle their food—or owner—if that's what they vomited up. She closed her eyes and took a breath. No speculating.

"There's a pile of dog vomit in the hallway," Ann said. "I need it for analysis."

"You want me to collect vom—" George gulped. "—it?"

Ann snatched the kit from his hands, dropped to one knee, and opened it up. She sorted through the supplies inside, found a mask, and put it on. Hopefully it would block the smell. After giving George a disparaging look, she went inside and got to work on the puke.

After they'd taken photos and collected everything worth collecting, including more of the like-human-umbilical-cord substance, they returned to the station with Pinky panting in the back seat. Ann parked and cleared her throat, dispelling George's disquieting silence.

"I'm assuming what we found belongs to Brent in some capacity." She opened the door. "I'd like you to drive the evidence to the Pine Valley Hospital and drop it off with a lab tech named Melissa. Tell her I sent you. Ask her to check for DNA against this." She handed him a hair sample she'd taken from Brent's brush in the bathroom. "If the DNA matches Brent's, we'll need to contact his parents to inform them he's . . . missing."

"You hesitated. You don't think he's missing, do you?"

Ann didn't answer.

"His dog . . ." He gulped. "Did she eat him?"

Ann stared straight ahead.

George turned in his seat and looked directly at Ann. She glanced side-long at him.

"Tell me Pinky didn't eat Brent." Tears wet his eyes. "Please. Even if you don't think it's true, just say it. I need to hear those words right now, out of *your* mouth." He glanced over his shoulder at the dog in question, who grinned the way only pit bulls could.

"She didn't eat him." Ann got out and opened the back door to let Pinky out and grabbed the box of non-bio evidence. She waved an ashen-faced George off to Pine Valley.

Ann went inside and set the box on her desk. She filled a bowl with water and set it on the floor by the kitchenette. Pinky ran to it and lapped frantically. She lifted her head, and liquid dribbled from the corners of her substantial mouth.

"You're with me until I figure out what to do with you," she told the dog. Pinky cocked her head to the side.

Marcie's copy of *The Local Inquirer* with the note from Brent sat on her desk. Inside were pictures of two suspects, clear as day, but they seemed too obvious. Louise and Teresa Hart. Motive? Libel, of course. Brent couldn't expect to do a false write-up without consequences, especially when those people being written about were both, well, crazy.

Suspect number three. Ann sighed. George Riley. He had motive for Marcie and Brent. He also had a set of keys to Sheriff McMichael's house.

She wondered how often Brent published *The Local Inquirer* and what it usually contained. Perhaps an earlier edition had more clues. She found the number in the phone book and dialed.

An elderly male voice answered.

"Hello, this is Ann Logan. I'm helping out a local case. Can you tell me how often Brent Winter publishes *The Local Inquirer*?"

"Annie Logan, the little girl who grew up to be a hero?"

She didn't say anything. Instead she cleared her throat and sniffed.

"It's random. He'll call me about a week before to let me know when he has enough content. Then we coordinate," Mr. Newspaper said. "That Brent Winter. What a character. He comes up with some pretty funny stuff, doesn't he?"

"Oh, sure." She didn't agree. "When was the previous one printed?"

"Let me check." The sound of movement and a drawer opening and closing came through the line. "Before the latest edition . . . looks like it was about four months ago."

"Did it include any pictures?"

"There's one of Louise Marga, but he's always got pictures of her." The rustling of a page flipping. "There's a picture from a town hall meeting—haven't had one of those in a while, until this week that is." He paused. "Caption calls 'em a local cult discussing how to take over Castle County." He laughed too loud.

"Anyone in particular stand out in that photo?" Ann asked.

"Louise Marga, again, but she's kind of all over the place around town, you know."

"How often does Louise feature in Brent's paper?"

"Every issue has a picture of her, I'd say."

"What about Teresa Hart? Is she in the town hall photo?"

"Teresa Hart?" He sounded confused. "Oh, you mean the doctor's wife. Let me see."

She could almost see his eyes scanning the picture. Maybe he held the page close to his nose for a better look.

"No, the Harts aren't present."

"Do you happen to recall what the actual town meeting was about?" Ann asked.

"It came out in June so probably upcoming summer events."

"Thank you so much for your time," Ann said.

"My pleasure. You stay safe."

"I will." She hung up and tucked the bagged copy of *The Local Inquirer* out of sight.

Louise shot to the top of Ann's suspect list. Another visit to the old loon's house would definitely be in order. But until she had solid proof, she was at a loss. How and where could she find more proof?

Right on cue, the phone rang. Pinky barked and ran to the door. Ann jumped, startled by both the phone ringing and Pinky's reaction.

She picked up the phone on her desk.

"Castle County Sheriff's Department, Ann Logan speaking."

"Are you a detective or a receptionist?" Joey's voice came over the line.

"Short-staffed. What do you have?"

"Fingerprints. Let's see . . . I'd email you my findings, but they are way too big, and you just have to see everything."

"Whose fingerprints were on the window?" That was all Ann needed to know.

"You're gonna love this," Joey said. His voice held a note of accomplishment. "After I ran the print, I did some extra digging. Found even more gold. You have to read the entire dirty write-up."

"Tell me who it was, and I promise I'll read the whole file."

"Let me give you some highlights."

Ann grumbled. "Fine. But you know you're obstructing justice by not telling me."

"Yes. But I don't care. Let me have this moment." He cleared his throat. "The perpetrator is a woman."

Check for both Teresa and Louise.

"She has had an extended stay in a loony bin twice in her life."

Ann didn't know about Louise, but she knew Teresa had been in Mountain View at least once.

"Those places were easy to hack. You'd think with confidential patient info they'd have better internet security systems in place, or at least have a firewall that's water tight like a frog's ass." She heard the shrug in his voice. "Their ignorance is my gain."

"Tell me more," Ann said through her teeth.

"Here we go—you ready for this?" He cleared his throat again. "The first time she went to the funny farm was after her mother died. The possible suspect was fifteen years old at the time. Mummy took too many lorazepams with too much whiskey. Maybe on purpose, maybe on accident. Maybe the fifteen-year-old daughter did it."

"Go on," Ann said.

"The second time she went was after her baby died."

Ann hit the top of her desk with her flat palm. "Teresa fucking Hart."

"Come on. You stole my thunder."

Joey sent her the files via file transfer. While she waited, she made another pot of coffee, played four games of Solitaire on the dispatch computer, checked the time every two minutes, and finally, a folder called, "You Can't Make This Shit Up" appeared.

Inside were the files Joey hacked right out of Mountain

View. Teresa's haunted past. Every single piece of it, complete with news articles from reputable newspapers, stories from gossip rags, police records, and photographs of her family. Joey had also included the fingerprint analysis.

Ann didn't know if a hacker's work would hold up in court, but for now, Ann needed Teresa in custody. She selected every file and hit print. Then she pulled on her jacket and grabbed the keys to the station vehicle.

When she stepped outside, her skin ached from the cold. No, not her skin. Ann pulled up her sleeve. Her veins glowed. Her blood tingled.

Maggie was in trouble.

CHAPTER 49

Mother? Dead?

Teresa snatched the phone from Derrick's hand and hit redial.

Three obnoxious tones rang out, then a robotic voice.

"We're sorry, your call cannot be completed as dialed. Please check the number and dial again."

She punched the numbers in. Then again. Then again. She was about to dial one more time when Derrick took the phone from her unyielding hand.

"She passed away when you were a teenager. Remember?" Derrick said in his giving-bad-news-to-a-patient voice.

Teresa turned away from him. Suppressed memories swirled out of the depths of her mind.

Her mother dead in the bathtub with an empty bottle of generic Ativan and an empty glass of whiskey on the bathroom floor.

A tear slithered down her cheek. She wiped it away.

Derrick took her by the hand and pulled her carefully toward him, then shifted his hand to her elbow.

"It's okay," he said, stroking her back. "Let's go out to the car, okay?"

She nodded but didn't know why they needed the car. They only used the car when they went grocery shopping. Was he taking her grocery shopping? Now?

"Okay." Shock tightened her throat. It came out a strangled whisper. Though she wasn't sobbing, tears dribbled from her eyes.

Derrick helped Teresa into the car and fastened her seatbelt for her. She stared out the window as he drove out of town.

"It's not true, is it?" Teresa asked. "I just talked to her on the phone."

Derrick's lips tightened. He didn't answer. Concern lined his forehead.

The car passed the sign wishing farewell to those who had visited Harmony. She turned in her seat. The other side of the sign welcomed people with a goofy looking bear wearing a hard hat and headlamp and holding a pickaxe.

The sign disappeared into the distance. They weren't going grocery shopping. Teresa forced her heart rate to stay steady.

"Where are we going?" Teresa stared at the side of Derrick's face.

His eyes shifted to her, then straight ahead. He gripped the steering wheel tighter.

"Derrick, tell me. I demand to know where you're taking me."

She couldn't stop her pulse from rising, her mouth from going dry. She already knew the answer, but one part of her hoped it wasn't true.

"Tell me." She pulled on his arm. The car swerved.

"Teresa, goddammit." He straightened the car.

Teresa slouched into her seat and crossed her arms.

After a few miles, he turned down an all-too-familiar winding road. The road to Mountain View. Teresa sat straight up.

"No." She shook her head. "You can't take me there. You can't!"

"Among other things, you've been talking to your dead mother on the phone. Something isn't right." He turned on the radio and tuned in to the local rock station, boosting the volume a little higher than necessary for casual listening.

"Don't turn the radio on to drown me out." Teresa jabbed the off button. "You can't do this to me," she said, hating the threat of hysteria in her voice. "Please don't do this."

He didn't care about what this would do to them, to her. He didn't love her anymore. He wanted to get rid of her so he could be with Ann. Ann, Derrick, and Maggie. The perfect family for this perfect little stupid town.

She reached for the emergency brake, desperate to stop the car somehow. Derrick slapped her hand away and glared at her.

She couldn't get a full breath. Though she hadn't had a hysterical breakdown in years, she remembered the first signs of one.

"I can't breathe," she said.

Something touched the back of her left arm. Teresa looked over her shoulder. Tiffany, buckled into the seat behind Derrick, waved to her.

"Hi, Mommy," she whispered. She held out her hands and presented Teresa with a hypodermic needle.

Blessed child. Blessed Yaldabaoth.

Teresa took the syringe.

"Would you turn around and sit still?" Derrick's voice was full of agitation. "What are you looking for back there?"

Teresa faced forward.

Out of the corner of her eye, Derrick's zoe line pulsed from his chest, oozed across the center console, and ended in her lap. A heavy living weight across her thighs. The cold glass of the hypo's barrel calmed her heart and lungs.

"I won't go back," she said in a steady voice.

"You have no choice," he said.

"I won't, Derrick. I can't. And I won't—I refuse!" She yelled the last word and, at the same time, twisted in her seat and plunged the needle into Derrick's chest.

The car swerved, tossing Teresa against the passenger side door. Derrick's eyes were wide, his mouth opened and closed as if he couldn't get any air. His hands on the wheel managed to get the car back on the road.

"What . . ." blood dribbled from his lips.

Teresa grabbed the plunger and pulled.

The car swerved again, went off the road, careened down a hill still spotted with clumps of snow.

Just as the barrel finished filling with Derrick's zoe, the car smashed into a tree. Even with her seatbelt on, Teresa smacked her head against the window, and the world around her blurred.

The familiar *whump* of a fire igniting sent a surge of adrenaline through her.

She fumbled for the door handle, her vision still foggy, got the door open, and fell into the grass.

She managed to crawl a few feet away before her world faded to black.

* * *

When Teresa came to, she didn't know where she was. The scent of smoke and barbecued meat assaulted her nostrils.

Camping? They'd never gone camping. Why now?

She sat up and rubbed her head. Her hand came away with blood on it. The barrel on the syringe warmed her other palm. The zoe inside swirled and pulsed.

She peered at the car and blinked a few times trying to remember what happened.

A mass sat in the driver's seat.

Teresa stood up so fast the blood rushed from her head,

and she nearly fell to her knees. Derrick's burned form. Not moving. Of course he wasn't moving. He was dead. She approached the car and looked in the back seat to see if her baby was okay. But Tiffany was gone. A sigh of relief. Then a wave of grief washed over her. Teresa dropped to her knees and put her hands over her face.

I've killed my husband. He's gone. All this work to make him happy—and now he's gone.

A sob escaped her. Movement from the car. She snapped her attention to Derrick. He shifted. Alive?

She dropped her hands. He turned his head, the movement jerky, and faced her. His eyes, which should have melted in the fire, were clouded white. Blind. Teresa's strangled cry caught in her throat. She flailed backward, tripped, and landed on her rear. Derrick sniffed the air in her direction. Then, with the same halting movement, he lifted his arms and reached for her. The center console kept him trapped. She reached up and closed the passenger door and crab-crawled backwards until the distance between her and the car felt safe.

When she got to her feet, her head throbbed with a probable concussion.

The sun had sunk low in the sky, casting ominous shadows. Teresa slipped and stumbled up the hill they'd careened down. At the top, she went back to town.

After she passed the sign welcoming her to Harmony, she stopped. Something was missing. Her hands felt empty.

The syringe. "Oh, God." It was gone. She looked back toward the crash site.

Petulant tears sprang to her eyes, and she bawled for a moment before regaining her composure.

She swiped a stray hair from her forehead only to find it stuck in the blood on her head, so she ripped it out with an angry shout. She stomped her feet, knowing she acted like a child, but all she could think about was slipping into a steamy bath and rinsing away the day's woes.

You just killed your husband—is that really just one of the day's woes?

Maybe she didn't want to turn Derrick over to Yaldabaoth. Maybe she could find the syringe and inject his zoe back into him.

A charred mess. He'd never look the same. What would the town think? Oh! The town would love her. She would stay with him even though he was horribly disfigured. A monster.

They would welcome her back. Her place in life would be restored. They would wash their hands of the baby's death in light of her devotion to her husband.

A smile made its way onto her lips but quickly vanished. A tear slid down her cheek, and her face contorted into what she knew was a horrendous visage.

Who would take care of Maggie now?

You have to take care of her.

She started walking toward town.

Maybe Maggie is next.

The thought startled her. She couldn't take a child.

You took Marcie's baby.

Teresa gripped her stomach and doubled over. She vomited foamy bile into a bush on the side of the road.

When was the last time she ate?

"I need my mommy," she whispered. Mother was gone, too. Teresa had no one. Nobody to help her, to take care of her, to love her.

Except Tiffany. Except Yaldabaoth. She had to go to him. She shook her head. To *them*. Tiffany needed her.

With renewed motivation, she set off toward the abandoned funeral home. If for no other reason than to regain a tremulous sense of purpose.

CHAPTER 50

"Hold on, Maggie," Ann whispered. Her first thought was Teresa was hurting her. Ann grabbed her radio while she maneuvered the old Jeep toward the Hart residence.

"Ann to George," she said.

"Yeah?" George responded.

"Be on the lookout for Teresa Hart," Ann said. "She is our prime suspect in the missing persons case. Likely armed, definitely dangerous."

"Is that a BOLO?" George asked, excitement in his voice.

"Yes. I'll radio you soon with more information." Ann pulled into Derrick's driveway and ran to the door. She pounded on it with the side of her fist. "Derrick!" she yelled. He was supposed to stop here to get Maggie's overnight stuff. Ann tried the knob. The door opened. She burst inside.

"Maggie?" she called. She held her breath and listened. No sound of anyone home, just the tick of a clock somewhere nearby.

The phone rang. Ann jumped. The answering machine picked up.

After the beep, a voice said, "Hello, this is Harmony Elementary calling. We have Maggie here . . ." Ann ran out the door, slamming it behind her. She jumped into her truck and hauled ass over to the school.

Maggie Hart stood outside with a woman about Ann's age. Tears streamed down Maggie's cheeks. When her teary eyes landed on Ann, Maggie ran to her and wrapped her arms around Ann's waist. The glow and the ache in Ann's veins ceased. The mark continued to burn.

"Daddy didn't come get me from school. No one came. My teacher took me home, but no one is there, so she took me back here. Where is my daddy?" Her words came bawling out of her, full of desperate fear. She looked up at Ann, and Ann's heart shattered.

This poor child. Stuck in the middle of crazy and crazier with the literal weight of the world on her shoulders.

Ann dropped to a squat, and Maggie wrapped her arms around Ann's shoulders, sobbing hot breath against her neck.

"It's okay, Maggie," Ann said. "I'm going to take care of you until they come back, okay?" She felt Maggie's head nod and heard a muffled agreement.

"Derrick Hart called the school earlier and said you would be picking Maggie up today," the woman said.

"Would have been nice if he told me I was supposed to

do that," Ann said in a tight voice.

That son of a bitch.

"We tried calling the number he left for you, but it didn't go through." She shrugged.

"Thank you. I'm sorry there was a miscommunication." She took Maggie's hands and extracted them from around her. Maggie took a step back and hitched in several breaths.

"Everything's going to be all right, okay?" Ann told her.

Maggie twisted her fists in her eyes and nodded.

"Let's go to your house and get some overnight stuff."

She nodded again. Ann stood and took the girl's hand.

As they drove to the Hart residence, Ann tried to contain her anger. She'd told Derrick to work things out with his wife. Not only did he not listen—and why should he? She wasn't the boss of him—he'd put his daughter at risk. He put *humanity* at risk.

On the other hand, if Teresa truly was behind the disappearances—murders—a mental health facility was exactly where she belonged. Ann was almost grateful. Almost.

"Why didn't they come get me?" Maggie asked with a sniffle.

"I'm sure there's a good reason." Ann followed the street into Harmony's suburbia. At Maggie's house, she parked in the driveway and went inside.

"Socks, underwear, clothes, toothbrush," Ann said. Maggie ran upstairs. Ann wandered into the front room and perused the pictures on the piano. Teresa and Derrick seemed like a happy couple in all of the images. She lifted one that sat in the middle. A photo of Teresa and their baby. She seemed so happy. Ann supposed a lot of women suffered from post-partum depression on the inside but hid it on the outside at the risk of letting it break them open.

Maggie clomped down the stairs behind her. "Got my teethbrush." She giggled. "I call it a teethbrush because I have more than one tooth." Finding her own joke so funny, she threw her head back and guffawed.

Ann couldn't help but laugh with her. She ushered Maggie back into the Jeep.

"I need to run by the station," Ann said. She hoped the printer had handled the massive print job. "Then dinner—and then I'm taking you to someone who is excited to see you."

"Who?" Maggie asked. "I want to stay with you."

"It's a surprise," Ann said. They got to the station a couple minutes later. Pinky greeted them with a *woof*. Maggie froze.

"Pinky?" she said. The dog bounded toward her and licked her face. Maggie squealed with delight and hugged the dog's head.

"I saw you in my dreams. You smashed through the glass." She stroked Pinky's scabbed-over cuts, then sobered and looked up at Ann. "Brent's gone, isn't he?" Her eyes filled with renewed tears.

Ann didn't know what to say. She cleared her throat and

went to the printer. By the grace of whatever, the station had a laser printer—not a dot matrix like she'd expected. Joey's hacked documentation from the mental institution Teresa went to as a kid and from Mountain View sat in the tray. She grabbed the missing persons case file from the desk and stuffed the print job inside.

"Are we bringing Pinky with us?" Maggie asked. She was on the floor with the dog's big head in her tiny lap. Pinky rolled slightly onto her back and opened her mouth. Her tongue flopped out as she gazed adoringly at Maggie.

"Please? I love her." Maggie wrapped her arms around Pinky.

Ann grimaced. Maggie may have known Brent was gone, but she didn't know how he went or what happened to his remains thereafter. So much inside of her said *no, leave the dog*, but Maggie's smile and Pinky's obvious contentment at having a child mauling her . . . Ann would just keep a close eye on the dog.

Ann found a rope in the storage cell to use as a leash. She tied it around Pinky's collar. Maggie climbed in the Jeep while Ann loaded Pinky into the back.

Behind the wheel, Ann glanced at Maggie, whose eyes were full of tears. She hitched in a shaky breath.

"Three people," she whispered.

Four, Ann thought. But she wasn't going to go there.

"It's okay," Ann said. "Don't cry. I'm here. You're safe."

* * *

Ann microwaved a frozen dinner tray for herself and threw together some noodles and sauce she found in the cupboards for Maggie. While Maggie slurped her spaghetti, Ann perused the file, dog-earing pages to come back to after she had Maggie safely with Raghib.

Maggie finished a second helping of spaghetti, and Ann cleared away the plates.

"I know you want to stay with me," Ann said. "And I really wish you could, but I have a lot of work to do." She tossed their napkins into the trash.

"I'll be quiet. I won't bother you," Maggie said. "Please, Ann."

"You'll be safe with this person, and I'll know if you are hurt or scared." She pulled her shirt aside and showed Maggie the mark again. "Even when you were scared and sad at the school, I knew."

Maggie wiped away a single tear that had fallen from her right eye.

"I can get to you in minutes if anything happens."

"Promise?" Maggie took in another hitching breath.

Ann nodded. Maggie grabbed her backpack with her overnight stuff, and they went out to the Jeep. A little way into town, Ann turned south toward Harmony B&B.

CHAPTER 51

Teresa hurried down the sloppy dirt road at a frantic pace. She stumbled up the front porch of Yaldabaoth's house and went inside. The walls didn't shift and transform. The cave didn't melt into view.

She didn't have the zoe. Yaldabaoth must be angry.

A figure emerged from the shadows down a hallway near the closet door.

"Who's there?" Teresa asked, peering into the darkness.

"It's me, Doctor Hart," Louise said.

Teresa took a step toward her and paused. That's why the cave didn't appear. Louise was there. Yaldabaoth only came to Teresa. Only *she* was special enough to talk to him. To touch him.

"What are you doing here?" Teresa asked in a voice riding the edge of a nervous breakdown.

"Oh my—what happened to you? You killed again, didn't you?"

Teresa took a shuddery breath and let out a soft wail.

Tears blurred her vision, and she nodded.

"How many now?" Louise asked.

"F–Five."

Louise's eyes widened. "You *have* been busy."

"I . . . I killed . . . my husband." She met Louise's eyes, shook her head, and looked away. "No. No I didn't. It was an accident. A car accident. He . . . he swerved off the road and we crashed. I hit my head and passed out." She looked at Louise. "When I woke up, the car was smoking. It had burned. Derrick—he didn't make it. He was inside. He burned up." Tears poured from her eyes now.

Louise came toward her with her arms out.

"There, there." She pulled Teresa into a hug. "I'm sure it was all an accident like you said."

"Yes . . . yes, an accident." Her voice took on a measure more of hysteria. "I would never . . . I would never . . ." She bawled against Louise's shoulder.

Teresa got herself under control and said, "I need to tell the police. I have to tell them. They'll find the car, the body."

You'll be atoned. They'll like you again. You'll be the sad widow.

"Calm down. We need to think rationally here," Louise said. "We need tea." She gave one curt nod.

Louise led Teresa out the door and through the woods. The lost souls floated on the cool air, but they didn't follow Teresa like they usually did.

Louise opened her front door and the two of them

went inside. She put the kettle on while Teresa watched from the entry, her entire body trembling.

The room spun. Teresa stumbled toward the kitchen, tripped on a cat, and leaned against a chair before sliding onto it. Her face fell into her hands.

"My mom . . . my husband . . ."

Louise gave her a glass of cold water.

"Let it out, dear. Let it out."

Teresa looked at the old woman and saw her mother's smooth, angelic face in place of Louise's.

She had to tell everything. From the start.

"My dad ruined our lives. My mother's and mine. He cheated on her. The media got hold of the news. A successful politician caught in the act with a woman not his wife." Teresa glanced at Louise, whose wrinkled old leather face had returned.

"She was so concerned with image. She couldn't take the hit to her reputation." Teresa's eyes drifted to the far edge of the table and rested there, not really focusing on anything in particular.

"But . . . no . . . That's not what happened. That's what everyone assumed happened. They didn't know. No one knew."

"No one knew what, dear?" Louise asked. The kettle screamed. Teresa jumped. Louise got up and made tea. When she returned to the table, Teresa met her eyes. Now that she had started, she wanted it all out in the open.

"I killed her." A sob erupted from Teresa's throat. "I

killed my mom. She's been dead for decades . . . but . . . I talked to her on the phone this week as if she were still alive." Renewed tears burst from Teresa's eyes. All this crying would wreak havoc on her skin and makeup.

Derrick is gone. You have no one to look beautiful for.

"The authorities took me to the hospital. I was only fifteen." Her voice softened as the snatches of memory drifted through her mind.

White walls, sterile rooms, over-starched sheets and gowns. The memories came to her as hazy reminders of a place she hated. Sessions with therapists, group therapy with people far worse off than her. People who didn't know who they were or why they were there. People who were delusional or acted like someone different every day.

Back then she knew she wasn't supposed to be there. She wasn't crazy like them. She was just depressed. Every day she had to take drugs that kept her in a constant state of muddled happiness. She didn't remember killing her mom until her therapist hypnotized her, a dangerous technique in therapy, and she spilled the whole thing.

"My mother was having an affair. I couldn't handle the hypocrisy—she pounded lessons on how to be a good wife into me my entire life, then turned around and cheated on my father." She had put an entire bottle of crushed lorazepam in her mother's whiskey.

When they released her she had done enough equivalent studies within the hospital's walls to graduate high school. Even though college wasn't part of her mother's plan, she went anyway, and when she met Derrick, life was back on track. Then Tiffany was born. Then Tiffany died.

To Mountain View. Only this time, she was committed for longer, and the drugs were so much stronger.

"I lost my identity and could never get it back even when the drugs were out of my system. I spent so many years in a fog, going through the motions of life but not feeling. I could only remember what my mother taught me. To keep my husband happy. To look beautiful for him. To do everything in my power to make sure he is taken care of. Meals prepared. Children washed and fed."

She couldn't let go, though. She knew they were happy once. Derrick seemed to dread spending time with her despite her upkeep of herself and the house. They weren't happy. He had moved the baby's furniture into the basement to store until he could figure out what to do with it.

"I went down there and I arranged it like the nursery. Just like it." Teresa smiled. "The changing table over there, and the crib—the pink sheets. A rocking chair." She looked at Louise, who had her chin resting on the backs of her clasped hands. "It was beautiful. But . . ." Teresa slumped back in the rigid kitchen chair. "He took it all away." She twisted her cup on the Formica table but didn't drink from it.

Louise cleared her throat. "Lovely story," she said. "Where is the fifth zoe? Did you give it to Yaldabaoth?"

Teresa looked up at her. "Lovely? The zoe? I'm telling you all this personal history about myself and you're concerned with where the zoe is?"

"Trying to keep you on track, dear," Louise said.

"Well, there is no zoe. Derrick lost control of the car . . ."

"Because you took his zoe."

"I would never!" She sat up straight again.

"You know what you did," Louise said. "You know you took his zoe and that's what caused the accident."

Teresa crossed her arms and scowled. "Everything else I told you is true." She pushed the cup away. Tea sloshed onto the table.

Louise didn't say a word. She slurped from her cup.

Teresa sighed and leaned forward. She put her face in her hands. "It's at the crash site."

"You must retrieve it. You need to complete your duty to our cause."

Teresa lifted her gaze. "Fine. I'll give it to Yaldabaoth, but then I'm going to the police to report the crash. Otherwise people will wonder what happened to him."

"That's a girl. Now we're thinking rationally."

She would be the sad widow.

The town will love you again.

CHAPTER 52

Ann parked her truck in front of room six at the Harmony B&B, which was actually a shitty motel that no longer served breakfast. She killed the engine and turned to Maggie. Pinky, on the seat between them, tried to lick Ann's face. Ann pushed her away, but it only made her try harder.

Maggie giggled. "She loves you." The girl hugged the dog. Ann patted Pinky's head and got out of the truck. She ran around to the passenger side and helped Maggie out. Pinky jumped out too and sniffed around. They walked to the door together, and Ann knocked. Maggie took Ann's hand.

"Who is it?" Raghib's voice came through the door.

"Ann."

"You shouldn't be here." He opened the door. His eyes landed on Maggie.

"Baba?" Maggie said, her eyes wide and round. "Baba?" Her voice raised twelve octaves and came out a squeal.

Ann couldn't tell if she was excited, shocked, happy, or horrified. Her face contorted, and she opened her arms to him. And then she threw up spaghetti all over the welcome mat.

Ann ushered Maggie inside and settled her on the couch with some blankets while Raghib cleaned up the mess. Pinky pushed her way past Raghib and jumped on the couch with Maggie. She gently lay down and rested her head on Maggie's body. The dog's noggin was nearly the size of Maggie's small torso.

"I'm sorry," Maggie whispered to Ann, her hands resting behind Pinky's ears. She looked over at Raghib as he closed the door and threw away the paper towels with a disgusted face.

"It is okay, my child," Raghib said. He washed his hands and came over to the couch. Ann backed away. "Even the mother of humanity is allowed to be sick." He looked at Ann. "How much spaghetti did you cram into my granddaughter?" He smiled.

Ann smiled back. Raghib moved to sit on the edge of the couch, but Pinky growled and shifted her head to block him.

"She's my protector, too, now," Maggie said with a smile. "It's okay, Pinky. This is my Baba." The dog made a content grumbling sound and nestled against Maggie's hand, but her eyes kept darting to Raghib every twitch he made. He pulled a chair over to the couch instead and sat down.

Ann felt like she was intruding on an important and private moment, so she stepped into the small kitchenette. She looked at her reflection in the window over the sink and wondered how she got here, to this place, to right here right now. How did she get here without knowing anything?

Raghib touched her elbow. "She's asking for you."

Ann went to Maggie's side. Pinky allowed her to sit on the edge of the couch.

Maggie relaxed against the pillows. "Will you stay here until I fall asleep?"

Ann nodded and pushed a stray lock of hair from Maggie's forehead. Though she liked kids, Ann had never wanted any ankle biters of her own. She didn't think she had motherly instinct. But this was different. Maggie was hers to protect. And part of protecting a child was making sure they were comforted, too. Right?

Maggie closed her eyes, and before long, her breathing grew deeper. Her hand slid off of Pinky's head, and the dog pushed closer to Maggie with a groan. Ann joined Raghib in the little kitchen area.

"I know I'm her Protector," Ann said. "And I know I'm the one to watch over her." She struggled to explain.

Raghib touched her shoulder. "I will take care of her," he said. "Besides, you'll know." He pointed at the mark.

"Right. Call me if you need anything. I'm sure she'll be hungry later since . . . you know." She motioned to the porch. "Do you have food?" Ann reached for the fridge to check out the grocery situation. Raghib stopped her.

"Yes. I am prepared."

Ann looked over at Maggie, then back at Raghib. "Thank you." She paused in the doorway. "Keep an eye on the dog, would you?"

Raghib smiled. "I think the dog is going to keep an eye on me."

As Ann drove away, a chill worked its way through her core. She felt weird. Like she was leaving her own child with a stranger. Her dad said she could trust Raghib. That small ounce of assurance was enough. Wasn't it? It had to be.

Ann pulled into her driveway and went inside, where Teresa's sordid past sat on her coffee table waiting to be reviewed.

CHAPTER 53

Teresa retrieved a flashlight from home and set out on foot to the site of the accident. The night brought a cold wind. The trees lashed the air. She pulled her coat tighter.

When she found the swerve marks, she climbed down the hill, aiming the flashlight's beam at the car.

The driver's side door hung wide open. From a few yards away, she shined the light inside.

Derrick was gone.

Fear boiled up to her throat, and she let out a whimper. He could be anywhere waiting for her to grab the hypo.

Would he chase her like Ruthie and the sheriff?

"Tiffany, where are you? I need you now. I need your strength."

"Here I am, Mommy." Tiffany stepped out from behind the tree the car had crashed into. "I'm sorry I disappeared. I was frightened."

Teresa knelt and opened her arms. Tiffany entered the embrace. A sob burst from Teresa's mouth.

"It's okay." Tiffany stroked her hair. "We don't need him to be happy, do we?" Tiffany leaned back and met Teresa's eyes.

Teresa shook her head. No. They would be happier without him and his constant desire to make pancakes for dinner.

Tiffany nodded. She stepped out of Teresa's arms and led her to the hypo.

Teresa hesitated.

"Pick it up, Mommy."

"I'm afraid," Teresa said. She shined the light around the clearing, shooing away the shadows among the trees, but the light only reached so far.

"Ruthie will chase us," Teresa said.

"She hasn't caught us yet."

Teresa took a deep breath and picked up the hypo.

Ruthie's shriek sounded in the distance. Teresa took Tiffany's hand, and they jogged up the hill.

Someone stood in the middle of the road, a black smudge against the darkness. Teresa shined the light toward it.

Derrick's milky-white eyes stared at her. He sniffed the air, then reached toward her with charred fingers. Skin sloughed off of him and hit the ground with a pattering-plop as he took a step in her direction.

Teresa shifted in front of Tiffany.

"He's not very fast, Mommy. But Ruthie is." Tiffany's little hand pointed beyond Derrick, where Ruthie lurched down the street in their direction.

Ruthie lined up next to Derrick and stopped.

Behind them, Sheriff McMichael waddled on bloated feet. He stood on Derrick's other side.

They'd come from the direction of town. How did they get there so fast?

There was no way Teresa could get past Ruthie. The others, yes, but Ruthie's vengeance fueled her need to stop Teresa from delivering the zoe.

"What do I do?" She looked down at Tiffany. Tiffany looked up at her with frightened eyes and shook her head. Of course a seven-year-old wouldn't know what to do. Teresa looked at the hypo in her hand.

It gave Yaldabaoth his power back. Would it make her powerful, too? Powerful enough to run all the way back to town? To outrun Ruthie?

She turned it needle-side up and looked down at Tiffany again, but her daughter was watching the living dead.

"They aren't moving," Tiffany said.

Teresa looked up and frowned. "Why are they just standing there like zombies?"

Tiffany giggled. "Or Like zoe-bies." Her laugh raised in pitch and hysteria.

Ruthie shrieked. Tiffany, suddenly silent, huddled closer to Teresa.

Teresa considered the needle again. Would the zoe kill her? Did she care? The last question surprised her.

Ruthie took a step toward her, then another. Teresa jammed the giant needle into her thigh and pushed the plunger.

At first the only thing she felt was a gouging, stinging pain where the thick needle stabbed into her skin. Then heat. Immense heat.

It coursed down into her calf and foot, and upward, spreading across her pelvis. When it tingled across her womanhood, she cried out and dropped to one knee. She tore off her coat. Her veins glowed red through her skin. The glow slid through her nervous system, and a peace overwhelmed her. Feelings of happiness and sadness all at once. She yearned to laugh, yearned to cry.

And then the feeling left her, frightened away by a hard beating in all of her pulse points. Her ears rushed with the sound of her own heart. She curled into herself. Each beat felt like a lash from a whip, a wallop from a baseball bat. Her head felt like it would explode. Even though it was painful, it was also pleasurable.

This was the pulse of power. Raw and unleashed. Wild. Uncontained.

It boiled in her loins and finally erupted.

She threw her head back and let out a sound so animalistic she couldn't tell if it was a wild cat's growl, a woman's scream, or both.

She crouched without thought, moved by instinct to adopt the attack pose of a predator.

Her breath mixed with the cold night air and formed

clouds with each panting exhale.

Tiffany was gone, but no matter. She couldn't contain the power ripping through her. It was better her baby didn't see her like this.

With keen night vision lent by the zoe, she stared at Derrick, then Sheriff McMichael.

Finally, her eyes landed on Ruthie. Ruthie let out a shriek, frail in comparison to the roar that had ripped from Teresa's vocal cords.

In less than a second, Teresa's muscles coiled and released. She sprang forward into a full sprint, charging straight for Ruthie.

The mummified woman jolted toward her with an enraged shriek. They crashed into each other. Teresa grabbed Ruthie's shrunken head, forced her fingers into the woman's mouth, and ripped her jaw off the rest of the way. She tossed it aside.

Ruthie stumbled backward, lost her footing, and fell.

Sheriff McMichael lumbered forward, bulging eyes intent on Teresa. He stepped on Ruthie's head and crushed it into the ground. The crunching sound distracted him. He looked down and lifted his foot as if to see what he'd stepped in.

Teresa sprinted past him and Derrick before they even knew what had happened to their scrawny leader.

She arrived at the abandoned funeral home in less than five minutes.

The lost souls crowded around her, as if they sensed

the zoe inside her. Where they touched her, they left tiny burn marks she couldn't feel. Her skin was numb from the cold, or from the zoe, she didn't know. She didn't care.

She needed to find Yaldabaoth. She bounded up the stairs and through the front door. The house melted. Yaldabaoth stood at his pool, gazing into it.

Teresa took long steps, grabbed him by the arm, and spun him into her. Her lips locked on his. She pulled away for a second.

"I can't contain this," she growled.

Yaldabaoth gripped her upper arms and forced her back from him.

"What have you done?"

"I had no choice," she said. She wanted him. Needed him. The energy inside of her begged for something—it could only be this. Lust seared her insides.

Yaldabaoth pulled her against him and squeezed her so hard she thought her ribs would break. Her body writhed in his grip. He lowered his lips to hers. She hungrily kissed him.

It wasn't sweet. It wasn't loving or warm like their first time together when he'd tricked her into believing he was Derrick. It was feral, angry, lustful. It was every deadly sin rolled into one blissful moment.

When he finished, his body glowed with the power, and Teresa lay back, drained. The zoe had left her. She was her simple, mortal shell, once again.

Shame replaced the power. She quietly righted her

shirt, pulled up her pants.

How could she do such a thing after losing her husband?

Yaldabaoth chuckled. Teresa glared at him. He held up his hands.

"I did not fool you this time." He grinned. Then his smile dropped. "Don't steal what's mine ever again."

He snapped his fingers, and Tiffany's pained screams came from the dark passage as they had once before. He snapped again, and the cries stopped.

Teresa said nothing. She walked to the police station to report the accident. Shame or no shame, the town needed to know their beloved doctor was gone.

CHAPTER 54

Ann sat on the couch. She opened the file and flipped through the pages. At the bottom of the stack were her dad's phone records. The phone company must've responded to Sheriff McMichael's subpoena and faxed them over. She scanned the list. Not a lot of activity. No outgoing calls for the past three months. Plenty of incoming calls from her number though.

She pushed the fax to the side and turned her attention back to Teresa's file. She had already read what the station had on her. Her interest lay in the documents Joey had sent her, hacked straight from the source.

She started with the patient file from Teresa's *first* admittance to a mental health institute.

Included within that set of documentation were the transcripts for three hypnotherapy sessions. Ann's eyes devoured the transcripts. When she reached the end, she set the papers down and wished she had more beer.

Harmony's Public Enemy #1: Teresa Hart.

Ann picked up the phone, but she realized she didn't need to bother Derrick about this. He knew who he was married to. He had to. Besides, he was probably still on his way home from Mountain View, assuming that was the reason he didn't pick Maggie up from school.

Teresa's mother hadn't committed suicide. She'd been murdered.

In session number three, fifteen-year-old Teresa confessed to killing her mother. She'd fabricated a story to cover it up as a suicide. In a delusion brought on by overwhelming guilt, she had convinced herself the story was true.

How the hell did she get out?

Ann flipped to the back of the stack, but there were no discharge papers included in the file.

Ann settled in with the documents from Mountain View. This time Teresa was admitted for manic-depressive behavior and as part of her sentence for neglecting her child. It corroborated the story Derrick told her the other night, except for one thing. Their baby was found *under* the giant teddy bear, not pressed against the crib bumper like Derrick said. Did he remember wrong?

Ann got up to retrieve the spiced rum from the freezer, but halted. Something about the discharge papers didn't sit right—something about one of the signatures at the bottom.

She rushed back to the table and sorted through the papers again until she found it.

The discharge papers were signed by the attending psychiatrist, Dr. Gail Park.

Ann knew the name. She had seen it somewhere in the past few days. She closed her eyes and tried to envision where.

She jumped to her feet, and a prickle went through her body. It was in the journal from the storage unit—and on the adoption certificate.

Ann grabbed the certificate. The signature matched. She flipped open the journal to the pages toward the back. Gail Park was in the collection of signatures. She compared them. They matched. But what did it mean? Why was her signature in her dad's journal? Who was she?

She looked at the other page full of scribbled words. She ran her hand over them, feeling the texture from the pen's pressure with her fingertips.

"Summon the angel," Ann whispered. She frowned. It didn't sound right. Because it wasn't. All her life he told her to summon *your* angel, not *the* angel.

Summon the angel. It is the key. Her dad's voice from the video came to her.

Ann scrutinized the words on the journal page letter by letter until an odd letter stood out. About a third of the way down the page he'd written, "SUMMON THE ANGE*T*."

She scanned the rest of it and found more instances in which a letter was replaced: SUMMON THE ANG*L*L and SUMMO*M* THE ANGEL. Heart pounding, Ann went back to the top and started circling the misplaced letters. She wrote them down and sat back with defeat. It was a bunch of nonsense.

TLMYWFZHMLCGVV

She checked again, just to make sure she didn't miss anything, then tried to unscramble the words, but there were no vowels.

"Think, Ann, think." She counted the number of letters, fourteen. Then counted them in the catch phrase. Fourteen again. Goosebumps broke out on her arms.

"Summon the angel. It is the key." The small key to her dad's lockbox had been taped to the opposite page. She grabbed the items from the box and shuffled through them and found the tabula recta.

She held up the slip of paper she'd written the random letters on. "If *summon the angel* is the key, then this has to be the cipher."

A cold prickle ran over her. She set the tabula recta on the table, found the first letter of the key, S, and went down until she hit the first letter of the cipher. Then she followed the line to the left. The first letter in the solution was B. She kept going until she had: BRAM IS.

Alive? Dead?

There were too many letters left. She forced herself to slow down. Her hand shook when she trailed the pencil across the grid to find the next letters. She moved to the next one, and the next, until the message revealed itself.

BRAM IS GAIL PARK.

I took care of both records.

Her father's voice from the video replayed in her mind once again.

Bram is Gail Park—her father had signed Teresa's discharge papers.

CHAPTER 55

Ann stared at the decoded message, then the discharge papers, willing the signature on the latter to change, to morph into someone else's handwriting, or a scribbled *just kidding* or something. Anything.

She finally let the paper drop from her hand. It floated to the edge of the table and onto the floor. She sat up straight. What if he hadn't signed it willingly?

Scenarios flashed through her mind. None of them made sense. What pull did her father have in the psychological world, or in the adoption world? She put it aside for now. She needed to focus on Teresa, on the case, and the fact that, despite killing her mother and baby, she had been freed.

And Ann's dad had freed her.

Ann consulted the phone book and dialed the number for Mountain View. A receptionist answered.

"This is Detective Ann Logan. May I speak with your privacy officer please?"

The hold music blared in her ear. After a few seconds, a man answered. Ann introduced herself again.

"I'm investigating a serial kidnapping and homicide case in Harmony. Will you or did you receive a patient by the name of Teresa Hart?"

"I'm sorry, ma'am," the man on the phone said. "Under HIPAA, I'm not allowed to disclose that information."

Ann suppressed a growl. Instead, she said through her teeth, "Lives are at stake here, sir."

"There's nothing I can do. Laws are laws." She could hear the dismissive shrug in his voice.

"I'm fairly certain you're allowed to disclose information to a law enforcement officer. Can you check the protocol?"

Humanity is at stake!

After a brief silence and a sigh, he said, "Sure. Hold on."

The rambunctious hold music came back on. Ann bit her thumbnail and bounced her knee while she waited.

"Hello?" a different voice said. "Are you the one holding regarding HIPAA protocol?"

"Yes." Ann gripped the phone harder.

"This is Dr. Smith, chief administrator of the hospital," he said. "I apologize for the delay. The privacy officer hasn't yet learned the protocol for enforcing HIPAA laws. He frequently says no—almost like a knee jerk reaction—without considering extraneous circumstances."

Ann perked up and pinched her lip.

He cleared his throat. "Now, we can disclose the

information to you, provided you fax us the proper form. I believe you can find it on our website. It's the one called Law Enforcement Official's Request for Protected Health Information."

"You've got to be kidding me," Ann muttered.

"I'm afraid not," the administrator said. "Laws are laws. As you well know."

"I understand," Ann said.

"Now, if the person in question does arrive at our facility and agrees to disclosing her personal information, we can call you and let you know."

As if Teresa would want to disclose to the Castle County Sheriff's office she was at a mental health facility. Ann gave him her phone number anyway, along with an ungrateful thank you.

She hung up and sat on the couch. There wasn't time for this.

Her father's fake signature stared at her.

Think, Ann. What are you missing?

Her keen attention to detail in the Salida Stabber case had identified one seemingly insignificant clue overlooked by the other detectives. A detail that had led her to the Stabber.

Ann sorted through the clues and evidence. Then reread her notes about the seven bloods.

Ancient, pure, tainted, loving servant, bastard, blind fool, devoted.

Nothing stuck out. She sorted through the contents of

her dad's lock box again.

Ticket stubs to Egypt. Same flight number on different days or years. The list of names with Louise's right on top. A list Louise claimed to know nothing about.

Ann wanted to believe her father left these items together for her to find, especially since the tabula recta was included. He knew she'd tie them together. He had to know.

Ann picked up the phone again and called Joey.

"Joey. I need another favor."

"Sure, sure. And what's in it for me this time?"

"My everlasting love if what you find is what I think you'll find."

He laughed. "You know I'd do anything for you."

"I need you to find the passenger manifests for the following Lufthansa flights." She gave him the flight numbers and dates. "How soon can you get those?"

"I've already hacked into the system. Do you want to stay on the line?"

"Sure."

A couple minutes passed. She paced to the sound of his clacking keyboard. A final hard tap.

"Done."

"Can you search for these names?" She read him the list.

"None of them were on any of these flights."

Ann slumped onto the couch. "What about any other Lufthansa flights?"

Clickity clackity.

"All of these people were on a recent flight to Egypt—like three months ago."

Ann's heart picked up. It was a wild guess, but she had to ask. "What about my dad? Bram Logan."

"He booked it but didn't check in."

Ann thought her head was going to explode.

"Oh . . . it looks like one of the other people you asked about also didn't check in. Louise Marga."

"Loony Lou?"

"If you say so."

"Thanks, Joey. Thank you so much. You've been incredibly helpful."

She hung up. Her dad was supposed to be on a flight just three months ago. Did that mean he'd been alive all those times she tried to call him? A brick of despair dropped into her gut. Raghib had said the Protectors had been forced into hiding. They left their families to protect them. And her dad, himself, said in the video it was all for the plan.

She turned on the TV and hit play on the DVD remote. She watched it twice before she noticed something about his eyes, and how, at the beginning of the video he scratched his eye. But, no. He didn't scratch it. She *thought* he scratched it. Really, all he did was subtly point at his eye. She stared at his eyes and listened to what he said. Sometimes he blinked slow, sometimes fast. She paid close attention to what he said and his corresponding blinks.

At the end, she sat back, butt on her heels, and stared at the DVD menu screen. She hit play one more time.

If you're watching this, I'm probably dead. Long blink, fast blink. Morse code for N.

I took care of both records. Long blink, fast blink, long, long. Morse code for Y.

Maybe it was a stretch, but her father knew her attention to detail. He knew she would catch his subtle hints.

If you're watching this, Raghib followed my instructions and contacted you. You can trust him. Long. Fast. Ann's heart rate picked up. She rewound the DVD and stared at his eyes.

You can trust him. Long. Fast.

N. No.

She couldn't trust Raghib. And he had Maggie.

CHAPTER 56

At the sheriff's office, Teresa took a long breath, let it out, and stepped inside. George Riley sat at the reception desk. He glanced up, and his eyes widened. He stood.

"Mrs.—Dr. Hart. What's wrong?"

"My husband . . ." She allowed her face to contort with grief. "He's dead. The car . . . he lost control and it crashed."

George rushed around and pulled a jacket off the coat rack next to the door and hung it on Teresa's shoulders.

"Please, sit down . . . uh . . ." He led her to a niche between two workstations and helped her ease onto the office chair.

"Can I have something to drink, please?" she asked.

George dashed off through a set of saloon-style doors and clattered around in the kitchen. The clock on the wall above the door said it was just after one o'clock. He came back out with a mug in his meaty hand.

"Excuse me just a minute," he said. He pulled the radio from his belt and went into an office behind the desks and closed the door behind him, but it didn't latch. It fell back open a few inches. Teresa heard every word despite the tinny speaker and static.

"George to Ann," he said. He repeated it. Finally, Ann responded. George went on. "Teresa Hart just walked into the station. She was in an accident."

"She's there?" Ann asked.

"Yeah. Dr. Hart, her husband, died in a car crash." A long pause. Derrick's sweetheart was probably processing that news.

"Arrest her. Don't believe a word she says."

"Okay, okay."

"I have reason to suspect she killed him and everyone else who's missing."

"What? Ann, you have to come down here. I can't do this on my own."

"Yes, you can. I know you can. I have something else I need to—" Ann cried out. "Maggie."

Teresa frowned. Of course Maggie was with Ann. Teresa knew it wasn't just because her husband's sweetheart was a cop. She bristled and crossed her arms. It was Derrick's plan all along. Dump her at Mountain View and live the life he dreamed of with *her*. His *one that got away*, as Louise said. Teresa scowled.

"Ann?" George yelled into the radio. "Ann?"

George took a deep breath and let it out. "I can't do this." The sound of a fist on a palm. "Yes, you can."

Teresa looked at the exit. She could run. But then what?

Where would she go? She had no one. Truly, now with Derrick gone. She was a fool to believe she could raise Maggie on her own. The girl didn't even like her. Teresa held out her hands and looked at them. Hands that had taken so many lives in the last few days, all in the name of saving a hopeless marriage and a dead daughter.

George's footsteps thumped across the floor in the other room. He paused at the door, likely alarmed that it hadn't latched and probably wondering how much she'd heard.

Eyes on the front door, the exit, Teresa listened. He was going to arrest her. She would go to prison. She would never be reunited with her baby. She ran her hands over her face, through her tangled hair. A hand touched her shoulder. She looked up. Tiffany with her beaming smile. She handed Teresa a hypo and grinned wider.

The door creaked open behind her. George thumped toward her, slow, steady. Did he have his gun drawn? She didn't want to look, but she had to. She turned.

George's zoe wriggled at his chest like a fat alien worm thrashing to eat its way inside of his body.

He stopped when he saw her looking at him.

"I don't know how to say this, but . . ." He rounded the desks and stood in front of her. The zoe pulsed with life. With power. She yearned to feel it again and nearly touched the protruding snake.

"What? What's going on?" She played dumb.

"You're under arrest?" George rubbed the back of his

neck with one hand and pulled his cuffs off his belt with the other.

Teresa lunged to her feet and plunged the needle into his chest. George Riley, dunderheaded buffoon, simply stood there as Teresa drained his zoe. The barrel filled, and she slid the needle from his chest. His head and shoulders drooped. He stood there, weaving.

Teresa didn't know what to do. He sort of had her caged in, standing in front of her the way he was, penned between two workstations. She looked at the zoe in her hand, craving the power Derrick's had given her—but no. Yaldabaoth would hurt Tiffany if she took what was his again.

Instead, she reached out and pushed George with one finger. He wobbled and fell over. Teresa bolted from the station. As soon as she stepped outside, Ruthie's strangled cries split the air.

Shit.

She had thought Ruthie was dead . . . er . . . re-dead after their previous encounter. Teresa ran in the direction of the abandoned funeral home. Ruthie appeared out of nowhere. The top of her head lay to the side, flopping with each lurching step.

The usual suspects were not far behind. Sheriff with his lumbering gait. Derrick's slow crawl.

Teresa darted down the dirt road, tossing glances over her shoulder. Ruthie was gaining on her. With the power of the zoe she'd easily outrun the mummified woman. She considered taking just a little hit off the hypo. The memory of her unharnessed desire and how she wantonly opened herself to Yaldabaoth stopped her.

Ruthie shrieked again. It sounded like she'd screamed right in Teresa's ear. Teresa looked behind her and tripped. She sprawled onto her front. The hypo bounced out of her hand and jangled along the rocks jutting from the road.

Don't break.

She was about to get up when something landed hard on top of her. It stole the wind from her lungs. Claw-like nails dug into her back, tangled in her hair. Teresa screamed and struggled. Ragged, rasping breath rattled in her ear. Ruthie had her pinned. She was done for.

The zoe lay glowing in a puddle of slushy mud. Teresa relaxed. This was it. The end.

Then Tiffany's beautiful form, glowing white in the moonlight, appeared at the edge of the woods.

"Mommy," she called, despair in her voice. She reached a hand toward Teresa.

All of this, all of the killing and the fear and the . . . everything—it was for *her*. For her Tiffany. Teresa ignored the pains shooting down her back. She bucked her butt upward, throwing Ruthie off-kilter, got her knees under her body, and staggered to her feet. Ruthie clung to her, digging her fingers into Teresa's shoulders. Teresa screamed again and ran toward the woods, dragging Ruthie with her. Cross the barrier.

She can't come with me.

Teresa lurched, her legs growing weak. A few more feet. She sloshed through the icy cold stream and crossed over, but something held her back.

Ruthie's screams doubled in volume. Her body convulsed.

The sound of electricity crackling made Teresa's head throb. Heat radiated across her back. Teresa tried to move forward, but Ruthie's arms, wrapped around her shoulders now, pulled at her. Even as the woman thrashed, her arms still held.

Finally, the barrier released them. Teresa cried out and fell forward.

The scent of burned flesh hung in the air. Ruthie's crispy corpse still twitched on the other side of the barrier. Teresa lifted her hand to her throat and recoiled in horror.

Ruthie's arms were still on her. She flung them away and crawled backwards in case they came to life and continued Ruthie's quest to destroy her.

Teresa let out a breathy sob. Derrick and Sheriff McMichael paced along the barrier, stomping on Ruthie's smoking body each time they passed it. Teresa stuck her lip out in a pout.

Could this day get any worse?

Then she realized she'd left the hypo outside the barrier, on the road, in a puddle.

CHAPTER 57

Wednesday, 0030

Ann crumbled to her side, gasping for air. She reached for the radio, but the pain searing her insides kept her curled in a ball. How was this agony supposed to be helpful for Sophia if it debilitated her Protector? Ann gritted her teeth and forced herself to her hands and knees. She took deep breaths and rose to a squat, using a dining room chair to steady herself. Her vision was haloed in blue from the light in her veins. They'd never glowed so bright before.

The pain started to lessen, but still burned. Her vision darkened. What a faulty alarm system!

"You've been . . . in worse . . . pain." Kind of true. There was a time in her training in which she was subjected to full-on pepper spray. Her eyes burned for hours despite washing with ice-cold water and resting her head in front of a fan to ease the burn.

Ann clipped the radio to her belt, pulled herself to her

feet, and stumbled to the door. She gripped the frame, and a low bass sound came from behind her. The book. She needed to protect the book, too. She grabbed it, then hurried outside. The cold air cleared her mind, and she was able to get a handle on the pain.

Deep breaths. Push through. It doesn't hurt. No pain, no gain.

She hauled herself onto the bench seat in her truck, threw the book on the floor board, turned the key, and backed into the mailbox. Old mail fluttered out and flipped and twirled on the blast of exhaust. She took off toward Harmony B&B.

By the time Ann pulled up to room six, the pain had lessened to a dull throb every few seconds, like a second, sluggish heartbeat.

Her headlights hit the wide-open door.

Ann jumped out of the truck. "Maggie," she yelled. The interior of the cabin was dark. "Raghib?"

Back against the door frame, she reached inside and flipped on the light. "Pinky," Ann gasped.

The dog lay on her side with a heavy lamp next to her. A small puddle of blood had pooled beneath her ear. Pinky shifted her head and fixed Ann with sad eyes. She let out a whimper. Ann rushed to her side. "Oh, Pinky. I'm so sorry. You tried to warn me, and I didn't listen."

Just like you didn't listen to George.

I hope everything went okay. . .

George could handle himself. He was big and burly

despite being so innocent, so saint-like, so . . . pure.

Blood of the Pure.

"Shit."

Ann stood but didn't go anywhere. Couldn't think of where to go, what to do. Maggie was in trouble. George could be next. Bram might still be alive. She needed backup and backup never came. On top of it all, the mark stabbed her with pain.

An overwhelming sense of responsibility and worry about making the wrong choice paralyzed her.

Condition Black.

Just like it had that night. She'd had to choose which one to save—the Stabber's victim, Elizabeth, or her partner, Bruce—and she couldn't decide. Both of them had died.

"What should I do?" She asked the air around her in a panicky voice.

Angel . . .

A voice whispered so soft Ann held her breath to hear it again. The light throbbed with the beating of her heart.

Angel.

Her father's words came to her.

Summon the angel.

Pinky sat up and flapped her ears, then slowly got to her feet. The wound on her head had crusted over. She stared at Ann, tail wagging in a low swish. She gave a half-growl-half-bark and moved toward the door.

One thing at a time. That's all she could do.

Ann followed Pinky out to the truck. First stop, the station. She needed a gun. The thought made her stomach flip, but it was a necessity given the circumstances. Raghib had Maggie, and Ann didn't have the slightest idea where he might have taken her, or to whom, or how many *whoms* there might be.

She arrived at the station a few minutes later.

"Come on, girl." Pinky groaned, shifted, licked her lips, and sighed again. "Let's go." Ann tugged on her collar, and the dog reluctantly crawled across the seat.

Ann peeked inside the station.

George lay on his back on the floor near the desks.

A mug of water sat on the desk. Probably a drink for Teresa. Ann, too, would have felt sorry for Teresa if she didn't suspect she'd killed Derrick and everyone else who'd gone missing. She'd have to dust the mug for prints later.

"Hello?" she called. "It's Detective Ann Logan. If you're in there, come out with your hands where I can see them."

When no one appeared, Ann crouched next to the dog.

"Pinky, seek and destroy." She pointed into the room.

The dog looked at her with the quizzical look dogs were wont to give, then grinned the classic pit bull grin.

"We'll work on that one." Ann crept inside. Pinky followed, looking up at her to see where she would go next.

"If you're in here, I have a dog who's trained to attack. Come out slowly with your hands up."

Ann scanned the area as she sidled over to George. She knelt by his side and felt for a pulse. There wasn't one. The crispy substance littered the floor near him.

"Dammit, George." She stuffed her emotions into the shadows and turned her mind to the work at hand. Number six. Assuming Teresa killed Derrick for his zoe and not just because he was a blind idiot.

Oh shit. Blind Fool.

One more and all hell would literally break loose.

Pinky sniffed George, sneezed, and went into the office. Ann heard her jump up onto the couch, circle around, and flop with a loud sigh.

Ann picked up the phone and dialed the county coroner's office to report the body.

The body. George. Her partner.

I've killed another one.

She should have listened to George when he said he couldn't handle Teresa.

The coroner's office didn't answer, so she left a message letting them know she'd found a body. The lack of resources in Castle County made everything so difficult.

She called the state and CBI. Where the hell were they?

Once again, the dispatchers who answered the phone told her they had no record of anyone from Castle County having called.

"I have a body here, and four missing persons who are probably dead. Get me some fucking back up." Ann slammed the phone down, rubbed her temples, then stared toward the locker room.

Her dad's gun. Her dad. He was still alive somewhere.

Keep it together.

Before she could change her mind, she stomped to the lockers and strapped her dad's belt to her waist. She ignored the pounding behind her breastbone as she checked the clip. No one said she had to use it.

She called Pinky's name, and together they strode back to her truck, but she had no idea where Maggie might be.

They climbed in, and Ann gripped the steering wheel. Raghib was still a Messenger of the Light, which meant he must be helping Teresa, or vice versa. She put the truck in gear and backed out of the lot. Brent had photographed Teresa coming out of the abandoned funeral home. It was the only lead she had.

I'm coming, Maggie.

CHAPTER 58

Teresa crept to the edge of the boundary and stared out at the hypo lying in the puddle. A soft sob broke through her lips. At least Ruthie couldn't get her now. Even if she could still move, she couldn't grab or bite.

Derrick and Sheriff McBloat were too slow. She could dash out, grab the syringe, and get back beyond the barrier before they even knew she was near them.

Her legs refused to move.

One . . . two . . . three . . . go.

Nope.

"Do it, Mommy," Tiffany's voice said. Teresa cast around, but her baby was nowhere to be seen. "You can do it." The voice carried like an echo on a whispered wind.

"I can do this. I can do this." Her legs still shook from the adrenaline of fighting off Ruthie.

She jumped up and down a few times. Then, before her brain could stop her, she lunged forward and dove past Derrick, dodged around the sheriff, and snatched the hypo. Her left leg slid in front of her right. She went down onto her hip.

Ruthie shrieked, but her body only twitched from side to side. Her legs kicked.

"Move," she yelled at herself. "Move it!" Her numb legs wouldn't cooperate. Her muscles twitched with fatigue and wasted adrenaline. She let out a sob.

I'm done. I've failed. I can't do this anymore.

She looked up. Derrick was only two steps away.

Beyond him, Tiffany waved to her. Teresa had to do this. If not for her happiness, then for Tiffany's. She had to get her baby away from Yaldabaoth.

Teresa gritted her teeth, got her knees under her again, and lurched into a sprint. She knocked Derrick out of the way. He grabbed for her, found purchase in the knit of her sweater.

Her forward momentum halted, and she crashed backward into him. They fell onto the ground. He let out a burnt-smelling *oof* into her ear when she landed on him.

"No," she yelled. His hands pawed her stomach, her breasts, below her belt.

She slapped at them and pushed them away, but it seemed like he'd grown extra arms. The smell of him turned her stomach, turned her vision foggy. She'd never eat barbecue again.

His hands raked her skin and forced their way down her pants. He breathed in ragged bursts in her ear and bucked and pressed his hips against her backside.

Teresa lifted her head and smashed it back against his teeth.

Again.

Again.

Again, until he let go of her.

She scrambled to her feet and backed away. He groaned and held his burned hands over his burned face. Teeth lay near his head, gleaming white in the moonlight.

She backed toward the creek and bumped into something soft and lumpy.

Sheriff McMichael's arms lifted to wrap around her. She elbowed him in the gut.

He let out a blasting belch, foul and stinking of rotten guts, stumbled but kept his feet. She spun around him and got across the creek.

Safe on the other side, she crumbled to her knees and collapsed onto her belly.

The lost souls bounced toward her, congregating around the syringe. At least *they* couldn't hurt her. She lay still for a moment, then got to her feet and stumbled to the house. She fell inside, and the cave appeared around her. Yaldabaoth turned from the pool.

"Back so soon?" He fixed her with his gaze. "My, you've been through quite a trial, haven't you?" He held out his hand and lifted her to her feet.

"S–six." She handed him the zoe and turned to shuffle back out into the cold world, but he held her hand and stopped her retreat.

"Please, stay," he said. His voice had changed.

Teresa closed her eyes, turned around, and opened them.

In Yaldabaoth's place stood Derrick. Teresa's heart shattered. Her world crumbled into nothing. She broke apart inside.

"I'm so sorry, Derrick. I'm so sorry." She cried against his neck. Even his smell was right. It was really him. Relief washed over her. He wasn't gone. He was here, now, in this cave.

"I love you so much. I'm so sorry for how I've behaved."

"There, there," Derrick said. "Don't get too gushy, my sweet. There's one more left." His scent shifted.

The soft flannel shirt under her cheek turned to cold snake skin covering a strong chest.

Teresa jerked out of his grasp. Anger tore through her now.

"I'll get you number seven," she said. "If I can have my husband back, too."

Yaldabaoth held out his hands and shrugged. "Sure. Why not. You deserve it all, don't you?"

"Just like that? Sure, why not?" She stared at him, skepticism lacing her judgment.

He'd tricked her so many times.

Yaldabaoth shrugged again. "It's inconsequential at this point. My power will be great. I can give you anything." He stepped toward her. "Of course, if you'd rather spend the rest of your days by my side, I wouldn't argue with that either." He slid his hand over her cheek and tilted her chin up. "My queen. My bride."

Teresa closed her eyes, and in her mind she saw Derrick on their wedding day. She gritted her teeth.

"No." She stepped out of his touch and paced away. "As soon as I deliver number seven, I'm finished." She turned around. "I want my daughter and my husband and my . . . my happiness."

"Suit yourself." He moved back to his pool.

Teresa backed away, turned, and ran out of the cave. She tripped on the porch steps, landed on her hands and knees, and vomited onto the ground. Everything hurt. Her legs, her lungs, the back of her head. Her heart. She wiped her mouth and sobbed.

The crunch of tires on gravel drifted through the trees. She wiped her eyes and looked up.

An old pickup truck stopped out on the road. Ann Logan stepped out. The dog from Brent's house followed. Ann locked the door manually and slammed it shut.

Teresa slunk to the side of the house and hid among the shadows until Ann and the dog went inside. She waited a little longer. She kept telling herself *one more minute* just in case Ann came out at the precise moment Teresa left her hiding spot.

When she couldn't take it any longer, she snuck out of the shadows and back to the barrier. The lost souls paid her no mind. She thought back to the times she was in here with syringes full of zoe, how the souls had flocked to her.

But, no. They only flocked to her that one time. Now they only flocked to the zoe. She stood straight.

Why didn't the souls come to her? The last shred of hope drained from her.

The lost souls disregarded her because her soul was lost, too, corrupted by the evils she had embraced. A sudden sensation of aloneness draped over her like a death shroud.

You can get it all back. You have to finish this.

CHAPTER 59

Ann held her free hand on the butt of her father's gun—the feel of it brought both anxiety and a sense of safety—and used the other to shine the flashlight's pathetic beam into the woods. She rubbed the mark over her heart. It still throbbed like a second pulse, giving her a strange feeling in her chest.

The flashlight beam landed on an armless body lying just this side of the creek. The smell of burning electricity and charred flesh lingered in the air. Ann took a step back and grabbed Pinky's collar, just in case.

She told Pinky to stay, and crouched over the smoking remains. The body had been burned and showed signs of having been crushed in some places, including the head, but she could tell it was female.

Ruthie.

How had no one seen her body lying here all this time? She supposed Sheriff McMichael really had cracked down on kids utilizing the old funeral home. Or maybe they'd found somewhere else to go or other things to do.

Ann looked up and peered into the trees. She called Pinky to her side and they stepped over the little creek at the edge of the woods. They trudged through the brush and went inside the abandoned funeral home.

The furniture in the room hadn't changed from the last time she was here, with Derrick long ago, and neither had the smell. Ann crinkled her nose against the scent of decay. Pinky sniffed around the room and down a hallway straight ahead.

"Pinky," Ann whispered, following. The silence in the house pounded in her ears.

The squishy carpet turned into linoleum in a kitchen tucked away at the back of the house. Pinky clawed at a door, whined, sniffed at the crack under it, sat and looked at Ann.

Ann swept the light over the kitchen, then turned back to the door. Pantry or basement?

If it was a basement, she needed to clear the rest of the house before descending. If Raghib or even Teresa were still inside and Ann wandered downstairs, they would have the upper hand. Ann envisioned the basement door slamming shut and locking her in its dark, decaying depths, leaving them free to kill Maggie.

She shuddered, circled back to the front of the house, and drew her father's gun, ignoring her stomach's clenching at the touch of the metal.

"Raghib? Are you in here?" she called from the hallway.

Silence. She tiptoed back down the corridor, cleared a bathroom on the way, and stepped into the living room.

At the back wall, catty-corner to the exit, a staircase led to the second floor. Next to that, another door. Ann opened it. Closet.

"I'm unarmed!" Ann shouted up the stairs. "I'm here to talk. Please come out." Keeping her back to the wall, she slid up, step by step. She cleared two bedrooms and another bathroom.

Ann returned to the kitchen. Pinky sat at the door, tail swishing across the linoleum. Ann gripped the knob. Pinky whined. Ann opened the door. Pinky blasted down the wooden steps. Darkness swallowed the wimpy light from Ann's flashlight.

Pinky's frantic sniffing came from somewhere down below. If there were remains . . .

Ann took the first few steps slowly. The wood bowed under her feet, creaking as it strained against her weight. She wasn't heavy, not by any standards, but the old wood cried out with each shift.

"Pinky," Ann whisper-yelled.

Sniff, snuffle, sniff.

The fifth step cracked. The sound sent a shock wave up Ann's spine. Then it gave.

With a startled yelp, her hand flung out to grab onto anything to stop her from falling. She dropped the flashlight to catch the banister, as if the screws bolting it to the rotten wall would hold her.

The flashlight bounced down the steps, landed at the bottom, and went out.

Ann let out a breath and felt her way to the landing, testing each step before applying her full weight to the edges where the risers would provide sturdier footing. She pawed the ground, found the flashlight, shook it, and clicked it off and on to no avail.

She crouched in the dark stillness and let her eyes adjust. A dark mass took shape in the middle of the space in front of her.

Please don't be the other bodies.

Ann shook the flashlight again, and the bulb or batteries or whatever spiritual force might be helping her, decided to work. The beam jiggled with the tremble of her hand. She lifted the light.

It revealed a medical table with some stained sheets piled on top of it. Ann let out a breath. Pinky had probably been drawn to the scent of the stains. The dog let out a sharp snort and moved on from the pile. She followed her nose into the dark corners of the basement.

Ann's racing heart slowed. She swallowed away the dryness in her mouth and throat. From the distant sounds of Pinky's claws clicking on the cement floor, and her sniffing, the basement seemed larger than the house above it. Ann put a hand against the wall and jogged along.

When the wall formed a ninety-degree corner, she stopped. A dark doorway stood out on the wall a few feet away.

"Pinky?" She listened, but didn't hear the tell-tale sounds of the dog.

Ann turned and shined the flashlight back the way she came, then passed through the doorway to a long, narrow hall not much wider than her arm span. She kept her hand out toward the opposite wall, willing it to not close in on her. The flashlight penetrated the dark only a few feet at a time.

After several yards, the air chilled. A couple more yards, and the hallway angled upward. Ann hiked up the concrete floor out into the night. Louise's house slumped among the pines a handful of yards away.

Pinky bounded out of the darkness and nearly gave her a heart attack.

"Where did you go?"

Pinky's legs were covered in black dirt. The dog reared up onto her hind legs and gave Ann an urgent poke with her nose. She took off with a sharp bark.

Ann ran to keep up, wondering if Pinky was on Maggie's trail.

Pinky's bounding hindquarters flashed across the beam. Ann changed direction. A tree root snagged her foot. She keeled forward and kept falling long after she should have hit the ground.

When her hands hit, she tumbled over and finally came to a crunching halt.

Miraculously, she'd managed to hold onto her flashlight and the gun.

The beam of light shined directly into a pair of bulging eyes only a foot away from where she landed. Muscle memory in her arm swung the gun to point at the face.

It didn't move.

Ann scrambled backward up the short incline and bumped into Pinky. She wrapped her arms around the dog and held on as if she were drowning.

She shined the light around. A shallow pit, roughly seven feet in crude diameter, held the remains of dozens of cats with two human corpses laying on top.

Ann slid back down toward them to get a closer view, though she was pretty certain she knew who they were.

Sheriff McMichael's body had bloated. The swelling stressed the elasticity of his skin, cracking the surface. The other body was charred almost beyond recognition. The blackened skin peeled up in chunks over the arms and face.

"Derrick." Ann covered her mouth with her hand and stifled the emotions crowding to burst out. She closed her eyes and fell to her knees.

You have your proof. They're dead. You have to stop her before she takes the seventh.

Ann collected herself. She had to keep a cool head. Teresa and Raghib and Maggie were out there somewhere, and time was growing short.

Ann climbed out of the pit and retraced her steps to the underground tunnel. When she and Pinky reached the entrance, partially hidden by overgrown brush, Pinky bellowed and took off again.

"Pinky—goddammit." Ann chased after but lost sight of her. The flashlight died in her hand. Ann shook it, but it only produced the faintest light. In the distance, Pinky let out an attack growl, then a pained yelp. Ann gasped, but Pinky had run back toward the funeral home, which didn't seem like the right direction. Ann's gut told her to check Louise's house.

Glass shattered, and someone—or some*thing*—crashed through the brush.

The book!

Ann sprinted toward the truck. Pinky lay on the ground a few feet from the vehicle, still breathing, knocked out by a heavy tree branch laying nearby. The truck door hung open. Tempered glass from the smashed window sparkled on the ground.

The book was gone.

CHAPTER 60

With nowhere else to go, Teresa stepped up Louise's front porch and rapped her knuckles against the door. Louise opened it.

"Come inside." She closed the door behind them. "Did you do everything we discussed?"

Teresa nodded.

"And the book?" Louise's greedy hands flexed. Her eyes searched Teresa.

Teresa shook her head. "I don't have it." She slumped into a chair.

A scowl worked its way onto Louise's horrible face. She was about to say something when Teresa glanced into the living room where an assortment of cats looked toward the couch with wide eyes. Maggie lay on the couch in a deep sleep.

"What's she doing here? I thought Ann had her."

Louise grinned. Someone knocked on the door.

"Don't answer it," Teresa said, twisting in the chair. "It's

Ann. I know it's Ann. She's out there."

Louise went to the door and peeked through the peep hole. "It's not Ann," she said and opened the door.

An older man stood on the porch. A satchel hung at his hip.

"My dear Raghib," Louise said. "Welcome back."

He came inside. To Teresa's horror, Louise embraced him, and they kissed—and not just the simple smooch of long-time friends. Teresa turned away, disgusted by the wet smacking sounds. She moved to Maggie's side to get away from their grotesque display of affection.

Maggie's breath was shallow. Teresa nudged her, but she didn't rouse.

"Is Maggie all right?" Teresa asked. Raghib snapped his attention to her.

"Who is this?" he asked.

"Raghib, this is Teresa. Teresa, Raghib." They nodded at each other. "Teresa is Maggie's adoptive mother. Raghib is Maggie's grandfather."

"I thought you were dead," Teresa said. He ignored her and pulled the satchel off over his head. Louise put on the kettle. Teresa stood where she could see Maggie on the couch and the two elderlies in the kitchen.

"She'll be okay," Raghib said. "A mild sedative. It'll wear off soon." He turned back to Louise. "I only gave her half of one."

"Good. We need her awake."

Raghib opened the satchel. Teresa moved closer. He

pulled out Maggie's book and presented it to Louise.

Louise's eyes landed on Teresa. She lifted an eyebrow. "He brought the book *and* the girl," Louise said. "You're almost worthless."

"I beg your pardon?" Teresa said. She came to the table. "He knocked out a child and stole a book. I've *killed* people."

Raghib looked up at Teresa with a smug expression, as if he, too, believed drugging a girl and petty theft outweighed multiple murders.

Teresa turned to Louise. "Are his tasks really more important than what I've done?"

"We couldn't complete the process without the book and the girl," Louise said. She dropped her gaze to the crinkled pages.

"You two are unbelievable." Teresa went into the living room while Louise paged through the book. She gazed down at Maggie. Just nights ago she'd swept the girl's hair from her forehead. She knelt by the couch and did it again. This time it didn't feel real. Grief bubbled up. She covered her mouth and stifled a sob. Maggie shifted.

"I think she's waking up," Teresa said.

"Ah, here it is." Louise tore a section of pages out.

Teresa returned to the kitchen. "What is it?"

"The instructions for harnessing Yaldabaoth." Louise scanned the pages. "You've, of course, carried out the necessary steps." Louise held up one of the pages. "Seven bloods. Seven souls," she read.

"No." Teresa shook her head. "I only took six."

Louise looked at her. "What do you mean you only took six?"

"What do you mean, what do I mean? I. Only. Took. Six."

Louise's eyes searched Teresa's face, then shifted back to the torn pages, then to Raghib.

"Six. It can't be. Tonight is the night. You should have been done by now. He said you would be done."

Teresa stood. "Who? Who said I would be done?"

Louise cocked her head and smiled. "Yaldabaoth, of course."

"Yalda—but I thought . . ." Teresa couldn't get the words out. Louise had never mentioned she, too, was talking to Yaldabaoth. The old bat had lied to her. Chills of realization broke out over Teresa's skin. Her eyes darted back to Louise's face.

Louise studied Teresa. "Yes, dear Doctor Hart. You have been a pawn in our grand scheme all along."

Teresa couldn't swallow. She couldn't speak. For a second, she thought Louise had cast a curse or spell on her. Then she realized she was having a panic attack.

The kettle whistled. "Tea, Doctor Hart?" Louise sneered.

Teresa shook her head.

"Water." The word came out strangled. "Please."

Louise filled a glass and set it on the table. Teresa took a few gulps, and her throat released whatever paralysis had taken it over.

"You tricked me. You lied to me."

Louise shook her head, an expression of pity on her wrinkled face.

"You've failed *him*," Louise said. "Does he know you've only taken six?"

It was Teresa's turn to be smug.

"Yes."

And he's chosen me as his queen, so there.

Louise waved a hand. "No matter, then. He must have a plan."

"Daddy?" Maggie sat up and rubbed her eyes. She peered around. Her breathing quickened.

Teresa went to her. "Don't worry," she said. Maggie latched onto her. "We're just at a friend's house."

"Why'm I so sleepy?" Maggie's voice was a whimper in Teresa's ear.

"It's nighttime. You're supposed to be sleepy." Teresa petted Maggie's hair and gently shushed her. Something inside her cracked a little. If it was just her and Maggie now, there was no need for jealousy. No Derrick, no judgment. Her heart ached. She pulled away from Maggie and looked into her eyes, but Maggie was looking off over Teresa's shoulder.

"Why is my Baba here? He's trying to kill me. He hurt Pinky."

Louise came into the living room. "Now, Maggie, he is your grandfather. He would never hurt you." She laughed.

"I'm sure it's just a misunderstanding."

Maggie looked to Teresa, then Louise, then Raghib. Her foggy brain was working out a puzzle she didn't understand. She jumped off the couch to run, but she collapsed into Teresa's lap. Teresa helped her to her feet. Maggie sprinted for the door, but Louise grabbed her. Maggie screamed and kicked, but Louise's gnarled hand kept its grip.

"Get the door," Louise grunted, indicating the basement entrance.

Raghib flung the bolt. The music played, but the white noise no longer blasted from the television.

Louise lifted Maggie so her feet just brushed the top step.

"Keep squirming, and I'll drop you down these stairs," Louise said.

Maggie struggled for two more seconds, then stopped.

"Please, let me go."

"Maggie?" Bram's voice yelled from the basement.

"Ah, yes," Raghib said. "Bram Logan, our dear friend." He grinned. Teresa shuddered. What would drive a grandfather to harming his own grandchild?

Louise hauled Maggie down the steps. Teresa followed.

Teresa swore she could still smell the scent of Bram's cauterized flesh.

Maggie squirmed out of Louise's grip and ran to Bram. She flung her arms around his neck and sobbed against him.

"Aw, a perfect reunion." Louise clasped her hands under her chin like it was the dearest thing she'd ever seen. "Oh, Brammy," Louise said. "Look who brought her to me."

Bram lifted his head. His eyes widened.

"You," he said in a harsh whisper. "You betrayed us, you sick son of a bitch!" Bram jerked and struggled against his bindings. When it did no good, he stopped. "Why, Raghib? Why did you do this? How could you betray your flesh and blood?"

"There is no greater light than Yaldabaoth," Raghib said. "You left me to fend for myself. The Messengers took me back in. They *care* about their people. It was *you* who betrayed *me*." Raghib spat on the floor, then let out a pained groan and fell to his knees. Louise stood behind him, a blood-coated knife in her hand and a twisted smile on her face.

Teresa let out a shriek. Raghib pitched forward and stopped moving. Louise tossed the knife aside. Maggie cowered against Bram, hiding her face in his shoulder.

Louise turned to Bram and Maggie and took a step forward. Teresa stood in front of her, blocking her path. "Don't hurt her. Please!"

Louise smiled at her, the sneer replaced by a sweet-little-old-lady face.

"Don't worry, dear. I won't." She touched Teresa's arm with cold fingers, then pulled her toward a work bench. Louise placed a thick, rough rope in Teresa's reluctant hands.

"We need to take them to Yaldabaoth," Louise said. "Behind my house is a passageway that leads directly to the basement of the funeral home. We'll take them that way, under the forest." She nodded toward Maggie. "Tie her up."

Teresa pulled Maggie's arms from around Bram's neck.

"I'm sorry, Maggie," she whispered. Tears burned her eyes but didn't well or fall.

"Don't you touch her," Bram's voice rasped. "Don't you dare touch her."

"What are you going to do, old man?" Louise asked. She kicked him in the shin. Maggie was eerily quiet and cooperative.

Bram struggled against his bonds.

"It's okay, Mr. Bram. I'm okay." Maggie said. "It's okay. We'll be okay." A tear slid down her cheek. "My angel . . ." her voice trailed off.

Teresa tied the knots at Maggie's wrists. The rope reddened Maggie's tender skin.

Louise checked the bindings, and Teresa guided Maggie to the stairs.

Louise knelt before Bram and gripped his knees. "Are you going to play nice, Brammy? Or am I going to have to remove a few more fingers?"

Bram spat at her. Louise dodged to the side. The glob landed on the cement floor.

"Teresa, give me the shears."

"No, no. Okay. I'll cooperate."

"Good boy." Louise brushed his cheek with the back of her hand. He flinched away.

"Not a word, either of you." Louise pointed at them with a horrific scowl. The four of them climbed up the stairs, the captives resigned.

Someone pounded on the front door.

"Louise!" Ann's voice. "Louise, let me in."

Louise slapped a hand over Maggie's mouth. Bram shouted, but she shoved him with her foot, cutting off his cry.

"Quick, to the back." Louise whispered. She pushed Bram ahead of her. Teresa followed with Maggie.

A door in one of the back bedrooms led outside. Louise ushered Bram through, then waved Teresa and Maggie forward. She closed the door behind them.

"The passage is to the north of the garden. It leads to the basement in the funeral home," Louise said.

Teresa nodded.

They tiptoed through Louise's lawn, past her overgrown garden, and into the forest. Teresa shuddered with fear.

Louise handed Bram's rope to Teresa. "The entrance is here somewhere," she said.

Teresa . . .

The word whispered on a nonexistent breeze. Teresa looked toward where the sound had come from.

Teresa . . . come . . .

It was male, but it wasn't Yaldabaoth's voice. It sounded like two voices in one.

Teresa let go of Bram and Maggie and followed the sound.

"Where is it?" Louise said under her breath. "Why didn't I think to bring a flashlight? Teresa? Where are you going?" Louise ran back over to Bram and Maggie and grabbed their ropes.

Teresa was dully aware of Louise behind her. She followed the voice a few feet away and stopped.

Clouds uncovered the full moon, and cold light shined down on a pit. Two bodies lay inside.

"What's this?"

"Oh, that's just where I bury my cats." Louise brushed a strand of hair from her forehead. "Come on, let's get into the passageway. It's just over here."

Teresa numbly took Maggie's rope. "How? How are they here?"

Louise gave her a bewildered look. "I put them there. After they die." She cocked her head and gave Teresa a strange look. "Is something wrong?" She stepped closer to Teresa. "Oh." She took a step back. "Are those . . ." Louise cleared her throat.

Teresa turned her gaze to Louise. The old woman's face, etched in the moonlight, held disgust and a measure of shock. Louise's eyes shifted to her.

"Why are they here?" Teresa asked.

Louise backed away from the pit, from the still bodies

lying in the bottom on top of countless cat carcasses.

"Didn't you put them there?"

Teresa shook her head.

Louise gave her a sad, close-lipped smile. "It's best to just let some things go unexplained sometimes." She touched Teresa's arm "Come on, Doctor. Ann's coming."

Teresa stayed by the pit for a few more seconds, looking down on the bodies. She flicked her eyes up to the moon and squeezed them shut against the burn of tears.

"Teresa," Louise whispered through the dark.

She turned and followed Louise into the passageway.

CHAPTER 61

Ann lifted Pinky into the truck and closed the door. She ran through the forest, dodging tree trunks and lifting her feet high to avoid tangling with any brush.

Too many things were happening at once, but her first priority was finding Maggie and getting her to safety. Then she could worry about everything else. Teresa, Raghib, Dad . . . the bodies in the woods, Pinky.

Just get to Maggie in time.

She tripped on a root, caught herself, and kept going in an uncontrolled sprint. She should take her time, have her wits about her, figure out a plan, but the voices in her head chanted in time with the dull throb of the mark.

Too late. . . Too late . . .

She ran for what seemed like too long. Too much time was wasted in these woods. Louise's house materialized in the darkness. She leaped up the porch steps and pounded on the door in case Louise had seen or heard anything.

"Louise! Louise let me in!" The knob turned easily in

her hand. She pushed, and the door thudded against the interior wall.

Cats scattered in every direction.

She clasped her dad's gun in front of her and peeked around into the house.

"Louise? Raghib? Teresa?" She took a breath. "Maggie?"

No one answered. She stepped around the jamb. Hugging the wall with her back, she took a cursory glance of the immediate area. The strange door at the entrance to the hallway, usually bolted shut, stood open.

She went to it and peered down a set of steps.

"Maggie?" Ann shouted into the depths. There was no response, but someone lay at the bottom of the stairs. "Hello?" The person didn't move.

Ann looked over her shoulder toward the kitchen, around the edge of the wall into the hoarder's den, then went down the stairs.

Heart pounding in her ears, she once again crouched next to a body and felt for a pulse. Weak and slow. Blood soaked the back of his canvas jacket. Whispers came from his lips. Ann leaned closer.

"Raghib," she said. "You son of a bitch."

He whispered again. The same phrase over and over.

"Lord Yaldabaoth, I am your servant. Take me to the seventh aeon." His hand shifted. Ann jumped back and aimed her gun at him. He dug in a pocket and moved his hand across the floor. There was something pinched between his fingers. Ann bent, gun still aimed at his head, and took it. Her father's ring. Raghib had taken the finger from her house.

"Why did you take this?" she asked. He didn't respond. She resisted the urge to break his neck and looked around the basement. It stank of human filth. A chair sat in the center; light and dark stains circled the floor around it. Urine, feces, blood.

A small, roughly cylindrical shape lay on the ground in the middle of a darker stain. Ann picked it up and sucked in a harsh breath. Another finger.

The edges of her vision faded out. She ran back up the stairs and slammed the door behind her, leaned against it.

"Jesus—fuck." She gasped for air that failed to fill her lungs.

Get it together. Find Maggie.

Where was she? She pushed away from the basement door and rushed around the rest of the house calling Maggie's name, but the girl was not there. On the kitchen table, the book lay open to where several pages had been ripped out. Ann picked it up.

"Help me find her." Ann's scalp tingled like someone was watching her. She turned around. A few cats sat behind her, wide eyes staring. Her shoulders dropped. Helplessness seeped in.

But the mark had stopped pulsing. Instead, it simmered constantly.

Angel…

She turned back around to grab the book, and the mark

pulsed again. Slow, steady. When she faced the hallway, it sped up and became a constant pain again.

She grabbed the book—warm in her hands—and followed this new beacon to one of the back bedrooms, paying close attention to the mark as she went. Ann burst out into Louise's back yard. She ran through Louise's shitty garden back into the woods.

The pit with Sheriff McMichael and Derrick's bodies was straight ahead. The mark beat, and as Ann turned to home in on Sophia's call, it pounded faster and faster until she faced the hidden passage to the funeral home's basement.

Angel…

Ann took a deep breath and stepped inside. She clamped the book under her arm while she jogged, keeping her shoulder close to the wall for guidance. Her other hand gripped the gun. With Raghib dying in Louise's basement, Ann had no idea who the real villain was. Louise or Teresa?

She made it to the central part of the basement with the stained sheets and took the stairs two at a time.

CHAPTER 62

Teresa sat on the arm of the moldy sofa. Louise paced back and forth.

"Six souls," Louise said. "Who will be the seventh?" She pounded her fist into her hand. "Blast. I should have kept Raghib alive."

Teresa wondered if Yaldabaoth would come to her with Louise hanging around. If the old woman was in cahoots with him, why didn't the cave appear?

A thrill of excitement coursed through her when she realized Louise's folly. The old bat turned around. Teresa couldn't help but smile.

Louise's zoe line hung from her chest.

"It can't be Bram. I picked him for the vessel—unless Ann is the vessel. Oh yes, this is so deliciously brilliant!" Louise rubbed her hands together and looked at Teresa. "Why are you smiling like that?"

Louise's zoe swayed and twitched like a cat's tail. The cold steel and glass of a hypo pressed against Teresa's palm. She wrapped her fingers around it and stood from the arm of the mildewed couch. She didn't need to look behind her. She knew Tiffany was there.

"Why are you smiling?" Confusion replaced the usual smug know-it-all expression on Louise's face, then fear.

"I know who the seventh is," Teresa said. She took a step toward Louise.

"We have the vessel and Sophia," Louise said, pointing at Bram and Maggie. "There is no seventh. Not without Ann here." Louise's voice wavered. Her eyes widened.

Some word of pleading formed on the old woman's lips. She took a step back. But Teresa rushed forward and plunged the needle into her chest. She didn't pull the plunger. Not yet.

"You lied to me." Teresa dug her thumb into the tender part of Louise's bony shoulder. "You say I was your pawn all along, but Yaldabaoth never came to you, did he?"

Louise's mouth opened and closed, her voice clicking in her throat.

Teresa squeezed harder. Louise's knees gave out. Teresa towered over her.

"No," Teresa continued. "He never did. If he had, this living room would be his cave." She threw her head back and let out a careless laugh from deep in her throat. "He never came to you. He came to me. He wanted me and he took me. You will never see your God's face hovering over yours. You'll never feel his flesh against your flesh. I am his choice. I am his queen."

She leaned into Louise, placed her lips close to the old woman's ear.

"We made love many times. He loves *me*. Not you." She pulled the plunger.

Louise's zoe line shriveled. Her skin turned powdery gray. The zoe line snapped off and fell to the ground in pieces. Her dusty form remained with an expression of horror and surprise locked on its face. Then it crumbled into a pile of ash.

Maggie screamed. Bram wrestled against the ropes binding his wrists. Ann ran into the room with her gun drawn.

"Teresa, freeze!" Ann shouted.

"Seven," Teresa said.

CHAPTER 63

Ann aimed the gun at Teresa and shifted her eyes to see if Maggie was okay. A bound man knelt next to her. He lifted his head and met her eyes.

Ann's world broke and crumbled into pieces. She couldn't speak, she couldn't move, it was all she could do to remain standing.

Her dad struggled against ropes tying his hands. Ann ran to him and began to loosen them. The ground tilted. Ann threw her hands out to the side for balance. The sound of stone grating on stone filled the air. The plaster walls shifted, warped, and transformed into brown, sandy rock.

A pool of water stood to her left. A man with a wild mane of hair gazed into it. Teresa approached him. He turned.

His face was a grotesque combination of man and beast. He took a step toward Teresa. No, not a step. He had no feet. To Ann's horror, from the waist down he was a serpent.

Yaldabaoth.

Chills broke out on her arms and sent an involuntary shudder through her body.

He took something from Teresa's hand—a large syringe by the look of it—and kissed her.

"Fr–freeze," Ann said again. The tremor in her hands coursed up to her elbows.

Yaldabaoth jammed the needle into his arm and injected it. Ann could only surmise it was the seventh soul.

The cave shook. Stones crumbled from the ceiling. The pool rippled and churned.

Ann ran to Teresa, who stood transfixed, staring at Yaldabaoth as the power of the seventh soul coursed through him. She pulled Teresa away.

"He needs to be harnessed," Ann shouted over the churn of water and rumble of earth. "Didn't you read the book?"

Teresa's eyes were wide. The woman didn't have a fucking clue. Ann ran to her father and worked on his ropes.

"What do I do?" she cried.

Yaldabaoth's booming voice said, "Sons and daughters, rise."

Ann looked over her shoulder. Yaldabaoth held his hand over the pool. The water boiled, thick now, like hot tar.

"Get Maggie out of here." Bram rubbed his wrists and stared over her shoulder at Yaldabaoth.

"How? There's no way out," Ann said. "We need to harness him. We don't have a vessel!"

She looked again. Seven figures rose from the pool. The seven bloods, the seven souls. All but one Ann knew. The seventh must have been a manifestation of Marcie's unborn child.

Bram turned to Maggie and untied her ropes. They left her wrists raw and bloody. He placed a hand on Ann's shoulder. "We have Teresa," Bram whispered. "You can be with Derrick again, like I wanted."

Ann flung a thumb over her shoulder toward the seven. "Derrick's dead." She searched her father's eyes. "We can't use Teresa—she's crazy. Having that woman carrying this evil around in her—no. It can't be her."

Bram pulled Ann into an embrace. "It has to be me then," he whispered.

"No, dad. You can't. Not after all this time. Please. It's supposed to be me. I'm the one. I'm the Protector."

"You keep Maggie safe. That is your duty." His voice held a commanding tone.

The ground bucked underneath them. More rocks fell from the ceiling. Ann lurched forward to protect Maggie from the debris.

Yaldabaoth's laughter rose above all other noise. "Poor simple mortals." He lifted his hands. "I bind thee."

Fleshy red ropes flew toward them. Bram slammed backward as the ropes made of umbilical cord, or something like it, bound him to the cave wall. Ann held on tight to Maggie and glanced toward a dark passage to the left of the pool.

No, she couldn't abandon her father. She could save them both. She stood and put herself between Maggie and the monster.

"You can't have her," she said.

Yaldabaoth laughed. "I don't *want* her," he said, slithering closer to them. "I want to *kill* her."

Another set of umbilici flew from his hands.

They pinned Ann, like her dad, against the wall. She struggled against them, repulsed by their living warmth.

Teresa stepped in front of Yaldabaoth, stopping him in his tracks.

"Where are they?" she asked. "Where is my Tiffany? Where is my husband?"

Yaldabaoth lifted Teresa by the arms. Her shoulders shot up to her ears, and she let out a surprised gasp. He pulled her close.

"There is no Tiffany." He leaned back as if to enjoy whatever look might be on her face.

"I saw her. I held her. She came to me." Teresa's voice climbed higher and higher with each phrase.

"There never was a Tiffany. It was always. Just. Me." He licked the side of her face with his forked tongue.

A high-pitched keen issued from Teresa's throat. She pounded his chest with her fists.

Yaldabaoth scoffed and tossed her to the side. She hit the wall and landed in a limp heap. He continued to slither toward Maggie, taking his sweet time. Drawing out the inevitable.

Maggie backed up against the wall between Ann and Bram.

"Don't touch her!" Ann cried. She struggled again. Maggie looked up at her. Her eyes glowed. She stepped away from the wall and from whatever protection being near Ann and Bram might give her.

CHAPTER 64

Yaldabaoth seized Maggie by the hair. Maggie cried out. The mark on Ann's chest flared. Yaldabaoth dragged Maggie toward the pool. At the edge, he released her and slithered back and forth. The seven figures clawed at the air toward him, releasing muted, anguished screams.

Maggie got to her feet and looked at Ann. Transposed over the child's body was a strong, powerful woman. Wind whipped her hair about her head. Her eyes glowed. The image shrank down until she was the size of Maggie. Ann's mark stopped hurting. Maggie held her head high, shoulders back. Maggie wasn't only Maggie now. She was Sophia.

She looked directly at Ann with glowing eyes.

I summon thee, Angel.

Ann heard her voice in her mind. Sophia's voice, the voice from the clearing days ago.

"I don't know what to do." Ann twisted in the flesh ropes. "He's going to kill her."

"Listen to me, Ann," her dad said. She locked onto his eyes. "You know what to do."

She tore her eyes from him and looked at Maggie, who stood with her chin raised, defiant.

"Believe, Ann. Believe in yourself. The power is within you."

Ann squeezed her eyes shut, but they wouldn't stay closed. Not with Maggie in danger. She struggled against the living ropes. Desperation replaced the frustration.

Yaldabaoth's laugh echoed around the cave. His voice slithered through her ears.

"Afraid, are we?" Yaldabaoth chuckled again. "I guess you'll just. Be. Too. Late." His face morphed into The Stabber's devilish visage.

Ann closed her eyes again, but Yaldabaoth's horrible laugh filled her head.

Your fear weakens you, he said in her mind.

Ann opened her eyes. Yaldabaoth's snake tail coiled around Maggie's throat. He lifted her. Her little feet kicked. The seven figures left the pool and lurched, lumbered, and crawled toward Ann and her dad.

Angel . . .

Sophia's voice held a note of desperation. Maggie's eyes shifted to Ann, her eyebrows angled with worry. Ann couldn't fail. Not again. She closed her eyes.

"Sophia called forth the angel to bind Yaldabaoth," Maggie's half-choked voice, rich with Sophia, said.

Who and where was the angel?

I am the Protector. I am the angel.

Stillness came over her—her mind hyper-focused. The cave's rumbling, Yaldabaoth's progeny, his cruel voice—all fell silent.

A tingling sensation began in her chest, softer than the pain associated with Maggie's distress. Suddenly, Ann stood outside herself and watched her own transformation. Blue light followed the trail of blood through her veins. It coursed up her feet, her legs, spread up her torso, and down each arm. It pulsed with each beat of her heart. When the light reached her center, it burst out of her. Pain erupted in Ann's shoulder blades, and great wings of blue light unfurled from her back, towering above her figure against the wall. The angel of light stood before her, and when Ann met the angel's eyes she wanted to weep. Ann stepped forward. The angel held up her hands. Ann did the same, and they pressed their palms together. Searing blue light flashed as their two bodies merged. Ann opened her eyes with a gasp that tensed her entire body. She and the angel were one.

The sounds of the cave rushed back with near-deafening force. The umbilical ropes shriveled into the crispy substance wherever they touched her glowing skin.

Blue light laced the edges of her vision. Her shoulder blades still ached.

Ann broke free of her bindings. She ripped the living ropes binding her dad.

"You did it," Bram whispered.

"Distract them. I'll get Maggie," Ann said. She drew her weapon and dashed away before Bram could stop her.

Ann pointed the gun at Yaldabaoth. "Let her go."

Yaldabaoth lifted his hand and swiped it to the side without even looking at her. Propelled by an unseen force, Ann flew and hit the ground a few feet away from the dazed Teresa. Stars flashed in her eyes. Her vision blurred. She shook her head and tried to focus.

The seven souls circled her dad, who gripped his ribs and fought to stay upright. Maggie screamed.

Yaldabaoth's tail coiled tighter, cutting off her cry. Her face turned red, and she gasped for air. He held his hands over her chest. Blue light pulsed out toward him. Ann cried out with pain from the mark as black veins crackled across Maggie's skin. Ann got to her feet, stumbled toward Yaldabaoth and raised her weapon again. Ethereal light from her hands encompassed the gun in its glow.

"I said, let her go," Ann said.

Yaldabaoth's hands coiled the air in front of Maggie, pulling her light from her heart. Tendrils of it wrapped around his fingers.

"You're too late. You can't save her." His face changed to the Stabber's again. "Look how your hand shakes." He said that to her that night in the old house outside of Salida.

Ann pulled the trigger. The gun bucked in her hand. The bullet sailed toward Yaldabaoth with a trail of red fire, like a tracer round. It struck him in the heart. He lurched backward with the impact. The light sucked back inside

Maggie, but she was so still.

When Yaldabaoth raised his head, his beast-face had returned.

"Mortal weapons cannot harm—" He made a choked noise in his throat and cried out in surprised agony.

"It's not a mortal weapon." Ann advanced. The angel fire from the bullet spread through his veins. Ann raised the gun again and blasted his tail below Maggie's feet, severing it in a gruesome splatter. Maggie tumbled to the ground.

"That's for Ruthie," Ann said. She shot him in the stomach. "That's for Sheriff McMichael." She shot him again and again, naming each of his victims. "And this," she said meeting his yellow, fear-filled eyes, "this is for Sophia." She shot him between the eyes.

Yaldabaoth's head rocked back, but he didn't fall. His gaze shifted over Ann's shoulder, and his eyes widened.

Ann turned around, took in the sight of the seven. The one representing Sheriff McMichael released his grip on Bram's neck. All of them turned and faced Yaldabaoth.

"No," Yaldabaoth whispered. He held up his hands. "I command you—"

Ann dove out of the way as the souls charged toward him and tackled him into the pool with a gooey splash. They all sank below the surface.

The cave was calm for a second, then Yaldabaoth burst from the depths with his arms raised like in Maggie's pictures. Two of the seven dangled from each arm. He let out a roar as his limbs were ripped from their sockets with the sound of rending leather. The rest of the souls rose from the water and tore his flesh, stripped his skin, and broke his bones until there was nothing left.

After Yaldabaoth's cries stopped, the seven turned and faced Ann. She held up the gun, but they stayed still. The mud recoiled from their bodies, leaving behind translucent representations of each victim.

Ann dropped the gun as if it had burned her palm, and looked from face to face. She let out a sob when Derrick smiled at her. He waved a silent goodbye. They slipped beneath the surface. The mud cleared. The water stilled.

Ann crawled over to Maggie's too-still form and rolled the child onto her back. No pulse. No breath.

"Please, no," she cried. She started chest compressions. Nothing worked. Then, the mark pulsed. Ann looked at her hands. Her palms glowed. She held them over Maggie's heart and willed the remaining angel light into the Child of Humanity.

The light left Ann's palms and surged into the mark over Maggie's heart. The mark lit briefly, then dissolved away, leaving behind only the faintest discoloration.

Maggie gasped. Her eyes still glowed but quickly dimmed and returned to normal.

Ann pulled her into a hug. "Are you okay?" She pulled back. Maggie nodded and pointed over Ann's shoulder. Ann turned.

Bram lay where the seven had left him. His chest

shuddered with shallow breaths. Ann ran to his side, Maggie followed and lay a hand on his cheek. He held her tiny hand in his, but his eyes found Ann.

"Annie," he gasped. "I held them off for you, but they were strong." A tear leaked from the corner of his eye. "They tossed me around like a goddamn rag doll until you started shooting." He panted for a second. "I think they remembered who they were—who the *real* bad guy was." His lips smiled, then contorted in pain.

Ann looked around. "How do we get out of here?"

Movement caught Ann's eye. Teresa sat up.

"We just walk out the front door." She pointed to the cave wall. "Through the woods to the road. Don't mind the lost souls." She tipped over and closed her eyes.

There was no door.

"Tartaros won't let us leave unless we replace Yaldabaoth," Bram said. "Soul exchange." Ann nodded over to Teresa's form. "Not her. She's still alive." He took a ragged breath. "It's gonna be me after all, my girl. I can feel it coming."

"It can't be. I have so many questions. I thought you were dead. Why didn't you tell me about all this? Where have you been?"

He shushed her. "I was supposed to board a plane to Egypt, to finish taking out the Messengers there. Louise got me first. One hundred CCs of sedative to the neck. I've been in her basement for I don't even know how long. She used sensory deprivation, beat me, starved me." He held up his bandaged hand and let out a pained laugh. "She cut off my fingers."

Grief and sadness and happiness mingled together. Ann couldn't tell if she should laugh or cry or both.

"Mr. Bram?" Maggie said.

"Yes, little love?"

"I don't want you to stay here."

"I'll be fine, sweets." His eyes found Ann's again. "I'm so proud of you."

Maggie lay her head on his chest, and Ann followed her lead. His arm wrapped around her. She listened to her father's heartbeat. She listened to his breaths gurgling in his punctured lung.

The time between the sounds lengthened, then stopped. The touch of his hand disappeared.

The air around them transformed. The sounds shifted from the echoing expanse of the cave to the muted sounds of the abandoned house. Sirens blared in the distance.

Something cold and wet snuffled against Ann's ear, followed by a warm tongue and a sad whimper. She sat up and fell against Pinky. Maggie joined them, sobbing against the dog's tawny fur.

Bram's body was gone.

CHAPTER 65

Three months after The Night

Ann and Maggie knelt at Bram's grave. Maggie placed a bunch of flowers at the foot of the headstone. They went to each victim in turn, leaving Derrick for last. It had become a monthly ritual.

With Teresa tucked away at Mountain View and Derrick gone, the state found some additional paperwork that named Ann as Maggie's legal guardian in the event of Derrick and Teresa's untimely death, or—in Teresa's case—parental unfitness. The papers were signed by Gail Park.

Maggie still carried Sophia within her. Every once in a while, she said something wise, older than her age.

When commercials begging for funds to help wounded warriors or starving children or anything of the like came on TV, Ann had to change the channel. If she didn't, it would send Maggie into a fit. She would swear Yaldabaoth was still out there doing things to cause these people suffering. She would be inconsolable.

Ann learned to give her time in these situations. And to monitor the television a little closer.

Maggie knelt at Derrick's grave when Ann's radio crackled.

"Sheriff Logan," a young man's voice said. He was her new deputy, a kid who reminded her of George in every way except his knack for law enforcement.

Ann stepped a few paces away from Maggie to give her the peace she needed.

"Go ahead, Deputy."

"The last of Louise's cats have been rehomed."

"That's great."

"Oh, and Rachel is complaining about the dog's gassiness."

"Did Pinky get in the trash again?"

"No . . . well . . . no. But I might have shared my sandwich with her."

Ann rolled her eyes. Being sheriff of her tiny town was what her father always wanted, and it was what she needed in her life right now.

"You know I have to live with that gas later tonight," Ann said. "Can you please follow the rules?"

"Yeah . . . sorry," he said.

Maggie finished at Derrick's grave. She always took a little more time at his.

"You ready to go?" Ann asked.

Maggie nodded and took Ann's hand. The scars on her wrists from the ropes had faded to a silvery reminder of that night, just like the mark on her chest. Ann's mark had also faded, but it still told her when Maggie was sad or angry or hurt.

Today was one of the days in which being Sophia was exhausting. Though they rarely spoke of that night, Maggie told Ann things, sometimes after her bedtime story when she was on the edge of sleep. She told Ann she could feel Sophia within her, though she'd never felt her before The Night.

Ann had called in Raghib's body, but when the coroner arrived, Raghib was gone.

Ann had trouble sleeping most of the time. Knowing the Messengers of the Light were still out there, still looking for vengeance and for Maggie, troubled her thoughts. Some day they could all rise up again and come after her, even though their god was gone for good.

All she could do was keep Maggie safe, and by doing so, the world would be as peaceful as it could be.

EPILOGUE

Six months after The Night

Six months ago, when Teresa had awoken in a hospital with a severe concussion, most of the memories of what had happened were gone. She knew she'd done something terribly wrong. The police guarding her hospital room door had told her a few things.

"Your husband is dead. Your daughter is in protective custody."

"Tiffany?" Teresa had said. "When can I see her?"

The officer had shaken his head. "No, Maggie."

"She's not my daughter," Teresa had said. "She's Derrick's daughter." She'd looked out the window at the familiar view of the Rocky Mountains. "Where am I?"

"Mountain View," the officer had told her.

Teresa now sat in a rocking chair in the common room, gazing out the window. An old leather-bound book, called *The Divine Messenger*, lay in her lap. She didn't know who sent it, only that it had been wrapped in paper with her name scrawled in black marker on the top. A red ribbon marked a page two-thirds in. Teresa opened the book and trailed her finger down the page. She'd read the inscription so many times, she had it memorized.

The seven mortal shells shall seek their souls and hunt the one who stole. And in their time of rest, they shall lay down upon the earth to be near to their master.

The page had a crude illustration of a pit with the 'mortal shells' laying inside. An image from that night flashed in her mind, forever burned there. The Sheriff and—she squeezed her eyes shut—Derrick laying on top of Louise's dead cats.

They really had chased her. Or, as the text said, hunted her. And they were in the pit resting, because that was as close as they could get to Yaldabaoth without crossing the barrier and burning up. That had to be it. She would tell her psychiatrist in a few minutes during their session. Her mind was clearer than it had been since they brought her here. Since The Night Yaldabaoth betrayed her.

A nurse came and guided Teresa to the therapy room.

"I'm ready to tell you the truth," she said to her therapist, her smile stretching her chapped lips.

The doctor turned on his digital recorder and nodded at her.

She began by telling him about Mother's desire to teach her to be a good wife, a good mother, and how social pressures got the best of her. Social pressures and Teresa's desire to be the perfect wife and mother and how the loss of her child was more than she could handle.

Dr. Andrews nodded, his eyes shining and hopeful.

"When my child came to me and told me we could be happy again, I promised her I would do anything it took." She nodded. "I stole their souls and gave them to a powerful being named Yaldabaoth. He would bring us all together again. We would be happy." Her words drifted off when the doctor's lips tensed. His eyes shifted to the notepad on his desk. A sharp exhale came from his nose as he jotted down notes.

He put the pen down and tented his fingers on the desk. "Is it possible," he started, his voice tense and a little short. A voice Derrick would have used on her. He took off his glasses and rubbed the bridge of his nose. "Is it possible you imagined any of this? Maybe you only thought they were chasing you because you were afraid of getting caught?"

Teresa didn't answer right away. She absorbed his suggestion. What it implied. She'd told him everything she learned from Louise, about the secret organizations, and Maggie's book. Louise torturing Bram in her basement. *She* was the town looney, not Teresa.

And still, he didn't believe her. She looked over his shoulder out the window at the rain clouds gathering in the west.

"Yes," she said. Her voice hitched. "Yes, that—that must be it." She lifted her hand and wiped a tear away with her fingertips.

But, the dead *did* chase her. Her baby came to her. Yaldabaoth promised her life back. Yaldabaoth used her body and her mind. He betrayed her.

Her hand dropped from her cheek and came to rest on her swollen belly. One of the babies inside pushed against her palm.

ACKNOWLEDGMENTS

Just as it takes a group of individuals with special skills to survive a zombie apocalypse, so, too, does it take such a team to produce a book. This book would not have made it into the world without my team:

Angela Alsaleem, who witnessed the first spark of this idea back in 2007 when I titled it *The She*, in my attempt to write about the "she" in the song "She'll Be Comin' 'Round the Mountain." I was so not ready to write a novel back then!

Lisa Baker, my brutal project manager and second #1 fan. Without threats from "The Baker" I may not have finished this book ever. Thank you for your encouragement, excitement, and love of my writing.

Pat Carroll, who read this in pieces while I wrote the first draft of this version a few years ago, and who read several subsequent drafts without complaint. Hey Pat! See you next Tuesday!

Michael F. Haspil, author of *Graveyard Shift*, for years

of support, encouragement, and amusing conversations about random topics, which lead to very strange places. You are a true storyteller to your core my friend!

My deepest gratitude goes to my beta readers, who read the "final" version and gave me valuable feedback and even more valuable encouragement and butt-loads of excitement. In addition to Lisa and Pat: Melissa McMurphy, Janice Hodge, Jennifer Baldovinos, Vicki Mullen, Andy Betsch, Amanda Keil, Rachel Whetzel, and Jill Hahn.

Another shout out to Melissa McMurphy, my Universe twin, inspirational goddess, comic relief, cohort in creativity, and so much more! We're doin' it! (that's what she said).

Thank you to Rebecca Rowley of Bexly for giving me permission to be my own target reader and for being with me when I came up with my "horror and more-er" author brand.

The Because Magic OG critique group: Michael F. Haspil, Nicole Green, Vicki Pierce, Chris Scena, Deirdre Byerly, LS Hawker (aka Uluru. Author of *The Drowning Game, The Throwaways* and other titles), Laura Main, and Marc Graham (author of *Song of Songs* and other titles). Without these people, I wouldn't be even a quarter of the writer I am today! You guys rock! Everyone should buy their books posthaste. Yes, I said posthaste.

A *huge* thank you to my editors, Jennifer Chesak of Wandering in the Words Press, and Michael Mann, developmental editor extraordinaire. These two took what I thought was a decently edited final draft of this book and tightened it, chopped it, reorganized it, pointed out its flaws, flogged it, stomped on it, and left it out in the rain like a cake, all while also making sure I knew I had something good here. Your balance of encouragement and red-line beatings pushed me to make this the best damn book it could be!

Another *huge* thank you to my cover designer and interior formatter, Michelle Argyle of MW Designs, who took the painting I did for a fake cover and used her mad skills to make it look like a real book cover. I cried when she sent me "The One."

And, of course, my family. My in-laws, Noreen and Daniel Fishback. Thank you for giving me your son. Without his love and support, this wouldn't have been possible. My parents, May and Barry Brouhard, who never stifled my creative spirit, but fostered it and let it grow and fester into the weeping flesh wound it is today (that's a good thing, in case you couldn't tell). My brother, James, for helping me add to my bone collection. Thank you for the cat skull and thank you for putting it on the ant hill to clean the residual flesh from it. And thank you for being weird.

My twin, Melissa "Wissa" Sirevog, who has always been my #1 fan. She pushed me to take this story from what it originally was and develop it into something that would knock her socks off. Thank you for always being by my side, even when we are apart. WTP!

Belle, my muse in the shape of a pit bull mix. Thank you for the long walks and for listening quietly as I explain why I'm stuck. Thank you for silently sending ideas and revelations and ah-ha moments with but a look. Even if that look said, "You are crazy, but I love you."

And last, but most important, my husband, Tim. My life wouldn't be what it is without you. You fill it with love, passion, excitement, adventure, and so much support. You understand that 50% of the time (or more) I don't live in this world. I couldn't have done this without you, and I wouldn't be who I am without you. Or alive for that matter.

Help Ann solve the Salida Stabber case and get FREE exclusive content!

Sign up at ClaireLFishback.com/stabber-puzzle to get a FREE cipher puzzle, like what Ann solved in *The Blood of Seven*.

Get the solution and you'll be rewarded with FREE and exclusive content!

Before you go . . .

Did you enjoy *The Blood of Seven?* One of the best ways to show how much you enjoyed it is to give a review on Goodreads or your favorite online retailer. Even if it is only a few words, it'll help exceptional readers like you find great books. Even better, tell all your friends about it!

CLAIRE L. FISHBACK lives in Morrison, Colorado with her loving husband, Tim, and their pit bull mix, Belle. Writing has been her passion since age six. When she isn't writing, she enjoys mountain biking, hiking, running, baking, playing the ukulele, and adding to her bone collection, though she would rather be stretched out on the couch with a good book (or poking dead things with sticks).

She can be reached at info@clairelfishback.com
for questioning.

Please visit www.clairelfishback.com and sign up to stay up to date on the latest releases and more!

Follow on social media:

Facebook: facebook.com/clairelfishback
Twitter: @clairelfishback
Instagram: @mrsfish2009

CPSIA information can be obtained
at www.ICGtesting.com
Printed in the USA
LVHW111342061019
633321LV00001B/19/P